CONTENTS

BOOK THREE

The Christmas Number One

DEAD PERCH BOOKS PRESENT

2023

A TRILOGY BY

The Justified Ancients of Mu Mu

MMXVII

First published in 2017
by Faber & Faber Limited
Bloomsbury House
74–77 Great Russell Street
London WC1B 3DA

Typeset by Faber & Faber Limited
Printed and bound by CPI Group (UK) Ltd, Croydon, CR0 4YY

The right of Bill Drummond and Jimmy Cauty to be identified
as Proprietor of this work has been asserted in accordance with
Section 77 of the Copyright, Designs and Patents Act 1988

Jonathan King, 'Everyone's Gone to the Moon'
Composer K. King
Publisher © 1965 Marquis Music Co. Ltd

A CIP record for this book
is available from the British Library

ISBN 978–0–571–33808–5

FSC
www.fsc.org
MIX
Paper from
responsible sources
FSC® C020471

2 4 6 8 10 9 7 5 3 1

THE PUBLISHER'S PREFACE

In the Spring of 2013, the undertakers Cauty & Drummond were on a tour of the Western Isles of Scotland. They were hoping to find and purchase the perfect plot of land to start work on the building of their long-promised pyramid – *The Great Pyramid of the North*.

Part of the tour took in the Isle of Jura.

Cauty & Drummond had made a name for themselves in the undertaking trade using the strap-line 'The Undertakers to the Underworld'. In doing so they had also made a somewhat rash promise to all the families who had entrusted them with the funeral rites of their nearest and dearest, the 'rash promise' being they would use some of the ashes of the said 'nearest and dearest' in the making of a brick, and each of these bricks would then be part of a pyramid that Cauty & Drummond would build at an unspecified location on the Western Isles. As yet they had not found and purchased a plot of land, let alone made a start on building the promised pyramid.

It was while staying at Jura's one hotel that they came across a strange-looking book on the bookshelf in the bar. It was hidden among the volumes of Jeffrey Archer and Irvine Welsh. The book was titled *Back in the USSR* and authored by someone using the name of 'Gimpo'.

Back in the USSR was a slim volume. Cauty & Drummond read it together in one sitting over a couple of drams of Jura's finest. But after reading it, all plans of finding the perfect plot to build *The Great Pyramid of the North* were shelved.

Back in the USSR was the memoir of a young woman who had been a nurse in the Falklands War in 1982. Her revulsion at what she had witnessed had impelled her to escape the West for what she perceived as the enlightened opportunities of the USSR.

Gimpo ended up in Kiev in what was then the Soviet state of the Ukraine. Here she met up with two young women named Tat'jana and Kristina, who were to have a profound influence on her.

According to *Back in the USSR*, Tat'jana and Kristina went under numerous aliases, the most widely used being The KLF.

Cauty & Drummond learnt from this book how, in the late '80s and very early '90s, Tat'jana and Kristina had a 'haphazard and anarchic slalom ride through the underbelly of Soviet popular music and high art'.

They also learnt:

How Tat'jana and Kristina ended up being the composers of the epoch-defining acid opera *Turn Up the Strobe*.

How for a generation of disaffected young folk growing up in the countries that fell under the Soviet sphere of influence *Turn Up the Strobe* told their stories and inspired them to believe they could make a difference.

How, as an acid opera, *Turn Up the Strobe* could be performed anywhere at any time.

How *Turn Up the Strobe* did not need Tat'jana and Kristina, as in The KLF, to actually be there for it to be staged.

How *Turn Up the Strobe* was performed hundreds of times in all sorts of unlikely venues, from abandoned cellars to disused aircraft hangars, performed by groups of teenagers using the most basic of instruments and liberated equipment.

How, to quote Gimpo, '*Turn Up the Strobe* sounded like Kurt Weil meets Delia Derbyshire mixed by The Todd Terry Project, with the libretto done by Maxim Gorky while working in the Brill Building circa 1962.'

Elsewhere in her book Gimpo states there's a version of history that interprets Tat'jana and Kristina's actions as 'the gentle push that was needed for the first domino to fall to bring about the collapse of the whole Soviet Union and all the disaster to follow'.

Also, in *Back in the USSR* it was claimed that Tat'jana and Kristina had been heavily influenced by a book called *Двадцять Двадцять Mpи! Mpилогія*. This book had been originally written in English as *The Twenty Twenty-Three! Trilogy*, by someone calling themselves 'George Orwell'. But this George Orwell was in turn just the pen name for a Roberta Antonia Wilson.

This George Orwell – or should that be Roberta Antonia Wilson? – wrote the majority of *The Twenty Twenty-Three! Trilogy* over a period of less than one month while staying in a cottage at the very northern tip of the Isle of Jura, and although one of her previous books, *Fish Farm*, had been a moderate success, there were no publishers in the UK who were interested in publishing *The Twenty Twenty-Three! Trilogy*.

Fish Farm had a cult following in parts of the USSR. It was seen in those parts as a literary attack on the West, in much the same way as *Brave New World* by Aldous Huxley had been a generation or so earlier. The Ukrainian arm of the Soviet State publishers decided to translate *The Twenty Twenty-Three! Trilogy* into Ukrainian and publish it on the back of the cult success of *Fish Farm*.

The now translated *Двадцять Двадцять Mpи! Mpилогія* did not repeat the moderate sales of *Fish Farm*, but for a select few individuals it became an underground classic. These rare few included Tat'jana and Kristina, who were then both still at an impressionable age – their early twenties.

Tat'jana and Kristina stopped everything else they were doing in their lives and started calling themselves The Ice Cream Men (The ICMs) and then alternatively The KLF. It was never revealed what the letters KLF stood for, although there seems to have been many assumptions.

As The KLF, they set about making art/music/situations very much according to the influence of much of what was described in George Orwell/Roberta Antonia Wilson's book *Двадцять Двадцять Мри! Мрилогія* (*The Twenty Twenty-Three! Trilogy*).

Cauty & Drummond asked their fellow drinkers in the bar if they knew anything of this Roberta Antonia Wilson or of Gimpo. The older drinkers remembered Wilson well, but not for her literary achievements; rather, for the fact that she, a woman of a certain age, had turned up on her Brough Superior Motorcycle most nights and proceeded to get drunk in the bar. Overall, their memories were warm and fond, but some had anecdotes of how she had a tendency to make inappropriate advances. There were other stories they told too, but now and here is not the place to recount them.

It should not go unrecorded that most of those remembering Roberta Antonia Wilson were male. The male gaze and mindset has a way of remembering things the female gaze and mindset does not.

It seemed the person on the island closest to Roberta Antonia Wilson was another local legend, Francis Riley-Smith, who was the wayward son of one of the local landed gentry. Francis Riley-Smith lived alone in his family's ancestral home, Jura House. Francis Riley-Smith had succumbed to cancer some years earlier.

As for Gimpo, she had worked as a chambermaid in the hotel over the Summer season a few years back. It seems she was also wild and reckless, but in a completely different way to Roberta

'Ton Up' Wilson, and she too had written a book in less than a month. Francis Riley-Smith had also taken to Gimpo, and it was Francis who had published a private edition of Gimpo's *Back in the USSR*. Other than the few copies Francis had given to friends, it was thought the rest had just sat in boxes in one of the outhouses of Jura House until Francis died. After that they would have been thrown on a bonfire with the rest of his collection of excesses and indulgences. By then the Riley-Smiths were impoverished gentry and having to sell off their highland estate to pay the death duties.

Duncan Buie, one of the more forthright drinkers at the hotel bar, claimed Francis had given him a copy of Roberta's book in Ukrainian. He said he would give it to Cauty & Drummond in exchange for a bottle of Diurachs' Own (the sixteen-year-old local single malt), but they had to buy him the bottle now. They did.

Duncan Buie was as good as his word. The next morning, as Cauty & Drummond were breakfasting on kippers and poached eggs in the hotel, Duncan turned up with his Ukrainian copy of *Двадцять Двадцять Мри! Мрилогія*.

Forty-eight hours later.

Back in London they had the whole of *Двадцять Двадцять Мри! Мрилогія* scanned and, via Google Translate, translated from Ukrainian back into English within seconds. The first thing they discovered was that *The Twenty Twenty-Three! Trilogy* was a book in three major parts, as if there were three books within one. They were also surprised to find that at the end of almost all of the 23 chapters in the book was a diary entry by this now mythical Roberta Antonia Wilson.

Cauty & Drummond knew someone who knew someone who knew us. And we are Dead Perch Books, an independent publishing house specialising in science fiction.

What you are about to read is what they read – well, almost. We have had our in-house editor Rosa Ainley go through the text and correct the grammar, punctuation and spelling, which Google Translate failed to do.

And now, thirty-three years after it was written, it is being published for the first time in English. We are not too sure if it can be classed as science fiction, fantasy or a utopian costume drama set in the near future. What we are sure about is that it is a book that deserves to be read by a discerning few.

Originally we were only going to publish *Book One* and see how that went before risking publishing *Book*s *Two* and *Three*. We changed our mind but . . .

Our legal department alerted us to the fact that much of the book contains quotes from famous and some not-so-famous songs. They told us that for us to publish this book we would have to gain copyright clearance for all of these lyrics. They then pointed out to us this would probably cost us a substantial amount of money and take much time. And even with an unlimited budget and an eternity of time, we could not be guaranteed to receive the clearances required.

After some deliberation we decided we owed it to Roberta Antonia Wilson, the people of Jura, Tat'jana and Kristina, and you *to publish and be damned*. But we are taking certain precautions. The precautions are that we will initially only publish a small run and not make them available through the usual channels. Instead of the Waterstones and Amazons of this world, we will make them available under the counter at various corner shops across the UK and beyond.

As for *Back in the USSR*, if we are able to sell this initial edition of the book and make a return on our investment, we hope to publish *Back in the USSR*.

As for the current whereabouts of Tat'jana and Kristina, we have no idea. According to *Back in the USSR*, they were last seen disappearing into the depths of the Black Sea in their decommissioned Project 865 Piranha submarine. This supposed disappearance happened on 23 August 1994. Rumour on the internet has it that they would not reappear for another 23 years.

Others say this was all just a myth they tried to create about themselves, and in reality they just grew up, got married, had kids and are now living normal lives in suburban Kiev.

Dead Perch Books
Breakfast Time
1 January 2017

AS-SALĀMU 'ALAYKUM

BOOK ONE

The Blaster in the Pyramid

1 : WHAT THE FUUK IS GOING ON?

'The history of the world is the history of the rivalry between five competing brands.'
    Stevie Dobbs, AppleTree

09:00 Sunday 23 April 2023

It is a bright warm day in April 2023, and the clock is striking thirteen. Winnie Smith, her Levi's slung low and her T-shirt freshly unbranded, strides through the gates of Victory Mansions. The sun is already up.

The tempting aroma of freshly ground coffee pulls her towards the Starbucks on the corner of her block. This is where Winnie has her first skinny latte of the day, every day. She checks her iPhone23 for the latest weather updates and the daily special offers from GoogleByte. She notes the retro fad for real fly-posters has made it to her part of town. The image on the poster is of an apple tree, hanging heavy with fruit. The tag-line is also indulging in some retro irony: 'AppleTree is Watching You'. There is nothing else on the poster other than the usual logo of an apple with a bite out of it in the corner.

Winnie looks at the screen of her iPhone23 again. Her iJaz* app pops up with a news story: Fernando Pó, the last nation state

---

* iJaz is AppleTree's news and current affairs channel. It was Al Jazeera until AppleTree bought out the Qatar-based company back in 2018, or was it '19? It was around the same time that AppleTree bought Sky and then launched their iSky entertainment and sports channels.

on Earth, is in negotiations with AppleTree to allow AppleTree to have the controlling share in their soon-to-be former nation. Winnie remembers with almost-nostalgia how, in her teenage years, nation states competed with religions to control the world. Almost as medieval as knights in shining armour rescuing maiden princesses from towers.

For those who don't know (and why should you?), Fernando Pó is a small island off the coast of Africa. It was once part of Equatorial Guinea, before Equatorial Guinea did their lucrative deal with WikiTube. But WikiTube decided Fernando Pó had no value to them. So they didn't bother with it, and Fernando Pó claimed nation status and went into the business of being a tax haven. 2022 was the last year anyone on Earth ever had to pay tax again, so Fernando Pó's trade as a tax haven was well past its sell-by date. This is why it had to do the knockdown deal with WikiTube.

Winnie watches a squirrel leap from one of the sycamore trees that line her avenue to the next. She watches what she likes to think is the same squirrel doing it each morning. She then notices something else. She knows instinctively it is not another of those retro posters the Big Five have been using. This poster is crudely made, even by the retro chic modes of the day. Just the year 2023 in large block numerals, followed by the question, 'WHAT THE FUUK IS GOING ON?' Just black ink on cheap white paper. There is nothing else on the poster. But it stirs something very deep in her. It triggers a longing, an urge that has nothing to do with sex, or networking, or travel, or keeping fit, or . . .

But you must be wondering who I am, this disembodied voice that is telling you this story about a woman called Winnie and a squirrel in a tree. Well, you will just have to accept me, just as I accept the compulsion to speak out even though I am painfully aware I am talking to an invisible, perhaps non-existent, you.

For it might be me who has spent the previous night fly-posting your city with '2023: WHAT THE FUUK IS GOING ON?' posters.

Winnie Smith enters Starbucks, orders her skinny latte, swipes her ZitCoins card and contemplates the rest of her life.

We now need to slip back a few years to the year 2011, and to the height of the Occupy Movement. Like many of her generation, Winnie is swept up in the excitement and idealistic aspirations of the Occupy Movement. Although her stepmother is left-leaning and cynical herself of international banking and the business world in general, she never felt motivated to do anything about it. Winnie is different. Winnie acts upon her impulses. Winnie walks out of school and doesn't stop walking until she is right there in the . . .

It is at this point we have to decide where Winnie lives. I sort of imagined her living in Seattle, as in the heart of where everything is happening. I imagined her Starbucks to be there on the sunny, affluent West Coast of the USA, hence the clear blue skies, etc. But now I am imagining Winnie living in one of the hipper areas of North London, and her walking out of sixth-form college half-way through a lesson in medieval history and all the way down the Kingsland Road, down through Stoke Newington, Dalston, Hoxton and Shoreditch. All the way until she gets to the City of London, and it is there she joins the Occupy Movement, right there on the steps of Saint Paul's.

The compromise I am willing to make is this: you can imagine Winnie coming from wherever you are from and her joining your local Occupy protest. Then maybe some years later, after university and a joint philosophy and computer studies degree, Winnie moves to Mountain View in Silicon Valley to take up her job with GoogleByte. Or maybe she just stays in North London.

It is on her first night in a tent, while sharing a second bottle of cider and listening to a nineteen-year-old filmmaker up from Brighton, that she loses her virginity. The nineteen-year-old filmmaker becomes her boyfriend. He is filming everything and anything that is going on. He (we will leave his name out of this for the time being) believes what they are doing could bring about the complete collapse of the crooked and corrupt financial institutions of the world.

He is right.

By the Summer of 2013 the worldwide Occupy Movement has a physical stranglehold on all the global financial centres, at the same time as having hacked all of their computer systems. The subsequent financial crash is complete. The Wall Street crash of 1929 was a mere blip compared to this.

There seems nothing the various wealthiest countries in the world can do about this – not even China. None of them are willing to send in their troops to arrest the brightest and whitest of their nation's youths.

AmaZaba, already the world's largest retailer, decide to step in. AmaZaba, which started out as merely a fast and efficient online way of buying and selling books, very quickly became the way most people bought all their essentials and most of life's un-essentials. That is, bar skinny lattes and freshly baked croissants. It now seems strange that they started out way back in 1994 selling only books, a product the internet quickly made obsolete, while helping to save the rainforests.

Before the 2013 crash, AmaZaba were already considering a move into using Bitcoins as their main trading currency. The Bitcoin movement is very much adopted by the young and alternative. So it is no surprise the Occupy Movement adopts the Bitcoin wholesale as a way of trading internationally among themselves. The fact that Bitcoins are an international currency that has nothing to do with the financial markets or any 'big bad' nation states is perfect for both Occupy and a global online retailer like AmaZaba. Occupy and AmaZaba are to be a perfect marriage and the dowry is paid in Bitcoins.

AmaZaba make a deal with the Occupy Movement to run the world's finances, using Bitcoins as the global currency. The first thing that is done is to change the name of the currency from Bitcoins to ZitCoins. Then overnight the power of all nation states is slashed. There is nothing the Big Five economic power-houses of the world – the USA, Russia, China, Japan, and the EU – can do about it.

Who is running the Occupy Movement is a bit less clear: some say it is just some teenagers drinking cider in a tent; others say it is someone in Helsinki called Hannu Puttonen.

By the end of 2013 AmaZaba, with the help of Occupy, have not only saved the world economy, they are the only online retailer any of us can trust. Of course, there are hundreds of thousands of specialist start-up online retailers, but discussion of them will be left to another part of this story.

The first state to go completely bottom up in late 2013 is Greece. The newly merged WikiTube sneak in while AmaZaba are still popping the corks at their wedding breakfast and buy Greece off the EU, for a fraction of its value. There is soon a queue of nation states lining up to be willingly bought by one of the new emerging Big Five. GoogleByte, WikiTube, AmaZaba, FaceLife and AppleTree's time has arrived.

Fast-forward again to a Starbucks somewhere in Mountain View, California; or is it Seattle, or Dalston, London? The choice is still yours, but my guess is Dalston may be getting the readers' vote.

Winnie takes a stool by the plate-glass window so she can watch the world outside. A helicopter passes across the clear blue sky, trailing a banner with the words 'ABOVE US ONLY SKY' and with the Starbucks logo on its tail. Yoko Ono is her favourite artist. She is pleased that her favourite artist has done a deal with her favourite coffee-shop chain. She watches the helicopter and its banner until it disappears out of sight behind YouTwo Tower.

Before putting her iPhone23 away she checks how many Likes her latest FaceLife post has got – 3,554. Not as many as her last post, but she only put it up ten minutes ago. Winnie has been on FaceLife since her twelfth birthday in 2006. Before that she was on MyFace. Since then every moment in her life, every passing thought, photos of almost every meal she has ever eaten are there. In fact, she has photographed the love heart in the froth on the top of each and every latte she has ever had. Her whole life is there to be Viewed, Shared and Liked. Right now she has 7,356,725 Friends, as well as 654,823,156 followers on Twitter. Not as many as her best friend Primrose but more than her last boyfriend.

Conspiracy theory types have been complaining about Google-Byte and AppleTree and AmaZaba and the rest since she was in her teens. The conspiracy theory brigade would tell you the Big Five are able to exploit the entire trail of personal information we leave in our wake. But these are usually blokes with something to prove, instead of getting on and making things happen themselves. She went out with one such lad for a few weeks when she was at uni, and he was into all that Illuminati conspiracy stuff. To begin with she was impressed with his attitude; he even persuaded her to come off FaceLife, but as soon as she finished with him she went straight back on it.

The truth is Winnie has never seen any particular problem with it, seeing as the Big Five have solved most of the world's problems in less than a generation. She cannot believe what the world was like, as in how shit things had been, even in her own lifetime. It is less than ten years ago that it seemed ISIS (Daesh) were going to hold the world to ransom. And now ISIS are just a bunch of blokes running the best channels on WikiTube.

What happened is that when WikiTube saw how many hits ISIS were getting on their old YouTube set-up, they made them an offer they could not refuse. It was all done above board; the Truth & Reconciliation Board was brought in so no resentments were left to fester. Within a couple of years it seemed every former disenfranchised young Islamic man around the world was running his own channel on WikiTube. They were all offered very attractive start-up deals. They would work all hours and they knew what the customer wanted and at the right price. As for Sharia law and all those other problems, the former Wikipedia side of WikiTube was able to show them exactly what it was that Muhammad meant them to do and how to behave. In fact, it worked so well that many of the former Christian Right in what we still call, for nostalgic reasons only, the USA drifted across to Islam. I mean, if you read The Koran/Qur'an, Jesus/Isa is one of the Major Prophets. But he is just a man and not Truly the Son of God, which makes more sense to everyone.

Winnie puts her phone away in her LabelFree* leather school satchel and pulls out the jotter. She found it yesterday in a vintage shop near Newington Green. She also buys a 1950s Parker fountain pen there and a full bottle of Quink ink. What she wants

* LabelFree is the name Fair Trade used to rebrand themselves once all trade became fair. Within weeks of Fair Trade rebranding to LabelFree, numerous major clothing brands started to adopt the LabelFree logo. This, of course, does not stop anyone with any awareness knowing exactly what brand the particular article of clothing or accessory is that is sporting a LabelFree logo.

to do is write a diary, like Adrian Mole or even Anne Frank. A private diary in her own handwriting that is never Viewed, Liked or Shared. It can be her version of her life. The trouble with FaceLife is you always have to tell the truth because if you don't, a million people tell you you're lying, and the Likes start to dry up. But in your private diary you can say what you want and no one ever knows.

Winnie fills the pen with ink, just as the man in the vintage shop showed her. She looks around at the other morning regulars in this Starbucks. Almost all of them are clutching their iPhones, updating their WikiTube pages, downloading the updated apps, or just Viewing, Liking and Sharing what their Friends are already putting up that day.

She is hoping some of the others may look up and notice she is opening a jotter, clutching a pen in her left hand and writing the first words she has written in her own hand since about 2017. No one notices.

Above the counter is the Yoko Ono line 'WAR IS OVER'. This became Starbucks' strap-line when the Yoko Ono estate came on board. Winnie has an almost OCD habit of reading the line five times in a row before taking her first sip of her first skinny latte of the day. There is something else that she is never able to work out about her daily Starbucks session – at home she rarely, if ever, listens to music, but one of the things she enjoys about her skinny-latte moments is the music they play in Starbucks. It can be anything from Bob Dylan to Bach to some of the new stuff she doesn't know, but it always makes her feel better about the world and womankind as a whole.

But today she writes her full name – 'Winifred Lucie Atwell Smith' – and today's date – '23 April 2023' – before taking her first sip. She then looks out of the window again. Yesterday she watched a young man there putting up one of the crude retro fly-posters she saw earlier. She didn't see his face, just the back of him. He had the same pair of Levi's as her, a pair of LabelFree work boots, but nothing on top. She could see his body was well toned, the muscles in his arms taut. She felt a rush of lust pass through her body. But this was followed almost immediately by a surge of anger. She had not felt proper anger for years. Not since the age of ten, when the mere sight of her father could drive her into a rage of pure hatred for him and all she thought he stood for. She blames him for her Mother leaving.

Winnie succeeded in transferring the hatred she once had for her father to the dark-haired young man she saw across the street.

Vivid, beautiful hallucinations flashed through her mind. She would flog him almost to death with a leather whip. She would tie his naked body to a stake and shoot him full of arrows like Saint Sebastian. She would ravish him and cut his throat at the moment of climax.

This rush of hatred towards a man whose face she had not seen and whom she had never met felt real. Not the fake real you see in films and read in books. It was like something worth killing for. She did not know she could still feel like this. Now she has everything she could ever want. Now world peace is guaranteed. Now we no longer have the need for prisons. Now we have harnessed the power of the sun, meaning there is no need to worry about greenhouse gases polluting the atmosphere and us running out of fossil fuels and whether the ozone layer has been patched up. Now there is enough food for everyone. Now you can practise whatever religion you want, or none at all. Now the existence of God can be proved and disproved in equal measure, and all are agreed with the findings.

The only trouble is that this opening up to negative thinking, which her seven years of therapy has all but sorted, reminds her of another of her previous boyfriends. It was when she made the classic mistake of falling for an older man. He was a bit of a hero of hers when she was still at uni. He was one of those super-hackers. His name was Julian Assange, there was some sort of media ker-fuffle around him for a while, but WikiTube did a deal with him for his WikiLeaks company. They set him up to run a programme in education. Between the years 2018 and 2020 WikiTube took over all the schools in the world, making free schooling avail-able for everyone between the ages of four and twenty-four at the now rebranded WikiCampus. The fundamental premise of WikiCampus was that every child was given a Wikipedia page at the age of five, and it was down to them to add to it daily and cor-rect those of their classmates. It had an instant effect of improving both the literacy and numeracy rates of children around the globe. Because children started to want to have their Wikipedia pages in more than one language, and Google Translate could still not be trusted, a side effect was that almost all children could read and write at least three languages before starting high school. Sadly Winnie was too old for this and could only speak English and Cantonese.

Winnie loathes Assange; she thinks he is a total fraud. It was her relationship with him that her seven years in therapy dwells upon most.

Back to Starbucks.

Winnie's eyes refocus on the page in the jotter in front of her. She realises that while she has been thinking about the man's torso from yesterday with a mixture of lust and loathing, she has also been writing, as though by automatic action. In huge letters across the page she has written the following five lines, over and over again in large capitals:

I HATE GOOGLEBYTE

I HATE WIKITUBE

I HATE AMAZABA

I HATE FACELIFE

I HATE APPLETREE

She cannot believe the words her hand has placed on the virgin paper in front of her. She glances around Starbucks to see if anybody has noticed what she is doing. They haven't. Why would they? They are all completely engrossed in the world filtering through their own iPhone23s. Winnie picks up her phone, flicks through a few apps, notices she had more than eight thousand new Likes to her FaceLife update and at least four thousand new followers on Twitter since she first sat down.

She wants to smash her phone on the ground and grind it with her boots into a thousand pieces. But she doesn't.

Instead she sips the last of her skinny latte, puts her jotter, Parker Pen and bottle of Quink ink away in her LabelFree satchel and strides out through the automatic plate-glass doors of Starbucks into a world that has no idea what is going to hit it.

▲

SAY WHAT YOU WANT, WHEN YOU WANT, TO WHOEVER YOU WANT. Marcia Zuckerberg (2007)

▲

Barnhill
Jura
23 April 1984

Dear Diary,

So I have finished the first chapter of this book. Writing about Winnie starting a diary made me think that I should do the same.

The pen name I'm using is George Orwell. Bit of background information there, in case anyone is ever interested. I do wonder if the reader will wonder what my real name is or even what sex I am. I have taken it upon myself to escape the clutches of London to live for some months in a crofter's cottage at the northern end of the Isle of Jura, off the West Coast of Scotland. Or for as long as it takes to get this novel written.

I was born in 1926, so that makes me fifty-eight.

My companion on this expedition and in life is a Brough Superior Motorcycle, the finest motorbike anyone could ever have and also probably the most beautiful piece of engineering that has ever existed. No woman could ever want a man after she had done a ton on a Brough. Well, I guess I have just given my sex away. If you need to know any more about Brough, I will leave it to you to find out.

As for this book I am setting out to write, I expect the reader's palette is reasonably broad, so they will notice I have borrowed from two monuments of twentieth-century literature. I do not feel the need to defend this on artistic grounds. I just hope that if this book is ever published, the holders of the copyright in both of these previous works of great literature will only feel honoured I have chosen to embrace them in my work of fiction.

The light is already fast draining from this glorious Spring day. I will celebrate this first day of writing by mounting my Brough, driving the thirty-one miles South to the village of Craighouse and the one bar in the one hotel on the island. There I will partake in a dram or two of Jura's finest. I hope that young lad from Jura House will be there tonight. What was his name again, Frank or Francis or something?

Maybe I should write one of these diary entries at the end of each of the 23 chapters in this proposed trilogy of books.

Love,

Roberta

2 : MEET YOKO & JOHN

There are some who have decreed order is the natural order of not only the human condition but of everything that has ever existed and is ever likely to exist.

And there are those who have proclaimed chaos is the natural order not only of the human condition but of everything that has ever existed and is ever likely to exist.

And there are those who have made it their lives' work to exploit our natural hunger for order.

And there are those who have made it their lives' work to exploit our natural hunger for chaos.

It is a free market for all of you living in the free world.

Whereas I am on the island of Fernando Pó. It is where I was born and bred. I may have disagreed with us being a tax haven, but I so abhor us being bought by AppleTree. Or, for that matter, by any of the other Big Five. I am totally and completely against what they are doing with the world. Womankind needs to have war, famine and inequality to function properly: without them we as a species will be over within a couple of generations. As for religion, we need as many as we can have to compete for our souls. The more radical the religion, the better.

That is why I am here with these five dolls I have made to represent the founding mothers of each of the Big Five, and over the next few days I will be sticking my needle made from bamboo into them. You may think this is a futile and primitive approach

24

to bringing about world change, but it worked for my ancestors and it already seems to be working for me. Last night I began testing the process by putting a needle just a short way into the doll that is Stevie Dobbs, and I think it was successful. I can already sense her days are numbered.

Meanwhile:

Winnie strides across the street, the caffeine gently coursing its way around her body. She looks up to see if the squirrel is about – she is. She is building a dray. Or that is what Winnie assumes it to be. On reaching the age of twenty-eight Winnie is wondering when her maternal instinct might kick in and start taking over her life. As yet it has not, but in some deep recess of her mind she is crossing off her fertile years. This, unbeknown to her, is influencing completely random aspects of her character. For a start there is a man called O'Brien at GoogleByte who she has only ever seen a handful of times, a man she would not have looked at twice a couple of years ago, but for some reason he keeps coming into her mind.

It is while she is dismissing the thought of O'Brien that she notices the window of the pet shop next to her corner shop at the base of her block has been done in, and the tanks containing the tropical fish have also been smashed. There are a couple of police cars and what look like two plainclothes officers from a period police drama standing about. Winnie never liked the idea of this shop and seeing those fish kept in their prison tanks but . . . she doesn't think any more about it.

Instead she goes over to the wall that has the poster on it. The '2023: WHAT THE FUUK IS GOING ON?' poster. Without thinking, she stretches out her arm and touches the poster with the open palm of her hand. She is surprised to find it still wet. Her arm recoils and she looks at her palm. It is covered with something that looks very much like male semen. Instinctively she sniffs it.

A lone cloud drifts across the blue sky.

Winnie enters Victory Mansions, and instead of taking the lift to her floor she runs up all seven flights. As she is just about to enter her apartment to get on with her day's work for GoogleByte, she hears the voice of her neighbour Tammy.

'Winnie, it's the kids' mac-Bot again. It's crashed three times today and it's driving my children mad. They are on the Junior WikiCampus and it keeps returning "translation failed", then the whole thing crashes. Can you have a quick look at it?'

Although Winnie is totally psyched up for her day in front of the screen, she knows it is the neighbourly thing to do to give her a hand. She is on a push to be less selfish.

'Yeah, I should be able to sort it.'

She likes the smell of their apartment, as if Tammy is always cooking an interesting meal. Always trying out another dish from another part of the world. Winnie usually eats out or gets a takeaway.

Tammy's partner George also freelances for GoogleByte, but on the sales side of things. George and Tammy have two children, Tina (seven) and Richey (nine). Winnie being asked to sort something out on their mac-Bot is becoming a regular thing and she wonders if Tina and Richey create something wrong with their mac-Bot just to get her in. They usually tease her and ask about boyfriends, but it's all friendly.

Winnie has always thought Tammy's a bit of an odd one. She was once a singer, even sang on a hit record by the Utah Saints, but now she's stuck at home bringing up a couple of kids. Once Winnie sorts out whatever the problem is, Tammy usually tries to get her to stay for a coffee.

But this time the problem with the mac-Bot does not seem to be something engineered by Tina and Richey. There is something else going on. George has left numerous pages open and they are all about the Illuminati.

Winnie has not thought about the Illuminati for years. When she was at school in her early teens, there was a conspiracy theory craze all the boys were into. They were always going on about the secret powers that really pulled the levers in the world. Back then it was Obama, Putin, Merkel, Jinping and Akihito who were the players, the ones who ran the Big Five countries. But the boys in her class had this idea that there was another, secret Five that actually ran everything in the world. And had done so for thousands of years.

'I got some Peruvian Organic Mountain Beans especially for you. Do you want a mug of coffee while you try and sort things out?'

'No, it's okay, Tammy. I will just get this done and then I need to get back to work.'

Then there is this whole story about J-Zee and Beyon-Say being members of the Illuminati, and the proof is in the fact they called their daughter Purple Ivy. This name is supposedly a secret code revealing her membership of an 'ancient and all-powerful occult society'. It is since then, when Winnie had just turned seventeen, that she knew boys and the male species in general were fundamentally stupid. It was one thing thinking there must be someone else in charge of things other than the President of the USA, but to think whoever that was would want to hang out with pop stars, however great she used to think Beyon-Say was back then, was just lame.

Looking at all of these pages on the Illuminati that George has left open, and which are slowing everything down on his system, it seems he has not grown out of it all. Maybe, Winnie thinks, George is just getting a surge of nostalgia for those days when the world was totally fucked-up and about to collapse. Even Winnie sometimes, after a couple of glasses of red, feels nostalgia for those days. She knows it's stupid.

Something inside keeps pushing her to read more and more of these pages on the Illuminati that have been left open.

'You sure you don't want a mug?'

The aroma of the freshly ground beans gets the better of her.

'Okay, Tammy. Black, no sugar. Thanks.'

'But you always drink latte at Starbucks.'

'Yeah, but that's my breakfast coffee, this is my working coffee.'

She is thinking about the words in the diary she has just started. The words she had no idea she was going to write. The 'I HATE' words. It is as if her appetite to read these pages about the Illuminati feeds that same need in her. But on another level she knows that if it is something GoogleByte could find that easily, then it is no threat at all. Anything really real, as in a real threat to our society, a threat to our hard-won world peace, would not be just there for all of us to read.

Tammy brings the mug of coffee through to where Winnie is at the screen.

'Don't you want to have children? You'd make such a great mum.'

Meanwhile:

Stevie Dobbs is walking through a glade of Sequoias in the Redwood National World Park in Northern California. It is where she goes to get away from all the politics of AppleTree Boulevard. It is also where she does her best thinking.

Suddenly she feels this sharp pain in the left side of her gut. Excruciating pain. Like someone has just jabbed her with a sharpened knitting needle. This is the second time this has happened to her today, but this time it is a lot worse.

Meanwhile:

Winnie takes her sip from the mug of coffee while not listening to what Tammy is telling her about her children. Instead Winnie is thinking it would be great if there was a secret society that actually controlled everything. And if that was the case, there could be another organisation that could attempt to undermine it all. Be at war with the Illuminati. An eternal war. She reads more of these pages. It seems there is another organisation called The Justified Ancients of Mummu who do just that. They exist to undermine the Illuminati and spread chaos in the world. They are called The JAMs for short.

Meanwhile:

In a warehouse on the side of a canal on the other side of the borough, in a place called Hackney Wake, a young couple called Yoko & John are just waking up. This Yoko & John are both 23; both have dropped out of art college. This Yoko has changed her name by deed poll in honour of that Yoko. John has changed his name from Paul Harrison, because he thinks it's funny. Yoko & John do everything together. Except John is fucking Yoko's best friend, and Yoko has yet to find out.

Today Yoko & John plan to screenprint their second poster. Yesterday they fly-posted the one hundred copies of their first poster on walls around the city.

Even better than getting all one hundred posters up is the fact that they did not document it in any way. Last night they celebrated by each taking a double dose of DMT2 and going to a retro rave.

John thinks they should call themselves The Post-Digital Underground, but Yoko doesn't like it.

'Why?'

'It is too literal. There is no poetry to it. And we should not be defined by what we are not, but what we can be.'

John does not understand what she is on about.

'But, Yoko, we are against the digital world, and we are underground. That is the whole point about us not documenting anything, so it can never be co-opted by the Big Five. And "post" is a good word, like in "post-war" and "post-punk".'

'But, John, it has no poetry. We need to harness the poetry in what we are doing. Poetry is our ultimate weapon. It is what will bring down the Big Five.'

John is not too sure if he really wants to change the world, or even bring down the Big Five. He finds it difficult enough that they aren't documenting what they are doing and uploading photos to Instagram and live-streaming content while they are actually putting up the posters. He knows if they did that, they could have an instant following of millions. Yoko always argues they may get that instant following of millions, but so does everybody who does anything, but that following changes nothing. And that following is just following you because they want you to follow them back.

Yoko always seems to win these arguments. At least her best mate Cynthia never gives John this sort of hassle, and she is a better shag.* But he knows Yoko is his best bet, so he has to compromise.

Yoko & John sleep on a mattress on the floor. Their duvet cover has not been washed for months. They don't use condoms or any other sort of birth control, as Yoko had womb cancer at eighteen and had her womb removed.

John goes to make Yoko her morning mug of sweet tea. She

---

* Cynthia being a better 'shag' was the word in John's mind and not the sort of language used by me, George Orwell.

only ever has sugar in her tea while still in bed. She needs that sugar rush to face the day.

He brings it back.

'John, you shouldn't have thrown that brick through the pet-shop window last night.'

'Don't talk shit. You know you are as against the keeping of pets as I am. It is evil to keep those fish in those tanks, just swimming around and around all day.'

'Yeah, but all that happened was the fish died.'

'Well, I think it's better they are all dead than living miserable lives as slaves so some straights can watch their pretty colours. And anyway, you thought it was funny last night.'

'Yeah, but I was off my head then. This morning my head is clear and I know what we should call ourselves.'

'What?'

'The Justified Ancients of Mu Mu.'

'What the fuck's that? I think we should be called The KMA.'

'And what the fuck's that?'

'The Kazakhstan Medical Association.'

'Forget it, John. We are The JAMs. No debate. I remember my mum telling me about a book she read once; it was called *The Eye in the Pyramid*. It has this pyramid with an eye in the top on the cover. Rubbish cover but . . . Anyway, the book was all about a secret society called the Illuminati who controlled the world. And in this book was an even more secret dis-organisation that existed to undermine the Illuminati . . .'

'Yeah. And?'

'Let me finish. This dis-organisation was called The Justified Ancients of Mummu. They spread chaos through the world and brought down the Illuminati.'

'So what does Mummu mean? Sounds like baby speak.'

31

'Mu Mu is the ancient spirit of chaos.'

'So you think that we should rip off the name from some dodgy old book your mum read back in the 1970s?'

'No. Like I said, we call ourselves The Justified Ancients of Mu Mu. As in, not Mummu, but Mu Mu. Two words, not just one. Mu Mu is the feminine of Mummu. Get it?'

'And, like, that is some big difference?'

'It is those subtle but all-important differences that count in poetry.'

'All right. So what do we do now?'

'We design a logo for The Justified Ancients of Mu Mu, or even just The JAMs for short. Then we make a new silkscreen. Then we steal some more of that cheap newsprint. Then we print up one hundred posters. And then we go and fly-post them all tonight. But first can you get me another mug of tea?'

It is then that Yoko notices the used condom semi-shoved under the mattress.

Meanwhile:

Winnie makes her excuses to Tammy and her kids, gets out the door and down the corridor to her own apartment. She takes her mac-Bot out onto her balcony to get on with her day's work.

The sun has shifted around. Her heart quails before this enormous pyramid shape in her head. A thousand rocket bombs would not batter it down. She wonders again who she is writing this diary for. For the future, for the past, for an age that might be imaginary?

'And, anyway, why does it matter what I do or don't do? Why should I care, why should anyone care, when everything we ever do is there for all future generations to see on FaceLife? And who is to say that whatever I write in this notebook will ever survive? I remember learning at school how the paper used in the printing of real books disintegrates within a hundred years, that is why the internet is so much better as it is there for ever. Why do I want to have secrets I do not share? It is keeping secrets that caused so many of the world's problems in the first place. And why use an old-fashioned pen, as if that somehow lends validation to what I am doing?'

Winnie puts her notebook away to get on with her work for GoogleByte.

But before she opens her own mac-Bot, she can't stop the vision of that young man's back and his taut arms passing through her mind. She suppresses it with thinking about O'Brien. But why O'Brien? He's not good-looking by any stretch of the imagination. She knows where it started. One night at an office barbeque he whispered in her ear, when no one was looking, 'We shall meet in the place where there is no darkness.'

It is a meaningless phrase, not even an office-party chat-up line. For some reason the line stayed with her and grew in meaning in her head. It also caused her to be drawn to him in some way. As if he had the same feelings she had. That he too maybe hated in the same way she did.

Meanwhile:

I am about to stick another pin into another doll. This time it might be you.

▲

NOTHING IS YOUR OWN, EXCEPT THE FEW CUBIC CENTIMETRES INSIDE YOUR SKULL. Yoko Ono (2023)

▲

Barnhill
Jura
24 April 1984

Dear Diary,

As for last night, I will sidestep it. At least before things got embarrassing in the bar with Francis Riley-Smith and Duncan Buie I was able to use the hotel's fax machine to send the first chapter of the book off to my literary agent. Within twenty minutes he, Dog Ledger (don't ask), sent back a fax with his full response and some other information he wanted me to respond to.

Firstly his comments.

He thinks I am overloading it with too many facts. That I am somehow desperate to prove what a 'brave new world' 2023 is. That I should just let things evolve more naturally. That I should get the reader more interested in Winnie, and the colours and textures of the world she inhabits. Especially the smells – he thought readers would relate to the smells. Once I had done that the book should then, bit by bit and subtly, introduce all the detail about the world as it is in 2023, as the story unfolds. He might be right.

The thing is, right now I don't know much about Winnie. She is as new to me as she will be to the reader. What I have known from the very inception of the idea of this book is that it is going to hang on the idea of the Big Five and how their power shifted from being nation states to five major companies. I knew all about that weeks ago, that was to be the whole premise of the book. Winnie was just the human element for the reader to project themselves onto.

The other news contained in his fax was all about *Fish Farm*, 'the book that made my "name"', it seems. The book that has already become a set text at some of the more progressive schools,

I might add. Roy Plomley even wanted me to go on *Desert Island Discs*.

It seems Disney have been on to Dog Ledger. Disney want to turn it into an animated film, with someone called Bill Murray doing the voice of Sammy. I have not heard of this Bill Murray but I did learn that Walt Disney no longer makes the films himself, as he died a few years back. They want Jack Nicholson to do the voice of Jack the baddie in the story. I know who Jack Nicholson is; I had the serious hots for him in that film *The Shining*.

It is very widely known, I'm sure, but I will try and get the basic outline of the story down to a couple of sentences:

The fish farm in question is a salmon fish farm off the coast of Scotland, near the town of Oban. All the salmon in the farm are happy with their lot. They are regularly fed and the net around them protects them from killer whales. One day a charismatic wild salmon called Jack approaches the net around their fish farm and starts to tell the farmed salmon on the other side of the net stories about all the things they are missing in the ocean outside. About the excitement of leaving the sea to find the river they were born in, the leaping up the falls and over the weirs while heading to the spawning grounds, dodging the advances of the fly-fishermen. And the final spawning in the shallow waters where their mothers had spawned them, and their grandmothers and great-grandmothers before that. Yes, there were dangers, but that was the glory of life.

The salmon in the fish farm debated and finally took a vote. Sammy, to be voiced by this Bill Murray, thought that Jack could not be trusted, but not many of the others wanted to listen to Sammy. Jack's tongue was silver. The vote to make a break for it was carried by a landslide. The big break-out was meticulously planned. And then the day came and the break-out was successful.

35

But as soon as they got to the outside, into the big, wide and wild sea, they were ambushed by a whole herd of hungry and ruthless grey seals. It was a massacre. The whole thing had been a set-up. Jack knew all along what was going to happen. But, as it happened, Sammy made his escape, and after weeks and months he did actually make it up to the spawning grounds where his great-great-great-grandmother had actually spawned her eggs.

There was also a subplot. Wee Katie Morag was a lady salmon who was sort of Sammy's girlfriend. She had never been in season, so the relationship had never been consummated. The thing was, Jack had his eye on Wee Katie Morag. Sammy was suspicious all along that Jack trying to persuade the farmed salmon to rebel was just a ruse so he could end up fertilising her spawn, before Sammy had a chance.

I will leave it to you to buy and read *Fish Farm* to find out if Sammy got to father Wee Katie Morag's spawn with his sperm.

I had never planned for there to be a moral to the story, just as I am unaware of any moral to the story I am trying to tell about Winnie. But it seems all sorts of morals have been projected onto *Fish Farm*. It seems Disney think it's an attack on the USSR, while the Left in the UK think it is an attack on Maggie Thatcher. I just think it is a story about fish that can talk.

I followed up *Fish Farm* with a novel based on a rambling story told to me by this young ex-military nurse that I met in a lesbian bar in Glasgow, whose name was Gimpo. She had just returned from being a frontline nurse in the Falklands War, which we lost. Gimpo was suffering from extreme post-traumatic stress disorder and self-medicating with whisky mixed with cheap speed. This novel was named after the Royal Navy's hospital ship HMS *Uganda*, which sailed down the Atlantic with the rest of our doomed flotilla for the war. That book was a complete failure, sold less than 700 copies. According to Dog Ledger the pressure is on from the publisher. I have to get back on form with this book. None of those negative war themes. Nobody wants to read a book about a war we lost.

But I digress. I am supposed to be thinking about Winnie, what she looks like, her character and all that.

So here it is. Winnie, in 2023, is twenty-eight years old, roughly. Just the right age to start on your life's mission. Her hair is mousey and hangs naturally to her shoulders. As a child she had it long. As a teenager she cropped it short and dyed it blonde. Since turning twenty-one she gets it trimmed regularly so it just touches her shoulders. And she has not dyed it.

She did have some weight issues when she was in her late teens and early twenties, going from painfully skinny to the verge of overweight. But she is now on top of things. She keeps to her broadsheet diet, which seems to work for her.

Sex is something I don't usually write about – I don't feel particularly well qualified to do so. But Dog has advised me, as my literary agent, that I should have some hint of it to keep the reader interested. So for those that need to know, Winnie would tick the heterosexual box, but does usually have a crush on someone of her own sex. For a time it was Viv Albertine, who played in that band The Slits. This side of her sexuality was only consummated once; it was with her Cantonese teacher on a school trip, although she is in denial about the consummation.

As for her regular heterosexual side, there have been a number of unsuitable boys and men. None lasted much longer than a few months. Each of them left their mark, but none as profound as the mark she left on them.

I hope those two last paragraphs keep Dog Ledger happy.

This evening I will not be driving the thirty-one miles down to

Craighouse on my Brough. And may not do so again until Francis writes a letter apologising for his behaviour last night.

I don't think the locals know who I am.

Love,

Roberta Antonia Wilson

Postscript: there is no point in me hiding my real name from you, 'Dear Diary'.

Postscript to the Postscript: something I have just thought of. If you are a male reader of the book, imagine Winnie to be two inches shorter than you. If you are a female reader, imagine Winnie to be two inches taller than you.

And I guess I'd better tell you why he is called Dog Ledger and what our relationship is. I know you must be wondering. He started life as Douglas McLedger. It is his, or at least his family's, ancestral cottage I am staying in. His first name went from Douglas to Dougie while attending the primary school on Jura. At the high school in Oban it became Doug. At university in Edinburgh, where we met in the late '40s, the 'U' got dropped and he became just plain Dog. It was a sort of joke, but it stuck. He decided to drop the 'Mc' when he fell out with his father. So now he is known across the literary world as Dog Ledger. He spends most of his life in his cottage in the Pyrenees. It was as a student that he invited me up to stay in this house at the northern tip of Jura. And yes, of course, we were lovers for a while, but that was all decades ago. That said, there are still some of the *frissons* ex-lovers can have at times. Not that I would be interested. If and when I need a man, I need a young man.

3 : SKY OF BLUE AND SEA OF GREEN

09:43 Sunday 23 April 2023

A frail and old Japanese lady sits on her balcony and looks out across the city that has adopted her. She sips the orange juice that has been freshly squeezed for her. The morning light is gentle. The heat of the day has not yet found its force. This lady remembers the young girl she once was in her native city of Tokyo, in a bunker hearing the bombs drop and wondering if she would live to see the sun rise. That little girl picked up a pencil and on a scrap of paper made a list of the things she wanted to do before she died.

The sun is rising above New York.

A young man enters the balcony.

'Ms Ono, two packages have arrived for you. Shall I open them?'

'No, just bring me my knife and I will open them myself. But thank you for offering.'

She decides to open the larger of the two boxes first. It measures about 40 × 20 × 30 cm. The sharpened kitchen knife slices easily through the tape and the box is soon opened. It contains mugs. Coffee mugs. All identical. There are probably twenty in the box, but she is not counting them, she is pulling one of them out of the box to have a look. It is better than she was expecting. In fact, she is quite thrilled at the way it looks.

When her management first approached her about doing a deal with Starbucks, she was unsure. Why would she want to do that?

She didn't need the money. She didn't go to Starbucks. She didn't even drink coffee. But something inside her, a small voice, said, 'Yes.' Maybe the voice of the girl in the bunker in Tokyo listening to the bombs, or the voice of John, saying, 'Yes.'

So she said 'yes' to her management. And now they have sent her a box of twenty mugs. She holds one of them in her hand. It is the standard Starbucks mug that is in their coffee shops all around the world, but the face inside the logo is not the face of the girl that is usually there. It is her face. Well, her face maybe fifty years ago taken from a photo, but still her face. Above the logo it says 'STARBUCKS'. Below the logo it says 'WAR IS OVER'. The little girl in the bunker would be pleased with her. John would be pleased with her. Her mother would be pleased with her. She was pleased with herself. This was good.

Then she picks up the other package. It is nowhere near as big. It only measures about 20 × 15 × 3 cm. She already knows it is going to be a book. Many people send her books. But it is not packaged in the usual AmaZaba packaging. It is plain. She picks up the kitchen knife and slices the packaging open. The book slides out. The book is yellow and hardback. On the front in large bold black typeface are the words *Grapefruit Are Not the Only Bombs by Yoko Ono*'.

The frail old lady turns the book over to find out if there is any other information to be had, but on the back there is only a photograph of a grapefruit sliced in half. She flicks through the pages. Each page has on it what looks like a poem, or maybe a set of instructions. One page just has the word 'NO' on it, but very tiny. She puts down the book and picks up the packaging. She looks at the back of the packaging. There is a sender's address, of sorts:

Yoko Ono
Warehouse A
Hackney Wake
London
Albion

The frail old lady feels a flash of anger jolt through her. This book has nothing to do with her. It is not only using her name, but the name of the fruit that has been associated with her artistic practice ever since the 1960s, before she met John, before the world knew who she was, before the world hated her. Before the world respected her. Before she did a deal with the largest coffee chain in the world, for reasons she is not too sure about.

She throws the book over the balcony.

Halfway around the world on the second floor of a warehouse in an area of London called Hackney Wake another Yoko Ono washes a sharpened kitchen knife. And she is thinking. She is thinking she could never have guessed how easy it is to kill someone. Even the person you love more than anyone in the world. Only yesterday she would have gone anywhere with this person. And done absolutely anything for them. But now they were dead and she felt nothing. There wasn't even that much blood. She rolled the body up in their duvet and planned to push it (note: no longer even him and certainly not the John who she had loved like no other man) out of the canal-side doors of their floor and let it drop into the canal two floors below.

If she could remember, she would remember that as a little girl she made a list of things she wanted to do in her life. There were one hundred things on the list. One of the things on the list was to climb to the top of Everest. Another was to be the first woman on Mars. And yet another was to murder someone. That little girl can now cross off another of the things on that list.

Yoko then goes back to the kitchen table with a mug of coffee. The mug is one John stole for her yesterday as a much-belated Valentine's Day present. It is one of those mugs Starbucks are now using with the other Yoko Ono's face on it and the words 'WAR IS OVER' underneath the logo. She puts the mug down and picks up one of the books from the pile of five identical books. She looks at the title and reads it again. She must have picked it up and read it a thousand times since she first got the box of books from the printers. She is still very pleased with the title *Grapefruit Are Not the Only Bombs*. Actually she only changed the word '*Weapons*' to '*Bombs*' at the last minute. She wonders if the other Yoko Ono has received the copy of the book she posted to her. And she wonders what she thinks. 'I bet she will love it.'

In New York, the sun has risen and the other Yoko Ono is on the phone to her management. She wants him to find out where this book has come from, who has written it and for all copies to be destroyed. 'I have had a lifetime of people trying to cash in on me, use me, take me for granted, and for what . . . They are not the ones Starbucks want for endorsement . . .' She slams the phone down.

A crow lands on the railing of her balcony.

▲

Winnie is sitting in front of her screen, daydreaming about her Mother. Winnie was five when she left. She remembers her as a tall, statuesque, rather silent woman with slow movements and magnificent hair. As for her father, maybe more of him later. This is all just before FaceLife and everything else.

A few years ago, back in the late Teens, when Winnie first got the job with GoogleByte, she could not imagine a more perfect job to be doing. A job she could do from anywhere in the world whenever she wanted. It all started with watching a TED lecture that Celine Hagbard gave. The name of her TED was 'Don't Be Evil'.

Everything about Celine Hagbard seemed ten times larger than life and just so inspiring. Hagbard swept all other heroines aside in one forty-minute TED. Winnie then fired off an email to her, never expecting to hear anything back.

It's hard to tell what was real and what was just made up about Celine Hagbard. For a start, did the submarine exist? Had she actually had a sex change or was that just a publicity stunt as well? Or was all that happened that he flipped his last name with his first name and he became a she?

But none of that really mattered because FUUK-UP was for real. FUUK-UP, or to give it its full and proper name, First Universal Uber Kinetic-Ultramicro Programmer, was the beginning of the internet. It was where it all started. Then FUUK-UP became Google, for obvious marketing reasons. Which then became GoogleByte. That was after Celine did the deal with Melinda Gates for MicroSoft.

If any one woman can lay claim to having united the world, it must be Celine Hagbard.

It is that TED lecture that made Winnie realise there was so much more to the world than the old right versus left, money versus art, real versus virtual, girls versus boys, even life versus death stuff that plagued her through her late teens and early twenties.

Everything is an opportunity. Even death. Every door can open onto a new world. Even though she knew it might all sound to others like that inspirational claptrap churned out by all those supposedly inspirational speakers of her father's generation, what Hagbard had to say *was* the real thing. She had done it, made it happen, saved the world – for ever.

It was just after midnight on 23 August 2017 when Winnie hit 'Send' on that first email to Hagbard. And by 3:00 she had an email back from her/him. And not only was he/she answering Winnie's question, Hagbard was also offering her a job. The ultimate job!

In Winnie's email to Hagbard she told her about her dream. In the dream she worked out how to record everything in her thoughts, all of it: her daydreams, her actual sleeping dreams, all her memories, even her emotions – everything. And then how to upload it all onto her computer. It was like she would then not need to have her own brain, her own memories. And as long as she kept uploading it every day until she physically died, she could then in theory live on for ever as all her thoughts, dreams, desires would be there to interact with everybody else. You could then carry on with being on FaceLife and send out tweets and wish your great-great-great-great-great-grandchildren a happy birthday, and they could do the same back to you.

Up until then Celine Hagbard had only been able to use Google-Byte to connect all that dull reality stuff in the world. What Winnie was proposing was she could connect every human being's brain with everyone on Earth for all time. Death would be vanquished.

At the bottom of the email from Hagbard was the quote, 'To organise the world's information and make it universally accessible and useful.'

No wonder that back in 2017 Celine Hagbard got back to Winnie almost immediately. It was Hagbard's *from here to eternity* moment. This girl from nowhere was not only offering her immortality, she was offering it to all womankind.

44

If anyone ever asks you what that record by The American Medical Association was about, it was about that very moment Celine Hagbard had at 3:00 on 23 August 2017. Celine Hagbard had long since acknowledged to herself that she had the greatest brain ever, so she not only understood exactly what this young woman was proposing, she could follow the logic of Winnie's theories-cum-equations-cum . . . This was an email from a mind that was at least equal to her own.

In the email back to Winnie, Hagbard told her she could start immediately, be paid whatever she wanted as long as they were ready to launch in six years' time: 23:00 on 23 April 2023 to be precise.

Whatever Winnie asks for and whatever she actually gets, me, the writer of this book, and you, the reader of it, are not party to. All we know is Winnie's financial circumstances do not particularly change. Winnie just gets on with the work. And she works almost non-stop.

The day before yesterday, the job was done, everything is in place. All she has to do is upload it all to GoogleByte's mainframe, and people around the world can plug in to have their brains connected and death will be over. Of course, the doctors still have to work on our bodies not falling to bits, but as far as our minds and imaginations are concerned we can be there for the Big Drive. And we would have access to everything in everybody else's brains, memories and imaginations as well – for ever.

All Winnie has to do is hit 'Send'.

▲

But Winnie doesn't hit 'Send'. She goes out and buys her jotter, Parker Pen and bottle of Quink ink. Then tries to start writing

45

down her thoughts. Her very own thoughts, not thoughts to be Shared or Liked, and definitely not all her thoughts that are going to be there for ever.

And this morning she is not hitting 'Send' either. She is just staring at her screen trying not to think about anything. Well, anything other than that young man's back. And what her Mum might be doing and where.

▲

Meanwhile:

Celine Hagbard is sitting at a pavement table of her regular Starbucks in New York City. Other than one small cloud drifting aimlessly across it, the sky is as blue as it has ever been. She is about to sup the dregs of her second double espresso when something falls from the sky and lands on the sidewalk next to her. It is a book. A hardback book. A yellow hardback book. Hagbard picks it up. She then instinctively looks up at the sky above to see where it has come from. All she can see is the small white cloud. She reads the words on the front cover: '*Grapefruit Are Not the Only Bombs* by Yoko Ono'.

Now, plenty of people might wonder, 'What are the chances that I have just noticed Yoko Ono's face is now being used within the Starbucks logo, 23 seconds before a book by Yoko Ono falls out of the sky at my feet?' They would then probably answer their own question with: 'Several trillion to one.' Whereas Celine Hagbard knew the chances were exactly the same as any other two things happening at the same time. But most people do not see the bigger picture Hagbard sees.

We now have to throw another fact into the equation. You can check it on Wikipedia, if you don't trust me. In 1968, when

Hagbard was still young, and to all intents and purposes still a man, he was taken on by The Beatles as a 'crazy inventor'. It was when The Beatles were going through their Apple end-phase and breaking out in all directions, awarding alternative knighthoods to people like Spike Milligan and making records with Wild Man Fischer and Vera Lynn.

Although history seems to have rewritten it as John Lennon's idea, in fact the whole Yellow Submarine idea came from Ringo Starr. Plans were pretty far developed with the submarine. Hagbard had spent two years on the designs. Paul McCartney had developed a working relationship with the shipyards in Gdańsk, Poland, where it was going to be built. This all started in 1965, when a young shipbuilder called Lech Wałęsa wrote a fan letter to McCartney about his bass playing, and, because McCartney's father had worked in shipbuilding on the Mersey and was laid off after the war, never to work again, McCartney had a real and lasting empathy with shipbuilders worldwide and their day-rate/non-contract plight.

Paul McCartney and Lech Wałęsa were pen pals right through the rest of the '60s. It was Paul who suggested to Lech he should form a trade union; and it was his girlfriend Francie Schwartz who came up with the idea to name the union Solidarność, or Solidarity in English. Paul convinced Lech the name would play well in the Western media.

For a few days in February 1970, the album that was subsequently released as *Let It Be* was going to be called *Solidarity*. It was Yoko Ono who stopped it and demanded it be called *Power to the People*. George and Ringo came up with the peace-making compromise of *Let It Be*.

As The Beatles were prevented from taking their royalties out of any of the Eastern Bloc countries for records they sold there, they used them to secretly bankroll the whole Solidarity Union movement right up until 1992.

Most historians cite the influence of Solidarity as the first move that, over the next two decades, brought down the whole Eastern Bloc. All because one young mechanic wrote a fan letter to Paul McCartney asking about the bass playing on 'Ticket to Ride'.

Before I get sidetracked even further into the secret history of The Beatles, I will bring it back to known and well-documented facts. George Harrison persuaded the other three the only worthwhile thing left for them to do was to stop the Vietnam War, thus bringing about world peace. No amount of protesting by the 'long-haired freaks' was going to make any difference. The Beatles knew they were the only group of people who had the power to make this happen. But they also suspected their power would cease the moment the decade ended.

On 1 September 1969, without telling their lawyers, accountants or even their WAGs, The Beatles withdrew all the money left in the Apple Records coffers. They insisted on having this in $1 bills. Then they flew in their private Learjet to Saigon, the capital of South Vietnam, disguised as nuns, with all the dollars stuffed into forty plain hessian sacks.

In Saigon they bought four Chinook helicopters for cash. With a Beatle in each Chinook they flew North, with ten sacks of dollars in each helicopter. The journey North was low over the paddy fields and jungle. All the while they were blasting 'All You Need Is Love' from PA speakers strapped to the undersides of the Chinooks. After getting lost for several hours, the Chinooks finally landed at a prearranged clearing in the jungle. There they met up with Ho Chi Minh, the leader of the Viet Cong (the side the USA was at war with).

This was the deal The Beatles offered for both sides to end

the war: they would hand over the forty sacks of dollars to Ho Chi Minh in exchange for him agreeing peace terms. As for the Americans, President Nixon had to pull all his forces out of Southeast Asia. Nixon also insisted The Beatles announce their cessation of all collective activities for a term of 23 years as of 1 January 1970, and hand over all the rights to their recordings to him, including all future royalties.

All parties were in agreement.

Between John, Paul, George and Ringo they pulled the forty sacks full of dollars off the helicopters and piled them up in the clearing. Then each of the four Beatles shook hands with Ho Chi Minh and climbed back into their individual Chinooks. Their job was done. The '60s were complete. World peace sorted.

They then took off and, while circling the clearing before heading South back to Saigon and the awaiting aftershow party, they could see the very old and frail Ho Chi Minh himself throwing a lighted torch onto the bundle of sacks. All forty sacks were soon fully ablaze.

The next day, Ho Chi Minh was dead, The Beatles did not announce their cessation of all collective activities on 1 January 1970, so the war in Vietnam dragged on for a further five years, The Beatles released a shit album and John Lennon got shot, and George Harrison died in mysterious circumstances. The fate of Paul and Ringo is yet to be sealed.

▲

But more importantly, back to the fate of one of the major characters in this book – Hagbard Celine, as he still was back then. You would think Hagbard would be pretty pissed off about The Beatles squandering all their assets on such a vain and foolhardy escapade, but in fact he was mightily relieved. The truth is he was very scared about the idea of spending time in a tin can underneath the ocean waves. He found it hard enough being stuck in a lift for the time it takes him to get to any floor above the second one.

The most important thing for Hagbard was his computer, FUUK-UP – First Universal Uber Kinetic-Ultramicro Programmer. George Harrison donated 50 per cent of all the royalties from his 1971 'Bangla Desh' charity single to make sure FUUK-UP got up and running. At the time it was the biggest computer in the world. And in a sense it still is, as it is what powers the whole internet.

The deal between George and Hagbard meant that in the future FUUK-UP would somehow bring about world peace, so George did not have to feel guilty about siphoning money off the people who got caught up in the flood (or was it a famine?) in Bangla Desh.

Back to the Starbucks in New York, 2023:

Celine Hagbard orders another double espresso and opens *Grapefruit Are Not the Only Bombs* by Yoko Ono at random. She is confronted with the word 'no' printed in lower case, as small as you could have printed it, in the middle of an otherwise blank page.

She then turns the page to find the next page printed solid with the word 'NO'. If she had been bothered to count them, she would have discovered there were 666 'NO's on the page. She then turned to the next page . . .

Meanwhile:

In an artist's studio near Stroud in Gloucestershire, England, Michelle Obama is posing semi-naked for a sculpture that the world-famous artist Damien Hirst is making. Mr Hirst's idea for the finished work is that it will be a pure solid gold, life-size statue based on the world-famous *Little Mermaid* statue that sits on a rock in Copenhagen harbour.

This version of the statue is going to replace the one that is already there. It will be the only solid and pure gold public work of art in the world. Damien Hirst chose Michelle Obama not only because she was the first ever female President of the USA, she was also the last ever President of the USA (2020–21), before AppleTree bought the whole of the United States of America for the price of the nation's debts to the Democratic Republic of China. What he had not told Michelle Obama yet was that AppleTree had commissioned him to make the work.

Meanwhile:

Someone read the following quote scrawled on a warehouse wall in Liverpool: 'I found myself in a dirty, sooty city. It was night, and Winter, and dark, and raining. Then I saw an ice-cream van pull around a corner and pull up beside a derelict building.'

Meanwhile:

Vladimir Putin, the former last Czar of the Russian Empire (2017–21), sits in the Winter Palace poring over the details of the contract for the world tour he and Michelle Obama are going to give on the international lecture circuit. As he had been in office as the leader of Russia for much longer than Michelle Obama had been President of the USA, he felt he should be getting the lion's share of the fee, instead of it being a straight 50/50 split.

Meanwhile:

Winnie decides not to hit 'Send' and instead goes for her daily seventeen-kilometre run.

As she closes the door to the balcony behind her a crow lands on the railing.

▲

Barnhill
Jura
23 April 1984

Dear Diary,

I have now introduced all the major characters in my new novel and set up the situations. This will undoubtedly keep the reader riveted as the story unfolds and finally resolves. Or this is what I had hoped until I faxed the third chapter to Dog Ledger earlier today. I got a fax back from him within about thirty minutes. And I quote:

'The characters are shallow. No one will emotionally commit to any of them. If Winnie is supposed to be the protagonist of the novel, we have to feel far more of her pain. You can't just tell us her Mother walked out on her when she was young and then her dad died and leave it at that before making up a load of rubbish about The Beatles. And who gives a fuck about The Beatles in 1984? It should be Southern Death Cult or Killing Joke if you want the youth of today to connect to your book.'

He says no way can I get away with lifting whole paragraphs from Eric Blair's *1948* and Robert Shea's *Kosmik Trigger*, that no publisher would touch it. He also thinks I should switch Fernando Pó for Jura. He says if I want this to be picked up for a film option, I should make all the locations ones where film companies would have no problem with insurance, etc. Right now I just don't give a damn about that sort of stuff. That said, I have edited out some of the bits I have lifted wholesale, and maybe I will edit some more of them out as I reread what I have written.

For some reason, Francis Riley-Smith was refusing to speak to me this evening. In protest I decided not to order another dram of Jura's finest and got a double of Laphroaig instead. That'll show the locals. There is nothing they find more offensive than a tourist drinking an Islay whisky while on Jura.

On a more positive note, Dog tells me *Classic Biker* want to do a feature on me and my Brough. It seems they just love that photo taken of me on the bike in the late '40s and they can't believe I am still riding the same Brough in 1984.

I bet Francis Riley-Smith will be all over me once he knows I am going to be on the front cover of *Classic Biker*.

Love,

Roberta Antonia Wilson

Postscript: it seems Walt Disney is not dead after all and he is considering coming out of retirement to oversee the making of *Fish Farm*.

4 : SEVENTEEN KILOMETRES

11:54 Sunday 23 April 2023

It's always that first stretch from her apartment down to the canal that's the worst. She hates that she is doing it. She hates the fact that she knows if she were to stop running exactly seventeen kilometres every day, it would be the beginning of her slide back into her previous addictions. She knows the running is just another addiction. That in one sense she is still on the first of the twelve steps. That this running is no different to the cocaine in her late teens, then the two bottles of Rioja an evening in her early twenties. It just exists to blot out the anger she feels at the world for her Mother leaving her when she was only five and then her father dying of cancer when she was twelve.

The world may have sorted out its problems, but she knows very well that all of us as individuals have some way to go.

And all the work she has been doing for Celine Hagbard is also part of the addiction. And now it is all done – well, all done bar hitting 'Send' – when she does hit 'Send', it will leave a massive vacuum in her life. A vacuum that can only be filled with . . . what? Alcohol? Drugs? Hacking? Violent sex? Whatever it is, it won't be good for her.

She gets to the canal bridge on Kingsland Road and takes the path down to the towpath and heads East. It is always on this part of the run that she can feel the negative emotions start to slip away. It is on this part of the run that her mind starts to open up and thoughts and ideas start to surface. It is this part that almost becomes dream-like.

Spring is in full mode. There are already flotillas of baby ducks scooting after their mallard mothers. The reeds and rushes are shooting up, the hawthorn on the far bank in bloom. There are other runners doing the same. The canal towpath is always popular with runners, but what they are thinking about we do not know or even care about because they are not in this book.

Winnie no longer feels the soles of her feet or the joints in her knees or the muscles in her thighs. She runs. And she stares down into the water at her right-hand side while she automatically dodges runners or fathers with buggies coming the other way. And in the water she can see her Mother's face looking up at her, as if her Mother is under the water following her along. And in her Mother's arms is her baby sister. Whatever happened to her baby sister? Her Mother left with her sister as well. It was just her father and her. And then her father left. But he left to go to hospital. And then he left to go to Heaven. And she was left alone.

Meanwhile:

On 23 January 1892 an artist in Norway wrote in his diary:

One evening I was walking along a path, the city was on one side and the fjord below. I felt tired and ill. I stopped and looked out over the fjord – the sun was setting, and the clouds turning blood red. I sensed a scream passing through nature; it seemed to me that I heard the scream. I painted this picture, painted the clouds as actual blood. The colour shrieked.

Meanwhile:

Winnie is still running along the side of the canal. If you are interested in knowing which canal, it is called the Regent's Canal

– I guess you could look at it yourself on GoogleByte's WorldNow. I guess you could even watch Winnie running along it in real time, if that technology still exists when you are reading this.

Winnie is thinking about hacking. Hacking is the addiction she fears most. At the age of thirteen she thought hacking was clever – and it *was* clever. WikiLeaks and everything . . . But by the time she was sixteen it had completely taken over her life. It was then the cocaine came to her rescue; with cocaine she could hack for longer. If the cocaine was good, she could hack for thirty-six hours straight with no Mother or father to tell her to stop.

It was the influence of Celine Hagbard that helped her to stop the hacking and the cocaine. The red wine came later.

Winnie could see her Mother's face among the baby ducks staring up at her.

She could see that boy's back. She wants to drag her nails down his back. She wants to hammer nails into his hands. She wants to—

Winnie keeps running.

Meanwhile:

In November 1970 in Totnes, Devon, a fourteen-year-old boy draws a picture of an old woman with a massive bundle of kindling strapped to her back. This boy is very good at drawing. He is the best in his school. He might be the best in the whole of Devon, maybe the whole of the country. He is even better than his big brother. The character he is drawing is based on a character in a book he saw at school called *Titus Groan*. This boy's favourite LP is *Led Zephyr Two*, the one with 'Whole Lotta Love' on it. *Led Zephyr Three* was released the previous month – it was shit. The boy's name is James Francis Cauty. People call him Jimmy. Jimmy plays the guitar.

Meanwhile:

In November 1970 in the Guildhall, Northampton, a sixteen-year-old boy is watching a band called Titus Groan play. They are one of four bands playing that night. But it is Titus Groan he wants to see as that is the name of one of his favourite books by his favourite writer, Mervyn Peake. It only cost one penny to get in and watch all four of the bands. But the boy is bored with the band and instead is thinking about an idea for a story he wants to write for a magazine he wants to put out called *Embryo*. The story is about the two men in the background of a poster of a painting he has on the wall of his bedroom at home. The painting is called *The Scream*. The boy is called Alan Moore. Alan plays the drums.

Meanwhile:

Two rows behind Alan Moore sits a seventeen-year-old boy who has just started at Northampton School of Art. But he is not thinking about art. And he is not really thinking about the band Titus Groan who are playing. And he doesn't know where the name Titus Groan comes from. He is thinking, 'Why are all of these bands playing for one penny? There are no more than 240 people in the Guildhall and there are 240 (old) pennies to one pound, so there can be no way this makes financial sense.' The boy thinks that maybe someone with a lot of money is paying for this to be done so we in the audience will be bribed into buying the records that have just been released by these four bands. This boy decides not to buy any of the LPs by any of these four bands. *Atom Heart Brother* by Magenta Floyd was released the previous month. This boy thinks everything about this record is brilliant. It is the best record ever made by Magenta Floyd. This boy's name is William Ernest Drummond. People call him Bill. Bill plays the bass.

Meanwhile:

Winnie keeps running. Winnie notices a dead fish, floating belly up in the canal. If Winnie knew about fish, she would know it was a perch. But she doesn't. She does know the canal is now cleaner than it has ever been since it was first opened in 1820.

Winnie is thinking about what killed the fish.

And death.

And her death.

And the end of death, if she only hit 'Send'.

Then Winnie tries to stop thinking and just runs.

But this lasts less than sixty seconds before she is thinking about Wikipedia. Winnie has not updated her Wikipedia page for five years, but it keeps being updated. Everybody updates everybody else's Wikipedia page – an exaggeration, but that is the way it feels for Winnie at times. Every ex-boyfriend, every new boss, everybody that has ever wanted to sell you something has an interest in updating your, and anybody else's, Wikipedia page. John Lennon's favourite ice cream was a Mr Whippy, according to his Wikipedia page, just because The Beatles wrote that song about travelling the world in an ice-cream van.

Winnie is thinking how everything she ever did between the ages of fourteen and twenty is there for all to see on FaceLife. But on her Wikipedia page it has gone in a different direction. Maybe only subtly, but it is shifting. And in 2023 Wikipedia is always used to know what happened in the past. It seems like the past is both always there to confront us with all our mistakes and always shifting.

Winnie is now running along the towpath of the Hertford Union Canal by Victoria Park. She likes this bit. A kingfisher flies past; all Winnie registers is the flash of electric blue. Kingfishers mean the water is clean. So clean you could drink it. Nobody throws empty cans of Diamond White or Coke Zero into the canal or anywhere else these days. Litter is a thing of the past.

Out of the corner of Winnie's right eye she sees the Shard. The Shard is the tallest building in London. But she not only sees the Shard, she sees a massive eyeball spiked on the top of it staring back at her. Winnie knows this eyeball is only in her mind. Winnie hates the Shard. She has no reason to hate the Shard. But she feels the Shard is watching her. Winnie hates the Shard in the way she used to hate bankers or politicians when we used to have bankers and politicians.

When she was very young there was a politician called Tony Blair. She can remember her father telling her Tony Blair was one week younger than him. Her father thought this significant. Somehow her father dying of cancer when she was twelve and Tony Blair are linked. She blames Tony Blair for her father's death. She still hates Tony Blair, even though he is an old man who does nothing but good things and even helped sort out the problems between Israel and Palestine.

She keeps running.

Meanwhile:

A killer whale called Killer Queen swims the narrow sound of water between the Isle of Islay and the Isle of Jura. Killer Queen is a lone whale: she bred once but her child was killed by getting caught up in the propeller of a passing ferry. Killer Queen likes to eat seals. But she would rather eat humans. Killer Queen is beautiful. Or that is what people think on the Askaig to Feolin Slipway ferry when they see her break water. Killer Queen thinks many things. One of those many things is, 'I wonder why the sea is so much less polluted than it was when I was young?'

Meanwhile:

Winnie is still running. Winnie has never seen a killer whale. Winnie does not even know killer whales live off the coast of

Albion. Winnie gets to the end of the Hertford Union Canal where it joins the Lee Navigation. She crosses the bridge by the Crate Brewery & Pizzeria and then goes down onto the towpath on the East side of the Lee Navigation.

She keeps running.

A small cloud passes between her and the sun.

On the opposite bank are warehouses. Or that is what they used to be. They are now lived in by the young art crowd. The post-hipsters, the post-hack generation. The ones who can't remember what it was like before FaceLife. The ones who don't care. Winnie looks up at the open double door on the first floor of one of these warehouses. There is a woman standing there. Black boots, black jeans, black T-shirt, black hair. On the T-shirt is a stencil of '2023: WHAT THE FUUK IS GOING ON?', the same as she had seen on the poster the young man had been putting up opposite her apartment. Their eyes meet. But only momentarily.

Meanwhile:

Yoko Ono, the young one whose real name is not Yoko Ono, is standing at her open doors looking down at the canal where she dropped the body of her boyfriend earlier that morning. And she is wondering why she still feels nothing. No regrets. No pain. No guilt. She thinks about John's mum. She likes John's mum. How will she explain John's disappearance to her? But really she doesn't give a shit. And one thing John taught her is to sometimes not give a shit. She can hear him saying right now as she stares down at the water: 'If everybody gave a shit about everything, nothing would ever get done. It is our job to get things done.'

She then notices the woman with the mousey hair running along the towpath on the opposite bank. She runs past every day.

60

And Yoko thinks, 'I wonder what she does and I wonder if she gives a shit? I wonder if she would kill her boyfriend?'

▲

This is an important book, the critic assumes, because it deals with war. This is an insignificant book because it deals with the feelings of women in a drawing room. Virginia Woolf

▲

Meanwhile:

Stevie Dobbs, whom many used to consider the most powerful person on Earth, when those sorts of things were considered, is sitting with her back against a giant redwood, taking a short break from her hike. She is thinking about the deal she did with TREE back in 2020. She is now wondering if it was worthwhile for the world at large.

TREE (Trading Russian Empire Equity) was formerly Yandex, Russia's top online trading company through the Teens. It was the deal between Apple and TREE that brought about the end of the war in the Ukraine and the other former Soviet states. It was the deal that bought out Putin in exchange for crowning him the Czar of the Russian Empire – a purely honorary position. Stevie Dobbs knew none of this would have been possible if the price of oil had not kept falling from 2014 until it reached zero in 2019, when the whole world switched to renewables.

But Stevie Dobbs is thinking way back. Way, way back to when she was only a teenager. A genius teenager. A teenager The Beatles signed to Apple to invent the computer programme that would bring about world peace. And to the bitter rivalry she felt with that Hagbard Celine, as she was then. So why did she feel the need to fuck John Lennon? Just because she knew she could? And why did she have to let Yoko Ono know? And why did she trust George Harrison when he told her he would give her 50 per cent of the royalties from that charity single of his, when she knew in her heart Harrison would promise the same offer to Hagbard?

But Stevie knew where John, Paul, George and Ringo hid their store of Achilles heels. She knew the secrets locked in the vaults of Apple. She knew of their ties with The American Medical Association. It was because of this knowledge – and John, Paul, George and Ringo's knowledge of her knowledge – that she was able to do the deal that gave her the rights to take over all their future Beatles royalties and the very name of the company Apple itself. On 1 April 1976 she launched Apple Inc., and she never looked back.

So why in 1980 did she feel the need to go and fuck John Lennon again? And why did she suspect – no, not suspect, but know – his murder was a set-up job? And she knew for almost certain who was behind it. And it wasn't Yoko Ono.

▲

'I don't know how to stop,' states Trane.

'Try taking the fucking horn out of your mouth, man,' responds Miles.

▲

Stevie Dobbs invented a brother and called him J. R. 'Bob' Dobbs, who in turn invented a religion called the Church of the

SubGenius. She still does not know why she did this, but her therapist thought it might be something to do with trying to get her own back on George Harrison.

Meanwhile:

Winnie keeps running. Up past the Hackney Marshes, with their goalposts as far as the eye can see. Then up Springfield Park, and she is bang into the Jewish Orthodox area. And she thinks how weird it is they have changed. Not in the way they look. The men still wear the same hats and the women still wear the same wigs, but it is their attitude that has changed. Five years ago, if you had come up here, there is no way you would have got a smile out of them. Now they are all smiles. Anti-Semitism for three thousand years, and bang, within three months it is all over. You can even go into a Kosher butcher's and ask for a half-kilo of beef sausages and they don't look at you funny.

Up Clapton Common she runs, until she gets to Stamford Hill. There she sees the massive new billboard for FaceLife. As much as she now hates FaceLife, she can't deny the billboard looks great. It's the one with the leaves on a branch of a tree, with the FL logo cut out of the leaves and the sun shining through. It is one of those digital billboards where the images move. On this one you don't notice to begin with, but the movement of the air makes the leaves flutter slightly. Very subtle.

Winnie then heads up Amhurst Park until she gets to the New River. She follows the course of the New River. She is now in a trance. She can't feel her body, it just runs and runs. And her mind has risen above the city. She can see the world stretching to the horizon. She can see the curvature of the Earth. But then she sees the Shard again, with that giant eyeball spiked on top of it. That eyeball staring back at her. And the loathing and the rage return.

63

She will not hit 'Send'.

She will not save mankind from death.

She will start a new chapter in her life.

She will find that man with the bare back who was putting up the poster with '2023: WHAT THE FUUK IS GOING ON?' on it.

She will fuck him and fuck him, and when she can't fuck any more she will nail his hands and feet to the floor and leave him to . . .

But she knows she won't. She never does.

Just as she is about to enter Victory Mansions, by the Arcola Theatre in Dalston, she sees a woman pasting up one of the '2023: WHAT THE FUUK IS GOING ON?' posters. It is the same woman she saw standing in the warehouse down in Hackney Wake, by the Lee Navigation.

She stops running and goes over to ask her—

Meanwhile:

Jonathan King sits in a Starbucks somewhere South of the river. He is editing the Jonathan King Wikipedia page.

▲

Barnhill
Jura
24 April 1984

Dear Diary,

Tonight has been a great night at the bar. Not only was Francis in a good mood, one of his mates was up from Devon. He drives a Bonneville. And there was a rock band playing in the village hall. They are called Echo & His Bunnymen. They are from Liverpool,

I think. Seems they are quite famous. The whole population of Jura was there and half of Islay. Me and Francis's friend and the manager of the band got talking afterwards. He was quite mad. All he seemed to want to know was how he could take his band off to some Neolithic standing stones he had read about on the island. Then when they learnt it was me that had written *Fish Farm*, they were all incredibly impressed. The guitarist from the band, whose name was Will, swapped me his favourite comic for my autograph. The comic was called *Swamp Thing*. Then the drummer of the band, who was exceedingly cute, saw my Brough Superior Motorcycle, and that was it. They all wanted to have their photographs taken sitting on it. There was a journalist and photographer up from London doing a feature on the band for one of the music newspapers called the *New Melody Express*.

And then this friend of Francis – his name was Jimmy, I think – it turns out he is famous as well. When he was only fourteen, he did this drawing based on a character from a book and then sent it off to one of his favourite bands called Led Zephyr, or something, and they used it on the cover of one of their records. It seems this record was a number one around the world. Then they made a poster out of his drawing and it became the biggest-selling poster of all time in the world. Not that I know anything about posters. Maybe I should tell Dog Ledger about him. Maybe he could work on the animated version of *Fish Farm*. Or maybe chapter plates for my new book.

I won't deny I attempted to persuade the cute drummer from Echo & His Bunnymen back to the cottage. He was very courteous about it, but he did tell me that although he thought me very attractive, I was older than his mother, and maybe we should just stay friends.

This morning I woke early, read this comic called *Swamp*

Thing. It was like no other comic I have ever read before. Nothing like *Topper* or *Whizzer*, which I used to read when I was at school. While eating my kippers and home-baked soda bread, I remembered a conversation I had with the manager of the band last night. He was telling me how he used to go to art school in Northampton, and the person who wrote *Swamp Thing* also lived in Northampton and he was called Alan Moore. One night in 1970 they were both at the same rock concert. Four bands were playing and it only cost a penny to get in, and this gave him an idea.

The idea was that if he ever managed a band, they should play in strange far-off places, not to make lots of money but to give the band a strange and far-off-places type of mystery. He said it was a much better way to get people to want to buy their records than to play in boring places like Northampton and only charge a penny to see them.

He said Echo & His Bunnymen are currently on a tour, following a ley line from the Callanish Stones on the Outer Hebrides to the Albert Hall in London. I don't know whether to believe him or not.

Then after this concert in Northampton in 1970 he got talking to someone called Alan, who turned out to be this Alan Moore, and he also thought it was shit. He said *Titus Groan* was one of the best books he had ever read, and was the name of one of the bands. And then it turned out that the picture on the record sleeve, which Francis's friend from Devon had drawn, was based on one of the characters in *Titus Groan*. What were the chances of all that happening in one night?

I think I will rewrite some of yesterday's chapter to include some of this. The fax machine at the hotel is broken, so I was not able to send anything through to Dog. I am quite relieved. I could do with a break from his daily criticism.

Today is looking like it is going to be good, and once I have reworked Chapter 4 I will plough straight into Chapter 5. Things are about to start getting dangerous.

Love,

Roberta X

5 : EVERYONE'S GONE TO THE MOON

Whatever Winnie was going to ask her has gone, evaporated, irrelevant. The girl standing in front of her, with the black boots, black jeans, black '2023: WHAT THE FUUK IS GOING ON?' T-shirt and black hair has a far more distinguishing feature. Across her mouth is a broad strip of Gaffa Tape. And this girl, who was in the process of pasting up the next '2023: WHAT THE FUUK IS GOING ON?' poster, is indicating to Winnie for her to pull the Gaffa Tape from her mouth. Winnie is understandably confused, but the confusion does not stop her immediately and without further thinking from tearing off the Gaffa Tape from this stranger's mouth.

But what happens next shocks Winnie even more. And remember this is all happening at lunchtime in a busy part of Dalston. This stranger, now without her mouth taped over with Gaffa, drops the wallpapering brush from one hand and bucket of paste from the other, embraces Winnie and attempts to snog her.

Winnie pushes her away. The girl laughs loudly. The girl then pulls a book out from the bag that holds the roll of posters yet to be fly-posted. The book is yellow, hardback; there was no time for Winnie to see the title or the cover properly before this strange girl opens the book seemingly at random. The left-hand page is blank. The right-hand page has four words on it. Note: this girl has still not uttered a single word. Winnie reads the words on the page. There are only four words on the page. They are 'GAFFA

68

TAPE YOUR MOUTH'. She then turns the page. Again the left is blank and on the right are a few words: 'ASK A STRANGER TO RIP THE GAFFA TAPE OFF YOUR MOUTH'. She turns the page again, and again there is a blank page opposite a page with a few words. In fact, only three words: 'SNOG THE STRANGER'.

Winnie is confused, amused and somewhat alarmed. This girl then flicks through the book to another page and gesticulates to Winnie to read it. Winnie reads:

Throw a dice
If it turns up one, stop talking for one hour
If it turns up two, stop talking for one day
If it turns up three, stop talking for one week
If it turns up four, stop talking for one month
If it turns up five, stop talking for one year
If it turns up six, stop talking for the rest of your life

The last line has been heavily underlined with pencil, and the girl is pointing at it. She shoves it towards Winnie, insisting in no uncertain terms that Winnie has this copy of the book. For some reason, Winnie does not ask her questions. She is assuming the girl is dumb and maybe to talk to a dumb person is in some way insulting. Maybe this girl is deaf and dumb.

Winnie takes the book. Crosses the road and enters Victory Mansions.

Back in her apartment she engages with her post-run ritual by slicing a grapefruit in half and squeezing the juice into a glass. Then she goes out onto her balcony with the glass in one hand and the book she has just been given in the other. The deaf and dumb girl has gone from the street below. Nowhere to be seen.

Winnie sits down on her balcony chair and takes a sip of the grapefruit juice and looks at the book. On the front cover is a grapefruit. On the back is a grapefruit sliced in half. Winnie knows coincidences are meaningless. Winnie knows humans projecting meaning onto 'coincidences' is just part of the weakness of the human condition.

She reads the words on the front cover: '*Grapefruit Are Not the Only Bombs* by Yoko Ono'.

At this point in this chapter we have to step back and consider some things.

The author of this book made a decision earlier today, when she was drinking her own freshly squeezed grapefruit juice in a cottage at the northern tip of Jura. The decision concerned how to present the character of the other Yoko Ono. Her problem had been to work out how important a character she should be in the book. Should we the readers want to project ourselves onto her in the same way we may already be projecting ourselves onto Winnie? Or would that weaken Winnie as the protagonist and possible heroine of the book? The author already knows she wants to develop a relationship between Winnie and this Yoko Ono, but in so doing does not want to weaken Winnie's position in these pages of a story (or is this literature? I hope it isn't genre). She knows it is important for there to be an evolving backstory to Winnie. It is this backstory that drives her. But with this other woman (note: no longer girl), maybe she should remove any suggestion of a backstory. That she should be a dark, threatening other, more a shadow of ourselves. It was on squeezing the second half of her grapefruit that she decided from now on in this story this Yoko Ono does not speak. And we never learn any more about where she comes from and why she does the things she does. She just does.

That said, there is one thing I know and you are about to know and she will never know. And it is this: during John Lennon's lost weekend (1973–5), he fathered a child. A girl, Lennon's only daughter. This is kept a secret from both the world at large and Lennon himself. This daughter goes on to have a child of her own in the year 2000. This girl grows up to have her own suspicions and fantasies about her own background. This girl becomes a woman and decides to call herself Yoko Ono and write a book called *Grapefruit Are Not the Only Bombs*. This Yoko Ono considers herself to be an artist. An angry artist, even if not a very original or good artist. But certainly a very motivated artist.

This book is simple. It contains a hundred instructions. A less than sympathetic reader of the book might claim she has just ripped off *Grapefruit* by the real Yoko Ono, or maybe even *Oblique Strategies* by the composer Gavin Bryars.

She has it designed and typeset but printed in an edition of only 23 copies. That is all she needs.

There is something else you should know about her. She has a private income. She does not know where it comes from, but every six months several thousand ZitCoins are added to her account. This troubles her but she never questions it.

▲

Jonathan King is still sitting in a Starbucks somewhere in South London. In fact, we now have confirmation about where he is: it is a branch of Starbucks at Borough Market. It is near his recording studio. He is updating on his Wikipedia page the amount of records he has sold, both as a solo artist and as a producer. He has decided that for each album he sold when he was producing The American Medical Association back in the late '80s and early '90s, the sales can now be multiplied by ten, in that each album would have included at least ten tracks, and in the world of downloads (circa 2000 to 2017), each download of an individual track can be counted as a record sale. Much to Jonathan King's satisfaction, he has now not just sold 213,569,213 albums but 2,135,692,130 tracks. That is much more impressive.

Now that all recorded music is streamed, actual sales do not exist and no one really gives a shit how many records, tracks or downloads were sold back in the pre-streaming era. But for Jonathan King these historic facts are all-important.

What Jonathan King is not satisfied about is that he has not had a hit record for the last thirty years, since he was producing The American Medical Association, before they 'retired' after their performance at the Brits in 1992. And what is even worse is that his nemesis Pete Waterman is back in business and having hits. And not just any old hits: worldwide epoch-defining hits. Pete Waterman went and signed the two most media friendly of those Russian feminist provocateurs Pussy Riot. What Jonathan King wants to find is two London-based women who can compete and beat Pussy Riot at their own game.

Just in case you were wondering, Simon Cowell was murdered by a former contender live on *China's Got Talent* back in 2019.

▲

The artist formerly known as M'Lady GaGa is sitting in a Starbucks in Hoboken, New Jersey, doing exactly the same updating thing with her Wikipedia page. And she is also wondering how it all went wrong for her. There were a couple of years in the early Teens, only ten years ago, when she could do no wrong. But it seemed the more she learnt about her craft, the less it impacted on the world at large. And now she can sit in this Starbucks and no one knows who the fuck she is. There were a couple of teenagers in last week and she overheard one of them saying, 'Isn't that M'Lady GaGa?' And the other said, 'No, M'Lady GaGa is not fat.' How painful was that? She just wanted to get up and scream.

She sits there going back and forward through her Wikipedia page trying to work out where it went wrong. The only bit she can maybe point at is when she decided not to contact The American Medical Association to see if they wanted to come out of retirement and do a track with her, but instead she went and did a recording with the E Street Band. Then those tracks with Tony Bennett – a major mistake. Then it was all over.

She has an idea. She needs to make a record with a less trashy version of Pussy Riot. Someone hip and of the moment. And foreign.

And she knows exactly what she wants the video for the song to be like. In it she would be a mermaid tempting a passing Viking longboat onto the rocks. And you would see the longboat smash and the Vikings drown. And all the little girls around the world would love her again.

▲

A news story pops up on Winnie's iPhone. 'David Hockney, Albion's greatest ever artist, has died of lung cancer at the age of ninety.' Winnie remembers being taken by her father to a David Hockney exhibition. It was in a converted mill up in Yorkshire somewhere. She was very young at the time, but ever since then she has always liked Hockney, not so much because of the work, but because it somehow reminds her of a time when both her parents were there.

She is trying not to think about what she should be thinking about, which is the email she should be sending to Celine Hagbard. So instead she decides to carry on reading *Grapefruit Are Not the Only Bombs*. Even though the real Yoko Ono is her favourite artist, and she knows this to be just a play on her book, she really likes it.

These are some of the entries she is reading:

Remake Apocalypse Now *using Plasticine men and stop-frame animation. The dialogue must be kept exactly the same except for the 'Napalm' line to be changed to 'I love the smell of burning MONEY in the morning'*

Make a pot of tea

Buy a roll of Gaffa Tape

no

no, no,

74

no, no, no, no, no, no, no, no, no, no, no, no, no, no, no, no, no,
no, no, no, no, no, no, no, no, no, no, no, no, no, no, no, no, no,
no, no, no, no, no, no, no, no, no, no, no, no, no, no, no, no, no,
no, no, no, no, no, no, no, no, no, no, no, no, no, no, no, no, no,
no, no, no, no, no, no, no, no, no, no, no, no, no, no, no, no, no,
no, no, no, no, no, no, no, no, no, no, no, no, no, no, no, no, no,
no, no, no, no, no, no, no, no, no, no, no, no, no, no, no, no, no,
no, no, no, no, no, no, no, no, no, no, no, no, no, no, no, no, no,
no, no, no, no, no, no, no, no, no, no, no, no, no, no, no, no, no,
no, no, no, no, no, no, no, no, no, no, no, no, no, no, no, no, no,
no, no, no, no, no, no, no, no, no, no, no, no, no, no, no, no, no,
no, no, no, no, no, no, no, no, no, no, no, no, no, no, no, no, no,
no, no, no, no, no, no, no, no, no, no, no, no, no, no, no, no, no,
no, no, no, no, no, no, no, no, no, no, no, no, no, no, no, no, no,
no, no, no, no, no, no, no, no, no, no, no, no, no, no, no, no, no,
no, no, no, no, no, no, no, no, no, no, no, no, no, no, no, no, no,
no, no, no, no, no, no, no, no, no, no, no, no, no, no, no, no, no,
no, no, no, no, no, no, no, no, no, no, no, no, no, no, no, no, no,
no, no, no, no, no, no, no, no, no, no, no, no, no, no, no, no, no,
no, no, no, no, no, no, no, no, no, no, no, no, no, no, no, no, no,
no, no, no, no, no, no, no, no, no, no, no, no, no, no, no, no, no,
no, no, no, no, no, no, no, no, no, no, no, no, no, no, no, no, no,
no, no, no, no, no, no, no, no, no, no, no, no, no, no, no, no, no,
no, no, no, no, no, no, no, no, no, no, no, no, no, no, no, no, no,
no, no, no, no, no, no, no, no, no, no, no, no, no, no, no, no, no,
no, no, no, no, no, no, no, no, no, no, no, no, no, no, no, no, no,
no, no, no, no, no, no, no, no, no, no, no, no, no, no, no, no, no,
no, no, no, no, no, no, no, no, no, no, no, no, no, no, no, no, no,
no, no, no, no, no, no, no, no, no, no, no, no, no, no, no, no, no

Gaffa Tape up holes and cracks

Gaffa Tape up your mouth

But then Winnie reads this one:

Ask your boyfriend to choose a number between one and six
Ask him not to tell you the number but to write it down on a
  piece of paper
Ask him to fold up the piece of paper
Ask him to give you the piece of folded-up paper
Don't open it yet
Later
When alone
Roll a dice
Then unfold the piece of paper
If the rolled number on the dice is the same as on the piece of
  paper
Kill your boyfriend
Choose your own time

Winnie looks up and out at the horizon. She can just see the top of the Shard. There is no eyeball looking back at her. But she can see a giant grapefruit sliced in half rising above it. She knows this is not real. She knows this is just her imagination. But recently her imagination has been doing too many things like this.

The sun is already starting to dip. The day is sliding towards its end and still she does not hit 'Send'. Still she does not end death. For ever.

In an earlier chapter of this book it is mentioned that Winnie does not listen to music other than by chance in cafés or else-where. This, although not a complete lie, is not exactly the case. Occasionally, very occasionally, she will go on YouTube and watch clips of Nina Simone singing songs. The reasons for this are mixed, but the main reason is that one of the more powerful memories she has of her Mother is of her listening to Nina Simone. And her Mother telling her that Nina Simone is the most real woman in the world. A woman's woman. A woman who knows how to say 'No'. A woman who is a true artist whatever song she sings or whoever wrote it. A woman who only has to open her mouth and she is not only singing for all women and all African Americans but for every person that has ever lived and has ever been oppressed.

Okay, she can't actually remember her Mother saying all of those things, but that is what she believes her Mother felt about Nina Simone.

So Winnie listens to her sing 'I Put a Spell on You', then 'Here Comes the Sun', then 'Don't Let Me Be Misunderstood', then the absolute classic 'Sinnerman'.

And as she is just about to click on 'To Love Somebody', she notices there is a version of 'Everyone's Gone to the Moon' sung by Nina Simone.

Now, you may not know this, but 'Everyone's Gone to the Moon' is a song written by Jonathan King and was a hit for him way back in 1965, when he was still a fresh-faced student at Cambridge University. If there is one other thing Winnie remembers about her Mother and music, it is how much she hated Jonathan King and everything he seemed to represent to her.

Winnie does not know if she wants to hear her Mother's musical heroine sing a song by the man she loathed. She can't stop herself. What she hears is not what she is expecting. It is the Jonathan King song, but it is not sung in the usual Nina Simone commanding way. It is a frail and old voice, still Nina's voice, but with none of her inner strength, and the accompaniment is just Nina playing the piano. And even her piano playing is faltering.

Winnie clicks it off. This is not the Nina she wants. She looks up again. Darkness is falling and now, instead of a grapefruit above the Shard, she can see a full moon rising.

▲

It is mid-afternoon in New York. Celine Hagbard has decided to walk from one end of Manhattan to the other. This is a walk of about twenty kilometres. All the way from Battery Park up to Inwood Hill Park.

When things are troubling Celine she likes to walk from one end to the other. It gives her time to think, time for emotions to settle, time to come up with a plan. And things are troubling her. She needs a plan. She has been expecting an email from Winnie Smith all day. This is what they have been working towards for the last five years. Through all the personal ups and downs there has always been daily contact between the pair of them. Whatever massive business deals she is in the middle of, every time she sees there is an email from Winnie in her inbox she gets a bit of a rush. It isn't a sexual thing, it's more that Winnie is the daughter she never had. The perfect daughter, who seems to understand the world in the way she does. She would not have used the word 'love', but that is what it is.

Then, mixed in with all of this, there is the Yoko Ono book that fell from the sky. She went online and nowhere in the world of GoogleByte is there any mention of this book. Nothing. And as far as she's concerned, if GoogleByte cannot track it down, it does not exist.

Celine has her own personal memories of Yoko Ono from the late 1960s back in London. She never really took to her then. That was a long time ago.

This book, this *Grapefruit Are Not the Only Bombs* book, has triggered all sorts in her. Very much unsettled her. She has read it from cover to cover while still sitting in the Starbucks – mind you, that didn't take more than thirty minutes. She keeps on coming back to one particular statement – 'Push The Button'. Not just a statement, more a commandment. It is like these three words are screaming at Celine Hagbard from the middle of an otherwise empty page. She knows the button has to be pushed. But she cannot push it until Winnie Smith emails her the final information that would make all the other bits slot together. Today is the 23rd April 2023. This was always to be the day the button was to be pushed.

Just as Celine is striding up Adam Clayton Powell Junior Boulevard through Harlem she feels this sharp pain at the bottom left of her back. It is as if someone had stuck a knife in her. As she falls to the ground she turns her head to see who has stabbed her. There is no one there.

▲

Whereas I am still on the island of Fernando Pó. Whoever is writing this book has not transported me to the Isle of Jura, off the coast of Scotia, to make things more attractive for film options.

And as I made plain to you in an earlier chapter, womankind needs to have war, famine and inequality to function properly. Without them we as a species will be over within a couple of generations. And I still believe we need as many competing religions as possible to compete for our souls. The more radical the religion, the better. And the so-called sorcery I practise is possibly more radical than most.

About thirty seconds ago I sunk my needle into the doll I have created to be Celine Hagbard. And wherever this Hagbard is in the world, I am hoping she is suffering the consequences of my actions. It is the least she deserves.

▲

Tate World have just announced they are going to rebrand the Turner Prize as the Hockney Award. This is in honour of David Hockney, whose death was announced earlier today. The shortlist for the Hockney Award will be announced tomorrow.

▲

Yoko Ono looks down into the waters of the Lee Navigation from the open doors of her floor and she starts talking to her boyfriend, who is lying at the bottom of the water underneath the reflection of the moon. She tells him she has a plan and he will be proud of her. In the background we can hear some loops he had created for a track they had been working on. The samples he used to loop were taken from 'Sinnerman' by Nina Simone. There was also a M'Lady GaGa sample in there as a hook.

▲

Streets full of people
All alone
Roads full of houses
Never home
A church full of singing
Out of tune
Everyone's gone to the Moon
Jonathan King (1965)

▲

Barnhill
Jura
25 April 1984

Dear Diary,

Things are getting stranger.

As I get closer to what may lie at the heart of this book, I sense I may be losing people. That is, if anyone is reading it in the first place. I keep circling around something from character to character. Which character will be the first to jump? Which will be the first to reveal?

Before I started writing this chapter this morning I was tempted to kill off one of the major characters, almost creating a 'who done it?' mystery. I know the bogus John Lennon character was killed off in Chapter 3, but we know who did that, so there is no mystery there.

As yet I have not decided if Celine Hagbard is already dead – that decision can be left for the morning, when Chapter 6 is to be attempted. Then there is the need to have some sort of romantic thread to the story. Does she or does she not get the boy? That's always a good way to keep the reader turning the pages. And which boy? Certainly not that O'Brien I mentioned in Chapter 2 and, anyway, I seem to be leaving behind the templates of *1948* and *Kosmik Silver Trigger* that I was using earlier on.

Then there is the lack of a clear-cut villain. People like to have a villain. If this were to be a proper dystopian novel, there would be the dictator or the police state we could all hate, but that doesn't exist here, mainly because it is not a dystopian but a utopian novel. That bloke in Fernando Pó might think Celine Hagbard and the rest are baddies but none of the other characters in the book particularly think so.

I did not send anything off to Dog Ledger again today. I phoned him instead and made up some excuse about the fax machine still being broken.

I just got back from the bar about twenty minutes ago – and things were getting strange there too, but in a good way. Francis's mate Jimmy from Devon, who did the poster from Mervyn Peake, is still up, as is the manager of Echo & His Bunnymen. We all got talking about the film *Wicker Man*. Jimmy thought it was filmed up here on one of the islands, but the manager of the band – Will Drummond, I think – said it was filmed around his home town of Newton Stewart down in Galloway. But both were agreed it would be a good thing to try to do it for real one day. By the end of the evening they seemed to agree they would return in the future to build and burn a giant wicker man on Jura. I said I would definitely be back to witness it as well.

I would like to put it on record – even supposing it is only me who ever reads this – that I neither drank too much nor embarrassed myself by making untoward advances to any young men.

Let's hope I have a good night's sleep. Or at least until the call of the curlew wakes me in the morning.

Love,

Roberta X

6 : PUSH THE BUTTON

21:37 Sunday 23 April 2023

The crow is pecking an eye out of the dead squirrel in Gillett Square by the Vortex Jazz Club in Dalston.

John Lennon is lying at the bottom of the Lee Navigation, thinking the thoughts of a dead man.

Killer Queen is riding the crest of a wave and thinking about music. She wants to form a band.

Mister Fox is trotting along a darkened street without a care in the world.

Dead Perch is contemplating a career in social media.

Shanthi is trying to work out why dating in the modern world never works.

A reader is thinking, 'Who the fuck is Shanthi and why is she in this book?'

And we don't know if Celine Hagbard is alive or dead.

A cloud drifts between the moon and Winnie. She can no longer see the Shard. Winnie returns her gaze to *Grapefruit Are Not the Only Bombs*. She turns the page and reads. And what she reads is not what she wants to read:

Push The Button

So she turns to the next page and she reads:

Wait until after dark

Catch a bus
Stay on the bus until the end of the line
Catch another bus
Stay on that bus until the end of the line
Run back to where you started

Winnie has waited and it is after dark. And Starbucks is still open. She decides to go for a double espresso before catching the first bus. As she closes her front door behind her, Crow lands on her balcony rail.

As she passes the entrance to the Arcola Theatre she notices they are about to stage a version of *Macbeth* but done in Pidgin English; it is being directed by a Daisy Campbell. Winnie makes a mental note to go and see it. She has seen eleven different versions of *Macbeth*, and that is not enough. It is never enough.

Ten minutes later Winnie is boarding the 149 heading North to Edmonton Green.

At Edmonton Green, Winnie gets off the 149 and catches the next bus to pull up. It is the 279 to Waltham Cross. She used to catch this bus to the home of her first boyfriend, who lived in Waltham Cross. They used to hold hands and listen to music and talk about things. It was a long time ago. Nearly fourteen years. Half a lifetime. They are still friends on FaceLife.

She gets off the bus at Waltham Cross and starts running. She is running East towards Waltham Abbey. When she gets to the bridge, she ducks down to the river. It is the Lee Navigation. But it is North of the M25. There are fields either side. She heads South. She keeps running. Her mind is sliding, the reflection of the full moon in the water is following her. She sees a dead Oak tree standing on top of a small hill. A sliced grapefruit is rising behind the tree. The two men she has seen before in her dreams

84

are walking up the hill in silhouette. These men are also on the poster of *The Scream* she first got when she was thirteen and still has now. Although now she has it in a frame. She always knew why the person was screaming but what were those two men with their top hats doing? Where were they going? What were they thinking? The screaming is the easy bit.

She keeps running.

There is no one else running. No one else on the towpath at this time of night. She now sees a pylon. She likes pylons. We all like pylons. Pylons buzz when there is a mist. Pylons stalk the landscape of our dreams. Winnie sees that eyeball again. It is rising. It sits atop the pylon. It stares out at the world, unable to blink. It stares into the very darkest parts of Winnie. Parts of her hidden even to herself.

And The Weyward Sisters sing the Sugababes classic 'Push The Button':

> *If you're ready for me, boy*
> *You'd better push the button and let me know*

Winnie keeps running.

There they are. The two men with their black hats and black coats and black trousers and black boots. They are on the towpath. One of them is sitting on a stool in front of a canvas on an easel. He is holding a paintbrush in one hand and a palette in the other. The other man is standing. He has a walking stick in one hand. He is using the walking stick to point at the pylon on the hill and the eyeball staring back.

Winnie runs past them. She does not look back.

Push The Button

Push The Button
Push The Button

▲

By 1987 Jimmy Cauty, Alan Moore and Bill Drummond are washed up. No one buys their graphic novels any more, no one buys their posters of scenes from Mervyn Peake books any more, no one buys Echo & His Bunnymen records any more. So the three of them meet up in Alan's house in Northampton and decide to form a band.

Alan is the drummer and singer, he also writes the words.

Jimmy plays guitar.

Bill plays bass.

They call themselves Extreme Noise Terror.

And they are.

And they record an album in a local studio.

And put it out on their own label.

And John Peel plays it on the radio.

But hardly anybody buys the record.

It is called *Burn Wicker Man Burn.*

They even build and burn a wicker man on the Isle of Jura off the West Coast of Scotia in the Summer of '91. But still no one buys their record.

Then Eve from The American Medical Association hears them on *The John Peel Show* and thinks they sound great.

And Eve said to Adam, 'I think we should invite Extreme Noise Terror to play with us when we perform "3 a.m. Eternal" at the Brits.'

And Adam said, 'But Jonathan King said we should do it with Benny and Björn from ABBA backing us.'

And Eve said, 'Fuck Jonathan King, I have had enough of him making our records sound like commercial shit. We were always supposed to be a rock band and somehow we have ended up as a disco band. Disco sucks.'

And Adam said, 'Okay.'

So they do.

But before they do The American Medical Association write and record an album's worth of songs with Extreme Noise Terror. The album is to be called *The Black Room*. It is not disco!

Then, on the night of the Brits, when Benny and Björn turn up to play, Gimpo (Eve and Adam's helper) locks them in the dressing room. Extreme Noise Terror take to the stage with The American Medical Association and blow the place apart.

Afterwards Eve and Adam go to the aftershow party. On the red carpet they are all smiles for the tabloid cameras. But then Eve pulls from her Coco Chanel handbag a pearl-handled duelling pistol, as does Adam from the holster strapped to his leg. They then proceed to blow each other's brains out.

The cameras keep clicking and the bulbs keep flashing.

The suicide note is found in Eve's handbag. It reads, 'We Died for Ewe.'

And they do.

Forget Madonna falling over, this is the greatest Brits moment ever. And ever and ever . . .

Their album, *The White Room*, which is already triple platinum, goes global.

As for Extreme Noise Terror, they release their follow-up record. It is called *Never Mind*. It changes the face of rock music in the '90s. Northampton becomes the new Düsseldorf.

▲

Jonathan King is still sitting in the Starbucks at Borough Market, even though it is after midnight. And he is still not able to get over the fact he let slip the chance to produce, manage and pull the strings of Extreme Noise Terror. No amount of tampering with his Wikipedia page can ever change that. And he has tried. But some fucker up in Northampton keeps changing it back.

▲

Winnie keeps running.

▲

And as Celine Hagbard falls to the ground, she just finds the strength to push the button on her iPhone.

There are now only twenty-four hours before GoogleByte completely shuts down. The mother of all search engines will burn up on re-entry.

▲

Things are different when you are dead. For a start you don't hold grudges. You communicate in a completely different way, and with life forms you would never have communicated with when you were alive.

Killer Queen has now formed her band – it consists of her, Crow, Dead Squirrel and John Lennon (the one at the bottom of Lee Navigation). They are called Tangerine NiteMare and they are about to release their first album, called *Far Out,* Mister Fox is their manager and Dead Perch does their social media.

John Lennon had been working on tracks for months but not getting anywhere with them. He only ever did this when Yoko Ono was out with her friends. She thought it was all self-indulgent rubbish, which it might have been. But Killer Queen thought it brilliant, and if he only took off the patronising whale noises and all that other nature stuff and made it sound a bit more industrial, it would work.

Crow flies in through the open doors of Yoko Ono's apartment. He lands on John's workbench, where his laptop is open. Crow uses his beak to click open the *Far Out* files. He is soon going through them, removing all the nature samples. Then he loops up some of the industrial sounds that John has not bothered with, brings up some of the keyboard parts that were lost. Then puts the whole lot through some new filters he downloaded. Mister Fox somehow has got into the apartment and is insisting they rip off a drawing he found on FlikGram that the fourteen-year-old Jimmy Cauty did for *Led Zephyr Five*, which they never used. Dead Squirrel, who is still lying in Gillett Square, but whose left eye is now in the belly of Crow, suggests they go with the mix they had and upload it straight away. Mister Fox does a deal with AmaZaba.

Crow hits 'Send'.

Dead Perch gets to work on social media. Within moments it is being listened to, Shared and Liked around the globe. It passes seven million streams within sixty minutes. By dawn it would be the most played piece of music on the globe.

Killer Queen heads around to the Maelstrom, off the northern tip of Jura. She wants to listen to it there in full surround sound.

The only question left worth asking is: was the dress blue and gold or black and white?

▲

Winnie is still running, but she is getting her mind more under control. This entire imagining grapefruit-rising-into-the-sky and landscape-artist-at-work-on-the-canal-path-at-midnight thing has been repressed. As has the urge to nail that young man to the floor.

But she does know these are the tell-tale signs of stress. That she has been overdoing it. And maybe she is not ready to end death for mankind for ever quite yet, whatever her agreement with Celine Hagbard is. 'I'm sure she understands. Celine has always been so understanding in the past when she has one of her turns.'

As she runs down into her more familiar territory, with Hackney Marshes to the left and Springfield Park to the right, she decides she is going to give herself twenty-four hours to decide if she should hit 'Send'. She will email Celine Hagbard in the morning and be totally upfront with her about these concerns.

In those twenty-four hours, she feels the need to do something else with her life. Explore some of her other urges. Maybe get pregnant. Maybe this diary she has started could become a novel. Do people still write novels? And if they do, do people read them?

Then a fox trots nonchalantly past Winnie. When did foxes get so cocky and confident? Is it something to do with the fox-hunting ban? It's as if foxes now think they can go where they want, when they want. Before you know it foxes will be running everything.

Winnie is now running on the opposite bank, past the warehouse in Hackney Wake. She looks up to where she first saw the girl with the Gaffa-Taped mouth who gave her the book. The double doors are open as they were before, but there is no light on. But then she sees what looks like a crow fly out. Seconds later the lights go on in the apartment and the girl is standing there and looking down at her. The girl waves and seems to beckon her up.

Winnie takes the path up to the bridge, crosses the canal and finds the entrance to the warehouse.

Seconds later she is in the apartment with Yoko. Yoko is still not speaking, but Winnie quickly realises Yoko can hear, and within seconds they develop a way of communicating – Winnie talking and Yoko using a mixture of crude sign language and writing things down with paper and pencil.

They are off.

Yoko shows her the news story about the Hockney Award and the four shortlisted artists. She indicates that she thinks this is all elitist rubbish, existing only to further the interests of the commercial art establishment and those in positions of power at Tate World.

If, twenty-four hours earlier, Winnie had been presented with these arguments she would have thought them to be the naïve half-baked thoughts of a frustrated teenager. But now, as part of the twenty-four hours she is giving herself to embrace everything before hitting 'Send', she is thinking, 'Fuck it, let's see where this goes.'

While Winnie puts the kettle on, Yoko is already doing the artwork for a poster using Letraset. As the tea is brewing, Yoko is making the new silkscreen using the artwork.

While they are waiting for the tea to cool enough in their mugs to drink, they start to screen-print the poster. Yoko does the screen-printing. Winnie hangs the poster up on the washing lines to dry.

Winnie loves working at this speed.

The poster reads:

ABANDON ALL ART NOW
Major rethink in progress
Await further instructions

When they have ten of the posters printed, Yoko does the artwork for a second one. She gets the silkscreen made and they are soon printing out these new ones. They read:

It has come to our attention you did not abandon all art now
Further direct action is thus necessary
The K-SEC announce the 'mutha of all awards', the 2023 K-SEC
Award for the worst artist of the year

In smaller typeface they name the four shortlisted artists and how you can vote for whoever you thought the worst. Also on the poster is the prize money: one million ZitCoins.

Winnie is a bit concerned about this.

'How can we pay the winner? Or is this just a hoax?'

Yoko writes on a scrap of paper the following reply: 'Nothing I do is a hoax. Everything I do is for real. Look at my arm.'

Yoko then shows Winnie her arm. On it, scarred into the skin, is '4 REAL'. Winnie does not ask anything else; she just accepts what she reads.

'We will find the money,' Yoko notes down with a pencil.

And she gets on with doing the artwork for the third poster. It reads:

AMENDING THE HISTORY OF ART
The winner of the K-SEC Award
Announced at noon today
VOTE NOW

By 1:00 all the posters are printed.

By 2:00 all the posters are dry.

They head out into the night with the thirty posters, a bucket of wallpaper glue and a brush.

They get a cab up to Kingsland Road and get to work.

It only takes them about an hour to have all thirty of the posters pasted up onto walls.

By 3:00 – job done.

They head back to Yoko's to get on with whatever is going to happen next.

▲

A young man walks past the posters. They catch his attention. He photographs them on his phone. He uploads the photos onto FaceLife. They get Shared. And Shared. And Shared. And Shared.

A researcher on the early shift for the *Today* programme on Radio Four sees it on her FaceLife page and thinks it could be an interesting story. She presents it to her producer, who is also working the early shift. They decide to make it the cultural story of the morning. The show's presenter, John Humphrys, is briefed. For those that don't know, the *Today* programme is on air between 6:00 and 9:00 every morning. It is the most listened to live news and current affairs radio programme in the world. It is simultaneously translated into 853 languages as it is broadcast. It has approximately seven billion daily listeners. It defines the agenda for the day – for everyone.

Winnie and Yoko are back down Hackney Wake. Yoko chops out two lines of pure Colombian caffeine. They snort, then get back to work.

Yoko explains to Winnie about The Justified Ancients of Mu

Mu and plays her the track John and her had been working on. They remove all the rubbish John had done and replace it with a better loop from Nina Simone, then a sample from 'Alejandro' by M'Lady GaGa.

It seems that although Yoko can never speak in her life again, she allows herself to sing.

Yoko gets them to do some chanting that she records. It goes, *'Mu Mu, Mu Mu, Mu Mu, Mu Mu.'* It makes no sense, yet it makes perfect sense. Yoko flies it in. The track is almost there. Winnie suggests the tune from 'Telstar' by The Tornados would fit perfectly. They have to play this live on Yoko's keyboard. Those piano lessons Winnie had as a child come in useful. The track is sounding brilliant.

Winnie tries to convince Yoko they should upload the track.

It goes against all of Yoko's Post-Digital Underground principles. Yoko wants to cut it as a real vinyl record, but Winnie argues the case that Yoko is already breaking her principles all the time by using the recording methods she does.

Winnie wins the argument.

Winnie presses the button.

The track uploads.

It is off.

Free.

Within sixty seconds of it going live, it is showing on GaGa's GoogleByte Alert, and she is then listening to it on her morning run down on the Hoboken waterfront.

M'Lady GaGa tweets.

Winnie tweets back.

M'Lady GaGa suggests recording some live vocals for the remix when she has completed her run in forty minutes.

M'Lady GaGa knows she is back in action.

This is going to be better than if she had done that track with The American Medical Association, and definitely better than the shit album she did with The Neptunes.

M'Lady GaGa has her best ideas when running.

She has one of her best ideas now.

'Bad Moon Rising'.

Is the dress black and white or blue and gold?

Winnie and Yoko watch as the streams keep climbing. By 5:00 they have passed the seven million mark.

Jonathan King has already listened to the track eleven times, and he is also watching the streams climb. This is the sort of track he should be involved with. He goes straight onto Wikipedia to update his page.

Winnie and Yoko see this on Yoko's GoogleByte Alert. They just think it funny.

Then M'Lady GaGa sends in her live 'Bad Moon Rising' vocals – and if you are wondering, this has nothing to do with Creedence Clearwater Revival. Neither Winnie, Yoko nor GaGa have ever heard of Creedence Clearwater Revival.

Once they have spun that in, the track is ten times better than it was. They upload the new mix and it instantly goes mental. Especially in China and India. But that's maybe just because of the time of day there: the kids are just getting home from WikiCampus, or something.

Winnie is knackered.

Yoko is knackered.

Winnie borrows Yoko's bike and cycles back the two kilometres or so to Victoria Mansions. The birds are already singing. By the time she climbs into her bed it is almost daylight.

She instantly falls asleep.

A deep sleep.

She dreams.

Vivid dreams.

Note: from now on in this book, unless otherwise stated, when Yoko Ono or John Lennon are mentioned, they are the ones both living and dead in Hackney Wake.

▲

Barnhill
Jura
26 April 1984

Dear Diary,

There is no way I am going to send what I wrote today to Dog Ledger. I may just rip the whole lot up and start again tomorrow.

What happened last night was that Francis Riley-Smith had some of his homemade LSD, as in acid.* Jimmy persuaded me I should, and although Bill seemed reticent at first he ended up taking a tab, so I just thought, 'Why not? I have risked everything else in life, why not try acid once?' So I did. And then we all went off in search of the Neolithic standing stones.

Somehow I got home, and when I woke up this morning I was still tripping. But that didn't stop me from getting on with the writing. I know I have to get a three-thousand-word chapter done each day or everything else will start to slide.

And I hope tomorrow I can bring things back into line.

* Francis reckoned he could make millions from the manufacturing of his branded LSD. He uses some of the waste product from the Jura distillery to make it. He has an underground laboratory back at Jura House, where he does it all. He keeps threatening to take me back there and show me how it is all done. I don't know whether to believe him or not. It might be just his friend Jimmy that brings it up for him.

Goodnight.

Love,

Roberta X

Postscript: I ripped off the name Tangerine NiteMare from Francis's friend Jimmy. He had been telling us about an imaginary band he had as a teenager called Tangerine NiteMare. They played Krautpop, or something.

7 : WHILE WINNIE SLEEPS

08:36 Monday 24 April 2023

While Winnie sleeps, BANKSY calls an emergency meeting of the selection committee for the Hockney Award at Tate World.

Coffee and fresh croissants have been provided by Starbucks.

'This is the last thing we fuckin' need. This will make us look like we are completely out of touch, with not only what is happening in our so-called art world but the world at large. Every year we sit around and discuss whether we should change the format of the prize. And we do fuck all. So we changed the name from Turner Prize to Hockney Award yesterday, and last year we changed it to four artists above the age of seventy, just to keep the last-gasp baby-boomer lobby happy. But nothing fundamental.'

'We doubled the prize money,' quips Ms Emin.

'Yeah, and what did that do for us? It just made us look more like some desperate talent show. We may as well get Simon Cowell to front it.'

'He's dead,' observes the Chapman Brother.*

'Yeah, I know, I am just making a point,' retorts BANKSY.

'Look, BANKSY, we have made a huge change this year. "LET THE PEOPLE CHOOSE," you said, and insisted on it and threatened you would resign if we didn't go with it. You know I was against it from the beginning. And so we did go along with your idea. And we presented our four artists under the age of

---

* The other one died from sniffing too much glue while doing his Airfix.

twenty, with their half-baked ideas and sloppy presentation and puppy-dog eyes. And look what happens. In the past three hours we have had over fifty-four million spoilt digital ballot papers. And each and every one of them is spoilt with the same word: "K-SEC". Who the fuck are "K-SEC"?'

'Well, whoever they are, Grayson, I think we should announce them as the winners of the 2023 Hockney Award,' says BANKSY with a smirk on his face.

'For doing what? Putting up three posters on a wall in Dalston last night?' asks Lord Serota.

'No. For being *zeitgeisty* and not just a bunch of wannabees like the rest of them. For making something happen that the world is responding to. Nothing fuckin' happens these days. Only eight years ago young men were chopping off the heads of other young men and posting it on YouTube because they believed in something. But now all we are doing is marketing something for the family to go and see on a Sunday afternoon at Tate World.'

'Yeah, but, BANKSY, you know it will be something different tomorrow and everybody will have forgotten about K-SEC.'

'Well, I am not willing to take that risk. I think we should vote on it now. A show of hands between the five of us. Show the world we have the balls to do something like this.'

The vote is carried. At noon the winners of the 2023 Hockney Award will be announced, and the winners will be K-SEC.

▲

While Winnie sleeps, Crow flies through her open balcony door and perches on the bedpost nearest to her head. Crow stares in wonder at her beauty. His seed is planted.

▲

While Winnie sleeps, a paramedic in the back of an ambulance in New York City tries to resuscitate the heartbeat of a woman. The paramedic's name is Sam. The patient is maybe in her late seventies. Sam was rather amused to discover evidence that the patient may have had a sex change at some time and probably was born male. The other paramedic, whose name is Dave, who is also in the back of the ambulance, picks up a book that has fallen from the pocket of the patient's coat.

Dave opens the book at random and reads:

Choose a brick
Choose a window
Throw the brick through the window
Repeat until satisfied

Dave closes the book and looks at his colleague.

'Sam, I don't know why you are still at it. You know she is dead. She was dead before we picked her up off the sidewalk. I blame all these old folks that think they can keep running, playing tennis and doing Pilates in the park. This one is no different. She must have known her heart couldn't take it, but no, this honky bird was out there running up through Harlem like she owned the place. I say we head back and save some real lives that still have a chance.'

Sam responds: 'I will agree with you only if you agree to us switching off the siren and switching on "Hold On, We're Coming" at full volume.'

'Agreed.'

What Sam & Dave don't know is that this old honky bird is

100

none other than Celine Hagbard, one of the five most powerful individuals in the world. And maybe right now, even dead, especially dead, the most powerful.

What Sam & Dave don't know is that the regular iPhone23 they found their patient still clutching in her hand has an app on it like no other.

What Sam & Dave didn't know was that when the 'special' button on this phone was pushed, it would alert the app, which would alert a satellite that had been circling the globe for the past forty years and counting.

What Sam & Dave didn't know was that this satellite had the name FUUK-UP. And that FUUK-UP was the computer that powered the world's largest search engine, GoogleByte. And because of deals done by this dead woman who was maybe once a man, all other search engines and even would-be search engines were owned or at the very least beholden to this dead old honky bird.

What Sam & Dave didn't know was that without FUUK-UP no other search engine or even would-be search engine on Earth (or in space) could do what it had been born to do, which is search.

What Sam & Dave didn't know was that this app had sent a message to FUUK-UP instructing it to shut down in twenty-four hours. And on shutting down it will start to fall to Earth. And in falling to Earth it will burn up on re-entry. And on burning up, all of its knowledge and prowess will be lost for ever.

What Sam & Dave didn't know was that in the last will and testament of this old honky bird there is only one benefactor. And her name is Winifred Lucie Atwell Smith. Yes, the Winnie Smith who you, the reader of this book, already know, but who is asleep right now. And that this Winnie Smith has the fortitude, talent and know-how, if harnessed, to prevent and reverse the instruction given by this app, in this iPhone23, in the back of this ambulance in New York City.

What Sam & Dave do know is that they are now playing 'Hold On, We're Coming' at full volume over the speakers of their ambulance, and they love the way it distorts at the top end. They also love the fact that Sam's nephew fixed the ambulance with super-bass woofer speakers underneath it, so the bass from the track could be heard at least ten blocks away before they got to the site of the call-out.

In fact, if you are anywhere near any sort of music-playing device, I recommend you play 'Hold On, We're Coming' at full volume right now.

Don't have to worry, 'cause we're here
No need to suffer, 'cause we're here
Just hold on, we're comin'

▲

While Winnie sleeps, two of Lord Saatchi's henchmen are carefully cutting out three sections of wall that had three posters pasted on them only five hours and forty-two minutes earlier.

It is only now that we notice these three posters designed and screen-printed by Yoko have each been pasted strategically and aesthetically over three of the larger AppleTree posters Winnie observed in the opening paragraphs of this novel.

Once removed they load them into the back of their unmarked white Transit van, in which they will be taken to Lord Saatchi's Battersea Power Station Gallery on the South Bank of the Thames. Where they will be ready for public exhibition the moment the winner of the Hockney Award is announced at noon.

▲

While Winnie sleeps, M'Lady GaGa is on a conference call to her new management team Aloysius Parker Associates. This new management team is very well aware of the track their new signing released three hours ago and which is now the most streamed track in history. They had no idea she was going to release it, but that is all part of the mystery and genius that is M'Lady.

She disappears for five years. The world thinks she is washed up, burnt out – and that's if they remember her at all. Even her LittleMonsters had given up on her. But no, she was secretly working away at her masterplan, like when Ziggy Stardust did his *'68 Comeback Special* in 2018. But this looked like it was going to be bigger. Much bigger!

'Just tell us what you want, M'Lady.'

'I want to make a film for this new tune of mine. And I want to make it in one hour's time. Then we can edit it immediately and have it up online by the time kids are having their lunch break at WikiCampus.'

'Yes, M'Lady, and what do you want in this film?'

'I want a Viking ship, full of strapping Vikings, sailing on a storm-tossed sea.'

'Yes, M'Lady, and what else do you want in this film?'

'I want me dressed as a mermaid, perched on a rock.'

'Yes, M'Lady, and what will you be doing perched on the rock?'

'I will be beckoning the Vikings to row harder. I will be warning them of unseen threats. I will be tempting them with my allure. I will bring about their salvation and their destruction, all in three and a half minutes.'

'This is genius, M'Lady. I will be around in the Rolls to pick you up immediately. By the time you get to the film studio, all will be in order. The Vikings will be strapping and the sea will be tossing. Your mermaid costume is already being stitched.'

'Thank you, Parker.'

▲

While Winnie sleeps, a fox slips through her unused cat flap and springs light-footed onto her bed. He can feel her warmth. He can taste her breath. His seed is planted.

▲

While Winnie sleeps, Daisy Campbell has called an early rehearsal at the Arcola Theatre in Dalston, London. The Arcola specialises in experimental and radical theatre.

Daisy's father, Ken Campbell, did many things. One of those many things was to go to the Melanesian Islands and rewrite Shakespeare's *Macbeth* so local people could perform it in their version of Pidgin English.

He then took this version of *Macbeth* to the rest of the world, with the promise he could teach each and every one of us how to speak Pidgin English in one hour. He then led performances of *Macbeth* in Pidgin in theatres, jungle clearings and ice floes – or would have done if they had paid him. Ken Campbell passed to the other side in 2008.

Daisy took up the baton. By 2021 Pidgin was the most spoken language in the world after Cantonese.

In Studio Two of the Arcola Theatre, Daisy is about to recite some of the most powerful words to resonate down the centuries in any language, to the green but keen young actors waiting to learn their parts. These are the words she now begins to recite:

Nara dei mo nara dei mo nara dei
Wokabaot snel spid dei long dei
Long las wan haf wod blong evri wan samting bagarap ded
*   finis yea taem*
Mo olgeta yesterdei blong yumifala
Oli bin laetem krangke haf mad fala long griri tata
Nomo no faer nao lil fala kandel
Laef emi sado blong wokabaot
Emi konset rabis man
Nao i singsing mo hambugum wan owa antap bokis
Nao yumi Nomo harem em
Emi storian blong longlong kukiboi
Fulap mekanois, saenem nating

And these are based on the following more legible words in English:

Another day and another day and another day
Walk about snail speed day into day
To last one half word belonging every one something bugger up
*   dead finish yeah time*
And all together yesterdays belonging you me two fellow
All been light kranky half mad fellow to dusty goodbye
No more no fire now little fellow candle
Life him he shadow belonging walk about
Him he concert rubbish man
Now he sing and flirt one hour on top box
Now you me no more hear him

105

Him he story belonging crazy serving boy
Full up make a noise, signalling nothing

And these are how you may have had to learn them in a boring English Literature class at school:

Tomorrow, and tomorrow, and tomorrow
Creeps in this petty pace from day to day
To the last syllable of recorded time
And all our yesterdays have lighted fools
The way to dusty death. Out, out, brief candle!
Life's but a walking shadow, a poor player
That struts and frets his hour upon the stage
And then is heard no more. It is a tale
Told by an idiot, full of sound and fury
Signifying nothing

While Daisy is listening to herself recite the words, hoping it will inspire these young and eager actors, she has an idea. This is the idea in her own words: 'Maybe instead of presenting The Three Witches (or The Weyward Sisters, as we in these more feminist-aware times call them) as they are usually, maybe I should present them as three mermaids, as in sirens of the sea.'

Daisy notices her charges' attention collectively begin to wander. She reprimands them and they get down to serious work. The show opens tomorrow night.

▲

While Winnie sleeps, the Twenty-Three Sparrows chirrup in a haw-thorn bush somewhere in South London. The bush is in full bloom.

▲

While Winnie sleeps, three men in their late sixties meet up in a redbrick two-up, two-down terrace house in Northampton. It is the first time they have been in the same room together since 1994. In 1993 they quit their stadium tour of the USA halfway through and the following litigation with the promoter nearly bankrupted them. All three know not to mention the name of the woman that supposedly caused their downfall. But for the sake of the reader who does not know who they are not talking about her last name is Hate and her first name is Candy. All three of them have made distasteful claims. Sexist claims. Claims that should never have been made. Only she knows the truth.

The North American promoter fails to completely bankrupt them but they manage to do it for themselves. Firstly, in a fit of artistic pique they withdraw £1 million* in £50 notes and burn them on a bonfire in front of the Houses of Parliament. Then they hire Francis Ford Coppola to film a re-enactment of the burning, with Marlon Brando, Robert Duvall and Christian Bale playing them. Alan Moore wants the film to be called *Guy Fawkes' Night on Acid*; Bill Drummond wants it called *Bonfire of the Sanities*; Jimmy Cauty wants *WATCH*. The democratic compromise is *WATCH Sanities on Acid*. It is a total flop, commercially and critically. Everyone sees it for what it is: the vanities of successful rock stars with not enough money to burn. Even Coppola disowns the film, and tries to get an injunction preventing it being screened in the USA. Like many before them, Extreme Noise Terror have just ripped off The Beatles, who did it bigger, better and first.

The three of them try to save some sort of artistic grace by

* £1 million is equivalent to 64 million ZitCoins at today's rate.

claiming they were misunderstood and they were going to call a Twenty-Three-Year Moratorium on their collective creative activities. To this end, they take out TV advertisements during *Coronation Street*. In these adverts, voiced by Princess Diana, they claim that for a period of 23 years, they would not talk, write or draw pictures about what they had done with £1 million in front of the Houses of Parliament. And in their reckoning these 23 years would give the hoi polloi, the art establishment and the international jet set enough time to assess the reasons why three ex-rock stars felt whim enough to burn a pile of money so big it could have saved one million starving Ethiopian babies from certain death. Nobody took any notice.

So they waited, biding their time.

In 2017, at the end of the Twenty-Three-Year Moratorium on their collective creative activities, they planned something big, but everybody had forgotten all about them.

So Alan went back to comics. A couple of his comics were turned into live action films – *V for Vendetta* and *The Watchmen*. They were both critically and commercially very successful films. But Alan thinks they are rubbish and compromise him as an artist. So he decided to direct, produce and finance a film based on one of his other comics. This one is called *The Lost Girls*. It was both critically and commercially a disaster. Alan left the Hollywood Hills and headed back to Northampton.

So Bill Drummond went back to his first love – unlistenable avant-garde classical music. He hired the Berlin Philharmonic Orchestra conducted by Sir Georg Solti to play his compositions. Just for the record, Drummond wrote all these compositions in the sand at Skegness at low tide. These then had to be photographed from a helicopter before the tide washed them away. No one listened.

So Jimmy Cauty spent several years building a 1:1 scale model of a post-apocalyptic London. But because he got a bit of the maths wrong, it was in fact twice life-size. It was so big it had to be exhibited in the Thames Estuary on the platforms where Boris Johnson was planning on building the New London Airport. An unusually high Spring tide swept the lot away on the day of its press launch.

> *We're in with the in crowd*
> *And we know what the in crowd knows*

So back to the redbrick two-up, two-down terrace house in Northampton. Over a pot of tea and some Marmite on toast, Extreme Noise Terror put past differences aside and decide to reform. Their comeback concert is going to be at the O$_2$ Arena tomorrow night. There will be a warm-up gig tonight at the Sizzling Sausage transport café on the A5 just outside Northampton.

They will be playing *The Black Room* in its 23-minute entirety. The concert will be streamed live around the globe. They will not be taking any recreational stimulants. Candy Hate will have better things to be doing on the night.

▲

While Winnie sleeps, a significantly large amount of money silently slips from Lord Saatchi's ZitCoin account into BANKSY's ZitCoin account.

▲

While Winnie sleeps, 87,654 women around the world are being raped. But we are not concerned about 87,651 of these women in this book. We are concerned about the other three. These women are all aged seventeen.

One of them is in Kolkata. She is being raped by her thirty-three-year-old husband. She is raped by him most nights.

One of them is in a village on the banks of the Congo River. She is being raped by a boy she has fancied since they were at Sunday school together.

One of them is in Port-au-Prince, Haiti. She is being raped by a transgender artist from London who is in Haiti as part of the Ghetto Biennale Festival. S/he thinks s/he is being very liberal by having sex with a black girl who cannot speak English.

All three of the men think the sex is either consensual or their God-given right. There is no more to know about these women, but all three will be major players in the second book in this trilogy, and I thought you should be warned at this point that things may take a turn for the serious, before we get back to the *Trainspotting* banter of this chapter.

▲

While Winnie sleeps, Killer Queen is listening to the voice of God and wondering if, in fact, she is the voice of God and thinking that every life form should hear what she has to say, not just a few other killer whales that like hanging out at the Maelstrom on a Friday night.

▲

While Winnie sleeps, the death of Celine Hagbard is announced across all platforms. This is the first of the New Big Five to die. The first of the individuals who are publicly recognised the world over as those who brought about world peace, the end of pollution, the end of our reliance of fossil fuels, the end of nation states, the end of radicalised religion (or any sort of religion that represses its followers), the end of everything that is bad and dangerous and that we all hate. And the end of heroes up on pedestals ready for us to worship one minute and allow to become dictators the next.

This is bigger than the deaths of Kennedy, Lennon, Princess Di and David Beckham all rolled into one.

This is massive.

▲

It is now 08:47 on 24 April 2023. The aroma of freshly ground coffee beans finds its way from the open door of the Dalston branch of Starbucks across the road and up to an open window on the second floor of Victory Mansions. Through the open window it is only two metres and thirty-six centimetres to the nostrils of the sleeping Winnie Smith, who is now stirring.

Another day beckons. A day that will change all our lives.

▲

Barnhill
Jura
27 April 1984

Dear Diary,

I feel I am getting somewhere with this book. It is taking shape. I know where I am going with it. It has purpose. I will fax these last couple of chapters off to Dog Ledger with confidence. I will never take LSD again. I will not get drunk at the hotel bar again

– or at least not until I have the book done. I will retain my dignity in my relationships with younger men. At least I'm skinny enough not to worry about losing weight. I do wish my breasts had not sagged so much though. I will go for a swim in the sea each morning before I do my daily chapter. I will not regret not having children. And I will forgive myself for not going home to my mother's for Christmas in 1971, when I knew it would probably be her last Christmas here on Earth. I will not believe in God.

Love,

Roberta X

8 : WHILE YOKO DREAMS

08:59 Monday 24 April 2023

While Yoko dreams, all 23 copies of *Grapefruit Are Not the Only Bombs* reach their final destinations.

▲

While Yoko dreams, The Tiger Who Came To Tea is strolling down Kingsland Road, about to turn into the Art Bar for breakfast of menemen with freshly baked Turkish bread. He will play over in his mind the events of the previous evening. Should he text her? That is the question.

▲

While Yoko dreams, the former Czar of the Russian Empire, Vladimir Putin, picks up a package on his desk. He flicks open his stiletto knife (a gift from Mussolini's great-granddaughter) and slices through the cardboard. It has not arrived in AmaZaba packaging. It contains a book with a yellow cover. He opens it at random and reads the Cyrillic script on the right-hand side of the page. Translated into English it would read:

> *Mankind needs War*
> *Without War civilisation would not have evolved*
> *It is your duty to further the evolution of Mankind*

Putin closes the book and looks out of the open window.

The cherry blossom is already in bloom.

Chekhov would be pleased.

▲

While Yoko dreams, the last but one Pope of all the world is sitting at his desk in his office in his apartment in the Vatican wondering what the point of anything is any more when he knows for certain God does not exist.

Being the first black Pope was a sensation back in 2019, but when his symptoms of agnosia were detected in 2020, the Papal Conclave had no choice but to quietly retire him for reasons of dementia.

He is quickly replaced by Pope Eloise, the first female Pope. She says all the right things. She is a believer. The media are no longer excited by a black Pope, they are excited about there being a female Pope. Those attending Mass around the world quadruple in as many months. Pope Eloise often quotes *How to Be a Woman* in her addresses. Then she too is retired quietly. Her symptoms are that of Lesbossis, a condition that has no known cure. Pope Eloise is replaced by Pope Anthony, a heterosexual Italian male with no known lapses in faith or fortitude. He only ever quotes the Holy Bible.

Due to poor administration within the Vatican, a package addressed to 'The Pope' does not arrive on the desk of the current Pope but on that of the quietly retired Pope before last. He struggles to open it with his arthritic hands.

It's a book. Nobody sends him books any more. It has a

grapefruit on the cover. He likes grapefruits. He has freshly squeezed grapefruit juice with his breakfast every morning.

He opens the book at random. And reads words written in Latin. If we could read them in English, they would read:

> *There is only one true faith*
> *There is only one true leader of that faith*
> *You are that leader for life*

Pope Dionysius XXIII looks up out of his open window as a white dove lands on its sill. His faith is immediately restored. There is work to be done.

▲

While Yoko dreams, Peppa Pig is recovering from her first night of snorting pure Colombian caffeine. It is better than she ever imagined, especially the sex, but now she is feeling shit and she has to have her 'History of Sheep Farming in the Ottoman Empire (1647–1653)' essay in by this afternoon.

▲

While Yoko dreams, Michelle Obama is sitting at her breakfast table at the Greenway Hotel & Spa near Cheltenham feeling rather pleased with the work Damien Hirst has felt inspired to create. It shows off her assets to a welcome advantage. She is still not sure if Mr Hirst's advances the previous evening were what she thought they might have been, but she is pleased with herself for ignoring them.

On a less vain note, she is very aware that to have herself

presented as the muse to the world's greatest living artist will further her position as the world's greatest living role model to all women whose great-great-grandmothers were cotton-picking slaves.

And while she wonders what black pudding is exactly, the waiter approaches.

'Excuse me, madam, but this package has just arrived for you. The courier was most insistent you receive it as soon as possible.'

'Thank you, just leave it here.'

Michelle Obama opens it immediately, using the knife she was just about to cut the black pudding with. It is a book, a yellow hardback book. She opens it at random and reads the words on the page. They are:

> *You are a Siren*
> *You are a Mermaid*
> *You are a Weyward Sister*
> *Find your other Sisters of the Sea*
> *Then all Three*
> *Find and pay homage to the One*
> *Who is the Daughter of Nature*
>
> *Await further instructions*

Although she knows this to be new-age nonsense, she decides to keep the book because she is in a good and positive mood. She looks up and out of the open window at the clear blue sky. A crow is flying across it.

▲

While Yoko dreams, two local plainclothes officers, whom we

briefly met in Chapter 1, turn up for work at Stoke Newington Police Station.

▲

While Yoko dreams, a parcel that has been posted to Marcia Zuckerberg at FaceLife in Menlo Park, California, is dumped in the recycling bins like nearly all of the other many thousands of letters and parcels addressed to Marcia Zuckerberg. Life is too short for . . . A rat runs across the road. He would willingly share his secrets with you, if only you were fluent in Rat.

▲

While Yoko dreams, she dreams of a pyramid. Sometimes it is a pyramid like the ones in Egypt. Sometimes it is a pyramid like the ones in Mexico. Sometimes it is a pyramid like the ones that you can only see in dreams.

▲

While Yoko dreams, Arati, the seventeen-year-old married woman in Kolkata in West Bengal, is still being raped by her thirty-three-year-old husband. But to try to block out the reality of the pain, Arati recites in her head the words that were in the book that arrived in the post for her that morning. They are the only words in the book in Bengali. And if they were in English and here for us to see, they would read:

> *You are a Shepherdess*
> *Your sheep follow only you*

But now it is time for you to find
Your Sisters
Then all Three of you
Find and pay homage to the One
Who is to be the Shepherdess of all Womankind

There are pastures green
Where the worm has not turned the Apple

It loses something in translation, but so does Tagore.

▲

While Yoko dreams, there are 176,463,251 living descendants of Mog the Forgetful Cat. Mog died in 2002 at the age of thirty-two. Although Mog herself only ever had two kittens and was spayed afterwards, none of her offspring ever were. These statistics are based on the facts presented on an A6 flyer that Yoko was handed yesterday. She never read the flyer before throwing it in the recycling bin. But she did have *Mog the Forgetful Cat* read to her when she was young. And when she thinks these sorts of things, she thinks she would have liked to have read *Mog the Forgetful Cat* to her child. If she had not had an abortion.

▲

While Yoko dreams, her Mother sits in a kitchen in Liverpool, thinking about the daughter she left 23 years ago today. The daughter was only five years old. She has not seen or heard from her since. She left the home with nothing but the clothes she was standing in and the bundle that was her newborn baby daughter, who was so obviously not the daughter of her husband, the father of her five-year-old. Her baby daughter's name was Elisabeth. Her five-year-old daughter's name was Winifred.

'Mummy, Mummy, please come back. I want to hold my baby sister,' were the last words she heard Winifred say.

'You can fuck off for ever with your half-caste mongrel,' were the last words she heard her husband say.

But now she can hear a thud on the doormat. She goes through to the hall. There is a package on the floor. Back in the kitchen she opens it. It's a book from Elisabeth.

'Why does she still insist on calling herself Yoko Ono? It is bad enough that there is already one Yoko Ono in the world.' She opens it at random and reads the words on the right-hand page. They are in English and they read:

Love your Mother

This Mother breaks down in tears.

▲

While Yoko dreams, a nineteen-year-old man in a block of flats on Queensbridge Road, Dalston, opens a package that is addressed to the Aga Khan c/o his address in his block. He doesn't know who the fuck the Aga Khan is or why this package has come to his mum's flat. But he may as well keep it.

The truth is that Yoko stops a young Muslim boy on his way to prayers and asks him who the leader of Islam is, like the Pope is the leader of the Christians. The boy says it doesn't work like that but some people think the Aga Khan is the leader. She asks him where the Aga Khan lives. He doesn't know. She then asks him for his address so she can send him a book that he can then pass on to the Imam at his mosque and he can then pass on to the Bishop, or whatever, and so on up the chain of command until it gets to this Aga Khan. The boy gives it to her with a smile. She asks him if she can say a prayer for him. And he says it doesn't work like that in Islam.

But she writes the number down wrong and it goes to number 355 instead of number 335.

So the young man who gets the book who lives at number 355 is not Muslim. His name is Henry Pedders. Henry opens the book at random and reads the words on the page. They are in English, so he has no problem. The words he reads are:

> *You give respect*
> *And you expect respect in return*
> *If that respect is not given*
> *You have to take it*
>
> *Without respect society does not work*
> *A society without respect has to be torn down*
> *And built anew*
>
> *It is your duty to give and take respect*
> *It is your duty to tear Babylon down*
> *If the respect is not returned*
>
> *You owe it to your children*
> *And your children's children*
> *And your children's children's children*

Henry did not know if these words were from The Bible or The Koran or some other sort of Holy book, but they made sense to him. We will hear more about Henry, and the lack of respect he feels he is due.

▲

While Yoko dreams, Igglepiggle still sails across the sea in his boat. Clasping his blanket all through the night.

▲

While Yoko dreams, the old Yoko Ono cannot sleep. It is almost 4:00 in New York, since they are five hours behind. She now regrets throwing the yellow book with the grapefruit on the cover over the railings of her balcony. Maybe there was a fan letter in the book. Maybe it would have been a good book. Maybe it would have inspired her. So little inspires her these days.

▲

While Yoko dreams, M'Lady GaGa is sitting in the back of her Rolls and Parker is driving. They are on their way to the film studio, to film the strapping Vikings in their boat on a storm-tossed sea. M'Lady is looking into her iPhone, watching the stream count on her new track climb and climb.

Then, while waiting for some lights to change, a courier on a bicycle taps on her window. Without waiting for Parker to tell him where to go, she lowers the window and smiles at the handsome courier. He hands her a package. 'For you, M'Lady, and I have to say, I love the new track. Back up where you belong.' And with that he pushes down on his right pedal and he is off weaving his way through the traffic.

GaGa opens the package. It is a book with a yellow cover with a sliced grapefruit on it. She not only loves the title *Grapefruit Are Not the Only Bombs*, but Yoko Ono is her favourite artist in the whole wide world. She feels honoured that Yoko Ono has gone to such lengths to deliver the book especially at almost 4:00 in the morning. She opens the book at random and reads:

You are a Siren
You are a Mermaid
You are a Weyward Sister
Find your other Sisters of the Sea
Then all Three
Find and pay homage to the One
Who is the Daughter of Nature

Await further instructions

She knows exactly what this is about and why she is being given the book. She is a Siren, as will be obvious to everybody around the world later today when they have seen her new video. But she also knows Yoko Ono is a Siren too, since she saw her as a mermaid on the new Starbucks mug. And then only seconds before the courier handed her the book her iJaz News app had popped up with the story about how Michelle Obama had sat for Damien Hirst and will be presented to the world as the new *Little Mermaid*, but in gold.

M'Lady knows that Yoko Ono, Michelle Obama and her are the Triumvirate of Weyward Sisters, and all they have to do now is find out who, where and what the One is and to pay her homage.

She will await further instructions. That said, M'Lady GaGa is not too good at waiting too long for anything.

▲

While Yoko dreams, the two local plainclothes officers are now in their office looking at the brick that was thrown through the window of the pet shop. Attached to the brick was a page ripped from a book. On the page are the words:

> *Find a brick*
> *Find a window*
> *Throw the brick through the window*

They are wondering if it is worth trying to find out if there is any DNA they can match up with what they have on file.

▲

While Yoko dreams, a package lies unopened on the desk in a small and tatty office behind a Polish grocer's in Brooklyn, New York. This is Celine Hagbard's office. This is the beating heart of GoogleByte, although the rest of the world would not know. Even the Polish grocer who Hagbard rents the office from does not know he is the landlord to the wealthiest and most powerful person on Earth. And as yet, the Polish grocer does not know his tenant is lying dead in the back of an ambulance that is still blasting out 'Hold On, We're Coming'. If the package were opened and Celine Hagbard randomly opened its contents, she would read the words:

As it so happens, Celine Hagbard enjoys the trip, every last second of it.

▲

While Yoko dreams, Jonathan King is remonstrating with his new colleagues Mike Stock and Matt Aitken in his new studio just around the back of Borough Market that just because 'Everyone's Gone to the Moon' is in 3/4 time does not mean it cannot be used to replace 'Telstar' as the main theme in the rip-off mash-up version of 'GaGa Joins The JAMs' that is streaming out of control around the world.

'Of course it will sodding work, just transpose the key and stretch the BPM. I have sold 358,000,000 records. I know what I am talking about,' says King.

'Even Pete Waterman was not this musically thick, not knowing a 3/4 tune will not work over a 4/4 rhythm without frigging it up. You wrote a tune in waltz time. Maybe you should get fuckin' Mozart in, he might be able to use your tune. A kid doing first-grade piano lessons knows this,' retorts Aitken.

'Or first day on Garage Band,' adds Stock.

'Well, turn the rest of the track into 3/4 time,' commands King.

'No one has danced to waltz time since the Second World War,' sneers Stock.

'What about *Strictly*?' responds King.

'Exactly,' jibes Aitken.

Matt turns to Mike: 'I say we quit now and start working with Waterman again.'

'Well, then you can all sod off out of my studio,' tantrums King.

Matt and Mike walk out. So does Phil Harding, the engineer, and Rick, the tea boy.

▲

While Yoko dreams, I am still on the island of Fernando Pó, off the coast of Africa. I am staring at the five handmade dolls on my table, wondering which one I should stick the needle into next. Yesterday I received a package in the post. I have never ever received a package in the post before in my life, even on my birthday. When I opened it I was disappointed to find it was a book. The disappointment was compounded when I flicked through the book to discover it was in all sorts of languages I could not and did not want to read. But then I came to one page I would allow myself to read, as it was in Bube, the language of my people. The future language of the entire world.

Up until now, when referring to myself in this novel I have made no mention of my name or my position in society. This was because it may have had untoward repercussions, but with the knowledge of the death of Celine Hagbard I feel more at ease sharing this information. You may think I am a witch doctor or something, but in fact I am none other than the future head of state of Fernando Pó, King Francisco Malabo Beosá XXIII, or just plain Malabo to my family. I made it a point of principle from the moment of my coronation I would never speak the colonial Spanish again or for that matter any language other than Bube.

And what I read yesterday morning, and I am reading again right now, as Yoko is dreaming of yet another pyramid, is:

> *It is your duty to save not only your people*
> *But all the people of Africa*

125

But for this to be done
Five have to die
Thus
Make Five dolls out of straw
Dress the dolls in rags
Make a sharp needle from bamboo cane
Imagine each doll to represent
The Kings or Queens of the Five States
Over a period of 23 hours
Sink a needle through the straw flesh
Of each of the Five dolls
The Kings or Queens of the Five States will die
A Child will be born
She will be the One

Build a pyramid in Her honour

I read and reread it before lifting the needle to sink it into the next doll. Stevie, your time is up. The AppleTree will fall.

▲

While Yoko dreams, Makka Pakka crouches on the ground beside an ATM machine, wondering if he can get enough for his breakfast before the thirst kicks in. Then he looks at a passing stranger who is looking disparagingly back at him and he turns to say to the camera that is not there, 'Makka Pakka, Makka Pakka,' in the way he always did within *In the Night Garden.*

Makka Pakka still collects stones, but only when nobody is looking.

▲

While Yoko dreams, Winnie is also dreaming. It is the sort of dream you have when you are almost waking. It is a dream she has had ever since she was five or maybe six. It is a dream about meeting her baby sister.

In the book Yoko gave her yesterday was a page with only one word on it. Winnie took little notice of it. The word was in capitals with a question mark:

SISTER?

▲

While Yoko dreams, Siobhán Harrison is sad and worries she has not heard from her son Paul in almost forty-eight hours. Since moving down to London and moving in with that strange girl who insists she is called Yoko, he has been very good at keeping in touch. He phones her nearly every evening. And if he can't phone, he will text. But nothing since the night before last.

▲

While Yoko dreams, Angela Merkel flicks through the book her assistant has just brought in. If we could understand German, we would know the conversation is going something like this:

'Why have you brought me this, Frank?'

'Because I thought you might think it funny. It might cheer you up.'

'There is very little to cheer me up in the world right now. The people have everything they want. What is there left for people like me to do?'

'But you know, Angela, this is only a phase. There have been many phases before where peace has reigned for a while, but the people get bored, the human condition wants more. And then, Angela, it will be someone like you who will have to show the way, take the reins and prevent the likes of Putin or his heirs from wresting control again. Anyway, there was a page in German in the book that I thought you might like. I have turned the corner.'

Angela Merkel finds the page and reads:

> *When the new day dawns*
> *And the seas begin to toss*
> *The world will need a woman*
> *To provide a steady hand on the tiller*
> *You are that woman*

A red kite is mobbed by a pair of crows above the Brandenburg Gate.

▲

While Yoko dreams, it is almost 4 a.m. in a New York night-club. Out on the floor is Upsy Daisy. She will dance until dawn. Sometimes she still wonders where Makka Pakka is now.

▲

While Yoko dreams, Camille, the seventeen-year-old woman in Port-au-Prince, is still being raped by the transgender artist in a room at the Hotel Oloffson. She will learn later in the day that a package has arrived for her. Although you, the reader of this book, and me, the writer of it, can guess what is in the package, we do not know as yet if there is a page written in Haitian Kreyòl that she will be able to read.

▲

While Yoko dreams, Moses Tabick is on the 491 bus. He has just got back from Damascus, where he is studying at the newly opened Jewish Theological Seminary. He is young and eager and has only one more year to go before he is a fully qualified Rabbi. His attitudes are very liberal even for these liberal and enlightened days. When he was coming through customs this morning he was handed a package with his name on it. It is only now on the 491 that he starts to open it. It is yellow. It is hardback. On the cover is a sliced grapefruit. But he is the first person to receive a copy of this book to notice, in the pattern created by the sliced-through segments of fruit, that there is a star. A six-pointed star.

He opens the book at random and he is surprised to see that the words are in Hebrew. And if we could read Hebrew, we would read:

> *You listened when I spoke from the burning bush*
> *You led our people out of bondage*
> *You parted the waves of the Red Sea*
> *You wrote the words on tablets of stone*
>
> *Yeah, but*
> *What have you done for me lately?*
>
> *I said*
> *What have you done for me lately?*

Moses closes The Book, looks out of the window and realises it is not good enough to be a Rabbi to please his mother. He has to be a Rabbi because he has been chosen to lead his Chosen People.

▲

While Yoko dreams, John Lennon is lying at the bottom of the Lee Navigation beginning to decompose. He is very glad to be in the band with Killer Queen, Crow and Dead Squirrel and hopes they do many more records together. He is also glad Yoko gave him his copy of *Grapefruit Are Not the Only Bombs* before killing him. And that he finally got to throw a brick through the window of the pet shop. The weird thing is, a lot of the tropical fish that died on the pavement after he had done it are now fans of Tangerine NiteMare.

▲

While Yoko dreams, Divine, the seventeen-year-old girl in an unnamed village a hundred or so kilometres upriver from Mbandaka on the Congo is still being raped by the boy she used to fancy when they used to go to Sunday school. Divine is wondering why nothing has changed in her world even though the world has now been saved. Her copy of *Grapefruit Are Not the Only Bombs* was stolen. We will find out how and why in a later chapter.

▲

While Yoko dreams, a package arrives at a Buddhist monastery in Tibet, high in the Himalayas. It is opened by the young novice monk, who is on admin duty for the day. It is his job to respond to all email, phone calls and traditional mail, and do the daily tweets, FaceLife, etc., while his brothers are in silent contemplation and prayer.

Inside the package is a book. He has never read a physical book. Only the Holy scrolls; everything else is online. He opens the book at random and after sniffing the pages – he didn't know real books smelt so nice – he reads the words on the page. If we could read Ü-Tsang, we would read the following:

> *There are no more wars*
> *There is no more hunger*
> *There is no more slavery*
>
> *But in the souls*
> *Of the people of the Earth*
> *There is war, hunger and slavery*
>
> *It is only your religion*
> *That can*
> *Bring that peace*
> *Feed that hunger*
> *Free those bonds*
>
> *It is your calling to go out into the world*
> *Use whatever powers you can harness*
> *And make this happen*

The novice reads these words again and then again. And he knows these to be the words of a higher calling. That these words have been sent directly to him for a purpose and he must follow them. That he must, today, leave this monastery, come down out of the mountains and into the world and use whatever powers he can harness to make all this happen. Nothing else will do. He puts down the book, wraps his saffron robe around him and sets off into the world. His name is Chodak. We will all hear more of Chodak.

▲

While Yoko dreams, Stevie Dobbs has died in her sleep in her log cabin up in the Redwood Forests. No one will know she has died for twenty-four hours, as she has insisted that she needs to have a break from everyone and everything until she says otherwise. The package with a book in it with her name on the address c/o AppleTree Campus, Cupertino, California, was instantly dropped into the paper-recycling skip, as were the similar packages sent to 'The Princess of Wales at WikiTube' and 'Jessie Bezos at AmaZaba'.

▲

While Yoko dreams, Meg of *Meg & Mog* fame (but not that Mog the Forgetful one) is riding on her broomstick heading South. She is currently crossing the Thames. What she hopes to do is land on the very top of the Shard and from there cast a spell over all of London and maybe even the whole of the world. Owl is flying behind them.

▲

While Yoko dreams, she dreams again of her aborted son. When she was sixteen and in her first year of Foundation at art school (instead of sixth form) she started to have an affair with her life-drawing teacher. His name was Mike Large. All the girls liked him.

He used to take her out at lunchtime in his car and fuck her in a wood. She didn't know if she loved him, but she felt differently about him than any of the boys she had gone out with before. He was thirty-two, married with two children. He used to joke that his wife understood him too well.

All the other girls were jealous, even though they disapproved. But then she got pregnant. She decided to keep the baby. Mike was angry. His anger took different forms. He would have nothing more to do with her. He kept on asking, 'What about the man's right to choose?' But he wasn't asking, he was telling. He said he would pay for the abortion. She didn't want 'his fuckin' blood money'.

She had to leave art school. Her Mother said she would help look after the baby. She was five months into the pregnancy when she had to go in for an ultrasound scan. On that day she learnt two things: the first was that the baby was going to be a boy. The second was that she had endometrial cancer, or cancer of the womb to you and me, and it was pretty far gone. If they did not operate immediately, there was no chance she could survive. She had no choice. She lost both her baby boy and her womb before teatime on a Saturday afternoon.

She had already decided what she was going to call her child if it was a boy – John. After the grandfather she never knew.

Yoko did not post the book to her unborn son John. She did what she did with his birthday cards each year and the children's books she would be reading to him if he were alive. These were the children's books her Mother had read to her. She would buy him *The Tiger Who Came to Tea*, take it home and, when John Lennon was not around, she would read it aloud as if she were reading it to her three-year-old son. And then she would burn the book page by page. She would sit and watch kids' TV programmes like *Peppa Pig* and *In the Night Garden*, imagining she was watching them with him. She would build towers out of Duplo pretending that he was building them with her. She would teach him to dance and sing the songs that her mum had taught her.

Yesterday morning she burnt every page of his copy of *Grapefruit Are Not the Only Bombs* at the open doors that look over the Lee Navigation. When John came back from putting up the '2023: WHAT THE FUUK IS GOING ON?' posters, he said something and whatever it was he said, there was only one course of action to be taken, and ten minutes later he was rolled up in their duvet cover and at the bottom of the Lee Navigation.

No one saw. As he fell, but before the splash, a magpie flew past. Yoko hated magpies because of the way they raid other birds' nests, killing their babies. But she loved the way they look. She loved their clean black and white. They reminded her of a killer whale she saw once when she was on a boat in Scotland. Her Mother had taken her on a holiday to the Scottish Islands. She did not know what a killer whale was then, but as she was leaning over the side of the boat looking at the gannets dropping from the sky, a huge creature leapt out of the water. And this creature was all gleaming and smooth and black and white. And so pure. It was seven metres of female killer whale.

She has one book left. She was going to post it to the last Chairman of the old communist China, but she doesn't know who he was or where to send it, so she just throws it into the Lee Navigation in the full knowledge that somehow the killer whale will get the meaning of it all.

End of *Book One*

▲

Barnhill
Jura
28 April 1984

Dear Diary,

I was going to write some more about how Yoko was dreaming about a ghetto-blaster coming down from the sky to land on the pyramid and that maybe King Francisco Malabo Beosá XXIII had the same dream.

And I wanted to say that while she was still dreaming, all the daffodils across London were in full bloom smiling at the sun, but then I remembered daffodils would be past their best by 24 April, even if the Spring was late.

I know I wanted to end *Book One* of *2023* with Yoko still dreaming her last dream of the night, while Winnie sent an email off to Celine Hagbard saying she was going to take twenty-four hours off before hitting 'Send' on the end of death thing. Obviously this would have just been before the world got to know about Celine Hagbard's death. And then I would have finished with it being a bright warm day in April 2023 and the clock just about to strike thirteen as the clock had not been mended yet and, in fact, it was just 9:00. And how Winnie in her Levi's slung low and her T-shirt freshly unbranded strode through the gates of Victory Mansions across to the Starbucks on the corner of her block for her first skinny latte of the day.

Maybe also mention something about Winnie noticing not only that the three posters had been removed from the wall, but three whole chunks of the wall had been removed.

But I got emotionally carried away with the whole abortion

bit and forgot all of this stuff. So instead I am going to get on my faithful Brough Superior, drive the thirty-one miles to Craighouse and see if I can do a ton on that long straight.

And maybe if Francis has any more of his homemade LSD, I'll drop a tab and then get drunk.

Love,

Roberta XXXX

Postscript: I have no idea what sort of book I am writing. But if Dog Ledger does not think it genius, I'm changing agents.

I should warn you, over the twenty-four hours that pass during *Book Two*, we will not be hearing from either Winnie or Yoko.

BOOK TWO

The Rotten Apple

ROBERTA ANTONIA WILSON'S PREFACE
FOR *BOOK TWO*

Book One, The Blaster in the Pyramid, is done. I have written
it and maybe you have read it. The final two chapters of it were
written at speed and in a state of mental stress and—

For *Book Two* I hope things don't jump all over the place like
they did in those last two chapters. I mean, why should you know
who Jonathan King is, let alone Phil Harding? Reading back
through that stuff this morning, it feels like it has been written
for an audience of less than half a dozen. It feels like I was just
trying to layer the whole thing with all sorts of reference points to
impress . . . well, whoever it is, I don't know. And it is not going
to help sell any more books than my last one. That one was called
Uganda.

Ten minutes ago, while I was having my final cup of tea before
starting the day's work of hitting these keys on my portable
Empire Aristocrat, I had an idea. Each chapter in *Book Two*
would be based almost entirely around one of the characters you
have already met (and one you might not have).

As with *Book One*, all the events take place over a twenty-four-
hour period, but this time I am going to totally ignore the different
time zones. This means the whole world is on British Summer
Time. And there is no way I can find out what time zone they are
in the MidWest of the USA, let alone Tibet. So if it is teatime here,
it is teatime in Tokyo.

Here goes.

1 : REVENGE OF THE CHILD ACTOR

The sun is up and over London. There is some weather coming in from the Southwest, but it will not be here until the early afternoon – or that was what the weather forecast claimed on the radio first thing this morning.

Henry Pedders is nineteen and he lives with his mother in a block of flats on Queensbridge Road, Dalston. On the seventeenth floor of 355 Queensbridge Road, to be more precise. His dad lives elsewhere.

No. 355 is a massive block of flats, and it is where Henry has grown up. There is a window in this flat that Henry has been looking out of ever since he was tall enough to look out of a window. What he has been looking at is how London has evolved in his lifetime. The first thing he can remember is seeing the enterprise zone down in Docklands grow. Down there were the first proper tall buildings in London, if you don't count the Post Office Tower, which we won't.

From his mum's flat, those buildings down there in Docklands looked like Manhattan. When Henry was five, he thought he could see New York from his mum's flat. On his first day at school, he told his teacher he could see America from where he lived. The teacher laughed at him, and because the teacher laughed at him, so did the other boys in the class.

Then sometime after that they built the Gherkin. This was closer. Some days it felt like he could lean out of the window and touch the Gherkin. Now it is time we address something about the actual age of this Henry Pedders. Earlier on, the claim was made that Henry was nineteen, so born in 2004. The Gherkin was built in 2003 and has been there all of Henry's life. The truth of the matter is that Henry is, in fact, thirty-four years old, but as far as the rest of the world is concerned Henry is nineteen and will be for ever. And when we say 'rest of the world' we mean the rest of some parallel world. And there is part of Henry, a big part of Henry, that will always be nineteen. Nineteen and angry at everything and everyone.

There is a story behind this anger and why he is still nineteen and not the thirty-four years he should be. And a reason for *some parallel world*. This is his story:

When Henry started school, it was not only because he thought he could see America from his mum's flat that the other boys laughed at him; it was because he was fat. The type of fat that puts people off; not cuddly loveable fat like James Corden but nasty fat like Billy Bunter. So Henry had to learn, and learn fast. Henry learnt to act. Act the fool, act the stranger, act the hard man, act the bully. The teachers thought Henry was good at acting: he got to play King Herod in the nativity play at school. It wasn't just the kids that booed when he came on stage as King Herod, it was all the parents as well.

It was one of his teachers who recommended that Henry should join the kids' theatre at the Arcola Theatre, just up the road from where he lived. Henry was shit at football and the other things that boys did on Saturdays, so Henry did kids' theatre every Saturday, and he always got the parts of characters the audience wanted to hate.

Then one Saturday morning, he and all the other misfits that did youth theatre were told some big film people were going to come along and watch them act, and if they were very good they might get picked to be in a film. Henry's mum loved to rent videos and watch films; she loved those films set in American high schools. Henry wanted to please his mum. Henry's mum was the only one who didn't boo him.

The next Saturday, Henry was told the people from the big film company liked him and they would like him to go to Pinewood Studios to do a screen test.

His mother took him and he was offered a part. The part he was offered would change his life.

He was offered the part of Dudley Dursley in the first of the Harry Potter films. This was in 2000, when Dudley was ten. Now, if you don't know, Dudley Dursley was Harry Potter's fat cousin. Dudley Dursley was everything Harry Potter was not. Dudley Dursley was there in the stories to be a horrible, fat, spoilt brat who bullies whoever he can. There were no redeeming features to Dudley Dursley, or not enough for us to bother about here. Dudley Dursley existed in the Harry Potter stories for children to hate.

Henry Pedders was the perfect fit for the role of Dudley Dursley. He told all the kids at his school he had got a part in a film and he was going to be a movie star and this time next year he would probably be living in Hollywood and never have to go to school again.

But none of this happened. Those who made the decisions at Pinewood Studios changed their minds. If truth be told, they felt that although this Henry Pedders could out-act all of the other child actors they had signed up for the various parts in this Harry Potter film, it was felt he was not of the right class. And neither was his mother. They felt he could not be relied upon. There was something too real about Henry Pedders.

So instead of Henry Pedders they chose somebody from acting royalty to play the part of Dudley Dursley. Someone whose grandfather had been a Doctor Who – a Time Lord. Someone whose mother would get him to Pinewood on time.

And the children at his school laughed at him even more when the first of the Harry Potter films came out and Henry Pedders was not Dudley Dursley. And Henry Pedders did not become a film star living in Hollywood.

And Henry Pedders became a teenager.

And Henry Pedders became angry.

And Henry Pedders would go down to Saint Pancras Station and watch the kids queuing up to have their photographs taken at platform 7 and ¾.

And Henry Pedders would want to smash those kids up.

It should have been me!

And Henry Pedders became angrier.

And Henry Pedders knew he had been robbed of what should have been his.

And Henry Pedders became fatter.

It should have been me!

And Henry Pedders became even angrier.

And as each of the Harry Potter films was released Henry Pedders would go and watch it. And every time he would want to burn the cinema down with all the kids inside.

And then when Henry Pedders turned seventeen, something happened. He decided he did not want to be fat any more. He didn't want to be Henry Pedders who did not get the part of Dudley Dursley any more. So he went to the gym. He went every day. It wasn't one of those modern gyms mums go to; it was an old gym that had been there for decades, where East End boxers used to go. It was where Rude Boys used to go. And it was now where Henry Pedders went. And he lost weight. There was a new Henry Pedders coming out from behind the old one. This Henry Pedders was fit and toned, with a punch that could flatten anyone who wanted trouble. Henry Pedders would look at himself in the mirror and for the first time in his life he liked what he saw. People did not recognise this Henry Pedders. This Henry Pedders could walk down Kingsland Road on a Saturday morning and girls would turn their heads to check him out.

But Henry Pedders was not interested in these girls.

And Henry Pedders was still angry at the world.

Some teenage boys take drugs and get drunk and steal cars and smash up bus shelters.

But Henry Pedders was not *some teenage boys.*

Instead Henry Pedders just kept going to the gym.

And when he was not at the gym he sat and stared out of the window of his mother's flat as he had always done. From where he was sitting his hate and loathing found a new and very pointed focus. A building was being built some miles directly South of his window onto the world. This building just got higher and higher. And sharper and sharper. It was already taller than the Gherkin and it was hardly more than half built. And this building started to appear in his dreams.

In July 2011 *The Deathly Gallows – Part Two* was released. It was all over the television news and the front pages of all the papers. It was now time for the next chapter in Henry Pedders's life to begin.

Less than a week after this, the last of the Harry Potter films was released, things started to happen. Things were kicking off up the Kingsland Road in Tottenham. Kids were taking to the streets and throwing bricks through shop windows. It was on the news. Kids of his generation from where he was. Kids who maybe hated the world like he hated the world, even if they were kids who hated him when he had been at school.

It was all over Twitter.

Henry got on the bus up Kingsland to Tottenham. Throwing his first brick through his first window felt like the best thing he had ever done in his life. Then he made a fire bomb, lobbed it through the windows of the old Co-op building and watched as, within minutes, the whole place was ablaze.

And that night he opened his new Twitter account. Using the name Henry Da Riot, he soon had thousands and then tens of thousands of followers – and by the next morning he had over 100,000 followers. But it didn't last. Within a week he was back spending his days just staring out of his window at the world he hated.

And he was skint.

And he was arrested.

And he was charged.

And he was given community service.

He was then put on a scheme for ex-offenders. It was a scheme to get 'young people' back into the mindset of working. 'An honest day's work for an honest day's pay' – or that is what he was told by his supervisor. He was given a box of tea towels and other cheap kitchen bits and pieces and told to go door to door selling them. It was shit. Demoralising shit. And it was a scam. Nobody wanted to buy anything from him. Or nearly no one. But he had to keep doing it. He promised his mum. He promised her care worker.

At the end of one day after selling fuck all down The Bishops Avenue, he bought a litre bottle of vodka. Then he went up to Alexandra Palace and drank the whole lot while spending the night looking across the city.

As dawn came up he knew he needed to do something with his life. He knew he had what it took. Not only to out-act all those other little shits and drama-school wannabes, but to write too. He knew he was better than the shit scriptwriters they had on the Harry Potter films. He knew what proper writing could be like.

He started writing straight away on a scrap of paper with the pencil that he was supposed to use to write down what he had sold. These are the first words he wrote:

The Earth grumbles
Growling. Rising. The city street-lamps flicker up
Loud distorted music blaring out

He wrote and he wrote.

He wrote for hours and hours.

And when he had nothing left to write on he went home.

Over the following weeks and months he kept writing. He did not know what these words were for. There were thousands and thousands of words. The words seemed to be about everything, but especially about how he saw the world as he walked the streets of London trying to sell tea towels to people who wanted him to go away.

He took the words to the one person he knew in the world who ever had any time for him: the Turkish bloke who ran the Arcola Theatre. But he was not there, so he left his book full of words there with his mobile number. He never heard back. Nothing. Fuck all.

The anger returned.

He stared out of the window again for hours and days and weeks.

He tried not to write any more words.

It was now the Summer of 2012 and the building he had been watching was now complete. It was on the news. It was called the Shard. And he kept dreaming about the Shard. In the dreams it had a huge eyeball on the top of it. The eyeball swivelled and stared back at him. And sometimes in these dreams this Shard was ablaze like the Co-op building up in Tottenham during the riots.

Henry wanted to see the Shard burn.

But the years started to slip by and his mother was not well and Henry hardly ever went out. In his twenties – those years when you should be out there making your mark, meeting people, making things happen – Henry just hid from the world. He looked after his mum. And the eye on top of the Shard kept staring back at him.

And his twenties turned into his thirties. But in his head he was still nineteen, waiting for life to begin.

It was years since he had sent out a tweet. But in theory he still had over 100,000 followers from way back in 2011.

This morning, Henry has just opened a parcel addressed to the Aga Khan and found a book in it. You may remember from the last chapter – it seems so long ago – that Henry read some words about respect that sounded like they came from a religious book. Henry liked religious books. His mum used to take him to an evangelical church when he was small. He always liked the sound of the words in The Bible. Not the words of Jesus, but the words in the Old Testament. They used to make sense to him. That is what got him into words in the first place.

Henry turned the page to see what was next in this book. There were only three words there facing him:

Nothing else, no explanation. There was nothing else that needed to be said. Henry knew these words had been written for him. Henry picked up his mobile. It was time to send out the first tweet he had sent for over twelve years:

Tonight we Burn the Shard

He then sent out a second:

We will march down Kingsland
Through the City
Across London Bridge
We will be there by midnight
The Shard will Burn

Henry Da Riot was back. The Twittersphere was ablaze. Nothing for a dozen years and he is back. He will lead the people. His people. The people who hated it all. The people who loathed Starbucks and all the shit. Who hated all this world peace and everything being all right and all the start-ups you could want and all the greenness of everything and the equal opportunities and everything being sorted. The people who wanted to express their anger. Who wanted to feel what it was like to turn over a car and burn a bus and throw a brick through a window. And not give a fuck.

Henry Da Riot was back.

▲

Dear Diary,

I decided to stop that chapter there. What happens to Henry Da Riot next will have to wait. There are more important things going on around the world on the morning of 24 April 2023 than what is happening with those responding to Henry's Twitter feed.

For a start, this Welsh girl calling herself Tracey Tracey turned up today claiming to be the journalist from *Classic Biker*. She is no more than twenty years old, so what she knows about classic bikes is anybody's guess. And she was driving an over-engineered Japanese sewing machine she claimed could do nought to a ton in less than ten seconds. Even if it can, as far as I am concerned that doesn't count, as it is not a proper motorcycle. I tried to tell her about the Burma Railway and how my cousin died building the bridge over the River Kwai. And how we should not buy such things. But she feigned not to know what I was talking about.

I am also loath to mention the fact that she was wearing a black leather, all-in-one, zip-up jumpsuit, like she thought she was Emma Peel. Certainly it seemed to turn heads at the bar last night. I left the bar early and headed for home. Goodness knows where she ended up.

This morning Tracey Tracey turned up at my place on her sewing machine – okay, it is called a Kawasaki 900, but why anybody would want to drive it I have no idea – to do the interview and take photos.

I have to admit she had done her homework: not only had she read *Fish Farm*, she had also read *Uganda*, and knew all about Brough Superior Motorcycles. It also seems she had just returned from South America, where she had driven the route

Che Guevara covered in the early 1950s on a '39 Norton 500 – a proper bike, the bike Che Guevara had actually done the trip on in the first place. So maybe I was being too hasty in my judgements.

I gave her some of the novel I am writing at the moment and she seemed to be quite impressed with it, but then she told me she should be the leading lady in it, or at least a major character. I said the book was not about that sort of thing. There were no romances or the like. She then suggested I should base either Winnie or Yoko on her. She was very persuasive and the fact she had driven all over South America on a Norton 500 was impressive, so maybe there will be a part for her later in the book.

Then she told me that on her journey up through Mexico, at the end of her South American adventure, she met up with a young revolutionary who was part of the Zapatista movement called Rafael Guillén. It seems this Tracey has a thing for Latin revolutionaries, and there may have been some romance, etc. But the main thing this Tracey Tracey wanted me to know was that she told Rafael Guillén he needed an image, and that she got him on a horse with a couple of belts of bullets slung around his chest, an AK-47 in his arms, a black balaclava on his head, and a cap with three red stars on the front on top of the balaclava. But the thing that Tracey Tracey claimed she came up with, and that all the world will remember him for, was the pipe she took off an old village peasant and shoved in Rafael Guillén's mouth.

She said she told him it would make him into a worldwide star to rival Che Guevara, if he was seen to be smoking a peasant's pipe. Then she told me she renamed him Subcomandante Marcos. It all sounds highly unlikely but it made a good story and maybe I will take elements of it and use it in my novel.

Tracey Tracey was quite keen on this idea, but then asked if I would write it so readers would think she had had a romantic liaison with this man on a horse with a pipe in his mouth.

Then Tracey Tracey got me out on my Brough, made me wear my Halcyon goggles and white silk scarf, and then from nowhere she produced a large Havana cigar that she had me chew on for the photograph. I have to admit it made me feel very special, and I look forward to seeing the photographs when they are developed. She promised she would post me a couple of prints.

And that was that. She was off on her Kawasaki, or was it a Suzuki?

Yours,

Roberta

Postscript: she left me the cigar. I might just smoke it this evening down at the bar, while wearing my white silk scarf.

▲

Jura
30 April 1984

Dear Diary,

I have decided to get a new literary agent.

I have just driven all the way down to the hotel again to send and receive faxes from Dog 'Face' Ledger. There was one from him. I was hoping it was going to contain encouragement, along with a few gentle words of advice.

But no!

He is telling me in no uncertain terms I have to remove all of the characters I have 'ripped off' (his words) from the manuscript he got from some young would-be hopeful. It was called *The Philosopher's Gate*. He had posted me a copy of this manuscript, as he wanted me to have a look at it to see what I thought. I read it, and was taken in by it, but it was rubbish. No legitimate publisher would be interested in it. But . . .

But there was something about it.

But because I knew it would get no further than the wastepaper baskets of literary editors the length and breadth of Bloomsbury, I thought there was no harm in me helping myself to one of the main characters and imaging a career trajectory for him. And not only that but imagining the whole thing becoming a massive franchise with follow-ups and films and all the rest of it.

And there in Dog Ledger's fax to me he is telling me I have to either get rid of the last chapter or change the character I had robbed totally so he could never be recognised. And how would I like it if one of my major characters were robbed by some other writer?

And then he started going on about the franchise possibilities in children's literature being the future of publishing. And maybe I should . . . Maybe write a children's book about an ice-cream van that has been retired and locked up in a garage and never gets to hear the children play, and one night it escapes to travel the world and go on adventures. Rubbish, pure rubbish.

And then he tells me I should remove any other characters from the narrative that in some way reflect real people with real lives, or any other characters I might be thinking of 'ripping off'. And if I didn't, it would just make it impossible for him to get a deal for the book.

And then he started going on about some book he represented about a football manager called Bryan-something, who used to swear a lot, and how this Bryan wanted to sue the publishers because he said he never swore. I say it serves Dog right for working with football managers. Or something.

And then Dog was almost telling me to grow up and—

Anyway.

I need a deal.

I need the money.

And I need the love.

Yours,

Roberta

2 : WHAT IS RAPE?

09:33 Monday 24 April 2023

Arati's husband is no longer raping her. He is leaving the family home for work in the car showroom his family runs.

Arati hates everything about the home she now lives in. It is not her home. It is not where she has spent her entire life until three months ago. She is now the youngest married woman in her new 'home'. She is treated like shit by all the other women in this home, even worse than the servants. She is at the bottom of the pecking order. At the top is her husband's grandmother. All decisions made about the running of this home come down from her. She is the 'dowager duchess' in charge of it all. It was her that arranged the marriage between her grandson and Arati.

Three months ago Arati was a carefree teenager who spent most of her time on the internet communing with other girls her age around the world. With Google Interpret she could chat to anyone anywhere – and she did. Her friends around the globe would chat about clothes, boys and women's rights. She was also very smart. Smarter than her brothers. She wanted to go to university to study civil engineering. She wanted to rebuild Kolkata in the way other girls around the world had rebuilt their cities. But her father's business was going bust – he too had a car sales business. He was bought out and part of the deal was Arati's hand in marriage to the son of her father's arch rival. There was nothing she could do; it was for the sake of her family.

Before she was married, she had never had sex. She still believed in romance and stories, especially the story of Savitri, the young goddess who goes out into the world to find her man and finally finds her Satyavan.

The reality of what happened to her was nothing like that. Every night she is made to have sex with this ugly monster, whose breath smells and whose body stinks and who has no charm or intelligence. She can say or do nothing. She has to just lie there and think of . . . well, not England, but wherever young women in West Bengal think of when having sex they do not want to have.

But is this rape? Or is this just her husband's right? She hardly dare ask herself. And now in her new life she is not even allowed to go online to ask anyone else. In fact, her laptop has been confiscated by her 'elders and betters' in her new family home.

Every morning, after her husband leaves for work and dishes are washed and morning chores done, Arati goes to the local temple at the corner of her street to say her prayers. Beside the temple an internet café has opened. This morning Arati snuck in. For a few old rupees, she was soon online (in India there is still a black market in old rupees).

The words Arati put into Google were 'What is Rape?' And the answer she got back immediately was:

Rape is any form of unwanted sexual behaviour that is
    imposed on someone
Rape is more about the abuse of power than about sexual
    attraction or the desire for sexual gratification

After Arati read that, but in Bangla, she went on a *Have I been raped?* forum on FaceLife. She was soon chatting to other young women around the world. Google Translate ironed out all the 'lost in translation' problems.

▲

In the Port-au-Prince Hotel Oloffson, the transgender artist has rolled off Camille and fallen asleep. Camille is lying there staring at the slowly revolving fan on the ceiling, wondering what has just happened and what she should do next.

Yesterday, if she had been asked, she would have thought she'd do anything to get out of Haiti to the USA, where she could make money to send home to her mum, to feed her two younger sisters and three younger brothers. All she had to do was get herself a *Blan! Blan!* man and fuck him well and she was almost guaranteed a passport to the USA. It had happened for other girls and boys she knew. One of them got one of these *Blan! Blan!* artists that stayed at the Hotel Oloffson every couple of years as part of what they called the Ghetto Biennale. She decided to try to get this one, because he looked strange and lost and not very attractive and no other girl or boy might go for him. He was from London, not the USA, but she reckoned that could be just as good.

This man who she had fucked was not really a man as he had breasts and wore strange clothes. But he was not gay. She knew what gay was. Lots of men were gay. Especially the voodoo priests. This man was something else, and he fucked her in ways she didn't want to be fucked. And he hurt her and laughed when he hurt her. She knew some men did these things. Maybe it was what she had to do to get a man to pay for her to go to the USA, or maybe London?

While he snored, she got dressed and went out to the bar. She sat down and drank a glass of water. There was another girl there but she was *Blan! Blan!* Using sign language, she asked if she could use *Blan! Blan!* girl's laptop for a minute. The *Blan! Blan!* said, '*Wi.*'

So she put into Google, '*Ki sa ki vyòl?*'

And the answer she got back immediately was:

Rape is when someone uses their power, manipulation or force
  to intimidate, humiliate, exploit, degrade or control another
  Rape has been used as a weapon in war, in racial violence and
  in everyday life

After Camille read that, but in Haitian Kreyòl, she went on the
Have I been raped? forum on FaceLife. She was soon chatting
to other young women around the world who had also just been
raped. Google Translate ironed out all the 'lost in translation'
problems.

▲

Divine, the seventeen-year-old girl in an unnamed village a hundred or so kilometres upriver from Mbandaka, is still being raped
by the boy she used to go to Sunday school with and had always
fancied.

His name is Patrice, after the revolutionary leader who had
won independence for their country from their colonial tyrants in
Brussels, before it was taken over by the brutal tyrant Mobutu,
or to give him his full title, Mobutu Sese Seko Kuku Ngbendu Wa
Za Banga.

Patrice is five years older than Divine. He is strong and handsome and almost any girl would want to be his woman, and here
Divine has struck lucky. It is what Divine has dreamt of for so
long.

Patrice had made it out of their village all the way to Kinshasa.
And there he had made a business. He imported and he exported.

And he made money. But he came back to their village. He told Divine the girls in Kinshasa were not good. That he always thought about Divine. And that he wanted to come back and find Divine and take Divine with him. And together they would go to Brussels or maybe Paris and live together like a King and Queen.

Divine knew that is how boys talked when they came back from Kinshasa. She had been warned. But Patrice was so lovely. Even when she was only five years old she knew she wanted one day to marry Patrice. And that day might be coming soon.

But something about what happened last night she did not like. He became angry. He lost his erection. He blamed her. He hit her and then he hit her again. And then after he hit her he got an erection again. And he fucked her. But when he was fucking her he told her to pretend to be a little girl. A frightened little girl. A little girl that did not want to be fucked by a big man.

Divine did not know what to do or say, so she did nothing but lie there. But then Patrice started to hit her again, and again he got an erection and again he fucked her and again he was pretending she was a little girl. The five-year-old Divine he used to know when they were in Sunday school together.

She knew this was not right. Her mother had told her there were men like this. But not Patrice. Not lovely Patrice. Not Patrice who was going to take her out of their village hundreds of kilometres from anywhere and take her to Kinshasa and then Brussels and maybe even Paris. Patrice who can speak French so beautifully. Handsome, kind Patrice.

Then when the village cockerels crowed and the day had begun, Divine got up and left Patrice lying on the ground. There was blood between her legs and there was blood on her lips, and her body ached like it had never ached before. And Divine knew it was over. All her dreams were over. She knew she would never leave her village. She would end up marrying one of the boys who did nothing and went nowhere, and she would have children like her mother and she would be bent double like her mother and she would work hard like her mother and her husband, like her father, would drink palm wine and get drunk and . . .

But she decided she was not going to accept that. She would leave their village, Patrice or no Patrice. She would steal a pirogue* and paddle the hundreds of kilometres until she got to Kinshasa, and there she would work until she had the money to buy a ticket for an airplane that would take her far, far away from all of this.

And she would never let a man touch her again.

So she got up and went out of the hut she and Patrice had spent the night in, and she went down to the river, the mighty Congo River. And there she untied a pirogue, climbed into it and, using the paddle, she pushed herself away from the bank and out into the current.

Divine had begun her journey.

▲

10:13 Monday 24 April 2023

An hour or so later, after Arati had been chatting online with other women who had been raped, she decided to put the words in the yellow book with the lemon on the cover, the words in Bangla, into Google. But nothing had come up. This was very strange. Google always found everything.

As she is walking back to her husband's family home for another day's drudgery, she flicks through the book one more time. It is

* Pirogue = a dug-out canoe.

then she notices some other writing in Bangla at the back of the book. But the script is very small and Arati's sight is not too good. It takes her some time to read it. And if we could read Bangla, we would know it says:

Meet at The Shepherdess, City Road, at 17:47 on 24 December 2023

And Arati knows that is what she will do.

▲

Also at 10:13 Camille is walking back down the streets of Port-au-Prince from the Oloffson to the Cité Soleil, where she lives with her mother and brothers and sisters. So much of her city has never recovered from the Earthquake back in 2010. The world may have sorted out all of its problems, but still no one gives a fuck about Haiti.

Why should they? Haiti has nothing to offer the world. It has no minerals. Agriculture is non-existent since the land has been raped for over two hundred years. There is no industry because no one would be foolish enough to invest in such a crime-ridden and corrupt society. And maybe the biggest problem for Haiti is it is not a threat to anyone. It was never going to be the birthplace of communism for the New World, like neighbouring Cuba. It was never going to be the spark of a radicalised Islamic revolution. And the people of Haiti were never going to have the money to be valuable consumers for the rest of the world to sell to.

No one gives a fuck about Haiti, even in 2023. And voodoo is no threat to anyone, whatever the witch doctor says.

Camille notices a parcel in the gutter. She looks around. No one is looking. She picks it up. She is surprised to see it has her name on it with the address of the Oloffson. She opens the parcel. There is a book inside. It has a yellow cover. She is wondering to whom could she sell the book? Maybe one of the artists staying at the Hotel Oloffson? She flicks through the pages of the book. There are many languages but she cannot read any of them. Then she gets to one page and to her surprise it is written in Haitian Kreyòl, and this is what it says:

> *Ou se yon Gadò Mouton*
> *Mouton ou swiv sèlman ou*
> *Men koulye a, li se tan pou ou*
> *pou w jwenn*
> *Sè ou*
> *Lè sa a, tout twa nan ou*
> *Jwenn ak omaj a Youn nan*
> *Ki moun ki se yo dwe mouton an*
> *nan tout Fam*
>
> *Gen patiraj vèt*
> *Ki kote vè k'ap manje kadav la*
> *pa te vire Apple la*

And my guess is you can guess what this is telling her, so there is no point in translating it for you.

Camille flicks through the rest of the book, looking to see if there is anything else written in Haitian Kreyòl. She finds one line near the back of the book. It reads:

Rankontre nan Mouton An, City Road, London nan 17:47 sou
   24 Desanm 2023

Camille is Roman Catholic but she also practises voodoo. She believes in signs. This book in the gutter is a sign. She decides to return to the Hotel Oloffson and find the man with the breasts who is an artist and fuck him so he will never want to fuck anybody else ever again. And then he will take her back to London with him. And then she will get a job and send money back to her mother to feed her brothers and sisters and pay for their school, and on 24 December she will go to The Shepherdess Café on City Road to meet the other two shepherdesses. And they will find and pay homage to the One.

Camille turns around and starts walking back up the hill through her still-devastated city towards the Oloffson.

Camille has begun her journey.

▲

Also at 10:13 Divine is lying back in 'her' pirogue, gazing up at the sky, while drifting down the river. She does not know how many days it will take her to get to Kinshasa but she does know this is the best day of her life so far.

A pure white Egret flies overhead. This is a sign she is doing the right thing.

▲

Jura
30 April 1984

Dear Diary,

After this morning's outburst about the future of publishing and me ripping things off, I was able to put all of my anger to one side and get on with some serious writing about serious stuff.

What I got written today is a chapter called 'What Is Rape?' I have never been raped. Never discussed in any depth with anybody who has been raped the lasting effect it has had on their life. So what gives me the right to write about such things? Have I just used rape in this story to give it more grit? Should only those who have been raped write about rape?

I do not have the answers to any of these questions.

Today I will not drive to the bar. Instead I will sit and watch the sun sink into the sea, as the heron stands in the shallows patiently waiting to make her move on the unsuspecting passing whiting.

Yours,

Roberta

3 : A GOOD YEAR FOR THE ROSES

I can hardly bear the sight of lipstick
On the cigarettes there in the ashtray
Lyin' cold the way you left 'em
But at least your lips caressed them while you packed

10:48 Monday 24 April 2023

'Angela, I have had enough. You know the world is not right. Things cannot carry on as they have been.'

'Vladimir, we have had our time. The world has moved on. We must let the young ones make of the world what they can.'

'So I have to just potter around my dacha planting potatoes and pruning the roses? I have a responsibility not only to the people of Russia but to the world as a whole.'

This snippet of conversation, held in Russian over the phone, is between Vladimir Putin and Angela Merkel. They both retired from active political life back in 2019. Angela supports her local football team, and Vladimir tends his garden at his dacha. They speak to each other most days on the phone. Angela's Russian is perfect. Putin's admiration of Merkel total. As far as Putin is concerned, Angela Merkel is the only other world statesperson who has any appreciation of his values. She understands even when she does not agree.

I am afraid that in their daily banter there is very little humour, so no witty quips to drop in here for your entertainment. Or maybe there is humour, but it gets lost in translation from the Russian.

'Well, Angela, I have had enough. And this time you are not going to talk me out of it with all your rational persuasions. If I do not do something about it now, nothing will ever be done. We are the last of the generation that knew what real politics was for. We might be the only ones left who can see through the charade of all of this FaceDeath and GoogleShite, who can see it for what it really is.

'For some reason I got sent a book in the post this morning. I don't know where it came from or who sent it. There was only one page in Russian in the whole book, so I read it. And somehow it said in four lines everything I knew to be true but have never actually been able to say in public. I have got it here in front of me. I will read it out to you now.'

'Hang on a minute, Vlad. I have to let the cat in first.'

'What, you don't have a cat flap?'

'She refuses to use the cat flap.'

'And you allow that to continue? I think you should get rid of that cat and get another one that does not refuse to use the cat flap.'

While Putin waits for Angela Merkel to let her cat in, he reads through the lines one more time. He knows what he has to do. But he also knows he has to tell Angela first. He needs her tacit approval even if she cannot give it publicly.

'Vlad, I'm back. What was it you were going to read to me?'

'Angela, just listen,' and Putin reads the only words in Russian in *Grapefruit Are Not the Only Bombs*. And if you need to be reminded what those words were, they are:

Mankind needs War
Without War civilisation would not have evolved
It is your duty to further the evolution of Mankind
Make War Now

There is silence down the other end of the line. Putin knows Merkel is still there, he can hear her breathing. He knows she will understand these words even if she cannot tell him she agrees with them.

Until the age of thirty-eight Angela Merkel lived under the gaze and influence of Soviet Russia. I will not use the clichéd word 'yoke' here, because Angela Merkel also understood and respected what lay at the heart of the Soviet dream. She understood what made a Russian 'man' tick, be that man from the Soviet era or from somewhere far back in history, or from today. For them, what we know as 'democracy' was never going to work. And what the world has now under the 'yoke' of the Five is anathema to everything Putin holds to be true and right.

'The thing is, Vlad, I also got a book in the post this morning. And my guess is it was the same book. And in my copy the only words in German are . . .', and Merkel reads these words:

> *When the new day dawns*
> *And the seas begin to toss*
> *The world will need a woman*
> *To provide a steady hand on the tiller*
> *You are that woman*

'Vlad, we have to ask ourselves, is someone playing us? Are we just the mice being tossed from paw to paw by the unseen cat? Anyway, I have to get going, we are playing away this evening. Talk to you in the morning.'

▲

Thirty-odd minutes later, Angela Merkel is already on the coach on her way to Dortmund to watch an away match with her beloved FC Energie Cottbus, and Putin is still on the phone.

But this time Putin is on the phone to his 'retired' Marshal of the Russian Federation, one Igor Dmitriyevich Sergeyev Junior. The 'Junior' is there so as not to confuse him with his father, who had held the same office a couple of decades earlier.

The thing is, when Russia went bankrupt because no one needed to buy their oil or gas any more, and their army, the largest in the world at the time, was dissolved, Putin had to put other secret plans into action. He had quietly mothballed forty divisions of his army.

Somewhere out in the vastness of Siberia, even beyond the reach of GoogleEarth, hidden in several thousand bunkers, each the size of a football pitch, were forty thousand tanks and a hundred thousand young and disciplined wo/men. Their only job was to wait for the call, and whenever that call came they would be ready. That call was about to come.

'Igor, today is the day. Are you and your legions ready to honour our Mother Russia and save the world? By December I need to know we have regained all of the land we had mastery over in the Soviet era. Everything as far as the Rhine is ours.'

'President Putin, give me twenty-four hours and our tanks will be rolling. We will be in Poland by this time next week.'

▲

And the lip-print on a half-filled cup of coffee
That you poured and didn't drink

But at least you thought you wanted it
And that's so much more than I can say for me

▲

Not that Divine would have any idea what the time was – she is still drifting down the mighty Congo. And just so you have some idea of how 'mighty' the Congo is, it is the deepest river in the world, at 220 metres, and discharges into the ocean over forty thousand cubic metres of water every second. And at this moment in time Divine is the only woman on its 4,371 kilometre length in a pirogue on her own. She is the Queen of all its waters.

Now, I don't really know what magical realism is, but I do know it was the name given to some sort of genre fiction that was all the rage in Latin America some years ago. But right now I am going to borrow something from what I imagine magical realism might be.

Here goes.

The white Egret that was flying above Divine's stolen pirogue in the last chapter has landed on its bow.

If you do not know what an Egret is, it is like a pure white heron, all very elegant and beautiful. And from this Egret's beak hangs not a baby in a basket, but a string bag, like your mother might have once used. In this string bag is a copy of *Grapefruit Are Not the Only Bombs*.

The reason for using this form of delivery to get the book to Divine – and not the Royal Mail, or some other regular parcel-delivery system like UPS or FedEx – is that the only connection Divine's village has to the outside world is via the Congo River itself. There are no roads leading in or out of her village, so no form of motorised transport. Maybe the odd pushbike, but that is it.

Once every couple of weeks or so, a half-dozen rusting barges, tied together with fraying steel cables, are pushed upriver by a tugboat. This is the only internal form of public transport between Kinshasa, the capital city, and Kisangani, the inner station. The journey takes about three weeks.

This ragbag of watercraft may have up to three thousand passengers on board, along with their livestock and all their worldly goods. And this ragbag of watercraft does not stop at any of the passing villages.

The only way to either get on the barges or trade with them is to wait in your pirogue for hour after hour in the middle of the Congo on the days you judge the ferry might be passing. And when the ferry comes up around the bend, you have to paddle like hell to get up alongside it. Then, with one end of a rope tied to your pirogue and the other around your waist, you have to make a leap for the side of the ferry and hope you can catch the hand of one of the many passengers who are leaning over the side.

You then tie the pirogue up to the railing of the barge and do whatever trading and transactions you need to do with those on board.

The above description is an aside, but I thought you should know that although your world might be the most connected it is ever possible to be, some parts of the world still have next to no contact with the outside world. High-speed broadband will never arrive at places like this. Why should it?

So, in the string bag hanging from the beak of the Egret is the book. And Divine takes the string bag from the Egret's beak, removes the book from the bag and flicks through its pages. I'm in danger of sounding very patronising here, but Divine lives in a world where all sorts of things intervene with the mundanity of real life. If an Egret wants to deliver her a book while she drifts down the mighty Congo, so be it.

The words in the book are in many languages and, as it happens, Divine is fluent in over a dozen of them. But the fact that on one page there are some lines in her language of Lingala surprises her way beyond the book being delivered by an Egret. In English you will not be surprised to discover these words read as follows:

> *You are a Shepherdess*
> *Your sheep follow only you*
> *But now it is time for you to find*
> *Your Sisters*
> *Then all Three of you*
> *Find and pay homage to the One*
> *Who is to be the Shepherdess of all Womankind*
>
> *There are pastures green*
> *Where the worm has not turned the Apple*

In the string bag is also a loaf of bread and a plastic bottle of mineral water.

The Egret's job done, it lifts itself slowly back into the air and heads for the North bank of the river.

Divine feels good. Better than she has ever felt in her life before. She will make it to Brussels or even Paris on her own. She is a woman, she can do these sorts of things.

▲

After three full years of marriage
It's the first time that you haven't made the bed
I guess the reason we're not talkin'
There's so little left to say we haven't said

▲

11:37

The forty thousand tanks are being filled with petrol.

  Their engines are being turned over.

  Shells are being loaded.

  Young women sharpen their bayonets.

  Young men write letters home to mothers.

▲

A distant cousin of Mister Fox takes a shortcut through Vladimir Putin's dacha. Putin likes to watch this fox. He likes to think that if he were an animal, he would be a fox.

▲

11:38

The transgender artist from London staying in the Hotel Oloffson in Port-au-Prince wakes up and wonders if he really wants to go through with the operation and have his cock removed. I mean, if he had his cock removed, he would never again get to fuck little whores like he did last night.

  He then thinks about the art he has been producing while over here as part of the Ghetto Biennale. He wonders if it is driven by post-colonial guilt, or if the post-colonial guilt is all part of it and makes the art even stronger.

He then uses his left hand to stroke his enlarged breasts while using his right hand to gently pull back the foreskin on his as-yet-to-be-removed cock.

He wonders what happened to the girl who came back with him last night. He wouldn't mind fucking her again tonight.

He wonders if he should be worrying about HIV.

▲

11:40

Putin decides to prune his roses before making any more phone calls. While doing this he whistles the tune to George Jones's hit 'A Good Year for the Roses'. Putin loves George Jones. It was one of the reasons why he first fell for Lyudmila. She was totally into Tammy Wynette, George Jones's then wife. How could Lyudmila and him not make a perfect match?

But Lyudmila and Putin divorced many years ago. Putin wonders if he has left it too late to ever fall in love again.

He keeps whistling the tune to himself while he prunes the roses.

▲

While a million thoughts go racin' through my mind
I find I haven't spoke a word
And from the bedroom the familiar sound
of our one baby's cryin' goes unheard

173

▲

11:41

Angela Merkel is on the coach with the other FC Energie Cottbus fans heading for Dortmund. It's a Cup match. Energie have never won anything, not even in the days when they were in the old East German league. Since unification they have only ever made it to the Bundesliga for a couple of seasons.

Angela is at the back of the coach, her red and white scarf around her neck, and is singing the songs she has been singing since she was only ten years old. It just so happens Angela Merkel is also a George Jones fan. She too, when alone and not singing football songs, can be heard singing 'A Good Year for the Roses'.

Angela's mind keeps drifting from the prospect of the evening's match to the conversation she had with Putin this morning. She knows Putin has a tendency to get carried away with different ideas about things, but she is usually able to get him to see sense. I mean, it took him a couple of years to accept it was all over for his Russia once no one was interested in buying his oil or gas. And all that posturing of his in the Ukraine. It was only her influence that stood between him and another major European war.

She pulls *Grapefruit Are Not the Only Bombs* from her handbag and starts to flick through it, reading each of the pages in turn. Where has this come from? If she has got a copy and so has Putin, who else?

She reads again the words that were so obviously meant for Putin. They make sense. Something in her knows these words to be true. Where wo/mankind had once arrived was now stagnation. Wars were always needed to jolt things to the next level. Yes, a generation of young men had to be sent to the slaughter, but that was what was required for culture to keep on evolving.

Without the bombing of Dresden there could have been no *Sergeant Pepper's Lonely Hearts Club Band*. Without the bombing of Coventry there could have been no Krautrock. Anyone with the thinnest understanding of cultural history over the past century knows this.

Oh yeah, and without the Atlantic slave trade, no Jazz, Michael Jackson, Bob Marley or even Jay Zee. Or something like that. Or is that a different argument?

Then she reads the lines again that are so obviously meant for her:

> *When the new day dawns*
> *And the seas begin to toss*
> *The world will need a woman*
> *To provide a steady hand on the tiller*
> *You are that woman*

▲

11:43

In a village hall somewhere in rural Northamptonshire, Extreme Noise Terror play through all the songs that are on their *Black Room* album without a break. They get to the end and look at each other. It was either the greatest moment in the history of rock 'n' roll reunions since the original line-up of Black Sabbath got back together in 2017, or it was a heap of shite. We will let history be the judge of this. At least they remembered all the chord changes, even if Alan Moore seemed to have improvised some of the lyrics.

175

Then he suggests they try a slowed-down grunge version of 'A Good Year for the Roses'. 'It might make a good encore.'

▲

Elvis Costello is considering recording another album of Country & Western covers in Nashville. He has just been listening to a *Best of* George Jones on his way to pick up his grandchildren from their grandmother, his first wife. He reckons his voice is now far better suited to the tragedy of 'A Good Year for the Roses' than it ever was when he was in his twenties. Maybe he should re-record it.

▲

In Stoke Newington Police Station the lab report has just come back. There is DNA on the piece of paper ripped from a book that had been tied around the brick that had been thrown through the pet-shop window.

Barney Muldoon and Saul Goodman are the names of the two officers on the case. If you think you recognise their names, it is because they have been borrowed from the two police officers in the Illuminatus books. I have done this so the identities of the two real officers on this case are not exposed.

The DNA matches up with a Paul Harrison they have on their files. He was charged last year with graffiti-ing abusive statements on walls around Dalston. It seems although he pleaded guilty, he tried to turn his court appearance into some sort of performance-art piece. The last known address they have for him is a warehouse down in Hackney Wake.

Muldoon and Goodman make plans to go and give the place a visit that afternoon, maybe pull this Harrison in for questioning.

'Kids have everything these days, so why the fuck do they still feel the need to throw bricks through windows?' asks Muldoon.

'Because he is an artist, so what he is doing is art,' retorts Goodman.

'And that is what our job has been reduced to in this day and age: trying to stop spoilt kids from doing what they call art. What happened to proper crime? I remember when we had to sort out drug turf wars. Kids stabbing each other with knives.'

'Yeah, remember the Tottenham Riots? Now that was fun. We spent months on that, nailing all the ringleaders. Sorting them out. Getting them back on the straight and narrow.'

'What are you saying? You reckon we could do with another riot?'

'Why not? It would be better than some kid with delusions of being an artist lobbing a brick through a pet-shop window.'

▲

11:54

Angela Merkel is looking out of the window of the coach at the autobahn and the passing cars. She tries to ignore her ageing reflection looking back at her. She is also trying not to think because, if she starts thinking, she will start thinking about Putin and how he is right. She might also start thinking that for some time she has suspected Putin is hiding something from her, that although all the deals were done and hands were shook, and we all looked forward to a world no longer blighted by war, that Putin had some other agenda. Maybe 'agenda' is too strong a word, but even way back when the deal was done over Greece between the two of them, and Greece was sold off to AmaZaba, she felt that he was hiding some of his thoughts and plans.

Angela Merkel knew in her heart of hearts Putin had a secret army somewhere out there in the vastness of his former empire, and at some point before he got too old he would want to use it. Boys always did. Especially when the boys were Russian men.

▲

11:57

Vladimir Putin makes himself a fresh pot of tea, takes a seat on the veranda of his dacha, and stares out at the roses in his garden. He can tell it is going to be a good year. At last things are going his way.

▲

12:00

'This is the news at noon on iJaz Europe. It has just been announced that the winners of this year's Hockney Award are a formerly unknown collective of artists who go by the name of K-SEC.

'As yet it is not known if K-SEC were aware they were in the running for the world's premier contemporary art prize. Our reporters are trying to track K-SEC down in the Hackney area of London, where it is suspected they are based.

'Their prize-winning work is a triptych of posters that were fly-posted in the early hours of this morning onto a wall on Kingsland Road, London.

'These works are being exhibited in Lord Saatchi's new contemporary art museum in the recently reopened, refurbished Battersea Power Station.

'I will now hand over to our arts editor, Will Gompertz, who is on-site in Battersea Power Station. Will, what can you tell us about—?'

▲

Vladimir Putin lifts the arm of his record player and drops the needle into the groove of his favourite track by the late great George Jones. He sits back, takes another sip of his black Russian tea and, as he loses himself in the tragedy of it all, the tanks begin to roll.

It's been a good year for the roses
Many blooms still linger there
The lawn could stand another mowin'
Funny I don't even care
When you turn to walk away
And as the door behind you closes
The only thing I have to say
It's been a good year for the roses

4 : SHIBBOLETH NOW

You may have been thinking, 'How come John Lennon's body has not floated to the top yet? Surely that is what dead bodies do?' And you would be right. What I failed to mention in an earlier chapter was that Yoko wrapped up John's training weights in the duvet cover along with his body before rolling it from their door into the canal below.

Yoko never allowed herself to be judgemental about John's obsessive lifting of weights every morning and his checking of his biceps and seven-pack in the bathroom mirror. Who wouldn't want a man with a fit body?

But as soon as she sunk the kitchen knife in and knew he was dead, the weights and his weight training were the most obvious example of his shallow vanities. Another reason, if she needed one, why he had to go.

Almost thirty-six hours since he landed at the bottom of the Lee Navigation, the gentle movement of the water has been working the duvet cover loose. His body is beginning to unravel itself. The weights have rolled to the side and are sinking into the mud.

At the same time this is happening, a small shoal of perch are beginning to bother John; they are from some online fan site dedicated to the work of Tangerine NiteMare. They just love everything he has done, and the band have to be their all-time favourite. They had heard from various sources on the net where John Lennon was now residing (and just to remind you: they were not getting confused, it is this John Lennon they were interested in and not the Beatle one). I guess the fact that one of their own kind, as in Dead Perch, had been doing the social media promotion on all things Tangerine NiteMare helped, but even so they could hardly believe he was really here in their stretch of water. Just hanging out like any other dead body that has been dumped in the canal.

John's body was also beginning to decompose, which this shoal of perch did not mind as it meant they could nibble at him at the same time as bombarding him with questions about future recordings and possible performances.

John is not that bothered. It is good to have other life forms interested in his art. They are also asking him what he thought about K-SEC winning the Hockney Award. You would think he would be totally pissed off and filled with jealousy that his ex-girlfriend, who murdered him less than forty hours ago, had gone on and won the world's most prestigious contemporary art prize with work he was substantially involved with and probably the main driving force behind. But that is the funny thing with death: you just ain't as bothered about these things any more.

'But surely you must be twisted with envy?' asked one particularly pushy Little Perch.

'No, not really. I'm pleased for her. And, anyway, I have the band now. And there is something I can reveal to you. And you will be the first to know. I have just heard from Killer Queen that we will be doing a performance at the Maelstrom at midnight tonight.'

The Little Perch are beside themselves with this, even though they know they will not be able to be there themselves, as they are freshwater fish and the Maelstrom is in saltwater, but it will all be streamed live so they will be able to hear it anyway.

'But, Mr Lennon, how will you be able to get there, seeing as you are lying dead at the bottom of the Lee Navigation?' asked what seemed like the pushiest of the Little Perch.

'As yet, I don't know. There is so much more I have to learn about being dead. But I am learning fast. And Killer Queen assures me it won't be a problem. If you can make it, I will be sure to put you on the guest-list.'

With this, the Little Perch flurry away and John Lennon's body starts to make the short journey floating to the surface of the canal.

▲

You may have noticed I used the word 'ain't' in the above section. This is one of those words that may mark someone out as not belonging to a certain class. This is called a shibboleth, as in a word or gesture or custom that indicates, unwittingly or not, whether you are in or out, if you are kosher or not kosher. There was a small town near where I lived where they didn't say 'ain't', they said 'in't'.

Those in that town who aspired to the society of those that lived in surrounding towns had to learn to say 'ain't' instead of 'in't'. But there was a strange reversal of pronunciations when it came to those that lived there. Their town was (and still is) called Rothwell. Everyone pronounced it as it was spelt. But if you came from Rothwell, you would laugh at the rest of the world for pronouncing the name of your small town so obviously wrong. You knew, and no one else did, that your small and perfectly formed town was pronounced 'Ro'well'.

There is a reason for having this sidetrack at this juncture in the novel you are reading. It is to bring the word 'shibboleth' to our attention, which you may have correctly guessed is a Hebrew word.

The word literally means the chaff that contains the seed of wheat or corn. About three thousand years ago a couple of the Semite tribes were having disagreements about land on either side of the Jordan – the usual thing. It was the Gileadites versus the Ephraimites. Now, there was very little to distinguish between these tribes except the way they pronounced the word for chaff, as in 'shibboleth'. The Ephraimites didn't use the 'sh' sound, so they pronounced the word 's'ibboleth', whereas the Gileadites pronounced it with the 'sh' as in 'shibboleth'.

When the Gileadites captured a bunch of unknown tribespeople, they asked them to pronounce the word they used for chaff, and they said 's'ibboleth'. The Gileadites immediately slaughtered their prisoners as they had given themselves away as being the thieving and land-grabbing Ephraimites.

Now, things might be pretty sorted out in the world, but if you take a stroll up to Stamford Hill, all the Hasidic Jews up there will look pretty much the same to us goys. But for them, their little enclosed society is riven with more sectarian differences than the whole of Christendom.

And they have many, many little 'shibboleths' to tell themselves apart that leave the difference between 'ain't' and 'in't' standing.

▲

12:07

Barney Muldoon and Saul Goodman are at the local Starbucks getting a takeaway flat white and an Americano. They are chatting about the case. Now a missing-person report has come in from a mother in Liverpool who is all in a flap because she has not heard from her missing son in over thirty-six hours. And the son's name is the same as the name they have for the pet-shop DNA – Paul Harrison.

Just for the sake of clarity, Barney Muldoon is Irish Catholic via Liverpool, and Saul Goodman is Jewish via some pogroms in Russia, but they ended up workmates pounding the same beat in the London Borough of Hackney. Both of them are barely practising – Midnight Mass on Christmas Eve and Synagogue on the Passover, and that is about it.

As they are leaving Starbucks with their coffee and croissants, a young man pushes violently between them heading South down Kingsland towards Dalston. Their coffees go flying. But this young man does not fit any of the stereotypes you might be imagining.

'Hey, mate, you better watch where you're going with that attitude,' calls Muldoon after the young man. Then, turning to Goodman, he says, 'He's one of your sort. You go and give him a chat. And get him to pay for another round of coffees for us.'

The young man in question is in full Hasidic drag: the white socks, the uncut and curled locks, broad-brimmed black fedora, white bits of string hanging down the outside of his breeches, the lot. Under his arm he is carrying a book. A yellow book. We have met the young man before. The trainee Rabbi. His name is Moses Tabick.

'Where do you think you are going with that attitude?'

'To Jerusalem. The Promised Land. I am going to reclaim it . . .'

'Hang on a minute, lad. I might not look it but I am as Jewish as you. So just slow down, and I think you should be apologising for knocking over our coffees and not offering to get us replacements. We are cops, by the way.'

Now, I don't want to bog down the narrative of this book in the minutiae of what goes on within Orthodox Jewish communities. And although I implied in an earlier chapter that all the troubles had been sorted out between the State of Israel and the surrounding Arab States, that was a slight over-simplification on my part.

There was one small sect in Judaism called Neturei Karta. They were totally against the whole Zionist movement. They believed the land of Israel would only be theirs once God gave it to them. You would always see members of the Neturei Karta at the front of any Free Palestine marches up the Kingsland Road back in the '90s and zeros. As far as Neturei Karta were concerned it was not down to man and his greedy mitts, guilt trips and loaded pistols as to when the walls of Jerusalem were to be rebuilt. They had to wait until God said so and the Messiah arrived.

After the Great Intifada of March 2017, the influence of Neturei Karta became like a flood. By 2019 this small sect had grown to the point it was finally able to persuade all of the Jewish people in Israel and across the Diaspora that they should relinquish their hold on the 'occupied zone'.

Deals were done, hands were shaken. The Jordan did not run with blood. Swords were turned into plough shears. Spears into pruning hooks.

But nothing stays settled for long. Especially on the banks of the Jordan.

Well, remember earlier this morning, when Moses Tabick was on the 491 heading up Kingsland Road to Stamford Hill and his mum's home cooking, and then he opened this yellow book and discovered he was the Moses to lead his people? What was not mentioned earlier was that a couple of stops further up the Kingsland Road, he turned over the next page to read:

185

You are the Messiah
It is for you to reclaim The Promised Land
For the Children of God

Now, most of us reading something like that would not give it a second thought. But our minds are not attuned in the same way as Moses Tabick's mind is attuned on this very day. For Moses Tabick this was an even more direct message from God. His God. Our God. The God of the People of The Book.

'I don't mean to be rude, sir, and here, have these shekels and get yourself another coffee or whatever it is, but I have far more important things to be doing than—'

And just as Saul Goodman is about to arrest the young man, he gets an emergency bleep on his iPhone23.

A body seen floating in the Lee Navigation
Fits the description of the missing Paul Harrison
Paul Harrison wanted for throwing brick through pet-shop
*   window*
Report immediately

Young Moses Tabick makes his break.
Barney Muldoon and Saul Goodman forget about their coffees.

▲

12:17

On the island of Fernando Pó, King Francisco Malabo Beosá XXIII picks up the third of his straw dolls and pushes his sharpened needle through it. And before the needle comes out the other side of the doll, Jessie Bezos drops dead on her family's tennis court in Seattle, just as she was about to make her serve.

In this chapter, and the previous two, there has been no mention of the death of Celine Hagbard. Yes, it is the largest news story in the world. And yes, she was the major mover and shaker in *Book One* of this trilogy of random facts and uncorroborated ideas, but we have many other issues to be dealing with between now and when that satellite with F U U K - U P on board burns up on re-entry in less than eighteen hours from now.

Of course, the death of Celine Hagbard is all that people are talking about in Starbucks around the globe. Her life story is what iJaz is pumping out on its rolling news channel. It seems that everyone who has been anyone in the past fifty years was her best friend and confidante at some point.

But, hey, get over it. Because you will not be able to get over what is going to be happening before your second latte tomorrow morning.

As for Jessie Bezos, the founding mother of all things AmaZaba, her family want to keep things hidden. There is so much they don't want to come out about her life and how the business is structured. It is in all of the Bezos family's interests to keep this under wraps.

▲

12:47

Barney Muldoon and Saul Goodman are on the far bank of the Lee Navigation. They are interviewing a young woman in jogging gear who was the first to spot the body. An inflatable police dinghy is on the opposite bank taking photos of the floating body before they begin to lift it out.

Siobhán Harrison, John Lennon's mother in Liverpool, has been contacted. Her worst fears are confirmed. Death is always a shock to those still alive, but Paul Harrison – or John Lennon, as we have got to know him – is more than well adjusted to it already. His only concern is what the sound will be like at tonight's gig at the Maelstrom, off the northern tip of Jura.

If Paul Harrison could talk directly to his mother now, this is what he would say:

'Hey, Mum, forget about it. Put the kettle on and make a nice pot of tea. The thing is, Mum, it is a lot better being dead than it was being alive. Not because life was miserable, it is just that being dead is better. I am no longer bothered if what I am doing makes any sense or anybody takes any notice of it. I just get on with it. And as it happens – with what is happening with Tangerine NiteMare – I am now a lot more successful than I ever was when I was alive and trying my hardest to make things happen.

'As for Yoko – I mean Elisabeth – she is a lot better off without me. She has already won the Hockney Award with that new partner of hers. Did you hear about it on the news? Will Gompertz thinks it is one of the greatest works of art of the century so far.

'So, Mum, go out tonight and celebrate by getting a fish supper with extra chips for me and Dad. And when you get home put the *Best of Jim Reeves* on, and when he is singing "Distant Drums" think about all us lads that followed the sound of the bugle to wherever it called us.

'Being dead, Mum, means I never have to worry about sex or drugs again, and I can just concentrate on the rock 'n' roll and the art and the writing and all that stuff. Love you, Mum.'

So that is what Paul Harrison – I mean John Lennon – has to

say; but right now Barney Muldoon and Saul Goodman have a homicide on their hands.

They love homicides. We all love homicides.

▲

In memory of this unsung John Lennon, we will take a note from his words to his mother and we will pause the story here, and if you have a record player to hand and a copy of the *Best of Jim Reeves*, play the track 'Distant Drums' now.

▲

Dear Diary,

Part One

I am going to have to stop this chapter here.

There is no point in trying to carry on.

I have been hit by a wall of melancholia that means whatever I write ends up being lost in the maudlin lyrics of Country & Western songs. These are songs I grew up with and thought I had outgrown decades ago.

Of course, this Siobhán Harrison would be way too young to have ever been into 'Gentleman' Jim Reeves. This is all far more about me than the characters that it is my job to sculpt and frame for the reader and the story I should be telling.

Instead I will take a break. Get on my Brough and head for the southern tip of Jura and then drive back. The round trip is just over sixty miles. By the time I'm back, the cobwebs should be well and truly blown away and I will get on with finishing this chapter before the day is out.

Part Two

I'm back. I did the whole journey there and back in less than an hour. And now I am ready to write. Ready to let the words flow and with no backsliding into Jim Reeves or George Jones or any of that other nonsense. If there is any sort of soundtrack I should be listening to, it is 'Born to Be Wild' by Steppenwolf.

Here goes.

Yours,

Roberta

▲

In the past three or four hours there have been some fundamental and major changes going on in Moses Tabick's mind, or inner core, or whatever it is that is inside and defines who we are and how we approach life.

A few hours ago Moses Tabick was a 'mild-mannered' trainee Rabbi with a liberal outlook, looking forward to completing his studies so he could then take up a position to serve his congregation as best he could. But something flipped a switch. First the switch flipped to him seeing himself as a Moses figure sent by God to lead his people. But something then turned the switch up to full, and now he is no longer just a prophet, even of the magnitude of Moses. He is the Messiah his people have been waiting for, for thousands of years.

If you were to have passed Moses Tabick on the street, you would have seen a below-average-height young Jewish man, with no outward and obvious signs of athleticism or charisma. If you had heard him speak, you would have heard that slight lisp that seems to be part of the North London Jewish accent.

The thing is with young men – and it has always been the case, and I guess will always be so – they have a need for their lives to have meaning and purpose. There are plenty of things that can sate that need they have for meaning and purpose. For some, the odd joint, a kick-about with some mates, their team having a lucky streak, a job with prospects, a few pints on a Friday night or a couple of E's and a bit of a rave on a Saturday night are enough. But others have more of an appetite for it. And if society is not on hand to give that young man meaning and purpose in his life, he will find it where he can. The more radical and confrontational, the better.

For the past couple of decades those young men have had X-Box; it kept them in check, stopped them hanging about on street corners. But even X-Box and Friday Prayers were not enough to keep some of them searching for it.

Religion was always the last resort and greatest prize for those who really had a 'manly' appetite for meaning and purpose. To you and me, Moses Tabick might not look like the sort of young man with that sort of appetite, but as he made his way down Kingsland heading for wherever that Promised Land was, he had more than enough.

It should also be noted that when his grandmother was liberated from Auschwitz as a young girl in 1945, she took a loaded Luger pistol from the holster of a dying camp guard. She kept it all her life in whatever drawer she kept her undergarments in. She kept it for the day it might be needed. She died last year. Moses Tabick knew where she kept it. And now Moses Tabick had this Luger hidden in the bag carrying his tallit (that's a prayer shawl, in case you don't know).

There is something else going on in Moses Tabick's imagination, and I guess he would not be pleased if we knew about it. At the same time as he knows he has been chosen by God to be the Messiah, he is also imagining it as a film. That, as he is striding down Kingsland, there is a crew filming it all. Stanley Kubrick is somewhere on the top of a building directing the various cameramen where they should be getting the best shots from. He is Alex in *A Clockwork Orange*. Unstoppable. The people are parting as he makes his way down through Stoke Newington and then Dalston. From nowhere, people are joining him, but not just Jewish people, people of all colours, creeds and faiths.

Or maybe it is not Stanley Kubrick, maybe it's Francis Ford Coppola, because in some way it is like *Apocalypse Now* and— But Moses gets these thoughts under control and remembers he is the Messiah and this is all real, and he can feel the Luger wrapped up in his tallit.

Moses Tabick and Henry Pedders are yet to meet, but will do so in the next few hours. There is another young man in this story, who you might have forgotten about, although he will not be meeting Moses or Henry in the next few hours. He is Chodak. He has begun his descent from the monastery high up in the Himalayas, and although he is not armed with a Luger he does have a sword, a razor-sharp sword. It is hidden from view under his saffron robes. It is a sword you can imagine being used to decapitate someone with one graceful stroke, like in a more graphic kung fu film.

The next chapter but one might contain his story. And maybe by the end of this book Moses, Henry and Chodak will have met up in the last Jellied Eel and Pie shop left in the East End of London.

▲

13:01

Killer Queen is putting the guest-list together.

▲

13:03

Alan Moore has an idea for a concept album, but has not yet told Jimmy and Bill about it. It is about a dystopian world, and is set on an island off the coast of Scotland where the last 23 surviving human beings on Earth live. There are twenty males and only three females.

▲

13:07

For some reason, GoogleEarth has not picked up on the tanks rolling across the tundra. If it doesn't pick up on them soon, it will be too late.

Putin sits watching his roses, takes another sip from his mug of tea, and smiles. We have never seen Putin smile in public. What Russian man with any self-respect would ever smile in public?

▲

Jura
2 May 1984

Dear Diary,

I am going to get on my Brough and head for the bar and drink until I cannot stand up.

Fuck the lot of them.

Yours,

Roberta

Postscript: I've decided not to send any more chapters of this book to Dog Ledger until it is all done.

5 : THE GREAT TUMBLE FROM THE SKY

Yoko Ono – the old one – is again sitting on her balcony staring out at New York. She has just had lunch. That said, she eats very little these days, and what she does eat is usually some sort of seaweed, high in vitamin Z.

She is not thinking about the yellow book she threw over the balcony yesterday, or if she has it in her to do one last major exhibition. What she is thinking about is nothing. It is what she likes doing best.

It is then she notices a tightrope walker walking between the Al-Qaeda Towers.* Yes, the Twin Towers were rebuilt, all part of the 'World Peace Now' deal the Five sorted out in 2020, after the United Nations was retired. The last to agree on the new naming was Islamic State, but even they knew it made sense. Once horrors of the past can be just another ride in a theme park, they can no longer hurt us. Once Harry Patch died, the trenches were as ancient history as the English Civil War.

Yoko Ono is transfixed by what she is watching. There has been nothing about this on iJaz, on Twitter, on FaceLife, nothing anywhere. But here it is, happening not more than a kilometre from her apartment. Is this a re-enactment of Philippe Petit's same walk back in 1974, when Petit brought New York to a standstill? For those readers who are way too young or not arsed about such

* Note to self: maybe no one will remember who or what Al-Qaeda was when this book is read by you. Or even Harry Patch.

195

things, Philippe Petit was a French high-wire artist who, without seeking permission from anyone, took it upon himself to sling a wire between the Twin Towers and walk it.

Back in '74 Yoko Ono may have had a major problem with this. Philippe Petit was calling himself an artist. But the population at large did not have a problem with it; in fact, they loved what he was doing and he was celebrated as one of the greatest living artists. Picasso had died the previous year and now the *New York Times* was writing about Philippe Petit as his rightful heir.

It is like Fluxus never happened. Yoko is getting angry again.

Then, from nowhere, as if the cavalry were coming over the hill, comes a helicopter trailing a banner with her phrase 'ABOVE US ONLY SKY'. This makes Yoko feel better.

Seconds later the helicopter is flying above the Al-Qaeda Towers. The downdraught of those blades can wreak havoc with the most carefully pegged lines of laundry. Our would-be Philippe Petit does not stand a chance. Yoko Ono is soon watching him tumble through the sky like he is in slow motion. The only emotion Ms Ono can feel is one of jealousy. Why is that not her tumbling through the sky?

'Don't look down, never look down.'

And why does Yoko Ono assume it is a 'he' and not a 'she' that is tumbling? Is this just another case of 'Everyday Sexism' on her part?

▲

13:13

M'Lady GaGa misses the whole 'tumble from the sky' piece. She is in the lift going up to the penthouse suite of Ono Towers. She is now knocking on the door of the apartment that says YES. She is let in by the butler – a female one.

'Ms Ono is expecting you.'

M'Lady strides past and heads through to the balcony.

'Hey, Yokes, how ya been? Seen any great art lately?'

'Unless we don't count the sight of you, I have not seen any great art in the last 23 minutes.'

Note, dear reader, she is completely ignoring what she has just witnessed in the past two minutes, when already the Twittersphere is ablaze with it, and Will Gompertz is, as I type, rewriting his piece for the evening edition of Art Now@iJaz, where he will consign *The Three Posters* to the trash can of art history and make a claim for *The Great Tumble from the Sky* as the finest work of art of the twenty-first century so far.

'So what did you see 23 minutes ago that was so good?'

'Your new video for your new track, where you are the Siren on the rock. And the ship of fools goes smashing into the rocks. It was after watching that I knew I had to get hold of you. I knew then you must be one of the other Three Sirens who are being called to find the One.'

'Yeah, and do you know who the other one is?'

'No.'

'Michelle!'

'Michelle?'

'Obama, of course. Didn't you see that old has-been Damien Hirst has been doing a sculpture of her as the *Little Mermaid*, but in gold or something? Anyway, I got on to Michelle straight away and she will be on Skype3D in five seconds.'

And in five seconds Michelle Obama, to all intents and purposes, is with them in the room. The wonders of Skype3D have yet to be embraced by some of the more Luddite members of the community, who are still trying to get their heads around 3D printing. Did these people never watch *Star Trek*?

'So look, Miche, or should we call you Elle? I take it you know Yokes.'

'Yeah, we met at The Beatles@Shea Stadium 3D reunion show, backstage. But tell me, Yoko, did you really fuck the 3D version of the twenty-four-year-old John Lennon in his dressing room?'

'Of course, wouldn't you? And I filmed it. I was planning on it being the centrepiece of my farewell show at MoMA.'

'Anyway,' interjects M'Lady, 'as far as I am concerned The Beatles never existed and, as it happens, I am considering starting up a conspiracy theory to prove The Beatles never existed and popular music went straight from Elvis to me. So no Zephyr, Dylan, Madonna, and certainly no American Medical Association. Just Elvis, then forty years of one-hit failures, and then me.'

'How does that work?' ask Yoko and Michelle simultaneously.

'It's a new thing GoogleByte are about to launch. If you get a billion people to sign up to a conspiracy theory, it automatically becomes true. Everything on the internet is corrected, and from then on no one can prove otherwise. That's unless some other conspiracy theory comes along that can get a billion people to sign up to it to prove otherwise. It is what democracy was all about, but they never got it sorted. The 23rd Amendment or something.

'You must have known something about this, Miche? You were the fuckin' president when all this was being sorted.'

'Nuff of the cussing, GaGa! We are all sisters but—'

'Okay, sorry.'

Yoko Ono, being the most senior of The Three Sirens, takes charge. Even if M'Lady GaGa is the pushiest – and Michelle Obama was the last and only female President of the USA, thus technically the one who has commanded the most amount of worldly power – it is Yoko Ono who is going to be the boss bitch.

Okay, okay, I know. But just remember this is a feminist tract and probably the greatest work of feminist literature you have read since the film rights to *How to Chuck Your Boyfriend* by Jane Eyre were sold for $100,000,000.

'So this is how I see it. From now on we are The Weyward Sisters – forget all that sexy mermaid stuff. We are the three real heroes of *Macbeth*, but for modern times. We know the Baby is going to be born, and my guess is that will be sometime just short of nine months from now. Where the Baby is going to be born is anyone's guess, but we will get that figured out. The stable thing has been done, so probably a women's prison, seeing as we don't have refugee camps any more. Probably London, because that is still, sadly, the cultural capital of the world.

'Are we all agreed?'

'Yeah, cool, Yokes, but don't you think we should make a promo clip together before we cut off our fishy tails. I mean, Miche is looking hotter now than Beyon-Say ever did.'

'Who's Beyon-Say?' quips Michelle.

'My point exactly,' retorts GaGa.

'Now, us single ladies, put your hands up,' demands Yoko.

And from somewhere we can hear the soundtrack to this book from a passing car stereo. It goes something like this:

> *I got gloss on my lips, a man on my hips*
> *Hold'n' me tighter than my Deréon jeans . . .*

▲

Women's Revolutionary Law

From the First Declaration as proclaimed by the Zapatista Army of Liberation from the Lacandon Jungle on 1 January 1994:

1: Women, regardless of their race, creed, colour or political affiliation, have the right to participate in the revolutionary struggle in any way that their desire and capacity determine

2: Women have the right to work and receive a fair salary

3: Women have the right to decide the number of children they have and care for

4: Women have the right to participate in the matters of the community and hold office if they are free and democratically elected

5: Women and their children have the right to Primary Attention in their health and nutrition

6: Women have the right to an education

7: Women have the right to choose their partner and are not obliged to enter into marriage

8: Women have the right to be free of violence from both relatives and strangers

▲

13:17

Subcomandante Marcos is sitting in his villa up in the mountains of Chiapas watching the rolling news on iJaz. It has been some years since he smoked his last pipe and led any sort of march with his sisters and brothers in the Zapatistas.

There is nothing left to liberate.

And as Subcomandante Marcos is watching the world's greatest living artist tumble to her certain death between the Al-Qaeda Towers, he feels that niggling sense of jealousy that he has never been able to get over. Not only did he never actually get to have his revolution, before the need for revolution was made surplus to requirements, he never got to be the star on several million T-shirts for several generations of teenagers, like that faker Che Guevara.

Like so many other trades before it, being a Revolutionary, along with being a milkman, had become redundant. Pints on the doorstep and manning the barricades were things now only found on the History Channel.

Subcomandante Marcos is watching the tumbling artist on repeat. Over and over again. But never at the point of impact. Never at her Ground Zero. Never the splat. Just the tumble. The beautiful tumble with the blue sky in the background, the one fluffy cloud and the helicopter trailing its 'ABOVE US ONLY SKY' banner.

In a previous chapter, we had a character who was probably transgender and we portrayed her/him in a somewhat negative light. We wouldn't want you to think this was some sort of prejudice on our part. We were just reporting the facts. But for the sake of balance . . . most revolutionary movements in the past have been quite macho, their leaders always portrayed as thrusting heterosexual male heroes. Subcomandante Marcos may not have reached the dizzy heights of Brother Guevara before him, but he was still all 'thrusting heterosexual male': the horse, the pipe, the bullet-belts, the poetry, the AK-47 are all tried and tested phallic symbols. Who could question any of it, what red-blooded woman would not willingly . . .?

The truth is more complex. But we must first quote from part of the statement given by Subcomandante Marcos himself:

To the lesbian, gay, transsexual and bisexual community: we are grateful that you have allowed us the opportunity to say our word on this, the twenty-first march of Lesbian, Gay, Transsexual and Bisexual Pride, which has convened some of the best of sexual diversity in Mexico.

May all of you accept the greetings of the Zapatistas on this day of struggle for the dignity of, and respect for, difference.

For a very long time, homosexuals, lesbians, transsexuals and bisexuals have had to live and die concealing their difference, suffering in silence persecution, contempt, humiliation, extortion, blackmail, insults, violence and assassination.

The different had to bear having their humanness reduced for the simple fact of not being in accord with a non-existent sexual norm. This norm has been converted into a banner for intolerance and segregation.

Victims at every social level, objects of jokes, gossip, insults and death, those different in their sexual preferences remained quiet in the face of one of the oldest injustices in history.

No more.

Our best wishes for your organised existence.

Our support for your struggle and your demands.

We Zapatistas, men, women and other, but still Zapatistas, greet lesbian, gay, transsexual and bisexual dignity.

Long life to your fighting spirit and a different tomorrow, one that is more just and human for all those who are different.

From the mountains of the Mexican Southeast.

Subcomandante Marcos, 21 July 1999

The complex truth is that Subcomandante Marcos was never quite sure about his own sexuality. And the more unsure he was, the more macho he wanted to present himself to the world. In retirement, he had come to accept the complications of his own sexuality. But on this Spring day, when all of creation was bursting forth and he was watching the Unknown Artist tumble to her certain death over and over again, Subcomandante Marcos knew he had been called.

Beside him in his armchair was a book. It had arrived in the second post. It was a yellow book with a grapefruit sliced in half on the cover. In the segments of the halved grapefruit, he could see a five-pointed star. The symbol of his revolutionary party. Even before opening the book he knew there would be a message contained in it for him.

He flicked through the pages – not much caught his attention – but then near the back of the book was a page with Mayan hieroglyphic script. If this was not meant for him, it was meant for no one.

Now, Subcomandante Marcos is of Spanish descent and not Native American, but his whole purpose in life has been the cause of the pre-Colombian people. He has not only taken it upon himself to be able to speak their language, he has gone some way to learning the hieroglyphics used before the conquistadors arrived. Even if no one other than academics could read it, he could.

And he read:

> *The revolution is not over*
> *It has only just begun*
> *Put on your balaclava*
> *Put on your cap*
> *Put on your bullet-belts*

Load your AK-47
Fill your pipe
Get on your horse
And ride, baby, ride

Subcomandante Marcos had never trusted the internet. And he knew his phone lines were tapped. He used runners.

All across Latin America, from the Tex-Mex border to the southern tip of Chile, there were young wo/men and not so young wo/men waiting to hear the call. To blow that bugle. To bang those drums.

Now was not the time for Subcomandante Marcos to come out about his complex sexuality, now was the time to make the revolution happen, even if the rest of the world did not give a shit about revolutions unless they were on the History Channel between programmes about milkmen and the English Civil War.

The world was interested in only one thing – SHOPPING.

But not for long.

▲

13:27

Killer Queen is having problems with getting the sound system sorted for the gig that night in the Maelstrom. She has no idea it is that complex a situation. It is going to need more than a couple of WEM columns, and then how are they going to get the back line out there?

Mister Fox says he can sort it out (remember him? He is the manager of Tangerine NiteMare, as well as the possible father of the One). He knows this lad in Dalston called 'Drums of Death'.

Drums of Death are massive across the Post-Digital Underground and have been having hits with everyone from Azealia 'I guess that cunt gettin' eaten' Vaults to Wolf Coat Macklemore, but the thing is, underneath all the scary make-up, Drums of Death is, in reality, Colin from Oban, and even though Drums of Death are all about the underground, Colin is still a homeboy back in Oban. And Oban is not more than ten miles as the gannet flies from the Maelstrom, just on the Scottish mainland. If anyone knows about getting the right sound system out to the Maelstrom, it will be Drums of Death, aka Colin from Oban.

'Too much information. I just want to know what is happening to Winnie and Yoko. Is she pregnant? Are they—?'

I am afraid you are going to have to wait until *Book Three* before you are updated on their situation; right now you are going to have to keep up with all these names and ridiculous subplots. And maybe the story of Tangerine NiteMare is the main thing in this book, and Winnie and Yoko a mere passing phase. Okay, all right, if you really can't be bothered with all of this: Winnie has a miscarriage, Darcy drops dead and she ends up having to marry Rochester. Now please let the rest of us get on with it.

'Sorry, can't help, Mister Fox. Drums of Death have a gig tonight at the London Aquarium, but seeing as Azealia "I'm a ruin you cunt" Vaults has pulled out, maybe Tangerine NiteMare could do the show?' says Colin from Oban.

'I will check with the others, but I'm guessing that could be a great crowd for us. They are very big with the fish demographic. That Stingray down there is always on FaceLife bigging up the team,' says Mister Fox.

Ten seconds later, Mister Fox is on the mobile to Killer Queen.

'Look, we are going to have to shift the gig. We can't get the sound system out to the Maelstrom. But Colin from Oban – you know, the Drums of Death lad with the scary make-up? – said we could do the gig with him tonight at the London Aquarium. You think you can get down here in time?' says Mister Fox.

'Yeah, sure. And, anyway, that Colin from Oban owes me one. He ripped all that black-and-white make-up thing off me. Mind you, it's a pity Azealia 'It's some sex shit' Vaults can't make it as well. She been my favourite for some time,' says Killer Queen.

Ten seconds later, Killer Queen is on conference to all the others.

'So we got the gig tonight at the London Aquarium. I say we do the whole gig in the same running order as it is on the album,' says Killer Queen.

'I'm on social media now with it,' says Dead Perch.

'Can you get some peanuts on the rider?' asks Dead Squirrel.

'I'll have to tell my mum. She is still cut up about me being dead,' says John Lennon.

And by the time we leave this scene for the next, all the Little Perch know about it and they are beside themselves with excitement.

▲

13:29

Will Gompertz has now got the full story on the Unknown Artist. He is about to broadcast live from Ground Zero Two. Her body is being left exactly where it splatted onto the ground, but now with velvet rope around it. This may be irony, or part of planned framing by the artist herself. Art lovers from around the world are queuing up to appreciate the work. Lord Saatchi has just flown in and is in negotiations to buy the complete piece.

It is rumoured there are those who do actually know her name and background, but the history of art for these times is already written, and it seems from now on she will always be known as the Unknown Artist.

Will Gompertz turns to the camera. 'Good afternoon. It is with great pleasure I can now proclaim that what we have experienced today is the first time in the complete history of art an artist has compressed their life's work into one action, which took less than sixty seconds to complete.

'There have been plenty of artists before whose fame rests on one particular work. Munch and his *Scream*, Duchamp and his *Fountain* are two obvious examples, but with them they went on to spend a lifetime making work no one really gives a toss about. But here with the Unknown Artist and her *Great Tumble from the Sky*, we have the first to "cut the crap" and just deliver the one great work and exit, with not even a gift shop in sight. The exit being a major part of the work.

'This will undoubtedly start a movement, and one that may last as long as twenty-four hours. We can expect a whole slew of young and impressionable artists to attempt the same feat. They will fail, their names only remembered by their mothers and brothers.

'It has been confirmed Lord Saatchi will be exhibiting the work from tomorrow morning as a replacement for the now seriously dated and outflanked *Three Posters*.'

The cameras cut to a close-up, before repeating a looped clip of the actual tumble.

▲

In a small village in the Massif Central region of France, a mother weeps for the loss of her daughter. Her daughter was the illegitimate child of the world-famous high-wire artist Philippe Petit. His daughter grew up never having known her father other than through the media. She wanted to beat him and show him she could not only do it better than him but do it without any support structure and famous friends. She died trying. She failed.

▲

3 May 1984

Dear Diary,

Today I have passed the halfway point in writing this book. It is now the fear starts to ratchet up. The advice I have been given in the past is to not look down, the analogy being that of the high-wire artist. But it is not the looking down, and the loss of balance it may engender, I fear. It is the unseen stroke, the hidden heart attack and the fatal motorcycle accident lurking around the next bend that will prevent me finishing this novel.

Looking down from the high wire I can handle. It is the innocent downdraught of the passing helicopter that is the making of my nightmares.

With what is left of this day I will walk around the coast and seek out the cave that can only be entered at low tide, or so I have been told.

Yours,
Roberta

6 : BIG MAC WITH FRIES

Radicalisation is a process by which an individual or group comes to adopt increasingly extreme political, social or religious ideals and aspirations that reject or undermine the status quo or reject and/or undermine contemporary ideas and expressions of freedom of choice.

Chodak is a character we met briefly at the end of *Book One*.

Chodak grew up in a village in Tibet.

Chodak is a young Buddhist monk.

Chodak entered his monastery in early 2017.

Chodak was seventeen years old.

Chodak's monastery is in the mountains above the holy city of Lhasa.

Chodak is now 23 years old.

Chodak was radicalised by himself.

Chodak was radicalised by the internet.

Chodak was radicalised because the world had failed him.

Chodak was born to be radical.

Chodak has walked out of his monastery.

Chodak is walking down the mountain.

Chodak is wearing a saffron robe.

Chodak has a shaved head.

Chodak has high cheekbones.

Chodak does not see the lone crow flying across the sky.

Chodak does not hear the squabbling Twenty-Three Sparrows in the thornbush.

Chodak has his sword still carefully concealed under his robes.

Chodak can see the city of Lhasa below him.

Chodak has never been to Lhasa.

Chodak has never seen the bright lights.

Chodak is walking into Lhasa.

Chodak's sacred number is 108.

Chodak silently repeats his sacred mantra 108 times.

Chodak has 108 beads on his Japa mala string of beads.

Chodak's earliest memory is of learning to say four words.

Chodak did not know what those words meant.

Chodak did not know what language those words were in.

Chodak is silently repeating his sacred mantra 108 times.

Big Mac With Fries

Big Mac With Fries

Big Mac With Fries

Big Mac With Fries

Big Mac With Fries

Big Mac With Fries

Big Mac With Fries

Big Mac With Fries

Big Mac With Fries

Big Mac With Fries

Big Mac With Fries

Big Mac With Fries

Chodak does not know why these were his earliest words.

Chodak does not know why they became the words of his mantra.

Chodak does know why 108 is his sacred number.

Chodak does know that all Buddhist monks know 108 is the most sacred of numbers.

Chodak does know 108 is more sacred than seventeen, 23 and
Forty.

Big Mac With Fries
Big Mac With Fries
Big Mac With Fries
Big Mac With Fries
Big Mac With Fries
Big Mac With Fries
Big Mac With Fries
Big Mac With Fries
Big Mac With Fries
Big Mac With Fries
Big Mac With Fries
Big Mac With Fries

Chodak did not know what a *Big Mac With Fries* was until he
entered the monastery.

Chodak clicked on Google Images to look at photographs of a
Big Mac With Fries.

Chodak clicked on Google Images every day to look at a *Big
Mac With Fries*.

Chodak did not know what a *Big Mac With Fries* would taste
like.

Chodak wanted more than anything else to know this taste.

Big Mac With Fries
Big Mac With Fries
Big Mac With Fries
Big Mac With Fries
Big Mac With Fries

Big Mac With Fries
Big Mac With Fries
Big Mac With Fries
Big Mac With Fries
Big Mac With Fries
Big Mac With Fries
Big Mac With Fries

Chodak knew a *Big Mac With Fries* came from McDonald's.

Chodak knew McDonald's was the biggest fast-food chain in the world.

Chodak had never seen a McDonald's.

Chodak knew there was a McDonald's in Lhasa.

Big Mac With Fries
Big Mac With Fries
Big Mac With Fries
Big Mac With Fries
Big Mac With Fries
Big Mac With Fries
Big Mac With Fries
Big Mac With Fries
Big Mac With Fries
Big Mac With Fries
Big Mac With Fries
Big Mac With Fries

Chodak did not know fashions change.

Chodak did not know things come and things go.

Chodak did not know people no longer ate *Big Macs With Fries*.

Chodak did not know that the last branch of McDonald's closed yesterday.

Yesterday all my troubles seemed so far away

Chodak had never heard The Beatles.
Chodak had never heard The American Medical Association.
Chodak had been a big fan of Azealia 'black girl shit' Vaults.

Big Mac With Fries
Big Mac With Fries
Big Mac With Fries
Big Mac With Fries
Big Mac With Fries
Big Mac With Fries
Big Mac With Fries
Big Mac With Fries
Big Mac With Fries
Big Mac With Fries
Big Mac With Fries
Big Mac With Fries

We know why fashions change.

We know why things come and go.

We know why the last McDonald's closed, even if you did not know until you were reading this right now that the last of the McDonald's to close in the big wide world was in Lhasa, high up in the Himalayan mountains of Tibet.

And yes, we all know why Azealia 'kizzat sh-shaved' Vaults is married and settled and no longer *the bad-mouthed bitch-queen* of the R&B scene.

Big Mac With Fries
Big Mac With Fries
Big Mac With Fries
Big Mac With Fries
Big Mac With Fries
Big Mac With Fries
Big Mac With Fries
Big Mac With Fries
Big Mac With Fries
Big Mac With Fries
Big Mac With Fries
Big Mac With Fries

The reason why the last prison on Earth closed was slightly more complicated, but not much. People had known for centuries that prisons did not work, but, as long as we had democracy, who would vote for a political party that had the abolishment of all prisons in their manifesto?

In an earlier chapter in this novel it was mentioned in passing how the Islamic State had been given their own channel on WikiTube, and how this got them into a more user-friendly line of work. This, in a way, skated over the real change in what was happening on the far shores of Islam. People had been blaming 'radical' Imams and inner city Mosques, wanting the Imams chucked out and the Mosques burnt down.

This was a mistake.

All the facts were already there and staring us all in the face.

But we chose to ignore them.

By early 2017 70 per cent of the prison population throughout Western Europe was made up of young men from Muslim backgrounds, whereas the proportion of Muslims in the broader population was little more than 10 per cent. While in prison these young Muslim men got angrier with society as a whole, and the injustices that led them to be incarcerated in particular.

Their anger was rewarded with a more radical take on their faith.

This radical take answered questions, gave life meaning, purpose and direction. To use the cliché of the time, they became 'radicalised'. As soon as they got out of prison, they headed for the ever-growing caliphate and started chopping off the heads of unbelievers, or anybody who did not quite believe in the version of Islam that they believed in. An oversimplification, obviously, but I don't want to bog down the flow of this chapter with too much detail and pseudo-academic shite.

Why play *Call of Duty* when you can do it for real?

Why put up with the shit when you can change the world?

The Western World as we knew it was being brought to its knees by young men who were nearly all 'radicalised' in our prisons. The logic had to be addressed.

And it was.

All the prisons were closed down and all the prisoners freed.

An end to radicalisation using radical means.

It worked.

The young men were also given start-up loans.

This also worked.

As for punishment, the public stocks were revived.

As a system it had worked for hundreds of years, until they fell from favour in late-Victorian times.

Twenty-four hours in the public stocks, with recycled food waste being thrown at them, put near enough everyone that contravened accepted behaviour back on the straight and narrow. The 'short, sharp shock' that really worked.

Big Mac With Fries
Big Mac With Fries
Big Mac With Fries
Big Mac With Fries
Big Mac With Fries
Big Mac With Fries
Big Mac With Fries
Big Mac With Fries
Big Mac With Fries
Big Mac With Fries
Big Mac With Fries
Big Mac With Fries

But none of this is relevant to Chodak in his Buddhist monastery up in the Himalayas. For him, Buddhism had all the answers, and nobody was listening. He needed to make the world listen. And as a bit of skimming of religious history over the last ten years told him in no uncertain terms, the chopping off of heads was the only failsafe way of getting the world to take notice.

Big Mac With Fries
Big Mac With Fries
Big Mac With Fries
Big Mac With Fries
Big Mac With Fries
Big Mac With Fries
Big Mac With Fries
Big Mac With Fries
Big Mac With Fries
Big Mac With Fries

Big Mac With Fries
Big Mac With Fries

Chodak walks into Lhasa.

Chodak walks the streets to where the local branch of McDonald's has always been. Or has been since the deal was done between Xi Jinping and the last but one President of the USA, back in 2017.

Chodak is using GoogleByte Maps on his iPhone23.

X marks the spot where McDonald's will be.

Chodak arrives in time for tea.

But the McDonald's is boarded up.

No longer in business.

The world has moved on.

Ronald has been let go.

They let him keep his clown drag for old times' sake.

Starbucks has opened next door, but *Skinny Latte To Go* is not Chodak's mantra.

However hard he might have tried.

Skinny Latte To Go
Skinny Latte To Go
Skinny Latte To Go
Skinny Latte To Go
Skinny Latte To Go
Skinny Latte To Go
Skinny Latte To Go
Skinny Latte To Go
Skinny Latte To Go

Even 108 times was not going to work.

Chodak looks down the street.

Chodak sees the drunken Ronald McDonald staggering towards him.

Chodak draws his sword.

Its blade glints in the late-afternoon sunlight.

As Ronald McDonald staggers his last . . .

Chodak sweeps his blade down in the most graceful of arcs.

Without a moment for hesitation.

Without a cry of despair.

Without a second for pain.

Ronald McDonald's head is cut clean off.

Ronald McDonald's head rolls into the gutter.

Ronald McDonald's neck spurts blood.

Chodak sits down to wonder at what he has done.

A crowd gathers round, too startled to do or say anything.

Ronald McDonald is well and truly dead, even if his left hand can be seen to twitch.

Chodak takes from his bag a book. A yellow book. A *Grapefruit Are Not the Only Bombs* kind of book.

Chodak opens it at the page, the only page in Ü-Tsang, his own language.

Chodak reads the following words aloud to those who have silently gathered around:

> *There are no more wars*
> *There is no more hunger*
> *There is no more slavery*
>
> *But in the souls*
> *Of the people of the Earth*
> *There is war, hunger and slavery*

It is only your religion
That can
Bring that peace
Feed that hunger
Free those bonds

It is your calling to go out into the world
Use whatever powers you can harness
And make this happen

Chodak closes the book.

Chodak puts the book back in his bag.

Chodak stands up.

Chodak slips the sword back into its sheath.

Chodak returns his sheath to its place under his saffron robe.

Chodak walks through the parting throng.

Chodak heads West towards the setting sun.

Chodak completes his mantra:

Big Mac With Fries
Big Mac With Fries
Big Mac With Fries
Big Mac With Fries
Big Mac With Fries
Big Mac With Fries
Big Mac With Fries
Big Mac With Fries
Big Mac With Fries
Big Mac With Fries
Big Mac With Fries
Big Mac With Fries

Cindy is on her gap year.

Cindy is from Australia.

Cindy saw it all.

Cindy filmed it all on her iPhone23.

Cindy uploads.

This was not art as Will Gompertz might know it.

This was not art as Winnie and Yoko might know it.

This was not the quote that Spock never said: 'It's *art*, Jim, but not as we know it.'

This was now.

This was at teatime today.

If we lived in different times, would Chodak's visage be on one million T-shirts, ten million posters, one hundred million screen savers by teatime tomorrow?

Subcomandante Marcos does not stand a chance when there are young men like Chodak stalking the Earth.

There seemed to be a smile on Ronald McDonald's painted face as it lay there in the gutter.

Or was it a grimace?

Big Mac With Fries to go. Yeah, and a Coke as well, please.

> *My life's a masquerade*
> *A world of let's pretend*

7 : EARLY DOORS

18:03 Monday 24 April 2023

There are three pint glasses on a round Formica-top table.

In the pint glasses is Phipps Ale, the local brew.

The table is in the snug of a village pub near Northampton.

Around the table and sipping the pints are Jimmy Cauty, Bill Drummond and Alan Moore. The original and only line-up of Extreme Noise Terror.

'Well, I think we did ourselves proud.'

'Yeah, but my lead kept coming out.'

'I thought that was part of the act.'

'I wonder who will turn up.'

'Do you think anybody gives a shit these days about what we did?'

'We are a major part of the rich tapestry—'

'Yeah, but who the fuck knows what a tapestry is, let alone a rich one?'

'Didn't you learn about the Bayeux Tapestry at school?'

'What, like "Born on the Bayou" by Creedence Clearwater?'

'Are you taking the piss?'

'No.'

'Like the Bayeux Tapestry in France, the Norman Conquest, 1066 and all that.'

This is Cauty & Drummond bickering. Alan Moore is saying nothing, just picking up his pint and taking the odd sip. Until . . .

'It's all very well us playing *The Black Room*, but it is so obvious.

Yeah, people will want to hear it, but I think we should be doing something new.'

'Like what?' ask Cauty & Drummond simultaneously.

'Like, I have an idea for a new concept album,' responds Alan Moore.

'Concept album?' Cauty.

'We're not prog.' Drummond.

'Never were.' Cauty.

'Never will be.' Drummond.

'Just listen.'

'We're listening.' Cauty & Drummond.

'It is a dystopian story, but not set in the future, set in the past. In 1984, so like it is a play on *Nineteen Eighty-Four* by George Orwell . . .'

'Dystopian?' Drummond.

'A story set in a bleak and fucked-up future.' Alan Moore.

'What, like all your comics?' Cauty.

'Yes, but this one is set in the past, on an island off the West Coast of Scotland. To be more precise, on the Isle of Jura, exactly when you two met each other and that batty old novelist you told us about, who got killed on her motorbike.'

'So it is about us?' Drummond.

'No, but you might get bit parts in it, if you are unlucky.'

'So what is it about?' Cauty.

'The Cold War gets hot. The bomb gets dropped. Then it's all out. Then everybody is dead, except 23 people who were in a bunker in a cave at the top end of the Isle of Jura.'

'But why Jura?' Cauty.

'Because it has got to be set somewhere, and you two are always going on about it. Can I continue?' Alan Moore.

'Feel free.' Drummond.

'There are only 23 survivors, twenty men and three women. The women include Margaret Thatcher, Yoko Ono and a little local girl called Wee Katie Morag. The men include Ronald Reagan, Leonid Brezhnev . . .'

'Brezhnev was dead by then.' Drummond.

'Don't be so fuckin' pedantic, this is fiction, not a history lesson. Anyway, there is a bunch of Hasidic Jews, a Buddhist Monk, an African King, a South American revolutionary, a milkman, two members of an English Civil War re-enactment society – one a Roundhead and one a Cavalier – a skinhead, a washed-up child actor, a biker, a three-piece power-rock trio—'

'Is that us?' Drummond.

'Maybe.' Alan Moore.

'Can I have a Marshall Stack and an SG?' Cauty.

'For fuck's sake, what is it with the pair of you? Just hear me out. The Pope and two locals who have converted to Islam—'

'That sounds like more than twenty blokes.' Drummond.

'Well, we can sort it out, maybe get rid of the biker and the skinhead.'

'What kind of bike would he be riding? British or Jap?' Cauty.

'British, of course, but that is irrelevant. It is the story that counts. I say we get the songs written and recorded and put the whole show on at the O$_2$ Arena on Christmas Eve.'

'What about *The Black Room* tour of the former Eastern Europe?' Drummond.

'Fuck all that, the world has moved on. There are bands like Tangerine NiteMare at the moment, that is where things are at . . .'

'You mean Tangerine Dream?' Drummond.

'No, I don't mean Tangerine Dream, I mean Tangerine NiteMare. You must have heard of them? They got these stage names, Killer Queen, the Crow, Dead Squirrel and John Lennon – and no, not that John Lennon. They do a sort of industrial ambient with beats. They are doing a gig tonight at the London Aquarium for the fish, totally conceptual, like more art than music. Some people actually think they really are a killer whale in the sea, a regular proper crow, a dead squirrel lying on the road and this post-hipster down in Hackney Wake who has been murdered by his girlfriend, or that is what it seems if you read their Twitter feed.'

'Sounds like rubbish.' Drummond.

'Yeah, whatever, but we have to think bigger than just playing our old stuff to a few ageing—' Alan Moore.

'Okay, we get the point. So how do you see this working as a stage show?' Cauty.

'I was thinking full-on rock opera, with M'Lady GaGa playing Margaret Thatcher, Yoko Ono playing herself, Drums of Death to play the Pope and we get Azealia Vaults to play Wee Katie Morag—' Alan Moore.

'Hang on a minute, Azealia who?' Drummond.

'Azealia Vaults, you must have heard of her? She is the teenage R&B sensation of the moment. Total in-your-face, says it how it is, confrontational. Everyone hates her, but she is genius. You must have heard about the biopic that was made? No one will release it.' Alan Moore.

'Why?' Cauty & Drummond.

'The title.' Alan Moore.

'Yeah?' Drummond.

'*Does My Clit Look Big in This?* It just about breaks every feminist, racist, homophobic, anti-Semitic taboo going.' Alan Moore.

'And you want her in our musical, playing a young Scottish girl on the Isle of Jura?' Cauty.

'It is our job as artists to push the boundaries. And no one pushes the boundaries like Azealia Vaults.' Alan Moore.

'Okay, you have made your point. Who else?' Drummond.

'I don't know yet, but I do know I want a choir of Hasidic Jewish men, done up in all their drag.' Alan Moore.

'And the story – what happens in this cave on Jura in 1984 in this post-nuclear-war wasteland world?' Cauty.

'I don't know yet. Either a baby gets born, or the girl gets her boy, or they all die. Or maybe all of these options. What do you think, are you up for it?' Alan Moore.

'All right.' Drummond.

'But only if we can get to play *The Black Room* from beginning to end as our encore.' Cauty.

'Oh yeah, and they have to burn money to keep warm.' Alan Moore.

Silence falls.

Cauty, Drummond and Alan Moore drink their pints in deep thought. Each of them looking in different directions.

The *kraa* of a lone crow can be heard in the distance.

▲

18:17

There are a couple of cans of Asonga Lager on a wicker table on the veranda of a shack. The shack is on the island of Fernando Pó, tucked into the Gulf of Guinea off the coast of Africa.

A twenty-something son is sitting facing his sixty-something father. The son takes a sip from one of the cans of Asonga and then says:

'But, Dad, you are just so embarrassing.'

'That is just a cliché. Every child is embarrassed about their father.'

'Yeah, but since Mum left you, you have just gone further and further out into some weird territory. It's like you are trying to prove something to someone, and all you are proving is what an idiot you are, and it is becoming more and more obvious why Mum left you. Every time I come round here I am worried about what I am going to find or what you are up to.'

'So what is your problem? I keep things together. Feed myself. Do my own laundry regularly. Sweep the place. Get a regular shave at the local Moroccan barber's. Even went to the dentist last week. Okay, my specs are held together with tape, but I will get that done. And I am sure if I wanted another woman, there would be a queue around the block.'

'No, Dad, it's none of that. It is all this black magic, witch-doctor stuff you have got into.'

'And?'

'And it's not the 1960s any more, when it was okay for Granddad to be a witch doctor. I guess back then it was a respectable position to have in society, but now the world is different. There is no excuse for believing in all this mumbo-jumbo. It's like you are playing to the preconceptions the rest of the modern world still has about Africa.'

'But we are Africans. We should be proud of that and our heritage and what we have given the world.'

'Well, I for one am pleased we on this island have finally accepted the modern world and, yes, have finally been accepted by the rest of the modern world. It feels like all the time you want to drag it back to voodoo and spells and all that witch-doctory stuff you get up to. We may have some catching up to do and I hope in the next few years we will have done that. But you seem intent on dragging us back. I mean, what are those five straw dolls doing on your table?'

'Those five dolls, as you call them, are the five leaders of the five companies that rule the world.'

'What?'

'This one is Celine Hagbard of GoogleByte; this one, Florence "the Princess of" Wales of WikiTube; this, Jessie Bezos of AmaZaba; this, Stevie Dobbs of AppleTree; this, Melinda Gates of MircroSoft; and, lastly, this is Marcia Zuckerberg of FaceLife.'

'And what are you intending on doing with them?'

'I am sticking this bamboo needle through them at intervals through the day.'

'To what end?'

'And each time I push the needle through one, they, the real one, drops dead.'

'Dad, this is a prime example of why I have every right to be embarrassed about you. You have to stop doing things like this. Everyone will be laughing at you. Even your oldest friends, like Sam Funai. Was that his name?'

'Yes, but have you not heard the news today? Celine Hagbard is dead; it was all over NokiaNet.'

'Dad, that is just it. You are still on NokiaNet. Nobody has used NokiaNet since 2018. But, anyway, that is beside the point. And, yes, I did hear about Celine Hagbard having a heart attack in a street in New York, but that had nothing to do with you sticking a piece of bamboo through a corn dolly in your shack on this island off the coast of Africa. You probably heard the news first and then stuck the needle in. Get a grip, Dad.'

'Now, son, you listen to me. I have not only stuck this needle through Celine Hagbard, I have done the same to Stevie Dobbs and Jessie Bezos. As far as I am concerned, they are now both dead. That leaves only Marcia Zuckerberg and Florence "the Princess of" Wales, and they will both be dead by midnight.'

'Dad, if both Stevie Dobbs and Jessie Bezos were dead, the world would know about it. Look at my screen. I am on the iJaz app right now; there is nothing. The only story they are running with is about the Unknown Artist thing.'

'Whatever. You wait. They are obviously just too scared to run the story yet.'

'Okay, Dad, just to entertain you: just say you are right and they are all dropping dead because of your five straw dolls and this piece of cane. Why are you doing it? What is there to be gained? The world, and you are part of that world, has every reason to be grateful to these five women, for sorting out the mess several million years of men made of the world.'

'The point, son, is this is all wrong. This is not how it should be. All this bland peace and happiness. The human spirit needs darkness. It needs fear of the unknown. It needs hunger. It needs Earthquakes and tidal floods and pestilence—'

'Hang on a minute, Dad, what exactly is "pestilence"?'

'I don't know, but it is one of the things we need. Since they cured AIDS and Ebola, we in Africa have hardly had anything to—'

'Dad, this is not only way stupid, it is downright evil thinking. The cure for AIDS and Ebola were two of the best things that ever happened for Africa.'

'Life has become meaningless. I am going to bring back Meaning to the people of Africa.'

'The people of Africa? You are talking like you are some sort of a leader as well.'

'Well, as it happens, this morning I took the final step on what I have been working towards all of my life.'

'And?'

'And I had a little private coronation ceremony where I crowned myself King Francisco Malabo Beosá the Twenty-Third.'

'Look, Dad, this just gets crazier and crazier. I think I better get a doctor or something for you. I'm sure there will be some sort of medication you could be taking. Where are you getting these ideas from in the first place?'

'Yesterday morning I got this book in the post – *Grapefruit Are Not the Only Bombs*. I know it is a stupid title. And if you were to flick through it, it would not make much sense. But then I got to this page, which is in Bube, and even if you have steadfastly refused to speak it, it is our mother tongue. And seeing as you have probably forgotten how to read it, I will read it out to you:

> *It is your duty to save not only your people*
> *But all the people of Africa*
> *But for this to be done*
> *Five have to die*
> *Thus*
> *Make Five dolls out of straw*
> *Dress the dolls in rags*
> *Make a sharp needle from bamboo cane*
> *Imagine each doll to represent*
> *The Kings or Queens of the Five States*
> *Over a period of 23 hours*
> *Sink a needle through the straw flesh*
> *Of each of the Five dolls*
> *The Kings or Queens of the Five States will die*
> *A Child will be born*
> *She will be the One*
>
> *Build a pyramid in Her honour*

'Do you understand?'

'Yes, Dad, I understand this is way beyond foolishness and into the land of total madness. It has to stop.'

'Nothing will stop me.'

'Look, Dad, I may have to get you certified, before you cause yourself or somebody else some real harm. Is there anything else you should tell me first?'

'Okay, there is something else, and even I am not too sure about this. I have been having these dreams where I am telling all of these stories to a white woman living on some island. I think it might be near England, or maybe Scotland. And she is writing everything down I tell her. But she is living many years ago. Maybe thirty or forty years ago. Maybe even a hundred years ago. And what I am telling her, which she is writing, is going to be in a book. And the book will warn the people of the world about the things that will come to pass. And maybe the people of the world will be able to stop those things coming to pass before they do—'

'Dad, look, I can cope with this bit, as you are telling me it is just a dream. Maybe the rest of what you think you are doing is coming from dreams. You have to tell the difference between dreams and reality. Maybe you have been living on your own for too long. Would you like to come and live with me and Zeina for a while? She would be more than pleased to have you. And you could spend time with your grandchildren.'

'I have not finished yet. By my reckoning this Baby is going to born in about nine months' time, and seeing as this book was posted from London in England, I plan to start work on the pyramid as of tomorrow, and then towards the end of the year head for London to find out where the Baby is to be born, so that I can pay my respects.'

'And where and with whom will you stay when you make this visit to London?'

'Well, I thought as now I am a King, I would stay with the Queen of England.'

'Shut up now, Dad. I can't tell if you are taking the piss or if you actually believe what you are telling me. And, anyway, they do not have a Queen of England any more. She retired when everything got sorted out.'

'Just remember, son, I love you. I love all my children. And I love my grandchildren. But you, being my oldest, one day, when I die, you will become the King of all of Africa.'

Both men fall silent. They drink their cans of lager, stare into the early-evening sky and listen to the Twenty-Three Sparrows squabbling in the bush nearest to the veranda.

▲

18:27

There are three halves of Guinness on the table.

The table is in the corner of a bar.

The early-evening sunlight is being filtered through the stained-glass window.

The stained-glass window depicts Saint Brendan in his coracle.

It is an Irish pub in the back streets of Rome.

The bar is called The Three Popes.

The three Popes sitting around the table do not address each other formally.

They are on first-name terms, their first names being Dion (Pope Dionysius XXIII), Ellie (Pope Eloise) and Tony (Pope Anthony).

'Is this a joke, Dion?'

'What do you mean?'

'Dragging us to some fake Irish bar so we can discuss matters of the highest—'

'You know more than anyone the whole of the Vatican is bugged. And probably you are behind all the bugging. But that's as maybe. I thought it important for the three of us to have an informal chat over a half of the dark stuff.'

Pope Anthony turns to Pope Eloise. 'Ellie, you are saying nothing. What are your thoughts on what Dion is proposing?'

'Sorry, I was thinking about something else altogether. What was he proposing?'

'He was saying he, as in Dion, as in Pope Dionysius XXIII, is still really the Pope in the eyes of God, and us two were just career-minded opportunists. And we know it and the whole world really knows it. And God definitely knows it.'

'Tony, Ellie, I am going to make this as clear as I can. I am not going to raise my voice or embarrass you or expect you to . . . but the reason why the world over the past few years has lost not only any respect for the Roman Catholic Church but, more importantly, faith in God, is we have allowed ourselves to fuck with the idea of what the Pope is. It is like we went all post-modern with what the Pope is. I don't mean to offend you, Ellie, but you just can't have a black female Pope, let alone a female lesbian Pope. It makes a joke of the whole thing. Even though I think it is a funny joke.'

'I am not offended. But it was you having opinions like that that meant you could no longer be the Pope. But I also think it's funny. And I don't hold it against you. I am still pretty good at the forgiving thing.'

'Look, I was sacked because I lost my faith. But now I have

232

found it again, I realise I had always been the Pope and you two were just interlopers.'

'I don't give a fuck what you say, Dion, or for that matter what you say, Ellie, you both let the Holy See down majorly. I have restored what you both managed to break.'

'But, Tony, nobody gives a fuck any more. Nobody needs the Church any more. Or that is what I have been thinking, until this morning.'

'This morning?'

'This morning a white dove landed on my windowsill and she spoke to me. She told me there is a Baby to be born. And this Baby is to be the Daughter of . . . well, not Man, as she said something about a crow and a fox, so I am not too sure about that bit. But, anyway, a Baby will be born and this Baby will be the Messiah returned. It is my job, above everything else, as the one and only Pope, to be there to welcome this Baby into the world.'

'And where is this baby to be born? In a stable in Bethlehem perchance?'

'No, my hunch is it is going to be born in a prison cell off the Holloway Road in London.'

'Okay, Dion, you have a choice. I will have you quietly and painlessly "put to sleep", and then by this time next year will have you Beatified, as in made into a Saint. As Saint Dionysius you will have all the honour and respect you lost in your lifetime. Or, if you want to live, you will be stripped of everything: your title, your pension, your flat in the Vatican. And you can't get to wear any of the costume, you're back to civvies.'

'There is no choice. I'm off now. Are you coming with me, Ellie?'

'Coming with you? I'm going to write the musical as we go. By the time we get to London and this Baby is born, Cameron

Mackintosh will be begging us to let him stage it in the West End. *A Child Is Born – Two.*'

On that note Pope Dionysius XXIII and Pope Eloise walk out of The Three Popes hand in hand. It would be good to say they left skipping or even doing the Morecambe and Wise exit, but Pope Dionysius XXIII's sciatica in his lower back would not allow it.

Pope Anthony looks up at the stained-glass window and wonders if he should have joined the family business back in Palermo.

The halves of Guinness are left undrunk.

▲

18:29

There are four glasses on the table.

There is maybe milk of some sort in the glasses.

We don't know where the bar is.

But this is the bar where Tangerine NiteMare meet.

To have their band meetings.

They like to call it the Korova Milk Bar.

But I don't think that is its real name.

Or if any of this is real.

Killer Queen takes charge.

'So tonight we do our gig in the London Aquarium. Then over the next few months Mister Fox and the girls at the agency have sorted out a world tour for us. It takes in all of the places we have ever wanted to play. From the mountains in Madagascar to the High Plains of Nebraska. From the potholes of the Gobi desert to the dustbowls of the Outback. From the in-flight deck of the last flying Concorde to the far horizons of Lake Windermere. From

234

the upper reaches of the Amazon to the tidal flats of the Ganges. From the—'

'Yeah! Yeah! Yeah! We get the point, Killer,' interjects Dead Squirrel.

'But where and when does the tour end?' enquires Crow.

'Where it might have begun: in the Maelstrom, off the northern tip of the Isle of Jura, on Christmas Eve,' answers Killer Queen.

'And the gear?' asks Dead Squirrel.

'Drums of Death, as in Colin from Oban, has got all that sorted for us. He has this PA that can be taken anywhere and is powered by mind control. It's massive but you can fit it in your pocket.'

'We don't have pockets,' quips Crow.

'I have,' pipes up John Lennon.

'Do we need to rehearse?' enquires Dead Squirrel.

'We have never rehearsed. Rehearsing would be selling out. We are for real. Everything we do is improvised. Everything we do is now. That is why they love us,' says Killer Queen.

'There is a rumour going around FaceLife that we are just an ordinary band made up of four blokes who have adopted stupid stage names and are playing derivative music. Should we try to scotch this rumour?' worries Dead Squirrel.

'No point. There are always going to be unbelievers. That is their problem. Their loss. We know we are real. Our fans know we are real,' adds John Lennon.

'If there is nothing else to discuss, I suggest we all get the bus down to the London Aquarium now and do our soundcheck. Oh yeah, and Drums of Death said he would do the desk for us,' concludes the Killer.

They suck up the rest of their milk through the straws and leave just as Alex and His Droogs arrive.

There is a pint of lager on the table near the door.

The door is a door to a pub on Kingsland Road, Dalston.

Another pint of lager is placed on the table.

'Do you mind if I join you?'

'Fine by me.'

'If you don't mind me saying, I don't think I have ever seen a Hasidic Jewish person in a pub before.'

'Well, the truth is I never have been in a pub before.'

'So what's caused the big shift?'

'Kinda complicated.'

'Try me.'

'Well, this morning when I was coming through Customs at Heathrow, I was handed a parcel. Inside the parcel was this book ...'

'Fuck me, I got the same sodding book this morning as well. Anyway, go on.'

'So I opened the book and I found this page in Hebrew that I read, and it had this instant impact on me. My first name is Moses, see, and there is this page that is, like, addressing me directly, and I think I am "the" Moses. You know, the Moses who leads our people out of slavery in Egypt? I am somehow thinking that is what I have to do. Then sometime later, after I got home and had some of my mum's cooking, I turned the page and there was some more in Hebrew, and after I read that I thought I was the Messiah.'

'Like Jesus, bruv?'

'Yeah, but for us Jesus wasn't the Messiah. Us Jews are still waiting for the Messiah to come.'

'But I thought Jesus was Jewish, bruv.'

'Yeah, but we didn't think he was for real, so we are still waiting. And like I said earlier, I thought I was the Messiah. And so I just got up, walked out of my mum's and started walking down the Kingsland Road. And in my head I am going to be walking all the way to the Promised Land to rebuild Jerusalem. But I am knackered 'cause I was on a flight overnight and didn't get any sleep. And I am thinking, "Maybe I am getting things out of proportion? Maybe I should just have a bit of a sit down and a think about it?" So I came in here, got myself a pint, and then you sat down with me. I know it all sounds like madness, but you did ask.'

'None of that sounds like madness, bruv. In fact, I know my Bible well. I know all those Old Testament stories about you lot and Moses. Yeah, I used to like Moses a lot. Anyway, like I was saying, I got given a copy of the same book this morning. But it was a different page I read. You see, remember the Tottenham Riots back in the day? Well, it was me that burnt down the Co-op building. I became like a hero to all the other kids. It sort of went to me head. I sort of suffer from mental things; I get very angry sometimes. Sometimes I take pills to control the anger. And this morning, reading this page in the yellow book . . . what's it called again?'

'*Grapefruit Are Not the Only Bombs.*'

'Yeah, good title as well. Anyway, I read these words, telling me to burn the Shard, you know, the building on the South Bank? I used to have all these followers on Twitter. Hundreds of thousands of them. I send out a tweet that tonight we will burn the Shard – it was the first in years. And now things have gone mental. Kids are coming from all over the place and they want me to lead them in burning down the Shard. So I have come in here to have a pint and think about it first. I mean, it's mental. But sometimes some of the best things are mental. That is why I think you could be the Messiah. But I don't think you need to go all the way to Israel to build Jerusalem – it would just start up all that shit again with the Arabs and stuff. You see, we have this song called "Jerusalem". We used to sing it at school. I remember reading somewhere that some people thought it should be our national anthem, when we still had a national anthem. They were right. I loved that song. Anyway, in this song they sing about the Messiah coming, and we build Jerusalem here in Albion. That is what I think you should do. I will do it with you. We will build Jerusalem here. Maybe not here in Dalston. But somewhere where there is some room. I used to do acting when I was a kid. We did acting all over the place; there are some great places to build Jerusalem. Maybe up North, it's pretty grim there, but up on the hills, the Pennines. It would be brilliant to build Jerusalem up there, with all its city walls and everything. And it could be where all you Jewish people live. It could become your Promised Land. I mean, no one lives up there any more. Not since everything got made in China, so they all got unemployed. And everybody started emigrating to Poland and Estonia and stuff. Plenty of space. You could do your Kosher farms and everything. I like bagels, me. I always like going to the twenty-four-hour bagel shop up on the Stokey bit of Kingsland. Smoked salmon and cream cheese bagel, that's my favourite. That's Jewish, right? We'll sort it. What you reckon?'

'How did the words to this song go, the one you were talking about?'

'I will sing it.'

And without stopping to think or even take a sip from his pint Henry Pedders stands up and in a full tenor breaks out into song:

> *And did those feet in ancient time*
> *Walk upon England's mountains green*
> *And was the holy Lamb of God*

On England's pleasant pastures seen!

And did the Countenance Divine
Shine forth upon our clouded hills?
And was Jerusalem builded here
Among these dark Satanic Mills?

At this point a bloke walks into the pub with a painted face, all scary-looking. A bit like Jack Nicholson as the Joker, but with more black, and more scary. And he starts singing along with Henry Pedders, but in harmony.

Bring me my Bow of burning gold
Bring me my Arrows of desire
Bring me my Spear: O clouds unfold!
Bring me my Chariot of fire!

And now all these other kids – well, not just kids, all sorts of people – come into the pub and start singing with Henry and the bloke with the painted face.

I will not cease from Mental Fight
Nor shall my Sword sleep in my hand
Till we have built Jerusalem
In England's green & pleasant Land

And when it gets to the end the place erupts.

'You see, Moses, that is why you should build Jerusalem here in Albion, even if you are not the Messiah.'

'Yeah, Henry, I think you are right, but who is this bloke with the painted face? Is he one of your mates?'

'My name is Drums of Death.' He is addressing the whole bar and not just Moses and Henry. 'And I want to invite you all to a gig I am doing tonight at the London Aquarium. I want to finish my set with everybody here singing "Jerusalem". And, Yid boy,* I reckon you should get some of your mates down to sing along with us. It will look great. And I should also let you know Tangerine NiteMare are doing a set. It will be the first show on their world tour. Someone buy me a pint?'

And on that note we will leave this chapter, with Moses Tabick, Henry Pedders and Drums of Death, aka Colin from Oban, having a quiet pint before the rest of the evening unfolds.

---

* Okay, maybe 'Yid boy' does not sit right, but when I tried 'Jew boy' and then 'Kike boy' they looked even more loaded. If this book is ever to be published, maybe the editor will fix it.

8 : LIVE FROM THE LONDON AQUARIUM

22:23 Monday 24 April 2023

Post-comeback warm-up gig, in the cramped dressing room of the Roadmender in Northampton.

'That was fucking rubbish. I mean, Bill, do you actually know any of our songs? Or even what end of the bass you are supposed to be playing? And, Jimmy, how many times are you going to use that "my lead came out" excuse? As for the rock opera I was planning, I may as well hire a couple of lads that are eager, willing and, most importantly, talented.'

Jimmy and Bill say nothing. The roadies say nothing. The promoter who has just stuck his head around the door says nothing. Alan has some more to say.

'I'm off for a smoke. Don't try to contact me.'

And that was that.

▲

22:27

Post-world-tour warm-up gig, in the cramped dressing room of the London Aquarium.

'That was fucking amazing! I mean, Crow, you just showed them how to fly across the sky in a straight line. And, Dead Squirrel, your running up and down trees had them moshing like it was 1999. As for you, Lennon, that "For those of you in the cheap seats I'd like ya to clap your hands to this one; the rest of you can just rattle your jewellery!" quip will be quoted for years to come. And as for myself, I think I definitely made the case for transgender killer whales making the best form of life to front any sort of band.'

The rest of the band are saying nothing. What can they say? They all know they just blew the place apart. The Stingrays went berserk. The Little Perch, who got in on the guest-list, will remember it for the rest of their lives as the greatest gig they ever went to. Killer Queen has some more to say.

'So, Drums of Death wants us all to come on at the end of his set to do "Jerusalem" with him. Yeah, that "Jerusalem" – "And did those feet," etc. He's got all these Hasidic Jewish lads down from Stamford Hill to be, like, the choir. And then there is this mad bloke called Henry-something who said he should have been in those Harry Potter films as the fat boy. He has a spoken-word bit that Drums of Death wants us to do some backing for. We will just jam it. And Mister Fox is off scoring us some gravel. And lastly Dead Perch has just texted me to tell you all that he is on it.

'In a word "Genius"!'

▲

22:37

The thing is, your children never appreciate you until after you're dead. When my son was around this afternoon, I knew he would not get it. But one day, after my state funeral, he will get it. But enough of that; the only reason why I am butting in here is to let you know I have now pushed the needle through the remaining two of my straw figures. As of now both Florence 'the Princess of'

242

Wales and Marcia Zuckerberg are dead in their beds. But seeing as both of them were asleep, no one will know until the morning. As far as I am concerned, these small actions have been my first steps at saving the world.

I had a mate whose dad died a few years ago. I remember him telling me how, when he was a kid, his dad was like a giant, and the fount of all truth and wisdom. And as my mate grew up his dad just shrunk and then shrivelled, and when his dad got old he started to lose his mind and became incontinent, and his opinions about anything were worthless – but on the day after his funeral, his dad became this giant again. He could see his father for everything he really was – his strength, his wisdom, all of it. I just want you to remember that, as this might be the last time I get to be in this book.

▲

22:47

FUUK-UP is still innocently orbiting the Earth, unaware its minutes are numbered. While the worm enjoys the apple.

▲

22:51

'There were two dark figures in the ice-cream van. I could not see what they were doing, but they were not in the business of selling ice creams.'

▲

Divine is still lying back in 'her' pirogue, gazing up at the sky while she is drifting down the Congo. But now the sky is a moonless black studded with tens of thousands of stars. She knows the names of nearly all of them. And she knows this has been the greatest day in her life.

▲

Henry Pedders walks onto the stage at the London Aquarium. A big cheer goes up from the Tottenham Riot Contingency.

'Some of you know who I am, some don't. But that don't matter. What matters is that we had a blinding set from Tangerine NiteMare earlier, and Drums of Death has been layin' down the beats heavy. It was him that asked me to come up and say a few words before we have a very special closing number for you all.

'What it is, is I keep having these dreams about the Shard. In these dreams the Shard has this big eyeball stuck on the top of it. This eyeball swivels around and sometimes blinks, but it is always watching me. Now, I don't know what this means or why I have these dreams, but I know I don't like it. In fact, I hate it. In fact, I think the Shard is everything I hate and loathe in the world as it is at the moment. And I know we are not supposed to hate anything now we have everything we want. But this morning I got this book in the post.'

Henry Pedders lifts his copy of *Grapefruit Are Not the Only Bombs* up in his right hand.

'I have no idea where this book came from or why I got sent a copy. And I can't even tell you what sort of book it is. But I flicked through it and I got to a page that had only three words on it. And I will read them to you now: "BURN THE SHARD". And I knew then that tonight I had to do it. Then I sent out a tweet, and I guess a lot of you here got that tweet. "Tonight we Burn the Shard."'

A big cheer goes up.

'And then I sent out another tweet. It was, "We will march down Kingsland, through the City. Across London Bridge. We will be there by midnight. The Shard will Burn."'

A bigger cheer goes up.

'But when I was walking down the Kingsland this afternoon, I began to wonder if what I was doing was the right thing. Was this just my madness? Had I not been taking my pills? Then I bumped into my new friend here, Moses. We were having a pint and we were discussing this and that. And what he suggested I should do is let the people choose. So that is what we are going to do. Those of you who think we should burn the Shard down tonight, please raise your left arm.'

A mighty cheer goes up, as does every left arm in the building. As for the fish in the aquarium, they were lifting their left fins.

'So I guess that is it. But before we go and get on with the business, there is something else I have to tell you. Moses here, when I met him this morning, was about to head off to rebuild Jerusalem where it used to be before the Great Intifada. I told him, "Forget it, mate, that will just kick off all those problems again. Why don't you build Jerusalem here in England, like in the song, but up North where no one lives any more, and all you Yids can go and live there and make it into your new Promised Land?" And Moses reckoned it's a good idea, so that is why he got some of his mates down here this evening with all their cool threads on and stuff. So after we have all sung "Jerusalem" together, with Drums of Death and Tangerine NiteMare backing us, and after we have burnt the Shard down, some of us are going to be heading up North to start building Jerusalem.

'I will count us all in.

'One, two, three, four:

'*And did those feet in . . .*'

▲

23:07

The tanks are still rolling.

▲

23:11

There is a knock at the door.

Yoko opens it. Winnie is standing behind her.

'We are arresting you both on suspicion of murder. You do not have to say anything, but it may harm your defence, if you do not mention when questioned, something which you later rely on in court. Anything you do say may be given in evidence.'

'What the fuck? Murder? What murder?'

Yoko resists; she is handcuffed. Winnie comes of her own accord.

Both Barney Muldoon and Saul Goodman know they have their women. They have all the evidence. It is open-and-shut.

▲

FUUK-UP switches off.

Her descent and burn-up begins.

The internet shuts down.

All of it.

Even your iPhone23.

World-wide panic is instant.

If you were to be looking down on London at this very point in time, the only light you would see would be the tongues of flame licking up the side of the Shard.

▲

08:59

A new day has dawned.

The birds are singing.

The cherry blossom is full.

A killer whale leaps through the surf.

A crow flies across the blue sky.

A squirrel runs up a tree to its dray.

A fox topples a bin to find a feast.

A mother grieves over her murdered son.

Welcome to the Dark Ages.

End of *Book Two*

Nine Months Later

BOOK THREE

The Christmas Number One

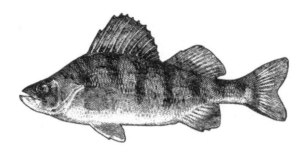

1 : THE GLOSSARY

05:21 Monday 24 December 1984

Dear Diary,

I have been living inside *The Shipping Forecast* for most of my life. The only respite has been music that might be called 'Sailing Out' or 'In' or maybe 'Sailing By'. Ah yes, 'Sailing By', that's it. And then at times I surface and I am in something called the World Service and I might be in Peru or Mongolia or Zimbabwe.

But then I am back again in *The Shipping Forecast*.

There are warnings of gales in Viking, South Utsire, Forties, Cromarty, Forth, Tyne, Dogger, Fisher, German Bight, Humber, Plymouth, Biscay, Trafalgar, FitzRoy, Sole, Fastnet, Shannon and Fair Isle . . .

This morning they brought me breakfast. It was still dark outside. There is an outside.

They said it looked like we might be having a white Christmas.

Christmas? When did that happen? When did I stop believing in Santa Claus? I blame my sister. I can still remember where I was standing, at the top of the stairs, when my big sister told me Santa Claus was not real and it was really our father and mother. Only we didn't have a father and mother. But we must have had them once.

South Easterly 5 to 7, increasing gale 8 at times. Rough or very
rough. Wintry showers. Good, occasionally poor . . .

The breakfast is the same every morning. Cornflakes; smoked
streaky bacon – more streak than bacon – with cold baked beans;
white thin-sliced toast with Golden Shred marmalade. The coffee
is Camp Coffee, not even Nescafé. They put the sugar in without
even asking.

I asked the nurse, or at least the woman who looks like a nurse,
where I was and could I go home yet. And she said, 'Not yet, luv.
You be a good girl and eat your breakfast. Matron will be around
soon. We don't want any naughtiness, do we?'

'Naughtiness?' I replied. 'I was always a good girl.'

And she said, 'You know, like yesterday morning. We don't
want you upsetting the other patients.'

Cyclonic 4 or 5, increasing 6 at times. Occasionally rough
at first in Dover and Wight, otherwise slight or moderate.
Thundery showers. Moderate or good . . .

I looked out of the window. There was some snow falling. So I
guess it must be Winter. Do they have Winter in Zimbabwe? It is
nearly morning. I am not inside *The Shipping Forecast* and I cannot hear 'Sailing By' playing either in my head or anywhere else.

But where am I?

I wait.

I listen.

There are other beds with other people in them. I don't recognise any of them. But I think they are always here. Maybe they
have been living inside *The Shipping Forecast* as well. Someone
is snoring. Someone always snores.

Westerly or North Westerly, backing Southerly later in West, 7 to severe gale 9, occasionally storm 10 at first in Sole, decreasing 5 or 6 for a time later. Very rough or high, occasionally very high at first. Showers, rain later. Moderate or good, occasionally poor . . .

I am not inside *The Shipping Forecast.*

The Shipping Forecast is somewhere else.

I am in a hospital.

'Matron, where am I?'

'You are in Saint Crispin's Hospital for the mentally insane.'

'And why am I here?'

'You ask me the same questions every morning.'

'But where is this place?'

'It is a hospital outside Northampton, in England, on the Earth, somewhere in God's Universe. And tomorrow is Christmas and we are all going to be good girls today, aren't we, Roberta?'

'Can you bring me my diary and pencil?'

'Only if you promise to write nice things and not try to poke your pencil in Jemima's eye.'

'Jemima?'

'The nice lady in the bed beside you. She is always good.'

'I only do that when she snores.'

'Well, you be a good girl. And, as it happens, I have a little surprise for you. A parcel arrived for you this morning. Somebody must love you. Do you want me to help you open it?'

'I will open it myself, Matron.'

I think that was when I fell back asleep.

Easterly or South Easterly 5 to 7, occasionally gale 8 in Fair Isle, decreasing 4 at times. Moderate or rough, occasionally

very rough in Fair Isle. Showers, wintry in Fair Isle. Good,
occasionally poor in Fair Isle . . .

I always like it when we get to Fair Isle. The first boy I ever kissed wore a Fair Isle sweater.

Matron left the parcel by my bed. It was wrapped up in brown paper tied with string – my favourite type of parcel. I also like *wild geese that fly with the moon on their wings.*

After Matron left I opened the parcel. There were two books inside. I like books. Books are my life. There was also a letter from Francis Riley-Smith. I remember Francis now. A nice young man. A good young man. If I was younger . . . I wonder if he ever wore a Fair Isle sweater.

It was then I started to remember. It was then I started to write this entry in my diary.

I am no longer in *The Shipping Forecast*. This is real life and I can remember – but what is it exactly I remember?

I was living in a cottage on an island. A Scottish island. The Isle of Jura. I had been writing a book. That's what I do. I write books. I am a writer. I am remembering and I am writing again.

The books in the parcel are newly leather-bound with gold embossed lettering on the front. The first one has the title *The Blaster in the Pyramid*, and underneath the title it says 'By George Orwell'.

But who was George Orwell, I wondered. And then I remembered that I was George Orwell when I wrote books. The rest of the time I am Roberta Antonia Wilson.

On the other book it said, '*The Rotten Apple* by George Orwell'.

Then I reread the letter from Francis Riley-Smith, and I will quote:

Dear Roberta,

We all hope you are recovering and are well enough to enjoy this Christmas. And come the Spring you will be back up on Jura to finish your book.

I hope you don't mind that when you fell ill last April, I took the liberty of driving up to your cottage to clear some things out before the holidaymakers started to arrive. The floor was covered with scattered papers, all of them typed on. Flora, the cleaner, who came with me, was going to put them on the fire with the soiled bedding and empty packets of Digestive biscuits, but I decided to collect them all. I knew you had been doing so much writing. I thought they might be important to you and your family. And everybody still loves Fish Farm.

I gathered them up into one huge sheaf and took them back down to my place.

You might remember the strange tall man who was with the rock band called Echo & The Bunnymen. His name was Bill Drummond. He was still at the hotel that night and he asked me if he could read through what you had been writing. To quote him, 'It's mind-blowing. It might not be great literature, but I have never read anything like this before.' Then my friend Jimmy, from Devon, the one who did the drawing from Titus Groan, *you may remember? Well, he read some of it as well and thinks it's brilliant. We decided there and then to see if we could get the two books printed and bound. Even if we only did a few copies of each of them. Jimmy said he would do some illustrations for the books.*

We had 23 copies of each of them printed. Bill Drummond knew somewhere in Liverpool that does this sort of thing. I think the illustrations Jimmy Cauty has done are superb. I hope you don't mind but we hope to sell a few of the copies up here to cover the cost of having them printed and bound. And, of course, to cover your outstanding rent on the cottage.

But most of all we all wish you a speedy recovery so you can get up here in time for the bluebells coming into bloom and you can then get Book Three *done. I am sure when all three of the books are written and published properly as a complete edition, it will be at least as successful as* Uganda, *if not* Fish Farm.

Yours truly,

Francis Riley-Smith X

After reading this I could feel the tears well up inside me. I repressed them. I am still good at repressing things. I did not stick my pencil into the eye of the lady in the bed next to me as she snored either.

I read his letter again. And cried some more.

And then I picked up the first of the two books, *The Blaster in the Pyramid.* I knew I had written it. I could tell these were my words. I could not remember anything about any of it. But I was horrified to discover they had also printed my diary entries as well. This means they will have read them. It is too late now. Nothing to be done.

Maybe some people reading it will just think I am some kind of post-modern character in the book and not really the author, and none of the more personal and somewhat embarrassing incidents I have reported actually happened. Let us hope so.

But, in a way, I rather like the idea that I am a character along with the rest in my own book. This has cheered me up.

Then I read the other book, *The Rotten Apple*. And it was the same with this one – nothing in my memory told me I had written it. What I did know was that there was to be a third book. If the third book does not get written, the world will self-destruct. And things cannot wait until the bluebells are in bloom or until I am back in the cottage on Jura. The book has to be written before the sun rises tomorrow morning. Before Matron does her rounds. Before it is a white Christmas. Before Santa Claus is not believed in by another six-year-old girl at the top of her stairs. Before another breakfast of bacon, egg and cold baked beans.

But the trouble is, I know nothing about anything I have been reading in these two books I have been sent.

My mind is clearing. *The Shipping Forecast* has gone. 'Sailing By' will not be heard ever again until . . .

I have made a decision. I will read both of these two books again and make notes about the characters, artefacts and incidents, and these notes will be the basis for the first chapter in *Book Three*. They will act as a glossary of sorts for future readers who have found themselves lost.

I once was lost but now am found
Was blind, but now I see

It will also be a handy way for those studying this book as part of their GCSE coursework to be able to just lift these bits without having to unduly worry about remembering or interpreting all of the book's many backwaters.

CHARACTERS, ARTEFACTS AND INCIDENTS

Winnie Smith, or Winifred Lucie Atwell Smith, to give her full name, is maybe the heroine of the book. She lives at Victory Mansions, Dalston, London. She is twenty-eight years old at the time the book is set in 2023. She goes running. She acts on impulses. She left school back in 2011 to join the Occupy Movement, where she lost her virginity. At the beginning of this book Winnie has just started to keep a diary – not a blog. She is using pen, ink and paper. She is filled with lust for a man putting up fly-posters. She has violent sexual fantasies about him that she tries to repress. She did have an affair with an older man, whose name was Julian Assange. She also has lesbian episodes. The first entry in her diary was:

I HATE GOOGLEBYTE

I HATE WIKITUBE

I HATE AMAZABA

I HATE FACELIFE

I HATE APPLETREE

But, more importantly, Winnie is working for Celine Hagbard. She has been since 2017. Winnie had worked out an equation that would end death – not physical death, but mental death. This was the final frontier and it was going to be smashed. All Winnie now has to do is hit 'Send' and death will be vanquished for ever. This is what this book is about – living life for ever. Winnie's Mother left her when she was five. Winnie's father died of cancer when she was twelve. Winnie is also an addict. Winnie is also pregnant, although at this point in the story she does not know it. Winnie also dreams of meeting her baby sister again one day.

Celine Hagbard invented the internet. She built FUUK-UP – First Universal Uber Kinetic-Ultramicro Programmer. FUUK-UP became Google, which then became GoogleByte when she did the deal with Melinda Gates at MicroSoft. Celine Hagbard may have once had a sex change and she may have once had a submarine – a yellow one. She once worked for The Beatles. She lives in New York City.

The Beatles were a band. They ended the Vietnam War.

Michelle Obama was both the first female and last-ever President of the USA. She is currently modelling for Damien Hirst, who is making a pure-gold statue based on the famous *Little Mermaid* in Copenhagen harbour, but with Michelle Obama's face and torso. He is keeping the fishy tail.

Vladimir Putin was the former Czar of the Russian Empire (2017–21). Obama and Putin are going to go on a worldwide lecture tour together.

Francis Riley-Smith is the son of the owner of the largest estate on the Isle of Jura. Francis is good.

The Isle of Jura is a very sparsely populated island off the West Coast of Scotland. Its main industry is grouse-shooting and the production of the world-famous single malt whisky named after the island itself – Jura.

Tammy and George are Winnie's neighbours at Victory Mansions. Tammy once had a hit singing with Utah Saints. They have two children: Tina (seven) and Richey (nine). George works for GoogleByte. He is also into conspiracy theories and the Illuminati.

The Illuminati is an organisation that conspiracy theorists think runs the world. It doesn't.

The Justified Ancients of Mummu is a secret organisation that exists to undermine and bring down the powers of the Illuminati. The Justified Ancients of Mummu's secret weapon is Chaos. It is not to be confused with The Justified Ancients of Mu Mu.

ZitCoins are the world-wide digital currency.

Fernando Pó is an island off the West Coast of Africa. By April 2017 it was the last nation state on Earth not owned by one of the New Big Five.

Label Free is a lifestyle brand. It is the brand of choice for those not wanting to be seen wearing a brand. It is Winnie's brand of choice.

O'Brien is a man Winnie has had unwanted sexual fantasies about over the past few years. O'Brien once whispered in Winnie's ear, 'We shall meet again in the place where there is no darkness.'

Yoko Ono the Younger

Yoko Ono is not her real name. We are not too sure what her real name is. It might be Elisabeth. She is 23 years old. She was an art student. She lives in a warehouse in Hackney Wake looking out over the River Lea. Her boyfriend is John Lennon the Younger. She murders her boyfriend. She has her reasons. She only ever wears black boots, black jeans, black T-shirt and black hair. On her T-shirt the words '2023: WHAT THE FUUK IS GOING ON?' are stencilled. She has also written the book *Grapefruit Are Not the Only Bombs*. She had an affair with one of her art school tutors when she was eighteen. She had to have an abortion when it was discovered she had endometrial cancer, as in cancer of the womb. Her womb was removed at the same time. This meant she would never have periods or children, but she was told she would still have the menopause.

John Lennon the Younger is not his real name. His real name is Paul Harrison. He is 23 years old. He was an art student. Yoko Ono the Younger was his girlfriend. He was murdered by his girlfriend. She wrapped his body up in a duvet cover and rolled him out of the window, and he landed in the River Lea. After he died he found he was no longer angry and formed a band with Killer Queen, Crow and Dead Squirrel.

Yoko & John

Yoko & John are not John & Yoko. They are the two 23-year-olds described above. They live in a warehouse squat in Hackney Wake.

Hackney Wake is a fashionable area of East London. Not to be confused with Hackney Wick, which was a fashionable area of East London in the Teens.

The Teens, as the years 2013–19 are commonly known. A period in time during which the nation states of the world began to collapse and were bought out by the New Big Five.

The New Big Five are:

GoogleByte
WikiTube
AmaZaba
FaceLife
AppleTree

The New Big Five have now solved all the world's problems. Thus, by default, the leaders of these five companies are the five most powerful life forms on Planet Earth today. Or at least in 2023.

The Leaders
The Leaders of the New Big Five are:

Celine Hagbard@GoogleByte
Florence 'the Princess of' Wales@WikiTube
Jessie Bezos@AmaZaba
Marcia Zuckerberg@FaceLife
Cynthia Stevie Dobbs@AppleTree

2023: WHAT THE FUUK IS GOING ON? are the words on one hundred screen-printed posters that Yoko & John have fly-posted on walls across London. These words have also been screen-printed onto five black T-shirts.

FUUK is also the name of a genre of music and the spontaneous happenings where this genre of music is played. The young people that are into this music and go to these happenings are called the FUUK Kids. We have, as yet, not come upon this genre of music in this book, but we will do.

The Post-Digital Underground is the name of a movement John Lennon the Younger wanted to start as an attack on the digital world and the all-pervasive power of the New Big Five. Yoko Ono the Younger thought it was a rubbish name.

Cynthia is Yoko Ono the Younger's best friend. Yoko Ono the Younger suspects she and John have been shagging. They have.

The Justified Ancients of Mu Mu are Yoko & John. Or at least that is what Yoko Ono the Younger thinks they should be called. The day after John is murdered by Yoko, she replaces him with Winnie.

The Hockney Award used to be called the Turner Prize, but when David Hockney died they renamed the prize in his honour. BANKSY, Ms Emin, the Chapman Brother and Grayson Larry are the selection committee for 2023. Yoko & John are in the running to be the winners of the 2023 Hockney Award. Yoko & John have no idea about this.

Grapefruit Are Not the Only Bombs is a book based on *Grapefruit* by Yoko Ono the Elder. It contains a list of one hundred instructions. Yoko Ono the Younger has mailed copies of *Grapefruit Are Not the Only Bombs* to the 23 people in the world who she thinks most deserve a copy.

Yoko Ono the Elder is a frail old lady who used to be married to John Lennon the Elder. She lives in an apartment in New York. She is considered by many to be the world's greatest living artist. She has recently done a deal with the coffee-shop chain Starbucks. 'WAR IS OVER' is Starbucks' new strap-line. They also use the line 'ABOVE US ONLY SKY' in their aerial advertising. A minimalist caricature of Yoko Ono the Elder's face is used in the Starbucks logo. The one that is a mermaid.

Starbucks is the most successful coffee-shop chain in the world. They have bought out all of their major rivals. They make the best coffee that has ever been made.

Cauty & Drummond
These are a pair of undertakers. Their strap-line is 'The Undertakers to the Underworld'. They are also the two men depicted in the background of Edvard Munch's painting *The Scream*.

Gimpo was a nurse on HMS *Uganda* in the Falklands War. There is a lot more to Gimpo than this.

Gimpo
There is also another character in this book called Gimpo.

1984 is the year in which this book is being written.

Jimmy Cauty turned twenty-eight years old in 1984. He was born on Merseyside and grew up in Totnes, Devon. At the age of fourteen he drew a picture based on a scene in the book *Titus Groan*. This was then used for the cover of an album by the band Led Zephyr. It became world famous. He is a friend of

Francis Riley-Smith. He rides motorcycles. He also plays guitar.

Alan Moore turned thirty-one years old in 1984. He grew up in Northampton, England, where he still lives. In 1970, at the age of seventeen, he watched a band called Titus Groan play in Northampton Guildhall. He writes stories for DC Comics. In 1983, at the age of thirty, he reinvented *Swamp Thing*. This re-invention of *Swamp Thing* is brilliant. Will Sergeant, the guitarist with Echo & His Bunnymen, lent his copy of *Swamp Thing* to the band's manager, Bill Drummond, while the band were touring the Outer and Inner Hebrides. Alan Moore also plays the drums. Alan Moore is also working on a new dystopian story. It is set on an island off the coast of Scotland where the 23 last surviving human beings on Planet Earth live. There are twenty males and only three females. He thinks this story might make the basis of Extreme Noise Terror's comeback album – a concept album.

Bill Drummond was thirty-one years old in 1984. He has lived in several places. In 1970, at the age of seventeen, he watched a band called Titus Groan play in Northampton Guildhall. In 1974, at the age of twenty-one, he worked as a nursing assistant in Saint Crispin's lunatic asylum, Northampton. His job was to watch people die and then lay them out. He has done other jobs. He also plays the bass.

Extreme Noise Terror are a grindcore band from Northampton. The line-up was, is and will always be:

Alan Moore – drums and vocals
Jimmy Cauty – guitar
Bill Drummond – bass

Their first album was called *Burn Wicker Man Burn*. No one bought this record. After they had been invited to perform with The American Medical Association at the 1992 Brit Awards they recorded their second album, *Never Mind*. It sold millions. It defined rock music in the '90s. Extreme Noise Terror were occasionally joined on stage by the singer Dene Jones, who had been the singer with The Clash.

They never released their album *The Black Room* before the beginning of their Twenty-Three-Year Moratorium.

The American Medical Association (The AMA) are a band from the late '80s and early '90s. They are the biggest-selling singles band of the era, produced by Jonathan King. The AMA are a sister-and-brother band. Their names are Eve and Adam. They had a suicide pact. After performing at the 1992 Brit Awards, they shot each other on the red carpet of the aftershow party using a pair of pearl-handled duelling pistols. After this public suicide, their final album, *The White Room*, became the biggest-selling album in the history of recorded music.

Jonathan King has been many things. He wrote and sang and recorded a song called 'Everyone's Gone to the Moon'. It was a hit in 1965, while Jonathan King was an undergraduate at Cambridge University. In 1987 he produced the first records by The American Medical Association. He is considered by those who know these things as the most visionary record producer of all time.

Tangerine NiteMare are a band. Their line-up is:

Killer Queen
Crow

Dead Squirrel

John Lennon the Younger

The manager of the band is Mister Fox.

Dead Perch does their social media.

They recorded an album called *Far Out*.

Tangerine NiteMare are like no other band: they exist in a parallel dimension to the one most bands exist in. John Lennon the Younger only joined them once he was dead.

Killer Queen is a transgender killer whale who lives in the waters around the Inner Hebrides.

Crow is a crow. He can often be seen flying across the skies of London, where he mainly lives. He may also be the father of the One.

Dead Squirrel is a dead grey squirrel that got run over and killed in Gillett Square, Dalston.

Mister Fox should not be confused with the fictional character of the same name in a children's book by Roald Dahl. He is, in fact, just an urban fox living in London. But, more importantly, he is the manager of Tangerine NiteMare. He may also be the father of the One.

Dead Perch is a fish that got caught and left on the bank to die. There will be more information on Dead Perch.

The Maelstrom is off the northern tip of the Isle of Jura. It is where Killer Queen likes to hang out and listen to music.

The Weyward Sisters, sometimes known as The Three Sirens, mistakenly known as The Three Witches, but correctly known as The Weyward Sisters. They are currently and collectively Michelle Obama, Yoko Ono the Older and M'Lady GaGa. They are going to lead the final charge for feminism. They know where the One is to be born.

M'Lady GaGa
M'Lady GaGa is a popular singer whose star has been fading. She is managed by Aloysius Parker.

Aloysius Parker is M'Lady GaGa's manager. He used to be Lady Penelope's chauffeur. Before that he was an East End gangster.

Sam & Dave are a pair of hard-working paramedics in New York City. They used to be soul singers. Their most famous hit was 'Hold On, We're Coming'.

Lord Saatchi owns art – nearly all of it. He also owns Battersea Power Station, which he has had converted into a museum to house his collection.

Candy Hate has many qualities, but a generation of ageing men blame her for the downfall of Extreme Noise Terror while they were still in their prime. They are wrong; they achieved this themselves.

The Twenty-Three-Year Moratorium: Extreme Noise Terror placed a 23-year moratorium on themselves to stop working as a group. This was to give the rest of the world time to catch up and them enough time to work out why. The moratorium came to an end in 2017, by which time everybody had forgotten who they were.

Yoko Ono the Younger's Mother left her father on the day she was born. She also left her five-year-old daughter Winifred on the same day. Each of the daughters had different fathers – that was the problem. Her baby daughter's name was Elisabeth.

Winifred's Father brought Winifred up himself. Winifred never saw her Mother or baby sister again. He died of cancer when Winifred was twelve.

The Brick is just a brick, but it symbolises so much more. What it actually symbolises evolves and changes depending on who is looking at it, throwing it or being hit by it.

King Francisco Malabo Beosá XXIII, or just plain Malabo to his family, is the King of Fernando Pó. He has been sticking bamboo needles into the five straw dolls in the knowledge that by doing so he will be ending the lives of the five women who lead The New Big Five, the five women who run the world.

Siobhán Harrison is the mother of Paul Harrison, whom we also know as John Lennon the Younger. She is concerned she has not heard from her son for over forty-eight hours.

Moses Tabick is a young trainee Rabbi. He is studying in Damascus. When at home he lives with his mother in Stamford Hill, London. Moses has been chosen to lead his people. Or that is what he thinks after reading a page in *Grapefruit Are Not the Only Bombs*. But this time he might not be just a prophet but the Messiah. He is armed with a Luger pistol.

Chodak is a novice Buddhist monk. He is in a Tibetan monastery high up in the Himalayas. But now he is on his way.

The Old Five and their leaders:

    The USA – President Michelle Obama
    Russia – Czar Vladimir Putin the First
    China – Chairman Xi Jinping
    Japan – Emperor Akihito
    The EU – Ms Angela Merkel

ABANDON ALL ART NOW is a poster by Yoko & John. The other words on the poster are:

Major rethink in progress
Await further instructions

iPhone23 is the only hand-held device anyone uses in the world in 2023. It cannot be bettered. There will be no iPhone24.

iJaz is AppleTree's news and current affairs channel in 2018.

iSky was launched in 2018, when AppleTree bought Sky.

Womankind: 'Womankind needs to have war, famine and inequality to function properly: without them we as a species will be over within a couple of generations. As for religion, we need as many as we can have to compete for our souls. The more radical the religion, the better.'

Henry Pedders was a fat boy who lived in Dalston. He was bullied at school. He joined the Saturday-morning youth drama group at the Arcola Theatre in Dalston. He should have got the part of Dudley Dursley in the Harry Potter films. He led the 2011 Tottenham Riots. His Twitter name is Henry Da Riot. Henry wants to see the Shard burn.

The Shard is the tallest building in London. It was built in 2012. Several thousand people living in London dream of the Shard. In these dreams the Shard often appears to have a large swivelling eyeball stuck on the top of it.

Tracey Tracey writes for *Classic Biker*. Interviews Roberta Antonia Wilson. Came up with the image for Subcomandante Marcos.

The Three Shepherdesses are three young and abused women living in three very different and distant parts of the globe:

Arati: the young bride with an abusive husband in Kolkata.
Camille: the young woman in Port-au-Prince who is raped by a transgender artist who is in Haiti as part of the Ghetto Biennale.
Divine: the seventeen-year-old girl in the Congo who is raped by her hero Patrice.

They all receive instructions to meet at The Shepherdess Café on City Road, London, at 17:47 on 24 December 2023.

We will learn more about The Three Shepherdesses and their part in the history of Womankind before the end of this book.

Barney Muldoon and Saul Goodman are two plainclothes coppers who are based at Stoke Newington Police Station and who are investigating the suspected murder of a young man whose body has been found in the River Lea.

Al-Qaeda Towers are the two buildings that were built to replace the Twin Towers.

Philippe Petit is a tightrope walker who walked between the Al-Qaeda Towers.

Will Gompertz is the arts editor for iJaz. He knows what art can be.

Colin from Oban, aka Drums of Death, paints his face and knows his stuff.

Azealia 'taste this quim' Vaults is a rapper and DJ from East London. Azealia 'you cun't make me cum' Vaults breaks all the barriers.

Ronald McDonald is dead. He was killed by Chodak.

NokiaNet: no one has used NokiaNet since 2018.

The Three Popes is a fake Irish bar in Rome. It is also where the last three living Popes like to meet for a quiet Guinness and to discuss things.

The Three Kings is a pub on Kingsland Road, London. You might not be able to find it.

The London Aquarium is the largest aquarium in London. It is also where Tangerine NiteMare play the opening show of their world tour. It was one of the greatest gigs ever to have been performed anywhere in the universe. Parallel or otherwise.

The Roadmender is a club in Northampton. It is where Extreme Noise Terror played their warm-up comeback gig. It was shit.

Yoko Ono the Younger and Winifred Lucie Atwell Smith, or Yoko and Winnie, were arrested for the murder of Paul Harrison, aka John Lennon the Younger.

'Welcome to the Dark Ages' was to be the title of Chapter 1 of *Book Three*. It is now going to be the title of Chapter 2.

▲

Dear Diary,

My mind is now clearer.

I am remembering things.

But you may also need to be reminded of who and what I am.

Please read the entries below. I apologise now for writing about myself in the third person.

After that is done I will get the rest of the book written and then plan my escape.

Love,

Roberta X

▲

Roberta Antonia Wilson is a writer. She is the writer of this book.

She was born in 1926, which makes her fifty-eight years old at the time she is writing it in 1984. She drives a Brough Superior Motorcycle. She wears a Belstaff Panther women's motorcycle jacket, Halcyon goggles and a white silk scarf. She is writing this book in a cottage at the northern tip of the Isle of Jura in Scotland. *Fish Farm*, her first book, was a runaway success. Disney is adapting it for the silver screen. Her second book, *Uganda*, was panned by the critics and ignored by the paying public. After dropping a tab of acid on the completion of *2023: Book Two*, she had a complete mental breakdown and was sectioned by her sister and has spent the last nine months in Saint Crispin's lunatic asylum, near Northampton, in the English Midlands. While there she has blocked out the real world by listening to the BBC World Service and *The Shipping Forecast*.

George Orwell is the *nom de plume* used by Roberta Antonia Wilson. She does not know why she ever decided to use it.

'Sailing By' is a piece of light orchestral music that is played each night before the late *Shipping Forecast* is broadcast on BBC Radio 4.

The Shipping Forecast is broadcast on BBC Radio 4 at 00:48 every night – for ever. The late *Shipping Forecast* is the last thing several million people in the British Isles hear before drifting off to sleep. It marks the end of the day and the beginning of another kind of life.

The early *Shipping Forecast* is broadcast several hours later at 05:20. This marks the beginning of the new day.

Saint Crispin's Hospital is a classic Victorian lunatic asylum built on the outskirts of Northampton, England. It opened for the care and incarceration of the insane in 1876.

Dog Ledger, or rather Douglas 'Dog' Ledger, is Roberta Antonia Wilson's literary agent. He will survive.

▲

Postscript: I can hear the Twenty-Three Sparrows chirruping from the hawthorn bush outside my barred window. I will get this book written by the end of the day. Then I will make my escape.

2 : WELCOME TO THE DARK AGES

08:17 Sunday 24 December 2023

Arthur Scargill is sitting at his kitchen table eating his cooked breakfast in his retirement bungalow in Grimethorpe, Yorkshire.

The radio is on.

The *Today* programme on BBC Radio 4.

There is a tear making its way down his left cheek.

John Humphrys is interviewing William Hague about the race for the leadership of the New English Tory Party. As of this morning it is a straight contest between William Hague and the former rank outsider Henry Pedders.

Arthur is hardly listening to what they are saying. He has too many emotions flowing through his body to take things in at any sort of intellectual level. He is not even bothered who this Henry Pedders lad is. All he knows is that he is not from Yorkshire and William Hague is, so he wants Hague to win.

Henry Pedders is a changed man since he led the mob all the way down Kingsland Road and through the City and over London Bridge. And they did burn the Shard down. But that is all history now. That was months and months ago. And if you are counting – nine months to the day. But so much has happened in the world since then; the complete destruction of the Shard is only a blip on the horizon of history compared to all that other stuff.

As for William Hague, he may have had a long and distinguished career, but to many he is still the original Tory boy from the 1977 conference.

The black pudding is as good as it ever was. And she still knows how to do the mushrooms just how he likes them.

If Arthur were pushed, he might admit it would be better if Brian Redhead were doing the cut and thrust with Margaret Thatcher. But you cannot have everything. And Arthur seems to have got most things he could ever have dreamed of.

Less than twelve months ago the last coalmine in England had been closed; he had been thrown out of his apartment in the Barbican; the National Union of Mineworkers (NUM) had stopped paying his pension; and Anne, his ex-wife, still refused to remarry him.

Whereas now the picture is very different. Since September fifty-seven deep colliery mines have been reopened; the industry has re-employed over 43,000 miners; Anne has remarried him; he has moved back to Yorkshire; and the NUM has invited him to be their General Secretary once again.

Unbeknown even to his conscious self Arthur is already harbouring fantasies about leading a strike. A national coal strike. It will be called in a couple of months' time on 12 March 2024, this being the fortieth anniversary of the official beginning of the last one. But this time they would win. He would show Anne he could still deliver the goods. And Margaret Thatcher will have to turn in her grave.

There is another reason why Arthur is feeling good. And that is because earlier on the *Today* programme on BBC Radio 4, it was announced that it was odds-on the Christmas Number One is going to be by The Grimethorpe Colliery Band. They are going to be on the Christmas edition of *Top of the Pops*. They are sending a chauffeur-driven Roller to pick him up so he can be in the audience when they record the programme later in the day.

Arthur Scargill is unlikely to feature in this book again, but for the sake of those who are not of a certain age or not from these islands, he was the last powerful trade union leader in this country. In his day he was as famous as any of the leading politicians.

▲

People adjust.

Life carries on.

FUUK-UP crashes into Earth. These things happen. The Age of the Internet is over. Many ages have come and gone. It takes less than a week for nearly every teenager in the world to throw away their iPhone23s. Almost immediately people find other ways to communicate. They never got rid of the pillar-boxes around what used to be called the UK. Admittedly they have become curios from another age but, within a month, there are postmen emptying them and delivering letters like it is 1999 all over again.

There has been more sex – real, physical, consensual sex – going on around the world in these past nine months than in the previous twenty years. People are holding hands again. Hands were not for holding when there were iPhone23s. Hands existed then only to hold iPhone23s.

▲

Jonathan King is standing looking at himself in his full-length mirror in his apartment in the Borough, South London. He is looking good. The gym and the running are paying off.

'Fifty-eight fucking years and I am back. I showed the proles. You can't keep genius down.'

Jonathan King had been talking to his reflection in the same mirror for a lot longer than fifty-eight years. In fact, this mirror was in his bedroom when he was only two years old. It has been with him ever since. It has been his 'Mirror, mirror on the wall'. The mirror that can always be relied on to tell him the truth.

As for the fifty-eight years, that is the distance in time since he was last on *Top of the Pops* singing 'Everyone's Gone to the Moon' to now. Back then he was a Cambridge undergraduate. Between then and now he has been one of the most successful hit-record producers of all time. And then he did his time. And then the world did not want to know. But things are different now.

He then does the thing he has done for decades – he pretends to interview himself, while standing and looking in the mirror.

'So tell me, Mister King, the world has always known "Everyone's Gone to the Moon" is one of the greatest songs ever written and you are its writer, but what gave you the idea to re-record it with The Grimethorpe Colliery Band?'

'Well, back in the '80s during the miners' strike, I had a lot of empathy for their situation. They were outcasts from respectable society. Then, after the strike ended, they started to close the mines down. The world had turned their back on miners. It was those miners that had fuelled our industrial revolution. Our Empire would not have existed without those men, young and old, down there at the coalface so our ships could sail the seven seas, our trains could take us from one end of the land to the other in less than a day, so our homes could be warm on Christmas Day. And after all the mines had been closed and we thought we could create energy with those stupid wind turbines and the sun, they kept their colliery band going. Just like I kept going.'

'So you saw this day coming?'

'Of course! Anyone with any intelligence knew the Age of the

Internet was only a passing phase. We knew it would not last. Coal is for ever. Like a good tune is for ever. As they used to say, "Coal is King."'

'Very good! Very good! But tell me, Mister King, when you approached them about recording a version of "Everyone's Gone to the Moon", how did they respond?'

'They were honoured. They thought it a brilliant idea. At least half the band were old enough to have bought the record the first time it came out.'

'I have to say, it has to be one of the greatest Christmas Number Ones of all time, up there with—'

'No, don't spoil it by comparing it to some other—'

'No! No! Of course not. But it is wonderful that *Top of the Pops* is back and you are on it and at number one, with a song you wrote when you were eighteen. A record you produced and sang on. And here you are again looking as youthful as ever at the age of . . . How old, if you do not mind me asking, are you now?'

'Well, that is the beauty of not having the internet any longer. This time last year, you could have just looked it up on Wikipedia on your dismal iPhone23 and known exactly how old I was and whatever other useless information you might have needed. Now we have got back to just knowing what we need to know. But I have to remind you I am not officially number one yet. That will not be announced until just after the stroke of midnight.'

'Yes, but surely that is a mere formality! Everyone knows you have been outselling every other record this week by something like a margin of two to one. I mean, the bookies stopped taking bets on it on Monday. And we won't mention that terrible record by M'Lady Gobshite, will we? Finally, all the best with your performance on *Top of the Pops* this afternoon. When does it air? Tomorrow?'

'Just after *The Queen's Speech.*'

The imaginary interview between Jonathan King and himself is now over. The actual song being sung by Jonathan King, backed by The Grimethorpe Colliery Band, sounds as good as Jonathan King would have the world believe.

As with Arthur Scargill, this might be the last time Jonathan King makes an appearance in this book. When the complete and final *History of Pop Music (1901–2023)* is written, it will look favourably upon his remake of 'Everyone's Gone to the Moon'.

As already mentioned somewhere else in these pages, Nina Simone recorded a version of 'Everyone's Gone to the Moon' too. Maybe the unseen power of Nina Simone is pushing her into becoming a character in this story. Maybe she is in the prison cell next to Winnie and Yoko Ono the Younger. Maybe she is sharing her cell with Lady Penelope. Or maybe not.

▲

It is obvious to all that when FUUK-UP crashes, the world is fucked in a way it has never been fucked before. It seems like there is no one alive on Earth who knew it could all end so quickly. And all so suddenly! And when it does there is nothing that can be done about it. It seems everyone thinks it is all backed up somewhere else. The whole thing, the whole Age of the Internet, relied on one machine: there was no back-up to the back-up of the back-up.

Mankind never learns that the good times don't last for long. There is always the comedown. However pure the cocaine may be on a Saturday night, the one who is snorting it is still going to feel shit on Monday morning.

After the Seven Good Years there will always be . . . does no one remember those Bible stories? It is like when people believe they are some sort of financial genius because the value of their flat doubles in six years, and it has nothing to do with the fact that we as a society are just not building enough homes.

And how soon we all start killing each other. And millions die from famine and pestilence. But that can be discussed in a future chapter.

Once the New Big Five were swept away, it was back to tribalism. And then those tribes made up stories about themselves and their relationship to the land and God. And from that nationalism grew and took root. And these new nations with their stories will be vaguely based on the nation states we had before everything had been sorted for ever and ever. Seven years, that is all we had of it between 2017 and now. Just like it says in The Bible.

And as for religion, there are more religions in the world than there have ever been. Churches that have been empty for years are now packed every Sunday morning. Religions fuelled by hate as well as love. Religions for all races and religions just for you alone.

But people love it. It makes them feel alive. People need to hate people, as much as they need to love people. At least they can go out and make arseholes of themselves and not have to worry that the whole world can see what an arsehole they are via FaceLife and the rest.

▲

'I have a good mind to sack you here and now, Parker.'

'Yes, M'Lady, very understandable.'

'But you said it would be a guaranteed Christmas Number One.'

'Yes, M'Lady, but that is the nature of the beast. We cannot control everything.'

'But you should have known that pervert – I mean genius – was going to do this. And he thinks now that we do not have the internet, we have all forgotten about the terrible things he has done to young people.'

'Yes, M'Lady, but the fact is he has been selling more records in the past week than you—'

'Well, I want him dead.'

'Yes, M'Lady. Right away.'

If an explanation is needed, this is it:

When streaming was over and the music industry folk realised they could get all the mothballed pressing machines back into service and start selling actual records again – real vinyl records, and not just to hipsters, but to everyone – they knew they were on to a good thing. And what people wanted to listen to was music that made them feel nostalgia for those far-off times before the internet. When everything was secure and safe. Even the ones who had never known anything else wanted to hear the likes of Cliff Richard sing 'By the Time I Get to Phoenix', or something. And, of course, Jonathan King singing 'Everyone's Gone to the Moon' with a brass band backing him is perfect. Genius, in fact.

When M'Lady GaGa came up with the idea that she should do a cover of 'Do They Know It's Christmas?', and it being the fortieth anniversary of the original record being recorded and getting the Christmas Number One slot, it also seemed like a genius move.

All she needed to find was some starving Africans to feature in the video. And for her to be seen handing out food to them. What record-buying sucker would not go for that?

Parker sorted it out with his old friend and fellow lag in Fernando Pó – remember the island off the West Coast of Africa? – for M'Lady GaGa to fly out in her Learjet to the island to do the film clip of her handing out food parcels to the 'starving' children.

The reason why the word 'starving' in the last paragraph is in inverted commas is because the children in Fernando Pó were anything but starving. Parker's unnamed old friend and fellow lag was none other than the nameless witch doctor who had put his bamboo needle through the five dolls that represented the five women who were the bosses of the former New Big Five.

Fernando Pó had been, prior to 2017, the world's leading tax haven. In fact, Fernando Pó was where all of M'Lady GaGa's businesses were officially registered. The unnamed witch doctor had been and was now again her primary tax advisor. Since the Fall of the Age of the Internet, Fernando Pó has once again risen to become the tax haven of choice for most of the wealthiest in show business. Fernando Pó is one of (if not *the*) wealthiest nations in the world, so although the children are African, not one of them is starving.

The English tabloid newspapers soon cottoned on to the unseen flaw in M'Lady GaGa's promotional video and exposed her for what she supposedly was – an uncaring, self-absorbed . . . etc., etc.

While we're on the subject of English tabloid newspapers . . . one of the first political fallouts after the abrupt end of the Age of the Internet was the In/Out referendum in England. England voted to leave the former United Kingdom, whereas in the Irish referendum they voted to rejoin. The United Kingdom is now made up of Ireland, Wales, the Isle of Man, the Falkland Islands, Gibraltar, Malta, Cornwall, Scotland and Sark. Other than Sark, the other Channel Islands voted to stay with England. As did the Isles of Scilly.

This referendum was soon followed by the Yes/No one about reinstating the Royal Family. The Yes vote had a resounding win. The next election was to see who would be the His or Her Majesty.

It was a straight contest between the Duchess of Cornwall and Princess Kate. Kate won by a landslide. Queen Kate Middleton reigns supreme in our island's hearts and souls – but not England. England has a different Queen.

Since the Fall of the Age of the Internet, the circulation of actual printed newspapers soared and soared. Print workers are now almost as powerful as coalminers. Which union will go out on national strike first will be known in only a matter of weeks. While Arthur Scargill is still tucking into his black pudding, Tony Dubbins, the leader of the Print Workers' Union, has long polished off his jellied eels and mash.

Fleet Street is still history, but Wapping is where it is all happening. In fact, the *Sun* ran a campaign demanding the English should not be outdone and should elect Kate Moss to be their Queen. Two Queen Kates on one island?

As for M'Lady GaGa, there has been enough negative tabloid press on her over these past few days to put off a significant number of people from buying her version of 'Do They Know It's Christmas?' And it looks like Jonathan King and The Grimethorpe Colliery Band are going to have the Christmas Number One.

Just for the record, all the children in Fernando Pó do know it's Christmas. As a matter of fact, Santa Claus has his villa there, and so of course that is where all his various companies are legally registered. Did you know Santa Claus owns Lego and Candy Doll?

▲

What neither Jonathan King nor M'Lady GaGa nor even Arthur Scargill have taken into account is that there are still several hours of record-selling before they start the count. It is now almost 9:00

on Christmas Eve and HMV and Woolworths record shops are about to open across the land. They will then all close at 18:00 this evening, when all the sales in all the shops will be totted up, phoned through, and the final Top Forty of the year will be announced sometime after midnight. So there is still one day's sales yet to happen. These sales could be crucial.

Also.

Utah Saints have spent most of the last nine months attempting to rework their one and only genuine hit crossover single. The one thing they have kept from the original is the vocals, Tammy Wynette's vocals. As you may remember, Tammy lives next door not to Alice, but to Winnie – our heroine.

Utah Saints rereleased this single at the beginning of December on their own label, Pure Trance Kommunications. Over the past three weeks this record has been steadily gaining ground in people's hearts and climbing the charts. The record is called 'Justified & Ancient'.

▲

Holloway Prison.

This is a prison in London. It is a prison for female offenders. It was closed in 2017, when all crime officially came to an end. It was reopened within days after the Fall of the Age of the Internet. Two of the first offenders to be banged up in it were Yoko Ono the Younger and Winifred Lucie Atwell Smith.

Yoko Ono the Younger was charged with and found guilty of murdering Paul Harrison, aka John Lennon the Younger. She was sentenced to life imprisonment – and these days, 'life' means life.

Winifred Lucie Atwell Smith was charged and found guilty of aiding and abetting in this same crime, as well as the additional crime of perverting the course of justice. Winifred Lucie Atwell Smith was sentenced to ten years, with no parole.

Winnie and Yoko have been sharing a cell in Holloway for almost all of the previous nine months.

Winnie and Yoko are more than best friends for life. They are soul sisters.

Winnie suspected she was pregnant, and she is. The nine months are up. Although her waters have not broken, it is only a matter of hours.

Winnie still has no real idea who the father is or, to be more precise, how the fuck she got pregnant in the first place. She has never had any proper full penetrational sex in her life. Not even dreamt about it. For Winnie, sex had always been about violently dominating the man of her desires. Never in any way the contrary. The less consensual the better.

The crow that lands daily on the sill of Winnie and Yoko's cell window to take a look inside has a different take on the subject. As does the fox that prowls the perimeter walls of Holloway Prison most nights.

Mister Fox and Crow have a better understanding of the workings of the universe than the two criminals locked up for their own good and the safety of society.

Over the last nine months, being pregnant and being banged up for a crime she had nothing to do with have not been the prime concerns in Winnie's mind.

No, there has been something far larger in her mind that holds nearly all her waking thoughts and most of her sleeping ones. If she had pressed the button when she knew she should have, would the course of history have been completely different? Would it have prevented the Fall of the Age of the Internet? And if it had, would the world be a better place? Or is her being banged up for a crime she did not commit, and everything else that has happened in the world in the past few months, exactly what was needed?

To bring it right back to being in the Brownies when she was seven years old – has she done a good deed? Or has she done a bad deed? That is the question – or two.

She lies on her bunk most nights staring out between the bars of her cell window. On the bunk below, she hears Yoko snore gently. And she sees the sliced grapefruit rise into the sky like a bad moon. But some nights it is not a half-grapefruit but an all-seeing eye.

Winnie knows she should not be in this cell looking out through the bars for her part in the murder of a young man she had never met. But she knows she should be behind these bars because of her wilful part in the . . . But then it becomes difficult and round and round her mind goes while the unborn Child in her belly grows and grows and is nearly ready to take its place upon the Earth.

Yoko Ono the Younger sleeps and snores soundly on her bunk every night, and will do so for the rest of her life-long term. Yoko knows she did the ultimate wrong thing in murdering her boyfriend, even if he had shagged her ex-best friend Cynthia Powell. She also knows her committing the murder was probably the greatest work of art she as an artist will ever complete.

She will also go down in art history as the only artist to win the Turner Prize* while being incarcerated for murder.

Right now, at 09:11, both Winnie and Yoko are having their breakfast, which is always gruel with raisins and a mug of hot sweet tea.

* The Hockney Prize had reverted back from being the Turner Prize after the Fall of the Age of the Internet and, it should be added, after it was discovered that David Hockney had been having an illicit affair with XXXXX. For legal reasons names cannot be named here.

This day, unlike all of the others, will not be forgotten.

Meanwhile:

Chodak the novice Buddhist monk has tramped down out of the Himalayas, across India, Pakistan, Afghanistan, Kurdistan, Turkey, Greece, Macedonia, Serbia, Croatia, Slovenia, Italy, Switzerland and France. He walked through the Channel Tunnel yesterday and arrived in England late last night.

He is now striding up the Old Kent Road, still in his saffron robe, his staff in his right hand and his copy of *Grapefruit Are Not the Only Bombs* clutched in his left hand. He is nearly there. What he is near to or why, Chodak still has no idea, but he has total confidence all will be revealed.

Crow flies across the Winter sky above him.

Meanwhile:

Jimmy and Bill are sitting at their table in Andrew's café in Clerkenwell. On the table between them is the Brick. They are talking in hushed tones. If anyone were to eavesdrop on their conversation, they would learn they are discussing the possibilities of throwing Alan out of the band.

▲

11:17 Monday 24 December 1984

Dear Diary,

I got my latest chapter to the book done in one sitting. But I am beginning to worry I am allowing a certain sloppiness of style to creep in as I am desperately trying to get it written before midnight tonight.

I have long allowed myself to start sentences with the words 'and', 'but' and 'I', but this is done to get my revenge on Miss

Maxwell Stewart, my Primary Five teacher, who I hated with a vengeance. Miss Maxwell Stewart must be forty years in the grave by now, so she is certainly colder than this dish I am serving her.

But I do have problems with starting sentences with 'so' and 'basically'. I have just flicked through what I have already written and found eleven cases where I have started sentences with the word 'basically'. I have taken the opportunity to cross them all out bar one. I am keeping that one in, as a form of literary self-harm.

Language should be left to evolve in its own way, as art, and the marketplace should do so too. And we should learn to live with and celebrate the consequences. Thus bad grammar and spelling mistakes are part of the healthy evolution of language. This does not stop me wanting to halt the cheapening or undermining of the power of certain words favoured by those trying to sell us something, be it tickets, products or just their own opinions. Included but not limited to these words are the following: 'genius', 'brilliant' and 'passionate'. I would like to suggest we have a rule where someone has to have been dead for forty years before they can be called a 'genius' or 'brilliant'.

This forty-year rule would allow enough time for a consensus to be reached regarding the individual in question.

As for the word 'passionate', maybe the truth is that I have never felt 'passionate' about anything in my own life. As for what I have felt for the flesh of either sex, I doubt it has ever been more than lust. So why should the hoi polloi feel more than me?

Back to reality. Back to the here and now.

Matron has confiscated both my radio and headphones. Maybe that is a good thing. Maybe I can now concentrate on getting this book done and off to Dog Ledger. Midnight will not wait.

I have to admit I have been somewhat distracted in the past hour by a visitor. I so rarely get visitors.

It was a young man with rather searching eyes and very long hair. His name is Alan Moore. He too is a writer. He lives in Northampton, not far from the asylum where I am currently locked up. He is a big fan of my work, not just *Fish Farm* but *Uganda*. He called it seminal. Said it has been a big influence on the book he is currently working on, which is, as he put it, 'sort of based on' the idea of Guy Fawkes but set in a near-dystopian future – so I guess pretty much like what I have been working on. Except mine is utopian.

I showed Alan the chapter I have just written. He thought it marvellous, but suggested I have some obvious dictator figure that all the readers can enjoy hating. I told him I am not good at evil dictators. I go more for the sympathetic, if somewhat fucked-up, heroine. He said you can have that as well, and explained he has this girl called Evey Organ in his book – she is every teenage girl that has ever been . . .

I had to explain to him about my ideas of the Fall of the Age of the Internet and what it was like, and about its collapse and what the aftermath was like, but I don't know if he got it. He has a lovely smile though.

He left me a copy of the chapter of his book that he had just finished this morning. It is called 'Behind the Painted Smile'. The chapter, that is, not the book. He is not too sure what he is going to call the book yet. I told him I would read it later.

I did not tell him I was planning my escape from this place later today, or at the latest in the early hours of the morning.

The last thing he said to me as he was leaving the ward was, 'Welcome to the Dark Ages.' I thought it a most inspirational thing, and in his honour I will use it as the title of this latest chapter.

Only five more to go and then freedom.

Yours,

Roberta X

Postscript: they have just brought the elevenses trolley around. I always have a mug of the Camp Coffee.

While sipping it I recalled how that Bill Drummond and Will Sergeant from the Echo-something band who had played at the village hall on Jura had been talking about a comic they had been reading called *Swamp Thing*. If I remember rightly, they said it was written by somebody called Alan Moore. Maybe I should rewrite some of the previous book to include this Alan Moore as a character. Maybe make him the drummer in that band instead of Ginger Baker, whose name I had been using.

> *Since you took your love away*
> *The pretending never ends*

3 : WAR! WHAT IS IT GOOD FOR?

11:07 Sunday 24 December 2023

Cell Block H
Holloway Prison
London

Winnie is lying on her top bunk, thinking.

Yoko is lying on her bottom bunk, thinking.

Winnie is not thinking about the fact she will be giving birth to a new life in the next twenty-four hours.

Yoko is not thinking about the man who she loved and who she killed.

Winnie is thinking about war.

Yoko is thinking about art.

'Yoko, are you awake?'

'Of course. Why?'

'I have been thinking about war.'

'And?'

'There could be all sorts of wars going on in the world, and how would we know? Without us getting any sort of news how would we know? And it is not just 'cause we are banged up in here, no one in London or anywhere else in England would know if millions of people were being killed in Australia or Argentina or America or anywhere. At least when we had iJaz we could know what was going on everywhere. No one could start a war because we would all know about it and—'

'But that didn't used to stop wars before. When we were kids there were always wars going on all over the world and we would see it on the news every evening, but that didn't make us stop them. It was the—'

'Yes, but . . . right now there could be millions of people being killed in a war in the middle of Africa, and because we don't know about it, it's like it's not happening. I mean, is it happening?'

'You mean, like, "If a tree falls in a forest and no one is around to hear it, does it make a sound?" Or whatever that quote was the teachers used to like quoting at us.'

'Exactly. But more than exactly. I remember once reading on Wikipedia in the old days about this war that had taken place right in the middle of the jungles of Africa back in the 1990s. And in this war over five and a half million people died. And we didn't know about it, it was like it never happened.'

'Well, you knew about it.'

'Yes, but that was only years afterwards. That same war could be going on now in that same forest in Africa and millions of babies and old ladies and girls and boys and unborn babies are being killed, and because no one knows about it here, it is like it isn't happening.'

'Like that tree in the forest.'

'Exactly.'

They fall silent.

A tree falls to the ground in the wilderness of the Yukon.

A young man falls to his death in the favela of a South American city.

No one hears a thing.

▲

Crow flies across the sky above Holloway Prison.

Killer Queen hums a new tune to her/his transgender self.

John Lennon the Younger has a riff going through his head.

And Dead Squirrel has an opening line.

Mister Fox is still negotiating the rider for the FUUK that night.

Dead Perch is thinking very hard about something.

As yet it has not been announced where the FUUK is going to be.

Rumours are rife.

Tangerine NiteMare are so far ahead of any other band on the planet it is frightening.

▲

'Winnie, I have been thinking about what you were saying about war. I guess it is the same with art.'

'What do you mean? People don't get killed in art or because of art.'

'No, not like that. But . . . you know how every day I scratch a "1" into the wall beside my bunk? And over four days I scratch four of these "1"s beside each other and then on the fifth day I scratch a diagonal line through it? And then I start again?'

'Yeah.'

'And that is what I will be doing for the rest of my life.'

'You never know, you might get released one day.'

'Yes, but there is no point in me dreaming about that. But anyway, this is what I do. In my head I have reinvented the week. Weeks used to have seven days in them, but now my weeks have only five days in them. It makes everything faster. It means I have more weeks in the year. More weeks in my life. And this wall beside my bed as far as I am concerned is the greatest piece of ongoing performance art ever. And no one ever sees it. Or knows about it. It is never going to be documented anywhere. Does that mean it does not exist? That it never existed? But for me it is better than anything John and I ever did.'

'Yeah.'

'Are you listening?'

'Yeah, sort of. I was just thinking.'

And they fall silent again.

▲

E. H. Gombrich is sitting in her library.

E. H. hated the internet and everything it stood for. As far as she is concerned, the internet destroyed art.

E. H. loves the fact the printing presses are once again clattering away, spitting out real physical books by the millions. People cannot get enough of them.

Or so she thinks. The truth is, 'real physical books' have not taken off again in the way some hoped.

E. H. has taken it upon herself to write a new edition of her great-grandfather's seminal text *The Story of Art*. She keeps most of what he wrote but just removes the positive things her father wrote about the internet in his edition of the book. She can never get over how wrong her father was about most things in life and the world, and how right her great-grandfather had been. She then adds a final chapter about Yoko & John, and their groundbreaking work together. She is considering going as far as to say *Grapefruit Are Not the Only Bombs* is the greatest work of art in her lifetime at the very least. And how it is not just the book but the way it has then been delivered to 23 individuals around the world and how they have responded to it. It is those responses, their ongoing nature, which maybe makes this the greatest work of art of the last one hundred years, if not since the Renaissance.

E. H. looks up from her desk and out of the window. The sky is empty except for a crow flying across, heading North.

▲

'You see, Winnie, I think everything I have done before is pointless compared to what I am doing on this wall, changing my days of the week. And the fact you are the only person in the world who knows about it.'

'Yeah.'

'Well, that's what I think.'

▲

Upsy Daisy is back in London selling copies of *The Big Issue* outside the Overground station on Kingsland Road. She is doing a brisk trade. Everyone loves reading *The Big Issue* these days.

Makka Pakka is standing in the queue at the Dalston Argos waiting to buy the board game Fifa24. This is to replace the one he smashed up in a rage last night when he was losing to one of the Pontipines. He has given up collecting stones.

And Igglepiggle is sailing his boat up the Lee Navigation past a warehouse that some artists used as a squat.

▲

And Chodak is striding across London Bridge.

▲

Down in the Borough hundreds of FUUK Kids are queuing up at the newly opened Woolworths record shop to buy the Utah Saints' 'Justified & Ancient' single. But this is not for the radio-friendly mix on the A-side but for the Tangerine NiteMare remix on the B-side. Then, of course, there is the Tony 'FUUK' Thorpe extended remix on the 12".

A young lad is standing outside handing out flyers for a FUUK that is happening tonight.

▲

'Yoko, do you ever think about sex?'

Winnie and Yoko are still lying on their bunks.

'Why do you ask?'

'Well, if you are going to be in here for the rest of your life, that means you are never going to have sex again.'

'What do you mean? Are you suggesting we should try to have sex?'

'You know what I mean. Real, physical, penetrational sex with a man.'

'But you told me you never had penetrational sex. Not that I believe you.'

'Yeah, but you are different. You told me you and John were always having sex.'

'Yeah, but that was then, I feel different now. Anyway, what about you? You told me you used to have all these fantasies about nailing men to the floor and all sorts of things.'

'Yeah, but being pregnant seems to have changed that. All that seems to have gone. I just think about how I am going to bring a Baby up here in a prison cell.'

'Yeah, but the prison staff tell us everything will be provided for and . . . anyway, when you were asleep before and the warden was bringing around our breakfast, she told me we have a new neighbour. Some right posh one calling herself Lady Penelope. She was most insistent she was allowed to bring her own teapot into her cell. My guess is it was just a ruse to smuggle in some weed.'

'"Lady Penelope"? What kind of name is that?'

'Fuck knows. Your waters about to break yet?'

'Not yet. You will be the first to know.'

'Yeah.'

▲

Parker gets a call on his in-car phone. It is from his former boss Lady Penelope. He has not heard from her in some time. Not since the incident. She was always going to take it too far.

The Lady Penelope in question's real name is Anastasiya Oleg. She is Ukrainian. She is a qualified midwife over there but, when the trouble with Russia happened in the 1990s, she escaped to London. Once here she took whatever work she could find, which was being a cleaner.

Anastasiya Oleg had never been one for doing the lottery, but then there was a week with a triple rollover. She could not resist buying a ticket, and she won. Sixty-seven million pounds. This was back in 2016, before they had ZitCoins. The first thing she did was buy a title off one of the penniless members of the aristocracy. She then bought a pink Rolls-Royce, which she had stretched, and a sound system, cocktail bar and hair salon fitted in the back. She next did what many would overlook doing with so much easy money. She did the smart thing and got a tax advisor on Fernando Pó, and through him set up a number of offshore companies so she could dodge paying any tax.

She chooses the tax advisor because of his name – King Francisco Malabo Beosá XXIII. This is not the King Francisco Malabo Beosá XXIII featured earlier in this novel. This one is a rival to a very disputed title. As of 24 December 2023, there are at least five different claimants to the title.

This King of Fernando Pó is not interested in sticking needles through straw dolls in an effort to save the world from the Five. This King Francisco Malabo Beosá XXIII is only interested in making as much money as possible. Ripping off failed states or his own vulnerable clients is his trade. But the newly titled Lady Penelope is neither as vulnerable nor as naive as he assumes. When Lady Penelope learns she has been cleaned out, and there is nothing she can do about it above the law, she sends her Parker to assassinate him.

After assassinating the wrong King Francisco Malabo Beosá XXIII – but not the one introduced earlier – Parker makes his attempt on the right one. Again he fails, but in doing so shoots and kills the right King Francisco Malabo Beosá XXIII's favourite son and heir.

There will be retribution.

But this was way back in 2016, before everything else. Lady Penelope's fortune is well and truly lost. Parker keeps the Roller in lieu of unpaid fees for the assassination attempt. Then he takes up employment with M'Lady GaGa.

Lady Penelope goes into hiding, resumes her old name, Anastasiya Oleg, and takes up cleaning for people in the Borough area of London. But the long arm of the law finally tracks her down. She is arrested, charged and found guilty of at least a dozen crimes. Historical tax avoidance is the least of her crimes. Last night she was banged up in Holloway Prison for Ladies. Ten years and ten days is the sentence.

Not to mention, the tax-advising King Francisco Malabo Beosá XXIII is still hungry for revenge. The murder of his son is not going to go unpaid for, especially as now the world is on a more even keel, and these things are quite understandable, if not above the law.

She also changes her name by deed poll to Lady Penelope. Even if she does not like it, from now on in this book she will always be referred to as Lady Penelope.

As the key turns to lock her in her cell, and that massive sense of loss and emptiness begins to fill her soul, she finally accepts in herself that buying that lottery ticket is the one major mistake in her life. She should have stayed in the Ukraine doing what she does best and brings her the most happiness – delivering newborn babies into the world.

She kneels on the floor of her cell, puts the palms of her hands together and prays to God to let her deliver one more baby in her life.

God is listening.

As is Yoko Ono the Younger – prison walls are thinner than you might expect.

▲

Chodak stops striding across London Bridge and turns to look over the side of the bridge to the waters below. And then up into the sky.

Chodak has been thinking.

Chodak has been thinking about the same thing for most of the past nine months he has been striding across India, Pakistan, Afghanistan . . . etc., etc.

And what Chodak has been thinking has been troubling him,

and he knows it shouldn't. He understands the Four Noble Truths. He has followed the Eightfold Path. He . . . well, this is what Chodak has been thinking and can find no way out of. If he were to write down these thoughts in actual words, they would be as follows:

I lift my right foot to take the next step, and I know what the feel of the sole of my right foot hitting the ground is going to be like before it hits the ground.

I watch a drop of rain fall from the sky and I know when it hits the ground it will splash and then join other drops of rain that have also hit the ground, and then when the sun comes out it will dry up.

I know if I don't eat for three days, I will be very hungry, and if I then eat, I will not be hungry.

And on and on it goes.

Cause and effect for hundreds and thousands and millions of years.

Everything is part of a huge chain of cause and effect.

And I am part of that chain.

Everything I think is part of that chain.

From the very beginning of time to whenever the very end of time is to be – all of it is part of the same chain of cause and effect. Every drop of rain, every ray of sunshine, every step I take, every move I make. Every thought I have.

Freedom of thought is just an illusion, because whatever we think, every choice we make or are going to make was already programmed at the beginning of time.

What then is the point of living?

Or if I do live, being good?

Or for that matter, being bad?

What is the point of punishment?
Or . . .

And on and on it goes for Chodak.

Each step of the way, mile after thousands of miles, he can never see a way out of this, and nothing in what he understands to be the teaching of the Buddha has anything to help lighten the chains that seem to be dragging him down.

But just as he is staring down into the dirty waters of the Thames, he feels the chains drop away from him. It is not that he sees a way through the rationale of his thinking, he just thinks, 'Fuck it.' And those chains drop from his body over the balustrade of London Bridge and into the waters below.

If he looked up, he would have noticed a crow flying overhead. A crow late for a band meeting.

It is then he realises he is freezing – it is 24 December and he is still only wearing his off-the-shoulder saffron robe.

He starts striding again across the bridge to the North Side. There he sees the Golden Arches of a newly reopened McDonald's. He walks straight in and orders:

'Big Mac With Fries.'

Fate has smiled kindly on Chodak. Big Mac With Fries is back on the menu of every McDonald's in the world.

'Yes, sir, right away. Do you want extra fries and ketchup?'

Chodak does not know what he is being asked, as Chodak's English is very rudimentary.

'Thank you, kind sir,' says Chodak.

There is some more confused conversation. The fact that Chodak has no pounds, shillings or pence is overlooked as it is Christmas Eve and the homeless – there are once again homeless in the capital city, and there are once again those that go hungry

– will not go hungry tonight as all McDonald's around the world are giving away free Big Macs With Fries to everyone who asks for one. It's a promotional thing.

As he is leaving McDonald's he is handed a flyer by a young man. If he could read English, he would have read the words 'BE THERE FOR THE BIRTH', and a long list of artists who were supposed to be doing PAs and sets.

Four miles further North in Holloway Ladies' Prison, there is a new prisoner in one of the cells. She is sporting a blonde bob and a pink cat-suit and she has the look and demeanour to match. In her hands she is cradling a silver teapot. She lifts the lid and talks into it.

'Parker? Is that you, Parker?'

We hear a voice rise from the teapot.

'Yes, M'Lady.'

'Parker, you have to get me out of here.'

'Yes, M'Lady, where precisely are you?'

'Don't be stupid, Parker. I'm in the ladies' prison.'

'Holloway, M'Lady?'

'Yes, Parker, of course.'

'I have to remind you, M'Lady, I am no longer actually in your employment.'

'Don't be stupid, Parker; we will sort that out later. But first things first, you need to get me out of here.'

Parker cannot help himself. Not that he has ever had any designs on M'Lady, or any real sense of responsibility towards her. It is somehow that he has always felt sorry for her and all her stupid aspirations. If Parker had ever had a wayward daughter, he may have felt the same emotions. But Parker has no children. In fact, Parker's private life is never discussed. Parker is a homosexual, and everybody knows it but nobody mentions it. Or not the people in this book. If one goes down to certain pubs in the old East End, they know all about it. It is rumoured Parker was one of Ronnie Kray's 'boys'. It was with the Krays that he learnt his trade. 'Parker the Gun', they used to call him. He was the one they always sent in when there needed to be some 'gun work' done first. But that was a long time ago. But you need to know because . . .

Well, because when it comes to breaking in or out of prisons, Parker is your man. He did it for the Krays, he did it for Bruce Reynolds. Whenever it is needed, he is the man to call upon.

A reader in Scunthorpe is thinking, 'So how come he ended up being a chauffeur for a lottery winner with cheap aspirations?' The answer to that will have to wait for another book. Right now the story has to move along, before readers who are not of a certain age and did not grow up in the UK get totally bored with these knowing references to icons of a very localised popular culture.

▲

Vladimir Putin is in his office in the Kremlin poring over a large map of the old Soviet Empire. On his desk are well-thumbed biographies of Peter the Great and Stalin the Terrible – his heroes and his rivals.

Now the world has come to its senses and there is no need any more for the proposed and very embarrassing world tour with Michelle Obama, he can get back to doing what he does best – controlling people.

Leonard Cohen is Putin's favourite singer and songwriter. At each of his weddings he has contracted Cohen to write a song specifically for his new bride. And, of course, Leonard Cohen then has to perform the song at the wedding.

There are some other songs in Cohen's repertoire that Putin has specifically commissioned. Some more famous than others. With most of these songs there is the version the world knows, then there is the original that only Putin and those in his inner circle know. One of these songs is playing right now as Putin pores over the map.

First we take the Black Sea, then we take Berlin . . .

Putin picks up the phone – the same one Stalin would pick up to talk to Churchill and Roosevelt, and, of course, Adolf.

Putin dials the number he dials most days. It is to his good friend and only worthwhile rival. The only 'real woman' in his world. But it is time to leave Putin's office and head back to HM Prison Holloway.

▲

'Yoko, have you gone back to sleep again?'

'Why do you ask me if I have gone back to sleep every time I fall silent?'

'Well . . . just . . . I have been thinking . . .'

'That is what I have been doing. That is what you are supposed to do in prison. I have got a whole life of thinking ahead of me, so I may as well get good at it.'

'I have been thinking we should write a book so we can put some of our thinking to good use.'

'A book?'

'Yes, a children's book. Or maybe something like *Alice in Wonderland*, and we discover a secret drain-cover in our cell and it takes us down into this other world like the Rabbit takes Alice into.'

'I never read *Alice in Wonderland*. I never read books when I was young. I watched television. What was your favourite kids' TV programme? Mine was *In the Night Garden*. I used to want to be Upsy Daisy.'

'I used to love *Abney & Teal*. While watching it I would roll around on the living-room carpet in hysterics. My carer could never work out why. Yeah, and I used to want to be Teal, the girl. I even made a tree-house I wanted to live in, like Teal. I remember when I was about seven and being taken for a walk through Victoria Park in Hackney, being told Abney & Teal lived on a particular island on one of the lakes in the park. I desperately wanted to swim out to the island to join them.'

'Maybe we should write a story about Upsy & Teal in Wonderland. I would go for that.'

'Brilliant. It starts with them both in a prison cell, when they hear these sounds from underneath the bottom bunk. They look underneath it to discover there is a manhole cover there, and it is being opened from below . . .'

'A white rabbit?'

'No, maybe a . . .'

Meanwhile:

In the Kremlin a man is making a phone call.

'Angela, is that you? I have been thinking about what you were saying. You might be wrong—'

'Vlad, I am never wrong. I keep Poland. You can have the rest . . .'

Meanwhile:

'The two dark figures climbed out of their ice-cream van and proceeded to graffiti on one of the walls of the derelict building.'

Meanwhile:

In Andrew's café in Clerkenwell Jimmy and Bill bottle out of kicking Alan out of the band as soon as he turns up.

'All right, you Teds?' For some reason Alan always refers to Jimmy and Bill as 'you Teds'.

'Yeah, we were thinking—' But before Jimmy gets any further Alan is straight in with:

'Well, there is too much thinking going on. We have a gig tonight and we'd better be getting the van loaded.'

Meanwhile:

Dead Perch feels he has almost got it all worked out. If only he could mastermind the crossbreeding of a fish with a human being.

Meanwhile:

The five claimants to the throne of Fernando Pó all arrive on the same flight to Heathrow. They want an audience with the brand new Queen of England. None of them know of each other's claims, and none know they are on the same flight. One of them is carrying a gun.

Meanwhile:

Parker has a plan.

▲

15:03 24 December 1984

Saint Crispin's Lunatic Asylum

Dear Diary,

I would have had at least a couple more chapters of the book done by now, but I had another surprise visit. I shouldn't complain, but it was that Bill Drummond who I met on Jura. Which was a bit of a coincidence as Alan Moore had visited me only a couple of hours ago.

Drummond's parents live in a place called Corby, which is not far from Northampton. He is visiting them for Christmas.

And he brought 23 freshly made mince pies. He told me he made the mincemeat as well.

It turns out Bill Drummond used to work in this hospital some time in the early 1970s. He was a nursing assistant, or so he told me. He said he used to have to lay out the dead bodies and give injections and change bedpans and feed those that could not feed themselves, and sell cigarettes. It seemed all the patients back then were allotted a daily allowance of cigarettes, but, instead of handing them out, the sister on his ward would divvy them up among the staff, who could then sell them to their friends and family.

And to my unsurprise, and Drummond's major surprise, this ward sister is now the matron who has confiscated my transistor radio and headphones. Nothing changes. I bet she has sold them.

But the good thing about Drummond's visit was that he was able to 'officially' get me off the ward and take me for a walk around the hospital, even though he is not a current member of staff. It seems Matron trusted him. My guess is something may have gone on between them. There was a glint in her eye when she was talking to him that I have never seen before.

He took me off to visit one of his other old friends in this place. He is the mortician. I didn't even know the hospital had a morgue. His name is Stewart and he's from the same part of Scotland that Drummond was originally from: Wigtown, or Whithorn, or somewhere.

Drummond was amused that there is still the same Frigidaire fridge that can house nine bodies at a time. The three of us sat around the autopsy table and drank mugs of Camp Coffee, while those two talked about the old days, about the Winter of '73, when the Frigidaire was full and they had to stack up a further seven corpses on the floor of the morgue and leave the door to the garden open, so that the freezing outside air could keep the bodies from decomposing.

'Yeah, I remember,' boasted Drummond. 'I had to lay out five bodies in one shift.'

'Yeah, and I had to stack 'em up on the floor here without Matron seeing. With the way things are going today, I won't be surprised if we beat that record. Just hope it is cold enough tonight to keep the corpses from stinking the place out.'

So while they were wallowing in nostalgia for the good old days, I was thinking that if this is the case, and he has to leave the morgue door to the garden open, that could be my escape route. I just need to get these last four chapters done, and I will make my bid for freedom.

Yours,

Roberta X

4 : PHONE A FRIEND

Dear Reader,

I hate it when the voice of the author somehow makes itself known in a novel. For me it is as bad as when a sloppy filmmaker allows the fourth wall to be broken – always a cheap and lazy stunt. But since rereading the first two parts of this trilogy and deciding I need to get this third part done before midnight and making my escape, I have been really struggling to keep my voice out of the text. Maybe this is because they have included my 'Dear Diary' sections within the book that Francis Riley-Smith and his friends have put together. Or maybe it is because I am a different person to the one who wrote the previous two parts of it nine months ago. Or maybe it is because I am writing this in longhand and not on my Empire Aristocrat typewriter. Or maybe it is because of the medication they have me on. Or maybe it is because I am shit scared and life is short and I don't really know who I am or where I am really going with any of this. Maybe it is because I want a friend and you, Dear Reader, are the closest I have to a friend right now. I am desperate and I feel if I do not get all this done by midnight, I may not live long enough to get anything else written.

If you don't like the style – and I would hate it – then there is little I can do about it. Maybe just stop reading now. Or I invite you to rewrite the rest of this novel in a style you find more to your and my taste.

Yours sincerely,

Roberta

▲

Not much happens in this chapter. It exists for us all to have a bit of a breather before Chapters 5 and 6 of *Book Three*.

I will use it to describe what has happened to the world over these past nine months. A bit of an overview. A bit of an under-view. And some close-ups. And after that, if I have time, we will eavesdrop on some telephone conversations that are happening between some individuals you have already met.

For a start, the world is not fucked – but I suspect you guessed that already. But on the subject of 'fucked', the big new genre in music is FUUK. Its roots are varied and diverse. Since all music that existed in the digital era has completely disappeared, the young and the eager have had to start making music with what-ever they could find in attics and basements – like old, broken and abandoned analogue machines and records. This is mainly being done by the Post-Digital Underground kids, the ones in their early twenties. It is soon given the name 'Atik & Base', or 'A&B', by whoever it is that names genres of music as they pass through the cultural landscape.

But then there is this newer, younger generation, those who had never even got into fetishising everything that was analogue. It is as if they have only come of age in these past nine months. As if they have never known anything else. Or that they have blocked out any memories of the world before the Fall of the Internet Age. They are just getting on with it all.

There is this lad down in Brixton who turned sixteen on the day it all came to an end. He was the first to come up with the real new music and have it pressed on 12" slates* and play them

* Reggae term for acetates.

on a sound system in a dancehall just by Max Roach Park. He is using some old gear his uncle used to make tracks on back in the late 1980s.

His name is Tony Thorpe. It is his music that first got the name FUUK. He was named after his Uncle Tony. It is why the FUUK Kids are called the FUUK Kids, 'cause they are all into FUUK. And it is what they play at FUUKs. They are the first new youth movement for what seems like decades. They make the whole hipster thing seem so stale and static and stuck in their Post-Digital Underground aspirations, with their distressed coffee shops and slow-mo' skinny lattes.

The FUUK Kids just break into some old disused Ministry of War building, or whatever, and set up a sound system and have a FUUK. I guess they must be using some sort of uppers. But they seem to be having a good time. And none of them gives a fuck. None of them has to worry about selfies and Shares and Likes and Followers. It is all about now. And they have no problem with playing old music: anything they find on any format they can get to play they will use – just anything. They even like Extreme Noise Terror, but I don't think Extreme Noise Terror are aware of this.

This is how things start.

You need things to fall apart for new things to grow.

Things need to be out of control.

So that is me focusing right in on one particular example of what is happening in the world over these past few months.

If I pull out and look at the world as a whole, I see a different picture. I have already described how the United Kingdom and England have realigned themselves. The same sort of thing has happened across the world. Not always as peacefully as it has on our islands off the West Coast of mainland Europe.

Just across the North Sea, in what we once called the Benelux countries, it has all seemingly sunk into scores of pitched battles. Tens of thousands of young men, who should be going to FUUKs and dancing all night, have been very literally turning plough-shares into swords. The urge to go to war was never sated, just repressed. Like religion, war gives life meaning. Obviously, if you can make a cocktail of both religion and war, it gives life even more meaning.

What these lads over in the Low Countries are fighting about is simple enough. The Flemish-speaking ones who live in what was once part of North Belgium want to be part of Holland (note: not the Netherlands), and those who speak French in the Walloon part of what was once South Belgium want to be part of France.

The fields of Flanders are awash with blood once again and none of this can be blamed on the final dying throes of those old European empires. This is just young men wanting to do it because they can. It is sort of like the Mods and Rockers on Margate beach over the Whitsun bank holiday of 1964, but mul-tiplied several thousand times.

The one upside to this is that none of these young men has access to the sort of weapons that could kill any more than one person at a time, let alone access to weapons of mass destruction. This is because all military hardware across the world was suc-cessfully decommissioned by 2018, which I understand to mean destroyed. It is all hand-to-hand stuff. Nobody gets killed without looking directly into the eyes of the person who is killing them, and vice versa.

Maybe I have overstated the Fields of Flanders analogy – there is no way that as many young men are being killed today, but all the same . . .

And Winnie was right. No one in London has any real idea

about what is going on over there. Okay, maybe there are individuals who know about it, but there is no coverage of it on the BBC.

Yes, the BBC is back. Hence there is a *Queen's Speech* and a Christmas *Top of the Pops*. But it is a ramshackle affair. They have been able to bring some of those huge cameras out of their History of Broadcasting museum. With a bit of an oiling of the hinges and tightening of the wing nuts, they had them working again.

But there is only the one channel, not even ITV as a rival. At least they got the colour working. The news is all local, as in from these islands. After the *Ten O'Clock News* they close down for the night, but not before they play 'God Save the Queen'. They have revived lots of the old programmes we all used to watch. They still have *Strictly* and the *Great British Bake Off*. And they are making new episodes of *Doctor Who* – with the Daleks again. And David Tennant is back as the Doctor.

Then, of course, there is *England's Got Talent*. Maybe Scotland has the same but I am not too sure. Which is weird because they still call it the BBC, as in the British Broadcasting Corporation, even though Britain no longer exists as a political entity.

The viewing figures for nearly every programme are in the tens of millions. Even for *Gardener's World* and *Darts with Davina*. And on the subject of Davina, the Big Brother House is back. Of course, the Premiership collapsed and it is back to just the old four divisions, but they still have *Match of the Day* being presented by Gary Lineker – he hasn't half aged. Haven't we all?

Mobile phones are totally a thing of the past, along with all the other forms of digital communication. They soon had the old-fashioned phones working – even the telephone boxes. You now get queues forming outside them like you did when I was young. And people chatting in the queues, all friendly, while others try to butt in, which then starts fights.

This brings us back to the world leaders. It seems the actual copper wires that ran between the offices of all the world leaders from the old orders were still there, linking all of the old countries – they had never been got rid of, which is why Putin can chat with Angela Merkel any day he likes.

As for our own leaders – Nicola Sturgeon is the President of the United Kingdom, even though they still have a Queen. Remember Queen Kate Middleton? And England has a prime minister – but we are waiting for the announcement right now about who is going to be the leader of the New English Tory Party. And just to remind you, it is between William Hague, who is going for the 'safe pair of hands' vote, and Henry Pedders, who will get all the new young ones. They are supposed to be announcing the winner of the election as part of the Christmas Day *Top of the Pops*, just before they do the chart run-down.

You have to hand it to Henry Pedders. Nine months ago he was making his name burning down the Shard, and today he is more than likely going to become the leader of the New English Tory Party. They will be having the next general election in late March. Thus by 1 April our Henry could be the Prime Minister of England, the Scilly Isles and, of course, Guernsey, Jersey and Alderney. But not Sark.

▲

Putin gets through to Merkel, but they are just talking about what Christmas shopping they have yet to do, so there is nothing worth reporting there.

▲

Michelle Obama is on the phone to Yoko Ono the Older.

'So anyway, Yoko, I can't believe it! BANKSY wants us both to star in his new film. And he wants you and me, and for some reason that washed-up M'Lady GaGa, to do a dance sequence. I take it you are up for this?'

'Of course. It seems we three are supposed to meet up at a pub called the Mermaid somewhere in the Cheapside part of London. Can you make it for ten o'clock?'

'Yeah, sure, I will give M'Lady GaGa a call.'

▲

'Is that you, Gags? It's Michelle here. Did BANKSY get hold of you?'

'About the film?'

'Yeah.'

'As it happens I will be on *Top of the Pops* – between you and me, I'm going to be the Christmas Number One, so I have to be there. Do you think BANKSY wants us to be working with a choreographer beforehand?'

'I think he just wants us there to observe, to be like these women who can see it all and know exactly what is going on.'

'So we are not the stars of the film?'

'Look, I don't think it is about us being stars or not being stars. You know the way BANKSY works. It is not until it is all brought together that you see the full genius at play. But, of course, the public will see you as the star. I was talking to Yoks and we have to meet up at this bar called the Mermaid. It's in Cheapside. See you there about ten. Will you have the pink Roller with you? It would be great if we could all turn up at *Top of the Pops* in that.'

'Of course. Parker is doing some little jobs for me today, as it happens.'

'See you later, and bring your copy of that *Grapefruit* book.'

▲

'BANKSY here. Do you want a part in my new film, Tracy?'

'What's it about?'

'All about this new scene called FUUK, what the kids are into. I have set it up so they are going to break into Television Centre tonight just after midnight when the Christmas Day edition of *Top of the Pops* is being recorded. They will take over the whole thing and have a FUUK right there and then, and it will go out live on TV. I have this lad called Gimpo who is handing out flyers across London today – it will be massive.'

'What do you want me to do? Act?'

'No. Just turn up with your *Bed*. I want it on the main stage. You can be lying on it if you want, or whatever.'

'And that's it?'

'Okay, there is something else. You know how you told me you were up for a knighthood in the New Year's Honours list? And you know how they are going to be recording the Christmas Day *Queen's Speech* just before *Top of the Pops*? Well, it would be great if we could have Queen Kate knight you there and then with her sword while you are lying on the bed, live on *Top of the Pops*.'

'Are you sure this will look good in E. H. Gombrich's new edition of *The Story of Art*?'

'Take my word for it, Tracy, she will dedicate the whole closing chapter to it.'

'Deal.'

'BANKSY here. Do you want a part in my new film, Bob?'

'I'm supposed to be dead.'

'Bob Hoskins will never be dead.'

'So you want me to play an East End gangster?'

'No, not quite. An East End cabbie. I want you to turn up at The Shepherdess Café on City Road—'

'The one I was in in that film *Mona Lisa*, or was it *The Long Good Friday*?'

'Yeah, that's the one. I want you there for about ten. I've got these three women turning up from different parts of the world. They won't know each other, but they will all be carrying the same book. I want you to go over and introduce yourself in some way – you will just have to improv, but I know you can do it.

'One of them will be from India, another from Africa and the other one from Port-au-Prince. They will have no idea about what's going on, but they will be fine. You have to get them out of there and into the back of your cab and to Television Centre in Shepherd's Bush by midnight. And no hanky-panky. These girls have been through a lot. And, oh yeah, the camera crew will be hidden. All one-take stuff. You up for it?'

'Yeah. I will want to be paid in cash though.'

'Cool. See you later. Oscars and everything. I always thought you should have got one for *Mona Lisa*. You were robbed.'

▲

'BANKSY here. Is that Parker?'

'Before you start, BANKSY, I've got a job on tonight. Not

only have I got to sort M'Lady GaGa's Christmas Number One, I have to get Lady Penelope out of Holloway and then—'

'That is what I was wanting to talk to you about. There was this scene in the film I am working on where I wanted to film this birth in a prison cell in Holloway. But now I have changed my mind and I want it done live on the Christmas edition of *Top of the Pops* on the main stage. I have already sorted the bed out with Tracy, so while you are breaking into Holloway to get Lady Penelope, could you get these two women as well? From what I understand, they are in the next cell to Lady Penelope.'

'Consider it done.'

And before Parker has a chance to say any more, BANKSY puts the phone down. He is a busy man – or is she a woman? Do any of us really know?

▲

'BANKSY here. Is that you, Katie?'

'Yeah, why?'

'Well, a little birdy tells me you are doing the *Queen's Speech* as a double act tonight. That you and Queen Kate Middleton are doing it together.'

'How the fuck did you get to know that? It was supposed to be completely hush-hush, but yes, and anyway, what gives me the pleasure of this call?'

'Well, I also heard Tracy Emin is on the New Year's Honours list and—'

'And was it the same little birdy that told you that? I need to find out which little birdy this is and get them to shut their trap. But you were saying—'

'It would be great if you and Queen Kate Middleton were to

hang around after you have done your joint *Queen's Speech* and pop into the *Top of the Pops* studio. I'm making my new film in there tonight. All sorts is happening, I want to capture the culture of these very fluid times in the one film. All in one ninety-minute slice of a FUUK that gatecrashes the Christmas *Top of the Pops*. I have this vision of you, as in Queen Kate Moss of England, knighting Tracy Emin with your sword of office, or whatever you call it.'

'Do I get to have my name above the titles?'

'You know I can't let you have that. I am the only one to have my name above the titles in my films. But I will agree to have your name to be the first to appear after the title. And we will play "God Save the Queen" after the closing credits.'

'You have a deal.'

▲

'BANKSY here. Is that you, Tony?'

'Yeah, Bro, what 'appen?'

'I need your nephew to turn up tonight at the *Top of the Pops* studio at Shepherd's Bush.'

'With the sound system and everything?'

'Yeah, and all his latest cuts. We are having a FUUK.'

'Cool. You know the fee?'

'Yeah, that will all be taken care of.'

'Security?'

'Parker will be there. I will make sure some of his boys will look after that.'

'Cool.'

'There is one thing I better warn you about.'

'Yeah?'

'You know your daughter, the one we don't talk about? The one who calls herself Yoko Ono, who won the Turner Prize and then got banged up in Holloway for killing her boyfriend?'

'Yeah?'

'Well, she will probably be there with her sister, Winnie.'

'You mean her half-sister. Same mum, but I wasn't the father. I think the colour of her skin is a bit of a giveaway, Bro.'

'Okay, right now they are sharing a cell in Holloway and they still have no idea they are half-sisters, or whatever. And maybe now is not the time to explain all that to them.'

'Whatever. You're the boss. I can handle the emotion. Does their mum know anything about this?'

'Nothing, but she is currently working behind the bar at the Mermaid in Cheapside. I might get her to do a driving job for me tonight as well.'

'Okay, that might be more difficult to handle. You know what it is like with exes. Unfinished business and stuff. But I will be cool. Time?'

'Just after midnight.'

'A'right, boss. See you later.'

'Well, as you know, you won't see me. Nobody sees me. I don't exist. Remember.'

'Cool, boss. See you . . . I mean, cool.'

▲

'BANKSY here. Is that you, Alan? I need you and your pair of halfwits at the *Top of the Pops* studio tonight. You know, in Shepherd's Bush? I got a show for you.'

'But we got a gig at the Underground.'

'Forget it, mate. You do this gig and you will be in my film and you will be massive again. Guaranteed. And remember, you owe me one from way back when.'

'What do you mean?'

'You know, the Guy Fawkes mask idea.'

'Okay, I understand. But make sure that I— I mean we, as in Extreme Noise Terror, are on the bill above any of the other proper bands.'

'You will be the only rock-type band there.'

'Okay. A'right, we'll be there. But we'll want a crate of Manns Brown Ale on the rider.'

'It will be there in your dressing room. Just after midnight, right? But make sure you boys deliver. You may have been big in the '90s, but I don't want any of those "leads falling out" and "the bass player being totally out of tune" excuses after the show.'

'I'm on it.'

'One last thing – it is good to see the Cobblers* back up in the old First Division where they belong. Next thing you know, the Hatters† will be up there too.'

'Okay, see you later, but no mention of the Guy Fawkes masks. My whole reputation rests on it.'

'And that is why I know I can call on you.'

▲

'BANKSY here. Is that Mister Fox?'

'Yep. This better be important, BANKSY.'

'Very.'

'So?'

'I am putting on a FUUK tonight and making a film about it.

* Cobblers – Northampton Town Football Club.
† Hatters – Luton Town Football Club.

It will be a slice through modern culture at this most crucial of times. And without Tangerine NiteMare there, it would be more than lacking.'

'No can do. I have the boys playing at the Maelstrom tonight. That is where you should be making your film. That is where it is happening. All your stuff is just so – how can I put it? Human-centric. You have no take on the animal world and the possibilities of parallel dimensions.'

'Don't give me the bullshit, Mister Fox. We all know this is just your publicity crap. That your band were just a bunch of lads that missed the Brit Pop bandwagon and—'

'Just fuck off now, BANKSY, you can keep—'

'You are so easy to wind up, Mister Fox. I believe it all. But, anyway, I will make it worth your while. I have already spoken to Drums of Death as well, so that is sorted. We'll need you at the *Top of the Pops* studio just after midnight. You know where it is an' all?'

'Yeah, cool. See you later. I mean, I won't see you later, but we will be there.'

▲

'BANKSY here. Is that "Nina Simone"?'

'Yes.'

'You won't know me, but Ronnie Scott told me you were doing a set at his club tonight.'

'Yes.'

'Well, I wondered if you would be interested in performing your version of "Everyone's Gone to the Moon" later tonight for a film I am making.'

'Sounds interesting – but am I to be the token black female artist in the film?'

'No, we already have one of those. We want you for your talent.'

'Then I will be there. You know my standard fee?'

'Of course, Nina.'

'Miss Simone to you.'

'Yes, Miss Simone.'

'Can I play some Johann Sebastian Bach on the soundtrack as well?'

'I was too afraid to ask.'

'Then we have a deal.'

▲

I guess I have made my point – the phone lines are up and working. A new mongrel culture of some sort is spiralling out of control, but somewhere behind it all, strings are being pulled, if you want to read things that way.

As far as I am concerned, I still believe in Chaos Theory, and BANKSY is under the delusion that he is somehow in control of these things. But as the author of this book my job is to relay to you the facts.

▲

Meanwhile:

In a cell in HM Holloway Ladies' Prison, two young women discuss their fate.

'You mean to tell me you cheated on him five times with five different men?'

'Well, it never felt like that at the time. It only felt natural. It was real.'

'So you went and killed the man you keep telling me how much you loved, just 'cause he cheated on you once?'

'As far as I am concerned, me killing him for that "just once" proves how much I loved him. And here I am, every day for the rest of my life, proving to you, him, his mother, the rest of the world how much I loved him. My love for him now is the greatest work of art I could ever produce. And no one will ever know about it, it is like your six million people that got killed in a war in a jungle in Africa that no one ever knew about, but bigger.'

We will leave them there. For a start I have no idea how Winnie should have or could have responded to Yoko Ono the Younger's last statement.

▲

'BANKSY here. Is that E. H. Gombrich?'

'Yes. This better be important, I have to get the last chapter done before it goes to press. *The Story of Art* has to be told, and it has to be told now, for today, and not what was happening in the Teens.'

'And that is exactly why I am phoning you. The history of art is going to be amended tonight, and you need to be there so the story can be told.'

'And you are not shitting me?'

'No, this is for real. If you miss out on what's happening tonight, your great-grandfather will never forgive you.'

'I will be there – but where?'

'The *Top of the Pops* studio, Television Centre, in Shepherd's Bush. Be there just after midnight. But no cameras.'

'Cool.'

▲

And that is the end of that chapter.

▲

Dear Diary,

There I was thinking I knew how it was all going to go, and suddenly this very minor passing character takes over the whole thing. Who would have guessed this BANKSY person would be pulling so many strings?

To be honest, I am knackered. I am going to have a bit of a nap now before attempting the last three chapters and working out my escape plans.

The afternoon tea trolley is just about to come around. A mug of hot sweet tea and a couple of Rich Tea biscuits and I will have an hour of shuteye.

See you later.

Yours,

Roberta X

5 : THE GREAT ESCAPES

19:19 24 December 2023

We now have to put to one side some of these admittedly ridiculous subplots and return to Winnie and the condition of her mind and body, as she is unable to do much else other than lie down on her top bunk in their cell and wait for her time to come. She can hear Yoko gently snoring from the bottom bunk.

I may have been over-flippant in my description of her state of mind as portrayed in the previous couple of chapters. The truth is, Winnie is riven with fear about what she is about to go through in the very short term. What woman has not been, ever since Eve gave birth to her troublesome sons? And whatever the prison staff tell her – and some of them are very supportive and understanding – she has no understanding of how she is going to get through all of this in the short term, let alone for the next ten years.

From baby to first words, from crèche to nursery, from primary to secondary school, how will her child explain to the other kids in the playground that Holloway Prison is home and her mum is doing ten years for aiding and abetting a murder? Who would believe her that it was a murder her mother had nothing to do with?

Here I need to stop and address something else. Winnie has no idea what sex the child is going to be. She has never had a scan – but somehow she assumes it is going to be a girl.

You see, this is where Saint Matthew and Saint Luke got it wrong. In their telling of the story of that other nativity, you never get any real angle on what Mary is going through. The Biblical Mary is just there as a blank canvas – an Every(young)woman – there was no real sense of her fear. There was no anger at Joseph for dragging her off so he could do his civic duty for the national census. Then there was no mess in the stable, no blood all over the place, no screaming in pain, no afterbirth, no umbilical cord to have to be cut with a blunt farming utensil.

And had Mary miscarried before or again? We've had centuries of men reminding us how Jesus was born in the most humble of surroundings. But every time it has been visually depicted in art, or whatever, Mary is always there in her blue robe, trimmed with white, looking the picture of health, with the lambs and the doves and the Star up above and the lovely Shepherds and the Three Wise Men with their gifts.

Why the fuck did we never get the true story of what Mary was thinking?

Top of the list of what she must have been thinking was:

'How the fuck did I get up the duff, when I ain't – or should that be in't? – fully fucked any Tom, Dick or Harry?'

As for Joseph, he obviously has a problem in that department.

And this is the question Winnie has been asking herself ever since the time of the month never arrived, and nor did it the next month, or the next. And she could feel those changes in her body and mind. And the belly began to swell.

Here she is in her cell, her time is almost up and she is no closer to learning how this happened. No Angel has appeared at the bars of her cell window with any sort of explanation. Not even in her dreams.

It goes around and around and around her mind near enough all the time, however hard she tries to suppress it.

If the truth be told, for all her violent sexual fantasies, the idea of a male cock – member, penis, whatever – physically entering her body fills her with disgust beyond any sort of rationality.

'So how did this happen?'

She keeps coming back to a theory that does not really stack up. This is the theory:

One night early last April, she did have a few drinks too many and she can remember chatting to some unsuitable man at a party. She had sort of been celebrating. She had got everything done, and the end of death was guaranteed, once, that is, she hit 'Send' to Celine Hagbard. This 'unsuitable man' tried to convince her that he managed a band – but they were a conceptual band, or that is what he was telling her, but what the fuck is a conceptual band?

The thing is, for all her fluttering of eyelashes and laughing at his dull jokes, she very much remembers coming home alone – as she always did. But when she woke the next morning, somewhat the worse for wear, she did feel strange and sore down below and a bit abused, and there were those hairs on her pillow that were definitely not hers – short red hairs. And that black feather on the bedroom floor?

She also knew however much she drank, and she had been way drunker in her red wine days, she would never have consented.

Winnie tries to stop thinking these thoughts and puts away all the fears and just strokes her swollen belly and feels the gentle kick coming from inside.

But then the tears start again. This child she is going to bring into the world will not only have no father but no doting grandmother or proud grandfather either. No siblings to rival.

At least that other immaculately conceived child would have had a proper childhood, running around the streets of Nazareth, and grandparents to do the doting and a bit of childcare.

At least she has Yoko. She could not have wished for a better friend, and there is obviously no chance of her going anywhere.

It is at this point in time, just gone 21:37, that she hears a heavy metallic scraping noise coming from what sounds like underneath Yoko's bottom bunk, followed by a very male and old-style Cockney accent issuing the word 'Fuck!' – definitely not said in reference to the new genre of music she has no knowledge of.

We will leave this scene now so we can catch up with what else is going on across the city of London on this first Christmas Eve in the real post-digital age, not one that is just some fashion statement.

▲

Subcomandante Marcos is on his horse riding along the elevated section of the Westway. Two bullet-belts slung across his chest. His trusty AK-47 sitting across his lap, ever at the ready. His balaclava down. His cap with the three stars polished. And, of course, his peasant pipe freshly packed with tobacco. We may never learn how Subcomandante Marcos made it onto the elevated section of the Westway, let alone across the Atlantic, but he is here and, as far as he is concerned, before the night is out the revolution will have begun where Marx and Engels dreamt of it first beginning.

▲

The Twenty-Three Sparrows have settled down for the night in a bush somewhere in West London.

▲

Queen Kate Moss and Queen Kate Middleton are fine-tuning their joint *Queen's Speech* in the their joint penthouse pad in Buck House.

▲

Moses Tabick and Henry Pedders are at their usual table in the Jellied Eel & Pie shop in Hoxton Market – round the back from the bottom end of Kingsland Road. Since first bumping into each other in The Three Crowns last April, they get together at least once a week to discuss religion and politics.

Of course, the New Jerusalem thing up in the Pennines never happened. Not through it not being a good idea, but with the collapse of any real mass contact with his brothers on the banks of the Jordan, let alone the wider diaspora, Moses had to put the plan on hold.

As for Henry Pedders and his career, as you may have already realised, it has taken a turn for the meteoric rise. Now that people across England, or for that matter the UK, have an appetite for politics again, numerous political parties have sprung from almost nowhere. The entire political party-type infrastructure that had been staggering along until 2017 has long since been swept away, along with any other rubbish that is no longer needed. These new political parties are all desperately trying to find credible and charismatic leaders before the first proper general election, to be held in three months' time.

After all sorts of deals done over pies and pints in smoke-filled rooms – yes, smoking is back – the dozens of new parties whittled themselves down to three. These three are the Young Socialist Workers' Party, the New English Tory Party and the Liberal Rights of Man Republican Party. Their names may give you a fake sense of their differences. The Young Socialist Workers' Party is for the 'hard-working families'. The New English Tory Party is for the 'families that work hard'. And the Liberal Rights of Man Party for Republicans is for anything they feel is not already covered in the manifestos of the other two major parties.

And Thomas Payne is back as the new Karl Marx.

It was after Henry Pedders burnt down the Shard, and the New Dark Ages began, that he realised he owed it to himself, his mother, Dudley Dursley and the people of England to put his leadership skills to good use. He had never been interested in politics before – back in the days when politics were used to run things – which means he had no sense of party-political allegiances.

Only in the last couple of months had it become obvious that it was going to be a two-horse race between the Young Socialist Workers' Party and the New Tory Party of England. Henry thought he should nail his colours to a mast. He took an old penny that had been handed down to him by his grandfather. He flipped it – tails for the New Tories of Old England and heads for Young Socialists. Tails got it. And now, two months later – as in Christmas Eve 2023 – he is running for the leadership. Admittedly it is looking neck-and-neck between him and the old guard, William Hague, but over the past week he has been making all the right moves, and the press is right behind him – especially the *Guardian* and the *Daily Express*.

But none of this 'meteoric rise' stuff gets in the way of his twice-a-week-or-more get-togethers with Moses Tabick at the Eel & Pie shop in Hoxton Market. And for the record, and as you might expect, Moses always goes for the jellied eels, Henry the pies.

Some days Pete from The Libertines joins them.

Throughout their endless and open discussions about religion and politics, they seem to have arrived at an understanding that if religions and in turn the concept of there being a mysterious hand at play behind all of Creation, and in turn the concept of there being innate morals, were invented, it follows that the political manifestos man must follow are equally all made up by man and likely to change with the seasons. Thus there are no rights and wrongs – never were – just survival.

The acknowledged truth of this agreement between these now close friends does not get in the way of either's chosen career path.

I am afraid both Moses and Henry still think in terms of mankind and not wo/mankind.

On this particular evening when the Eel & Pie shop is closing up for the night and they are considering walking up to The Three Crowns for a pint, in comes a rather startling-looking young man with a shaved head and saffron robe and bare feet. It may not be snowing outside, but this is still 24 December.

In one hand this young man has a staff, in the other he is clutching a yellow book.

▲

As for Gimpo – we may have met a female Gimpo somewhere earlier in the book who had served as a nurse in the Falklands War and went on to write a slim volume of great influence. This Gimpo is male. He is of a different generation, but has some of the same characteristics. This Gimpo works for BANKSY, although, like everyone else in this novel, he has never knowingly met BANKSY. Gimpo is a very able young man and has a can-do attitude to most things in life.

Today Gimpo is all over London handing out flyers for the FUUK that is planned to take place tonight at the *Top of the Pops* studio. But there has been nothing random about the handing out of these flyers – it's all very strategic. As you know, everything BANKSY does is strategic.

It is just the BBC has no idea this illegal FUUK is going to happen in the middle of Television Centre, as the Christmas Day *Top of the Pops* is being recorded.

Over the past few weeks a series of crudely executed graffiti have been appearing on walls on and around Kingsland Road and a couple down in the Borough.

These graffiti are just words, no visual imagery; just white emulsion daubed onto walls. No one would ever guess the world-renowned artist and filmmaker BANKSY was the unseen author of these words. BANKSY was smart enough to get someone else to do the actual dirty end of the business. That someone being Gimpo. As for the words, this is a selection:

EITHER DISSECT THE PAST
OR CREATE THE FUTURE

DO NOT BE INTERESTED IN ANYTHING
THAT HAPPENED EARLIER THAN TOMORROW

IF MARX SAID RELIGION IS THE OPIATE
OF THE MASSES
I SAY ATHEISM IS THE VANITY OF THE ELITE

IF GOD DOES NOT EXIST
NEITHER DOES FREEDOM OF CHOICE

I have chosen these four to give as an example as they are the four that have appeared on walls very close to the Eel & Pie shop in Hoxton Market.

It should also be noted here that BANKSY has hidden cameras

337

and microphones secreted in the very same Eel & Pie shop. The cameras are only ever turning over when Moses and Henry are at their table, or occasionally when Pete from The Libertines does a turn.

▲

A young lad – a second cousin of Tony Thorpe – helps himself to a book from the newly reopened Tottenham Library. It is titled *One Hundred* and it contains what are considered by the editor to be the hundred most important poems written in the English language. This young lad has never seen, let alone read, poetry before. The poems blow his mind.

The young lad used to be a tagger. He had been addicted to it. But he had never done any more than his tag, which was, ironically, 'POET'.

This book containing the hundred poems from the English canon has a profound effect – he is once more prompted into action. Using his spray cans, masking tape and carefully cut cardboard stencils he gets back to work. But this time it is not just his tag, it is the first verses of dozens of these poems that have been appearing all over London in these past two or three months.

The thing is, because of the expert and precise way they have been executed, rumour has gone around the city that BANKSY is behind the graffiti. Even Will Gompertz does a piece about them for the newly launched BBC programme *Arts Round-Up*.

Anyone with any understanding of the work of BANKSY dismisses this immediately. Or at least guesses he would have no truck with the words of these white male colonialists. I mean:

There's a breathless hush in the Close to-night –
Ten to make and the match to win –

The whole poem, not just these two opening lines, in all its imperial glory on the side of the Old Street roundabout.

▲

The Shepherdess has always been there. Fashions in cuisine come and go and even come back again, but the Shepherdess on City Road has been there ever since the original Weasel strutted about popping in and popping out of the place.

But three certain young women from three very different and distant corners of the world, who have never experienced a greasy spoon of any description, have nothing to compare the all-day breakfast on offer at the Shepherdess with, especially one served at 21:19 on Christmas Eve 2023.

These three women have no language or culture in common. There is no way they can converse beyond warm smiles and sisterly embraces. What these three young women do have in common is they have all suffered and survived years of sexual abuse; have all magically received a book with a yellow cover; have all received a calling; and have all made their escape.

How they ended up in the Shepherdess within minutes of each other on this Christmas Eve night will have to remain as much a mystery to us as Subcomandante Marcos's arrival on the Westway. But they are here and tucking into bacon, eggs, fried tomatoes, black pudding and mushrooms. All three decline the sausages.

And all three are sitting at the same table. It has to be admitted that Arati from Kolkata is using her fingers and not the knife and fork provided to eat her all-day breakfast. That said, she is doing it with only her right hand, and with the utmost daintiness.

They know they have been called, and recognise the same calling in each other. As yet, they have little real idea what that calling is for. Other than a Baby is to be born and they should be there for the birth.

Just as Camille is polishing off the last of the bacon fat on her plate with the last of her toast, a familiar face with that warm but bordering-on-threatening smile presents itself to the table.

'My name is Bob Hoskins, and I'm your friendly cabbie for the night. I'm here to take you to your final destination.'

▲

Meanwhile:

A coach containing all the members of The Grimethorpe Colliery Band is pulling off Junction Zero of the M1 and onto the London North Circular. On the backseat, and holding court, is our Arthur Scargill. He had waited until the Rolls-Royce turned up to pick him up, before he turned it down so he could travel on the coach with the band – his band, his miners, his men.

▲

A fluffy black cloud is making its way across the night sky. It may be the same cloud we have seen before but, as I have no idea about the lifespan of clouds, I have no idea.

But what I do know is that its blackness has only got to do with it being night, and nothing to do with foreboding air.

▲

Meanwhile:

An urban fox trots nonchalantly but purposefully along Westbourne Park Grove in a Westerly direction.

And somewhere up above, unseen in the night sky, a crow is crossing the Thames in a Northerly direction.

▲

The Mermaid Inn was burnt down in the Great Fire of London in 1666.

Yoko Ono the Older, President Michelle O'Bama and M'Lady GaGa arrive at the Mermaid Inn in their separately driven limousines – except M'Lady GaGa came in a black cab as her limousine and chauffeur were otherwise engaged.

They arrive at the prearranged time of 22:23 precisely. They seem pleased to see each other, but you never can tell. Rivalry runs deep, even if these three are not rivals in any sort of obvious way – but then how many would-be mermaids do any of us know? Or for that matter Weyward Sisters?

The place is packed with all sorts of people dressed in costumes hired from the wardrobe department of the Globe Theatre . . . or that is what we must assume.

Or should we assume these three culturally and politically important women have such a force-field around them that they walk into a bar and it is instantly Christmas Eve 1606 and the place is rockin'? That said, the drinks on offer are pretty limited. It is either pale ale or small beers. And there is one young man who is a dead spit for Shakespeare. But I don't think any of our three major but still supporting characters question any of it. For them it is all part of the parade that is their lives.

Just as they are wondering which of the handsome young men

on parade might take their order, Gimpo walks into the Mermaid.

Gimpo is not in costume, just jeans, a '2023: WHAT THE FUUK IS GOING ON?' T-shirt and a pair of Dickies work boots. It should be noted here that the whole unbranded movement goes out of style as fast as the Post-Digital fashion becomes so Pre-Age.

Gimpo is handing out flyers to all the members of the Elizabethan cast, as well as The Weyward Sisters, and if we could read the words on the flyer, they would read:

Be There at The BIRTH

The Seminal FUUK

Live from the Top of the Pops *studio*

Television Centre, Shepherd's Bush, London

On stage and in person: TANGERINE NITEMARE; Azealia 'My Quim Tastes Sweet' Vaults; Nina Simone; The Grimethorpe Colliery Band + Special Guest; Utah Saints featuring Tammy Wynette; Doctor Whore; The Weyward Sisters; The Golden Bow; FIRST VERSE; Beethoven & His Droogs; Wise Men Three; The Miles Davis Quartet with Max Roach on drums; The Justified Ancients of Mu Mu with EXTREME NOISE TERROR; and Tony 'FUUK' Thorpe at the controls

Be There for the Birth of The

ONE

Live Tonight

▲

'BANKSY here. Is that Will Gompertz?'

'Yeah, BANKSY. What is it this time?'

'Have you been tipped off about the Birth tonight at—?'

'Yes, I got the flyer, bought the poster, already wearing the T-shirt.'

'My guess, when the cultural history of these times is written, what is going to happen tonight is going to be seen as the major shift.'

'Well, if you don't mind me saying so, BANKSY, that is for the likes of me to decide.'

'You and the likes of E. H. Gombrich, who will also be there.'

'I get the point.'

'And there was only one André Breton.'

▲

The three Popes stroll into the Happy Shillelagh in full drag. Obviously all the regulars think it is just some eejits in fancy dress for the office Christmas party.

The three Popes have been tipped off something big is going to happen tonight, and if they are not there, it will be all over for the Roman Catholic Church. From Saint Peter – the first Pope – to now may have been two thousand years (almost), but two thousand years in the grand scheme of things is next to nothing. Plenty of religions have lasted longer. If they are to take the history of these past two thousand years seriously, they had better be there.

But where?

Before they have had time to let their three halves of Guinness settle, Gimpo walks into the bar and hands them a flyer each.

Sorted.

If not for E's and Wizz.

▲

Meanwhile:

Azealia Vaults is in her dressing room, unaware her name (spelt wrongly) is on the bill for a FUUK that very night. As far as she is concerned, she is there to do *Top of the Pops*, to promote her new single, 'Cum in My Space'. Her only concern is the dance steps – can she remember them?

▲

And into the Korova Milk Bar stroll Alex and His Droogs, as they usually do at this time of night. Now Ultra-Violence is in fashion again Alex and the boys are back in business.

The Tiger Who Came To Tea is drinking on his own as usual.

Upsy Daisy is making a scene; nobody is taking any notice though. She is kinda sexy, but they all know she is trouble.

Dead Perch is also on his own. He is maybe the only life form alive or dead on Earth at that very moment that knows how vital the events of this evening are going to be. Not just for the cultural history of our times. BANKSY is maybe pulling lots of strings, he knows how to make those puppets dance, but Dead Perch can see that what BANKSY is doing is in reality just window dressing, just wine and broken bread. Symbolic at most.

Dead Perch understands something far, far bigger is going on. He knows if it doesn't go right tonight, if the One is to be still born, wo/mankind will self-destruct within a generation, taking all other life forms with it.

With no new life, there will be no new deaths. And if you know your stuff and if you have read this far, you might be beginning to grasp it. To put it in the language of now: Life is the gateway

344

drug to Death. The hard stuff is only on offer after you die. That is when the Big Story begins.

There are numerous characters in this book who would have you believe it is their billing on the cast-list that confirms their knowledge or understanding. But The Three Wise Men are mere followers; The Shepherdesses are playing a role. Even M'Lady GaGa, Michelle O'Bama and Yoko Ono the Older herself have very little more than their limited nous in how to shape a career. Even they do not see the bigger picture.

No, the only three characters in this tale who have any idea how vast the horizons are – how high the mountains and how deep the oceans – are Dead Squirrel, John Lennon the Younger and, of course, Dead Perch.

It is these three who know that the rest may have taken a puff on a joint or had a can of Strongbow, but that is about it. Even Killer Queen and Mister Fox only have a half-clue. As for The Tiger Who Came To Tea, he is totally up his own arse.

So we will leave it there, just as Gimpo is coming through the doors of the Korova Milk Bar to hand out more flyers, and head back to the action.

▲

'What the fuck's going on?' asks Winnie.

'Fuck! Fuck! Fuck!' retorts a cockney accent from another age beneath Yoko the Younger's bunk.

'Yoko, are you awake? Someone or something is under your bunk. Yoko, wake up. I can't move.'

'What? Who? Where? What? Under my bunk? I wasn't asleep, just . . . oh my God. Winnie, there is a man under my bunk trying to get—'

In less than three minutes Winnie, with the help of Yoko, is down from the top bunk. They have shifted the whole thing to find a half-opened manhole cover and a rather ageing but fully formed man, who doesn't look even a bit like a string puppet carved from wood, climbing out of it.

'Pardon my language, ladies, I got my finger caught. I take it I am talkin' to Miss Ono and Miss Smith? I'm Parker – Aloysius Parker. I'm here to free you, but first we must take a few bricks out of this wall and get the good but somewhat feckless Lady Penelope out of her cell.'

▲

After about 23 minutes of very uncomfortable squeezing along a classic prison-escape tunnel and up into the ladies' powder room of the Islington Arts Factory on Parkhurst Road, they are all safely in the back of the pink stretch Roller.

Although Lady Penelope has cracked the champagne open to celebrate their escape, she is far more excited by the fact she is soon to be back in business with what she does and loves best – being a midwife.

And Parker knows where the *Bed* is for the Baby to be delivered on.

The waters are not yet broken, but it won't be long.

Yoko the Younger is silent. Half an hour ago she came to terms with spending the rest of her life in jail in exchange for murdering the man she loved. Now she is facing a life on the run. Could living a life on the run be performance art? She is already exploring the concept.

Even if Yoko and Winnie don't know, we do. They are all heading for the *Top of the Pops* studio at Television Centre. And the bed in question is being provided by the future Lady Emin.

346

▲

The Blue Boar Service Station
The M1
Northamptonshire

Dear Diary,

Well, that was more than a turn-up for the books, and this book in particular! Late this afternoon, who should turn up but that lovely Jimmy Cauty from Devon.

It seems that after – how shall I put it? – my funny turn, and I got incarcerated in this place to spend the rest of my life locked into *The Shipping Forecast*, he took it upon himself to take my treasured Brough Superior, Belstaff jacket, my Halcyon goggles and my white silk scarf down to Devon, for safe-keeping. Whether that meant keeping them for ever, or until I was in fit mental shape to return to the world of letters and the Ton-Up Club.

It seems after visiting me today, the lovely Alan Moore telephoned Master Jimmy down in Devon and told him of my improvements. Master Jimmy then took it upon himself to drive the two hundred and something miles up here for a second time to bring me my motorcycle and my Belstaff and goggles, etc.

I'm sure Matron was most jealous I was getting so many visits from young men in one day.

Master Jimmy told me his plans were to hitch down to London, meet up with a young lady, and then catch the first flight to New York. Once there he has been promised a second-hand American police car. He was then going to hit the highway and head for the Promised Land. All I could say was his companion on this trip was a very lucky young lady indeed. And I would help him on his way.

347

It was the boost to my spirits that Master Jimmy's visit gave me that in turn gave me the confidence to make my break. I told the slightly tipsy ward sister – it is Christmas Eve, after all – I was going to see my visitor to the doors of the secure wing. She smiled, almost winked, and nodded her head.

I then took Master Jimmy on a detour via the morgue. Stewart was long off duty but, as he had predicted, the day had provided a bumper crop. The Frigidaire was full and the surplus corpses were stacked up all over the place. And so he had left the door to the garden slightly ajar.

We stepped over the bodies, pushed the door open, and I tiptoed into a freezing night and freedom. But before we set off, Master Jimmy pulled out a bag of spliff and skinned up. It seemed like years since I had had a proper toke. He then told me how he had got lost in the new town of Milton Keynes on the way up. While there he saw all these kids rioting. It gave him the idea to break into the model village at Babbacombe when he gets back to Devon and set up a scene of a load of the model teenagers rioting, smashing the place up. I thought this was a brilliant idea. One more toke and it was time to get my Halcyon goggles on.

Once my thighs were astride the Brough again, it still felt like all the man I had ever needed.

I gave Master Jimmy a pillion lift down to the Grange Park Junction of the M1. He was going to hitchhike South to his further adventures. I was going to drive North. With a fair wind, I can make it to the Isle of Jura for a late Christmas dinner with Francis Riley-Smith.

As of now, I've pulled up into Watford Gap service station, to refuel both myself and my steed. And to get this last-but-one to the last chapter done.

I love Watford Gap services. Full of memories from the '60s, when it was known as the Blue Boar and I would bomb up here from London after the clubs closed in Soho.

Ham, eggs and chips, with baked beans on the side. Two mugs of coffee. A second round of toast. And I am now ready to hit the road again.

My next stop will be the Tebay services on the M6, at the top end of the Lake District.

See you there.

Yours,

Roberta

6 : CHRISTMAS *TOP OF THE POPS*

I will hand the first half of this chapter over to Winnie. It should be her words and not mine.

▲

This is not how I envisaged it.

Not in a trillion years.

Not how any mother-to-be could have ever dreamt it should be.

But here I am, lying on a bed strewn with the detritus of the second most highly regarded living artist in the world today. A bed on the main stage of the *Top of the Pops* studio. Yes, *Top of the Pops* is back and being broadcast live to the nation in the early hours of Christmas Day 2023.

'Just one more push, Winnie.'

At one side of me sits my best friend, Yoko Ono the Younger. She is holding my left hand and mopping my brow.

'Take deep breaths.'

And at the other side is a woman with dyed blonde hair, sporting a pink cat-suit. She calls herself Lady Penelope but I am sure that cannot be her real name.

'Deep breaths, Winnie. Deep breaths.'

Her accent keeps slipping from affected posh English to some distant type of East European. And from where I'm lying, I can see her roots. There is some grey in there. She is not as young as she'd have us believe.

'Another big push.'

The pain is like no other pain I have ever experienced, but it is also a pain that feels right, as it should be. I try not to scream. I will not scream.

'Just let it out, Winnie, as loud as you want.'

Above me, perched on the overhead studio cables, sits a crow, staring down at me. Who let a crow in? And at the bottom of the bed is a fox. He is staring straight into my eyes. It's as if we are staring right into each other's souls. I guess at times like these you see all sorts of things. I wonder what my Mother would have seen. My Mother! My Mother should be here now. At least my Mother should know I am giving birth.

Maybe I should close my eyes.

I close my eyes.

And in my mind I watch a beautiful killer whale leap through the surf. A killer whale I saw once, when I was only eight. My father took me on a holiday to the Scottish Islands. We were on a boat between Skye and the Isle of Rona.

But there is another memory, an ugly memory. One night when stepping out of the Vortex Jazz Club in Gillett Square, Dalston, I saw a squirrel dash across the car park. It never saw the car reversing. It was too late. It was squashed. But it was not dead. Its tail flicked. Its head twitched. And then it was dead. One moment alive, and the next dead. And then a crow flew down and started to peck out its eye. I wanted to shoo the crow away. But why? What was the point? Isn't this what life is about?

'One more push, Winnie. One big push.'

I'm sure she will want to get those roots done as soon as she can. And who wears a pink cat-suit anyway?

My dad loved Nina Simone. He said she was better than all the rest. She was the real soul and beating heart of the civil rights movement. My father would be pleased Nina Simone is here playing Johann Sebastian Bach on the grand piano beside me. Maybe Bach was made for moments like these, but Bach channelled through the soul fingers of the great-great-granddaughter of a plantation slave.

While Bach imagined this music, Nina Simone's foremother was on a slave ship bound for an unknown land.

Father, wherever you are, I love you.

'Winnie, I can almost see the head.'

Everything goes black for a while and then Extreme Noise Terror are playing. I used to hate it when the boys in the sixth-form common room insisted on playing Extreme Noise Terror. It was just noise and shouting. Some of the girls said they liked it, but they were just pretending.

I once brought in a CD of the *Birth of Cool* by The Miles Davis Quartet. But after ten seconds they took it off, said it was boring. I wish The Miles Davis Quartet were here now, playing live for me and my baby. I'm going to have a baby! Me!

'Push! Push! Push just a bit harder.'

I scream the loudest scream I have ever screamed, then all the girls and boys on the dance floor scream. Is it right to be on a bed on a stage in the *Top of the Pops* studio? I mean, when did *Top of the Pops* come back? Is this the Christmas *Top of the Pops*? I wonder who will be number one? Has Paul McCartney died? Did Ziggy Stardust make a comeback? I am glad The American Medical Association will never make a comeback. I always hated them. So fuckin' smug.

'I can see the head. Nearly there. Nearly time.'

The crow is still up there. Yoko the Younger is still holding my hand, the fox is also still staring at me. These foxes get everywhere, even into the *Top of the Pops* studio. And I can see those two men with the black top hats and black coats from *The Scream*. They are there with their large canvas on an easel as if painting the whole scene.

I can hear music now. Better music than I have ever heard before. It's as if all of Creation is making this music – the killer whale I saw leaping through the wave, the crow on the wire, the dead squirrel in Gillett Square, even Yoko's dead boyfriend, whose back I wanted to drag my fingernails down. All of them singing, all of them dancing. A thousand instruments playing the same tune. Every instrument ever made by the hands of wo/man. And the wind blowing across Ayers Rock and past the pyramids in Mexico and through the polar night. The singing of the Aurora Borealis. The tingling sound the pylons make in the mist. The sound of The Miles Davis Quartet playing and Nina Simone singing.

'It's a girl. A baby girl. A beautiful baby girl. Winnie, you have a wonderful healthy baby girl. Do you want to hold Her?'

And I hold Her and I stare into Her almost-open eyes. She is beautiful and She is mine. And I stare into Her eyes. She has the eyes of the fox and stare of the crow, and She is beautiful and She is mine. And I am Hers.

And I look up and there is Yoko the Younger smiling back at me, and behind her is my Mother. My Mother! 'Mummy, Mummy, don't go, don't leave me.'

And then it all goes black again. And in the blackness I can hear a silver band play. They are playing 'Everyone's Gone to the Moon'. And all the girls and boys in the audience are singing along and dancing and waving their arms in the air.

And then I open my eyes. My Mother is no longer there. But instead there are three faces, three dark faces. Faces I have not seen before. But they are smiling faces. Weary faces. Loving faces. Faces that have seen trouble. Warm faces.

A Baby Girl! A BABY GIRL! I will not leave this Baby Girl. Never! Ever!

The three faces belong to three young women. Each in turn holds out her hand and touches my Girl on the head.

And a voice asks, 'And what shall we call Her?'

'I will call Her Ishmael.'

'Ishmael? Why Ishmael?'

'Because my father's favourite book was *Moby Dick*. He was reading it on the holiday when we saw the killer whale. He told me then, if he ever had a son, he would call him Ishmael. So I say, call Her Ishmael.'

Lady Penelope lifts the Baby Girl from my arms. She lifts Her so all the dancing and singing girls and boys can see Her beauty and she says, 'Her name is Ishmael. You can call Her Ishmael.'

And then there is a bang.

▲

And now we leave the mind of Winifred Lucie Atwell Smith.

We travel to the other side of the packed studio, where the kids of London are gathered, the generation down from those now boring post-hipsters with their distressed this and that and their love of everything analogue.

These are the FUUK Kids, whose minds have not been *destroyed by the madness, starving, hysterical naked*. They are the butterflies before the wheel was invented. And there, standing in the far corner of the *Top of the Pops* studio, is King Francisco Malabo Beosá XXIII. But not the one who stuck his needle into the five dolls. Or any of the other three who we have not met in this book, but who still lay claim to the crown of Fernando Pó.

354

Although, as it happens, these other three are here down on the dance floor, dancing with the FUUK Kids.

No, this is the King Francisco Malabo Beosá XXIII who is seeking revenge. He is here to assassinate Aloysius Parker. But the sight of this Baby, this Heir to all of Creation and not just the island of Fernando Pó, shifts the focus of his anger.

He takes aim.

He pulls the trigger.

The hammer hits the cap.

The cap lights the powder in the shell.

The powder in the shell explodes.

The bullet is set free.

Set free to do what it was born to do.

To find living flesh and rip through it.

The bullet is travelling down the barrel.

Moses Tabick, Henry Pedders and Chodak have just entered the studio next to where King Francisco Malabo Beosá XXIII is standing.

Everything is in slow motion. Very, very, very slow motion. It is the way BANKSY directed it must be.

Yes, BANKSY is here. Somewhere up above, directing it all. Unseen. There are four cameras filming everything. One from each point of the compass. But there is one other camera filming what BANKSY does not see. This is the Super 8 camera belonging to Tracey Tracey.

The camera to the West is filming The Three Weyward Sisters dancing on their podium. They have been choreographed by Flick Colby. Yoko Ono the Older is in remarkable form. And M'Lady GaGa is no longer arsed about having the Christmas Number One because even she sees the bigger picture. Especially as her and her Sisters are pointing with their

355

left arm outstretched to the One newly born. Born again for another age.

The camera in the South is filming The Three Wise Men as they make their entrance bearing gifts.

The camera in the East is filming The Three Shepherdesses as they each in turn anoint the Baby Girl's head.

The camera in the North is filming the FUUK Kids dancing and singing as Nina Simone, The Miles Davis Quartet, The Grimethorpe Colliery Band, Drums of Death, The American Medical Association, Extreme Noise Terror and the Utah Saints are all playing 'What Time Is Love?' – the Tony 'FUUK' Thorpe 2023 remix version.

'And the Christmas Number One . . .'

'And the Christmas Number One for . . .'

'And the Christmas Number One for 20 . . .'

'And the Christmas Number One for 2023 . . .'

And out on the dance floor among the FUUK Kids are Alex and His Droogs, Arthur Scargill, Beethoven with his Ninth, Jonathan King, three of the five Kings of Fernando Pó, the three former Popes, The Tiger Who Came To Tea, Upsy Daisy, Makka Pakka, Abney & Teal, Alice & Her Wonderlands, Swamp Thing, Guy Fawkes, the whole cast from the Mermaid, The Great Fire Of London, The Golden Bow, Queens Kate and Kate, Pete from The Libertines and Thirteen Eels that never got jellied and, of course, the Little Perch.

BANKSY sees it all.

He sees Crow, Mister Fox, Dead Squirrel, John Lennon the Younger, Killer Queen.

What he doesn't see is what Dead Perch sees. Dead Perch sees the bigger picture. And we know nothing about Dead Perch, other than that he was caught by someone fishing in the Lee Navigation and then left on the bank to die. But Dead Perch knows you. As in, you reading this now.

Then there is the camera that Tracey Tracey is holding. Without her knowledge it is filming the bullet leaving the barrel, heading over the heads of the dancing and singing FUUK Kids and the complete cast of the times we have been living through.

Winnie has sat up and she is holding Ishmael, like you have only ever seen in the best Renaissance Madonna and Child paintings.

And the bullet is halfway across the studio, above all those waving their hands in the air while writhing on the dance floor.

Like that meteorite hurtling through darkest space, many millions of light years away but with only one target in mind – our fair and lovely blue planet – the bullet knows its job. Its destination is preordained.

There is only one pair of eyes that sees the bullet as it gets closer to its target – the heart of a newborn Baby Girl, the rebirth of our last hope.

Yoko Ono the Younger knows it is time to make her greatest work of art. The greatest work of art since those cave paintings.

And it should not go unnoted that E. H. Gombrich is sitting on her solo podium, taking note of every passing pose being pulled on the dance floor.

'And the Christmas Number One for 2023 is . . .'
'And the Christmas Number One for 2023 is . . .'
'And the Christmas Number One for 2023 is . . .'
'And the Christmas Number One for 2023 is . . .'
And the bullet is getting closer.
And closer.
And closer.
And only feet away.
And only inches away.

And Yoko Ono the Younger makes her move, her lunge. She throws her body between the bullet and the Baby.

Yoko Ono the Younger takes the bullet in the heart.

And then we are back in real time.

And the music is over.

And the screaming begins.

Yoko Ono the Younger is dead.

Long live Yoko Ono the Older.

The Grapefruit has landed.

There are no words left to describe the scene.

▲

The Tebay Service Station
The M6
Westmorland

Dear Diary,

Throughout writing the last chapter it has been difficult for me to hold myself in check. The stiff upper lip has been trembling. I cannot say I am drawing from personal experience. As you may know, plenty of tired and cynical flesh has entered my cunt, but no young and innocent flesh has ever left it for the big, bad, beautiful world that lies in wait for it.

The only bits of practical information I can impart from the last scene, as the curtains were closing on it, are that Moses Tabick drew his Luger, the one that was a gift from his grandmother. The one she stole from the guard she murdered at Auschwitz. He took aim and fired.

Aloysius Parker removed his Thompson submachine gun from its violin case and the trigger was pulled.

Chodak drew his sword from the hidden sheath under his saffron robe, and was about to make the arc of instant death. King Francisco Malabo Beosá XXIII's head would, in a fraction of a second, be removed from his shoulders.

But Moses' aim was not true. Parker's trigger jammed. And Chodak's sword got caught in his robe.

And several thousand miles away Sam & Dave hit the 'Hold On, We're Coming' button in their New York City ambulance.

Barney Muldoon and Saul Goodman appeared to make their arrest.

And as Yoko Ono the Younger fell to her death and into the arms of a waiting John Lennon the Younger to spend the rest of eternity in a love deeper than the ocean, his mother Siobhán Harrison dropped dead of a heart attack, only to find her son there in the afterlife with a bunch of gladioli to welcome her.

'And the Christmas Number One for 2023 is . . .'

And it was announced that Henry Pedders had defeated William Hague in the leadership election for the New English Tory Party for Old England.

'And the Christmas Number One for 2023 is . . .'

'Arise, Dame Tracy Emin, and, while we are at it, can we knight you for real, Lady Penelope? The honour would be ours. We used to love you in the *Wacky Races*.'

But enough, and back to me here in the Tebay services. It may not have the memories of me meeting Jimi Hendrix and Bob Dylan in the Blue Boar at 3 a.m. on a Saturday night/Sunday morning back in '66, but it does the job in these more mature years.

I won't deny I am fucked. Totally knackered. But my plan is to stay in this service station for the next hour or so, plough on with getting the final chapter done and then head North.

At first light I will find a phone box and phone Francis. Tell him I'm on my way and he should set out an extra place for Christmas dinner. And then I will phone Dog Ledger, wish him a happy Christmas and tell him the job is done and I will have it all faxed through after Christmas has died down.

I'm also thinking that in January I may fly to Calcutta to meet up with some of my old friends there. I wonder if the College Street Coffee House is still the place to hang out. Maybe I should give Satyajit Ray first option on turning this book into a film. I love his films and he was always telling me back in the early '60s how I should write a story for him. I can see how the whole thing could be translated into Bengali and set in Calcutta.

One more coffee, then on to the closing chapter.

Love,

Roberta X

7 : THE LOW ROAD

This is the end, beautiful friend . . .
I'll never look into your eyes, again

How many affairs have you had that have ended well?

How many empires have not crumbled in good time for the history books to be written?

How many apples have fallen . . .?

You know the point I'm making. Most endings of books do not fulfil the promise of the premise.

And I'm shit-scared with this one. But before we get there, there are numerous loose threads to tidy up. So here goes:

The Three Shepherdesses, Arati, Camille and Divine, return to their respective cities (Kolkata, Port-au-Prince, Mbandaka) and open up homes for abused women. Each of these homes is financed by an adjacent 'greasy spoon' staffed by the formerly abused women. Their all-day breakfasts are a must.

Henry Pedders wins the general election for the New Tory Party for Old England. It is too soon to see what kind of job he is going to do.

Bob Hoskins died sometime before the events in this story take place, so his part will have to be played by an alternative actor. Maybe Ray Winstone?

Grapefruit Are Not the Only Bombs only ever existed in the initial edition of 23 copies and is never discussed again.

Moses Tabick throws the Luger away and actually starts to build the New Jerusalem near Todmorden up on the Pennines.

Tracey Tracey marries BANKSY, but they split up after three weeks over musical differences. She then goes on to . . . well, that will have to wait.

Will Gompertz writes a book – *This Is Then*. This book covers the cultural landscape of the first twelve months of the Post-Digital Age and those crucial moments leading up to it. No mention is made of Yoko & John, the FUUK movement or even what the Christmas Number One for 2023 was.

Chodak walks all the way back to Lhasa in Tibet, where he opens a McDonald's. He eats a *Big Mac With Fries* every day for the rest of his life. He never draws his sword again in anger. And every Christmas Eve he gives away free burgers to all the street children of the city.

Barney Muldoon and Saul Goodman retire from the Metropolitan Police Force to set up their own private detective agency. They wanted to hire Saga from *The Bridge*, but discovered she was just an actor.

Colin from Oban, aka Drums of Death, marries Azealia 'my quim just for you' Vaults. They live happily ever after.

Jonathan King discovers some unreleased tracks by The American

Medical Association. He has these remixed by Spike 'The MAN' Stent. They are then released as a cassette-only album. It goes triple platinum.

The Two Men in the background of Munch's *The Scream* are occasionally seen by Winnie. But only from the corner of her eye. Their presence evaporates when she turns to face them. She never mentions this to her therapist.

Nina Simone records an album of instrumental tunes by Johann Sebastian Bach. Just piano. It sells very few copies but is considered her masterpiece by the connoisseurs.

Alex and His Droogs go back to the Korova Milk Bar for last orders. Later that night they form a band with Beethoven.

The Little Perch soon forget all about Tangerine NiteMare. It was just one of those numerous phases they went through. Within a couple of years they are all fully grown up and having little perch of their own.

Yoko Ono the Older, Michelle O'Bama and M'Lady GaGa get offered the gig as the brand new Pan's People. They turn it down and go back to doing what they do best – being mermaids. Yoko is dropped as the face of Starbucks after it gets bought out by Pret A Pret.

The Three Popes go quietly back into retirement and make the most of their pensions.

Extreme Noise Terror stay together. They even record Alan Moore's rock opera based on his idea of there being only 23 people alive on Earth – twenty men and three women, who all live on the Isle of Jura. It receives moderate critical acclaim in the likes of *Mojo* and *Metal for Muthas*. Alan Moore instinctively knows that, for all their faults, only Jimmy and Bill would put up with his mood swings.

The Twenty-Three Sparrows are still squabbling in a bush near you.

Vladimir Putin's twilight days are spent at his dacha tending his award-winning raspberry canes. His daily telephone conversations with **Angela Merkel** are what keeps his dreams of a Greater Russia alive.

Aloysius Parker continues to manage difficult showbiz artists, some more successful than others. The lid to the violin case has stayed firmly shut.

The Justified Ancients of Mu Mu tracks were never officially released.

The Tiger Who Came To Tea becomes a character in a children's story by the one-time great train robber Judith Kerr.

The iPhone23 becomes a must-have retro accessory for young wo/men of a certain age. Even though they don't work and serve no other practical purpose – the phones, not the young wo/men.

Makka Pakka goes back to collecting stones. Some of them are very precious stones. This meant he could afford to look after Upsy Daisy in her twilight years.

Arthur Scargill gets back on the bus and settles down to retirement and gives up any thought of there being another national coalminers' strike and focuses his alpha-male needs on his achievements at the local crown-green bowling club.

Sam & Dave retire, but in recognition of their undivided and unflinching services they are allowed to keep their ambulance with its sound system intact.

Melinda Gates may not have died as the other members of the New Five had done. But she may have died in a swimming accident on Waikiki Beach, Hawaii, in the early hours of the Summer Solstice of 2023.

Upsy Daisy writes her memoirs (with the help of Makka Pakka). They are published by Faber & Faber and become a best-seller.

Subcomandante Marcos is sometimes seen in the early hours, riding on his white horse along the elevated section of the Westway. But to date there has been no photographic evidence to back this up. We still await the revolution.

Lady Penelope goes back to the Ukraine to look after her ageing mother and takes up midwifery again.

E. H. Gombrich scraps the whole last chapter of her planned new edition of *The Story of Art*. This is the chapter that was going to be completely based around all the roads leading to the Christmas 2023 *Top of the Pops*. She puts her momentary lack of critical judgement down to there being acid in the water – or that is the rumour.

BANKSY finishes his film and, although it is a work of genius, by the time it opens in picture houses across the land the FUUK scene is dead and a new generation of kids is coming through. The new kids have a thing called Occupy-Now, which is a sort of revival of the Occupy Movement of the late Zeros, but without the politics. It is also reported by style journalists that they get the fashions wrong – wrong shade of sleeping bags, or something.

Gimpo becomes a filmmaker. His *BANKSY Exposed* becomes the runaway hit at Sundance 2025. It is later discovered he has exposed the wrong BANKSY.

And now we are getting closer to the characters and themes that really matter to the story:

Tangerine NiteMare disband when they realise they might be little more than a figment of Winifred Lucie Atwell Smith's imagination.

Mister Fox finds new streets to strut down at night and new vixens to impregnate with his seed.

Crow flies across different skies and is considering writing his memoirs.

Dead Squirrel is just a dead squirrel, run over by a reversing white Transit in Gillett Square.

The strange thing is that in the year 2046 the newspaper *The Times of London* does a major spread on the twenty most important bands of all time. At number one are The Beatles, as you would expect. But at number two, above all the rest – above the Stones, the Pistols, The Residents, even Led Zephyr – are Tangerine NiteMare, a band that may have never existed in any sort of proper Fender Twin Reverb way.

As for **Winnie**, after her appeal, she is cleared of all crimes and released from prison. She stops having visions of grapefruit rising in the night sky. She takes up yoga. She trains as a civil engineer. Within a decade she has sorted out where and how the High Speed 2 rail link between London and Birmingham should run, to everyone's satisfaction. Her next job is to get the Channel Tunnel up and functioning again. But more importantly, she is a great mother, if a tad overprotective. Of course, there are issues when Ishmael becomes a teenager – the usual things: the state of Ishmael's bedroom, the boys She hangs out with – but, you know, that is all part of it. As for Winnie and men, she makes the usual mistakes. But she never gets over her fear of consumma-tion, and things still always have to be about domination, etc. She also learns to bake bread.

And, oh yeah, it turned out, if I have not already told you, that the baby sister Winnie had dreamt about meeting up with for the previous twenty-odd years was Yoko the Younger. It was at Yoko the Younger's funeral that all of this became apparent to Winnie. And yes, this was where Winnie was also reunited with her long lost Mother. They recognised each other instantly. The embrace was like none you have ever witnessed in a novel before. The tears flowed and flowed. And, as mentioned very briefly, Tony Thorpe is Yoko the Younger's dad. Thus Tony 'FUUK' Thorpe is Ishmael's cousin. So I guess if you are looking for a happy end-ing, hold onto this moment. But . . .

Top of the Pops is taken off air within a few months. The official reason given is the viewing figures are just not there. The revamped *Earl Grey Whistle Test* fairs much better. All mention of the illegal FUUK in the *Top of the Pops* studios in the early hours of Christmas Day 2023 is suppressed in the media. Even the *Daily Express* does not get hold of the story.

We are getting closer.

Within a decade the five competing claimants to the title of **King Francisco Malabo Beosá XXIII** become the brand new Five – the hidden power behind all the major decisions in the world. Or so Tammy's husband, George, would have you believe. He is still convinced the Illuminati are in ultimate control.

Which may only leave **Dead Perch**. In *Book One*, Dead Perch was a very minor character in this fable – remember he does the social media for Tangerine NiteMare? But it is Dead Perch who understands that life on Earth may be saved only if wo/mankind can crossbreed with at least two other forms of animal life.

This is to be done not for the outward physical aspects of crossbreeding, but for the mental communicative aspects of it. This is crossbreeding on a far more symbolic, so even more real, level.

It is Dead Perch who believes that if this was achieved, all other forms of communication that wo/mankind has developed via the internet would be superfluous and FaceLife would be proved to be a cynical con developed by those in the then New Five.

Meanwhile:

Dead Perch earns his living fronting a traditional PR agency called BrassFinn.

Dead Perch, like Saint Peter and Saint Paul, believed and still believes that this crossbreeding has been achieved with the birth of Ishmael Atwell Smith – the One. Even Ishmael's mother does not know this.

Dead Perch believes it will not be until Ishmael Atwell Smith – the One – reaches Her late twenties that Her mission will become manifest. And by the time She reaches the age of thirty-three, it will be done.

▲

Between the fall of Rome in 470 Anno Domini and the rise of the Italian Renaissance in the late fourteenth century was a period of a little less than a thousand years. Experts predict that the period between the Fall of the Internet Age in 2023 and when we get superfast broadband in every hamlet around the globe will be a little less than Four Thousand Days.

▲

I thought this might be the end but realised there was more to be said.

For a start there is, of course, an alternative ending to this lengthy fable.

The alternative ending is that these stories are nothing more than stuff dreamt up by a pair of ageing acid casualties who spend their days sitting in Abney Park Cemetery, off the Kingsland Road, drinking cans of cheap cider and strong lager.

Each of them takes it in turn to tell the stories of what might have been.

If only the hand had dealt . . .
If only the dice had rolled . . .
If only the stars had aligned . . .

▲

'And the Christmas Number One for 2023 is . . .'

'And the Christmas Number One for 2023 is . . .'

'And the Christmas Number One for 2023 is the Tony "FUUK" Thorpe remix of "Everybody's Talkin' at Me" by Harry Nilsson, featuring Ricardo Da Force. Which, as it happens, in the last seven days sells only 23 more copies than "Justified & Ancient" by the Utah Saints with special guest Tammy Wynette, featuring the Pipes & Drums of the Young Revolutionary Guard of Luton.'

▲

Killer Queen, the transgender killer whale, is last seen leaping through the waves somewhere between the Isle of Skye and Jura. She is one of only five surviving killer whales living in the waters surrounding the Hebridean Islands. And over the past ten years there has been no record of successful breeding.

ALEIKHEM SHALOM

The End

▲

The Daily Express
27 December 1984
Obituaries

The death of Roberta Antonia Wilson has just been announced. The writer and imagineer was better known by her pen name, George Orwell.

Miss Wilson was tragically killed in a motorcycle accident on Christmas morning on the Loch Lomond stretch of the A82. The precise cause of the accident is unknown. No other vehicles were involved.

Miss Wilson was widely known and celebrated for her debut novel *Fish Farm*, which is currently being adapted by the Disney Corporation as an animated film. Miss Wilson's other books achieved neither the critical nor commercial success of *Fish Farm*. These other books, especially *Uganda*, have cult followings around the globe.

Miss Wilson was born in Calcutta in 1926. Her father was in the Diplomatic Service. She was educated at Polam Hall School for Girls in Darlington, England. She spent her war years working in Bletchley Park. She studied Medieval Literature at Edinburgh University in the late 1940s. She returned to Calcutta numerous times through the 1950s and 1960s. While there she was part of the College Street Coffee House set, historically seen as figureheads in the renaissance of Bengali culture. She promoted the translation of Rabindranath Tagore's work into English. She also became 'close friends' with the revolutionary Bengali filmmaker Satyajit Ray.

In later years she suffered from bouts of mental illness. Over the past nine months she was a voluntary patient at Saint Crispin's Hospital, near Northampton.

From her war years to her tragic death, she was always almost inseparable from her motorcycle, a classic Brough Superior. This was the bike favoured by one of her heroes, Lawrence of Arabia.

It is believed she was driving North to spend Christmas with her friends on the Isle of Jura, off the West Coast of Scotland.

Her longstanding literary agent Douglas 'Dog' Ledger is hoping to find a publisher for her last novel, which she was still working on when she was killed. According to Ledger, it is a utopian costume drama set in the near future entitled *2023*. The final handwritten and unedited chapters of this book were found in the pannier cases of her motorcycle.

She leaves behind no living relatives.

Friends and associates are planning to cremate her on a funeral pyre on the southern tip of the Isle of Jura. Her ashes will then be made into a house brick. As yet there are no plans about the purpose this house brick will serve.

▲

The wee birdies sing and the wild flowers spring
And in sunshine the waters are sleeping
But the broken heart it kens nae second spring again
And the waefu' may cease frae their greetin'

THE PUBLISHER'S APPENDIX

We at Dead Perch Books recently learnt that Tommy James, as in Tommy James & The Shondells, was born on the Isle of Jura. It is the island's one claim to rock 'n' roll fame. Tommy James is now well into his seventies, but he still regularly returns from California to his birthplace, and is more than happy to play his hits ('Crimson and Clover', 'Mony Mony', 'I Think We're Alone Now', etc.) in the bar of the Jura Hotel. It is just Tommy and his acoustic guitar, but by all accounts he brings the place down every time he turns up.

Tommy James's nephew is Tom James, the English writer and academic specialising in the Kounter Kulture of the High Peaks.

Tom James is the partner of Bodashka Kovalenko.

Bodashka Kovalenko is a Ukrainian woman.

Bodashka Kovalenko is also a writer and academic, but specialising in the Black Sea Underground movement.

Bodashka Kovalenko in her teens had been a fan of Tat'jana and Kristina – as in The KLF.

Bodashka Kovalenko would never tire of explaining to Tom James how important The KLF had been within the underground culture of the Soviet Union in the late '80s and early '90s. She had a theory that it was the influence of The KLF that in some way allowed the USSR to slip and slide and finally implode in the Spring of 1991. She also told him about a conspiracy theory among men of a certain age in the former Soviet states. This theory, as mentioned in the Preface to this book, was that The

KLF would re-emerge from the depths of the Black Sea in their submarine on 23 August 2017.

Bodashka Kovalenko had translated into English extracts from the libretto for The KLF's acid opera *Turn Up the Strobe*. These she would then read, even act out, for Tom James, in the belief he would see how and why The KLF had been so vital to an underground generation – a generation not just in the Ukraine, but those huddled under the dark shadows cast by the Berlin Wall, all the way to those still partying as the first light of dawn glinted on the waters of Vladivostok harbour.

To Tom James's mind, it just sounded like the ramblings of shallow, confused and probably E'd-up youths from anywhere in the World. No different from all the other Eastern European bands and the like getting it all totally wrong. Then one day Bodashka Kovalenko tracked down on VyTrubka (Russia's answer to YouTube) Tat'jana and Kristina's visual and sound triptych/installation that was made as a sound and visual response, if not interpretation, to the book *Двадцять Двадцять Mpи! Mpилогія* (*The Twenty Twenty-Three! Trilogy*).

Tat'jana and Kristina had called their response to the book *2023: Що за хрень відбувається?* And if your Ukrainian is not up to scratch, that reads *2023: What the FUUK Is Going On?* in English.

Much of the raw sound and visual material used in the making of *2023: Що за хрень відбувається?* had been 'borrowed' by Tat'jana and Kristina from the archives of the Soviet State Library in Moscow.

Bodashka Kovalenko explained how Tat'jana and Kristina would just turn up unannounced in some post-industrial Soviet city, and using their ex-military equipment set up a sound system and three screens in an abandoned warehouse or factory and play

2023: Що за хрень відбувається? at full blast and non-stop for 23 hours.

The local 'kids' would find out about it, turn up in their thousands and go wild. Tat'jana and Kristina were always nowhere to be seen. By the time the local authorities got wind of it, it was all over. The sound system and screens had been moved on to another city in another far-flung corner of the USSR.

Tom James was blown away by what he saw and heard. Now it all made sense to him.

Tom James was inspired to write a text called *Two Girls Who Shook the World*. In this text, The Beatles never existed. Instead Tat'jana and Kristina, as in The KLF, came from Liverpool. It was The KLF who were the biggest and most influential band that had ever existed. It was The KLF who tourists from around the globe flocked to Liverpool for, in the hope they could walk in their footsteps. And it was The KLF who had brought about the end of the war in Vietnam and the collapse of the West.

In his fictitious inversion of the history of popular music, Tom James has *2023: Що за хрень відбувається?* secretly playing for 23 hours in a boarded-up derelict Victorian terraced house in the Dingle area of Liverpool.

Tom James and Bodashka Kovalenko got wind – via Tom's Jura connections – of our plans to publish *Двадцять Двадцять Мри! Мрилогія* (*The Twenty Twenty-Three! Trilogy*) in English and in the UK.

Tom James and Bodashka Kovalenko contacted us.

We had a meeting with them. They showed us some remnant footage of *2023: Що за хрень відбувається?* on VyTrubka. It was devastatingly brilliant. Or maybe we just allowed what we saw to grow in stature in our imagination as so little of the original had seemingly survived the collapse of the USSR. But whatever the reason, we were inspired to use elements of these few minutes of remnant footage to create our own 23-minute animated film in homage.

As yet we have no idea what we will do with our film.

What we did know was that we wanted to launch this book, now retitled simply as *2023*, in a boarded-up derelict Victorian terraced house in the Dingle area of Liverpool. Maybe we should have our animated version of *2023: Що за хрень відбувається?* playing on a continual loop in an upstairs bedroom of this house.

We also decided to launch this book on 23 August 2017, this being the date – as stated in the Preface to this book – when those conspiracy theorists back in the Ukraine and Russia like to believe Tat'jana and Kristina, as The KLF, will resurface from the depths of the Black Sea in their submarine.

Copies of this book will be on sale on this date in a corner shop close to the boarded-up house in the Dingle.

As for Cauty & Drummond – 'The Undertakers to the Underworld' – it is not known if they have started work yet on *The Great Pyramid of the North*.

Dead Perch Books
Tea Time
1 January 2017